Michele Hauf ~~~~~~~~~~~~~~~~~~~~~~~ who has been writing ~~~~~~~~~~~~~ ntasy ~~~~~~~~~~~~~~~~~~~~~~~~~~~~ eteers, vampires and faeries usually feature in her stories. And if Michele followed the adage "write what you know," all her stories would have snow in them. Fortunately, she steps beyond her comfort zone and writes about countries and creatures she has never seen. Find her on Facebook, Twitter and at michelehauf.com

Linda O. Johnston loves to write. While honing her writing skills, she worked in advertising and public relations, then became a lawyer…and enjoyed writing contracts. Linda's first published fiction appeared in *Ellery Queen's Mystery Magazine* and won a Robert L. Fish Memorial Award for Best First Mystery Short Story of the Year. Linda now spends most of her time creating memorable tales of paranormal romance, romantic suspense and mystery. Visit her on the web at www.lindaojohnston.com

WITNESS IN THE WOODS

MICHELE HAUF

COLTON 911: CAUGHT IN THE CROSSFIRE

LINDA O. JOHNSTON

MILLS & BOON

First Published in Great Britain 2019
by Mills & Boon, an imprint of HarperCollins*Publishers*
1 London Bridge Street, London, SE1 9GF

Witness in the Woods © 2019 Michele Hauf
Colton 911: Caught in the Crossfire © 2019 Harlequin Books S.A.

Special thanks and acknowledgement are given to Linda O. Johnston for her contribution to the *Colton 911* series.

ISBN: 978-0-263-27448-6

1119

MIX
Paper from
responsible sources
FSC™ C007454

This book is produced from independently certified FSC™ paper to ensure responsible forest management.

For more information visit: www.harpercollins.co.uk/green

Printed and bound in Spain
by CPI, Barcelona

WITNESS IN THE WOODS

MICHELE HAUF

Chapter One

Joseph Cash raced toward the admittance doors of St. Luke's emergency room. He'd driven furiously from Lake Seraphim the moment he'd heard the dispatcher's voice announce that an elderly Indian man near death had been found crawling at the edge of County Road 7. A young couple had spotted him, pulled over and called the police.

Joe had responded to Dispatch and asked if he could take the call. She'd reported back that an ambulance was already at the scene and the man was being transferred to Duluth. The patient was seizing, and the initial report had been grim. They couldn't know if he'd arrive alive or dead.

The description the dispatcher had given Joe could have been that of any elderly Native American. Sun-browned skin, long dark hair threaded with gray and pulled into a ponytail. Estimated age around eighty.

But Joe instinctually knew who the man was. His heart had dropped when he'd heard the location where the man had been found climbing up out of the ditch on all fours. That was the one place Max Owen had used to rendez-vous with Joe when he brought him provisions, because from there it was a straight two-mile hike through the thick Boundary Waters to where he'd camped every summer for twenty years in a little tent at the edge of a small lake.

Joe hadn't seen Max since June, two months earlier.

He'd looked well, though his dry cough had grown more pronounced over the past year. Max had attributed it to the bad habit of smoking when he'd been a teenager. If anything happened to end that old man before Joe could see him—no, he mustn't think like that.

Now he entered the too-bright, fluorescent-lit hallway of the ER intake area. Three people queued before the admissions desk, waiting to be assessed for triage. Normally, Joe would respectfully wait his turn, as he had occasion to check in on patients he'd brought here himself while on duty as a conservation officer with the Minnesota Department of Natural Resources.

Fingers curling impatiently in and out of his fists, he stepped from foot to foot. He couldn't wait. If the emergency crew hadn't been certain about Max's condition…

"The Native American man who was brought in," he said over the head of a stooped elderly woman at the front of the line.

The male nurse behind the bulletproof glass glanced up and, at the sight of Joe, smiled. Though weariness etched the nurse's brow, his eyes glinted. "Hey, handsome, who you looking for?"

"An old man was found on County Road 7 about forty-five minutes ago. Dispatch says they brought him here." He wore the conservation officer's green jacket over his matching forest-green cotton shirt, so he had the official gear to grant him authority. But it probably wouldn't matter, Joe decided, as the nurse winked at him.

"Please, I don't mean to interrupt, ma'am." Joe flashed a smile at the old woman who was giving him the stink eye. "I think I know him. I can provide identification. He's eighty-two, Native American…" Joe thought about it less than a moment, then clasped his fingers at his neck. "And he always wore an eagle talon on a leather choker at his neck."

The nurse nodded. "We got your guy." He glanced at the computer screen before him and then muttered, "Oh."

That single utterance dropped Joe's heart to his gut. Because he knew. The nurse didn't need to say anything more.

Wincing through the sudden rise of sadness that welled in his chest, Joe nodded toward the doors that led to the treatment rooms. The nurse touched the security button, which released the lock on the doors, and Joe dashed through, calling back a mumbled thanks.

He hadn't bothered to ask for a room number. There were only two rooms designated for those bodies that awaited the coroner's visit. He knew that from previous visits. Walking swiftly down the hallway, he beat a fist into his palm as he neared the first room. The walls were floor-to-ceiling windows. All the curtains had been pulled, and no light behind them shone out.

"Officer?" A short blonde nurse in maroon scrubs appeared by his side and looked up at him. She smelled like pink bubblegum.

"I heard the dispatch call on the old man," Joe said. "I may be able to identify him."

"Excellent. We thought he was a John Doe. I'll just need your badge and name for our records. Why don't you step inside the room and take a look to confirm your guess while I grab some forms?"

"Is he…? When did he—?"

"He was DOA. Dr. Preston called it ten minutes ago. Presented as ingestion of a poisonous substance, but we're waiting for the coroner to do a thorough workup. I'll be right back!"

She was too cheery, but then Joe had learned that the ER sported all ranges of personalities, and it was those who exuded cheer who survived longest the grueling emotional toll such work forced upon them. Either that, or she was faking it to get through yet another endless shift.

He opened the sliding door, which glided too quietly, and stepped inside the room. Though the body on the bed was covered from head to toe with a white sheet, he just knew. The ten-year-old boy inside him shook his head and sucked in his lower lip. Not fair. Why Max?

Carefully, Joe tugged back the sheet from the head. Recognition seized his heart. He caught a gasp at the back of his throat.

"Oh, Max." Joe swore softly and gripped the steel bed rail. The man had been so kind to him over the years. He was literally the reason Joe currently worked for the DNR.

Poison? But how? It made no sense.

The sudden arrival of the nurse at his side startled him. She moved like a mouse, fast and stealthily.

"Sorry." She handed him a clipboard and then turned on a low light over the bed. "Just need your signature. Do you recognize the deceased?"

"I do." Joe scribbled his name and badge number on the standard form and handed it back to her. "His name is Maximilien Owen and he's Chippewa. The Fond du Lac band. Doesn't live on the Fond du Lac reservation, though. Hasn't associated closely with his tribe for decades. Eighty-two years old. Has never seen a doctor a day in his life. I thought he was healthy, though he'd had a dry cough of late. Are you sure it was poison?"

"That was the initial assessment. You know these Native Americans have herbs and plants they use for rituals and whatnot. Probably ate the wrong plant or something. It's very sad," she added.

Joe lifted a brow. She had no idea.

"Max would never eat the wrong plant," Joe insisted. "He lived off the land his entire life. He knew the Boundary Waters like no one else. His dad used to be a tracker in the Vietnam War, and he taught Max everything he knew."

"Oh, that's touching."

She wasn't in the mood to hear the old man's life story, and Joe wasn't going to gift her with Max's wonderful tale. He pegged her cheery attitude as a false front.

"I'm going to stick around for the coroner," he said. "I want an autopsy."

The nurse's jaw dropped. "Do you…know his family? We don't usually…"

"He didn't have family. I'll pay for the autopsy. This is important."

Joe wasn't about to let the old man be filed away as an accidental poisoning. That was not Max. At all. Something wasn't right. And Joe would not rest until it was confirmed that Max's death had been natural—or not.

Two weeks later…

BURNING CEDARWOOD SWEETENED the air better than any fancy department store perfume Skylar Davis had ever smelled. Pine and elm kindling crackled in the bonfire before her. A refreshingly cool August breeze swept in from the lake not thirty yards away and caressed her shoulders. She breathed in, closing her eyes, and hugged the heavy white satin wedding dress against her chest.

It was time to do this.

Beside her on the grass, alert and curious, sat Stella, the three-year-old timber wolf she'd rescued as a pup. Skylar could sense the wolf's positive, gentle presence. The wolf was there for her. No matter what.

She opened her eyes and then dropped the wedding dress onto the fire. Smoke coiled. Sparks snapped. Stella sounded an are-you-sure-about-this yip.

"Has to be done, Stella. I can't move forward any other way."

Using a long, charred oak stick peeled clean of bark— her father's fire-poking stick—she nudged the lacy neckline of the dress deeper into the flames. The tiny pearls glowed, then blackened, and the lace quickly melted. The frothy concoction, woven with hopes and dreams—and a whole lot of reckless abandon—meant little to her now.

Stepping back to stand beside Stella, Skylar planted the tip of the fire-poking stick in the ground near her boot and nodded. She should have done this two months earlier— that Saturday afternoon when she'd found herself marching into the county courthouse with hell in her eyes and fury in her heart. An unexpected conversation with her uncle an hour earlier had poked through her heart and left it ragged.

Her world had tilted off balance that day. The man she'd thought she was ready to share the rest of her life with had a secret life that he'd attempted to keep from her. She'd had her suspicions about Cole Pruitt, which was why she had been the one to approach Uncle Malcolm in the flower shop parking lot that morning she had intended to say *I do*. Normally she'd find a way to walk a wide circle around the family member who had done nothing but serve her and her father heartache over the years. But she'd had to know. And Malcolm had been just evasive enough for her to press—until he'd spilled the truth about Cole.

Since then, life had been strangely precarious. Not only had she ditched a fiancé, but her uncle had been keeping a close eye on her, as well. Hounding her about the parcel of land he wanted her to sell to him. And so close to making threats, but not quite. Still, she was constantly looking over her shoulder for something—danger, or…a rescuer?

Hell, she was a strong, capable woman who could take care of herself. She didn't need rescuing.

Maybe.

"Stella, I—"

Something stung Skylar's ear. It felt like a mosquito, but immediately following that sudden burn, she saw wood split out, and a small hole appeared through the old hitching post three feet to her right.

"What the—?"

Clamping a hand over her ear and instinctively ducking, Skylar let out a gasp as another hole suddenly drilled into the post.

Stella jumped to all fours, alert and whining in a low and warning tone. The wolf scanned the woods that surrounded their circle of a backyard. Cutting the circle off on the bottom was the rocky lakeshore. A cleared swath in the thick birch and maple woods opened to the lake, where Skylar saw no boat cruising by. Was someone in the woods?

She opened her hand before her. Blood smeared one of her fingers. What had just happened?

The holes in the post answered that question. And set Skylar's heartbeats to a faster pace.

"Stella, stay here." Still in a squat, Skylar patted her thigh. The wolf crept to her side and Skylar ran her fingers through her soft summer coat. "Someone just shot at me," she whispered.

And, unfortunately, that was no surprise.

Chapter Two

Finishing off a ham-and-pickle sandwich he'd packed for a late lunch, Joe Cash sat in his county-issue four-by-four pickup truck outside the public access turnoff to Lake Vaillant. He'd just come off the water after a long day patrolling, which involved checking that fishermen had current licenses, guiding a few lost tourists in the right direction and issuing a warning to a group of teens who had been trying to dive for "buried treasure." The depths of the lake were littered with fishing line, lost hooks and decades of rusting boat parts. Only the beach on the east shore had been marked for safe swimming.

All in a day's work. A man couldn't ask for a better job. Conservation officer for the Minnesota Department of Natural Resources was a title that fit Joe to a tee. Ninety percent of the time, his office featured open air, lakes, trees, snow and/or sun. Joe's job was to keep the public safe, but also to protect and guard the wildlife that flourished in this county set in the Superior Forest. Not a day passed that he didn't get to wander through tall grasses, spot a blue heron or, if he was lucky, spy on a timber wolf from a local pack.

He smiled widely and tilted back the steel canteen of lukewarm water for a few swallows. This job was what made him wake with a smile and dash out to work every morning. Nothing could give him more satisfaction. Except, that is, when he finally nailed the parties responsible for the rampant poaching in the area. Someone, or many someones, had been poaching deer, beaver, cougar, turkey and the animal most precious to Joe's soul, the gray wolf. But tops on the list was the bald eagle. Taking down the other animals without a proper license was considered a gross misdemeanor. Taking down a bald eagle was a federal offense. And recently he'd begun to wonder if the poachers were using something beyond the usual snare or steel trap. Like death by poisoning.

The autopsy on Max Owen had shown he'd been poisoned by strychnine. He hadn't consumed it orally, but rather, it had permeated his skin and entered his bloodstream. And even more surprising than the poison? His lungs had been riddled with cancer. That discovery had troubled Joe greatly. If he had known what was growing in Max, he would have taken him to a doctor long ago. The poison had killed him, but it was apparent the cancer would have been terminal. The coroner had ruled his death accidental. There had been no evidence of foul play. Max must have handled the poison improperly, it was determined.

Joe knew the old man was not stupid. He didn't handle poison. Strychnine was rarely used, and if so, only by farmers for weeds and crops. Max had immense respect for wildlife and would never use or put something into the environment that could cause harm.

After saying goodbye to his mentor in the ER that night, Joe had gone directly to the site where Max set up his campsite from April to October. It had been past midnight, but Joe had tromped through the woods, confident in his destination. Yet when he'd arrived at camp, he had been too emotionally overwhelmed to do a proper evidence search. Instead, he'd sat against the oak tree where Max had always crossed his legs and showered wisdom on Joe. He had cried, then fallen asleep. In the morning, Joe had pulled on latex gloves and gathered evidence. There hadn't been clear signs of unwelcome entry to the site, no containers that might have held the poison, but Joe had gathered all the stored food and the hunting knife Max used and taken it in to Forensics. The forensic specialist had reported all those items were clean. Whatever Max had touched was still out there, had been tucked somewhere away from the campsite or had been thrown.

And while the county had seemed to want to brush it off—the old man was dead and he hadn't had any family—the tribe had seen to the burial of his body.

Joe had insisted he be allowed to continue with the investigation. The tribal police had given him permission, as they were not pursuing the death, having accepted the accidental poison ruling as final.

He might not have been family by blood, but Max was true family to Joe. He'd been there for Joe when he was a kid, and had literally saved his life. And he had been the reason Joe had developed his voracious love for the outdoors and wildlife.

Touching the eagle talon that hung from the leather cord about his neck, Joe muttered, "You won't die in vain, Max." He'd been allowed to take the talisman from Max's things after the lab had cleared it as free from poison. The talon had been given to Max by his grandfather; a talisman earned because he had been a healer. It had been cherished by Max.

But the tracks to whoever had poisoned Max—and the reason why—were muddled. Did Max have enemies? Not that Joe had been aware of. He'd strayed from close tribal friendships and had been a lone wolf the last few decades. Not harming any living soul, leaving peaceably. A life well lived, and yet, it had been cut short.

The thought to tie Max's alleged murder to the poaching investigation only clicked when Joe remembered Max once muttering that he knew exactly who poached in the county, and that they would get their own someday. Joe had mentioned a family name, and Max's jaw had tightened in confirmation. Everyone knew the Davis family did as they pleased, and poaching was only one of many illegal activities in which they engaged—and got away with.

Now he needed new evidence, a break in the investigation, that would confirm his suspicion. So far, the Davis family had been elusive and covered their tracks like the seasoned tracker-hunters Joe knew they were.

The police radio crackled on the dashboard, and Dispatch reported an incident close to Joe.

"Anyone else respond?" he replied. Generally, if the disturbance was not directly related to fish and game, Dispatch sent out county law enforcement.

"We've got two officers in the area, but both are at the iron mine cave-in."

This morning a closed taconite mine had reported a cave-in. It was believed three overzealous explorers who had crossed the barbed wire fence closing off the mine could be trapped inside.

"No problem," Joe said. "I can handle it. What's the call?"

"Skylar Davis reports she's been shot at on her property. Her address is—"

"I got it." Joe shoved the canteen onto the passenger seat and turned the key in the ignition. His heart suddenly thundered. He knew Skylar Davis. Too well. "Is she hurt?"

"Not sure," Dispatch reported. "Sounded pretty calm on the call. You know where she lives?"

"I'm ten minutes from her land," he said. "I'm on my way."

He spun the truck around on the gravel road and headed east toward the lake where Merlin Davis—brother of Malcolm Davis, who owned Davis Trucking—had owned land for decades. Skylar had inherited her father's land years ago after cancer had taken his life. His daughter now lived alone on hundreds of forested acreage set at the edge of the Boundary Waters Canoe Area. She was a strong woman. A beautiful woman.

She was…the woman Joe could never sweep out of his thoughts. The one who had gotten away.

And she'd been shot at?

He slammed his foot onto the accelerator.

SKYLAR OPENED THE door and sucked in a gasp. Joseph Cash stood on the front stoop, dark hair swept over one eye and looking smart in his uniform. The forest-green short-sleeved shirt and slacks served to enhance his tan skin. Hand at his hip where a gun was holstered, he had been looking aside until she'd stepped onto the threshold. When he turned to her and his stunning green eyes connected with hers, she clasped a hand over her heart.

"Skylar, are you all right?" She heard genuine concern in his urgent tone.

She had so many things she wanted to say to him. Yet at the moment, she didn't know how to assemble a coherent sentence. Joseph Cash was the kindest person she'd known, and had always seemed to be there when she'd needed protecting. Be it in high school when she'd been bullied for sitting at the unpopular kids' table, or even when she'd had to struggle for customers when she'd been working as a small-animal veterinarian in town and most took their animals to the big city of Duluth. And yet, despite his kindnesses, she'd pushed Joe away, wanting to prove to him that she was her own woman. Independent and strong. That she didn't need a man to look over her.

Her rushed choice in fiancé had proved just that point. What a fool she had been.

"Joe," she said. "I didn't expect you. I called the county sheriff. I thought…"

"Well, you got me." He cast her a smile that surely made every woman in the county swoon. But Skylar had never known how to react to his easy charm and shyness, save with a thrust back of her shoulders and, admittedly, a stupidly stubborn need to prove herself.

"I was close when the call came in," he offered. "Just down the road coming off Lake Vaillant after a patrol. You okay, Skylar? Dispatch reports you were shot at? What's going on?"

"I'm okay. And yes, I believe I was shot at." She absently stroked her fingers over her ear, covering it with her loose blond hair. "I didn't expect you," she said again, rather dumbly.

Because if she had known Joseph Cash would be the one standing on her front stoop, she might have brushed on a little blush and combed her hair. At the very least, changed into some clean jeans.

A squawk from behind Joe made him turn sharply on the creaky lower wood step. Skylar noticed his hand instinctively went to his hip where his gun was holstered. A chicken in a pink knit sweater scampered across the crushed quartz pebbles that paved the stone walk up to the front steps.

"What the hell?" Joe said.

"That's Becky. She wants you to see her. She's very concerned about her looks. Do you like her sweater?"

The man scratched his head and then bobbed it in a nod, even while squinting questionably. "Yes?"

"She's one of my rehab residents."

"That's right, you rehabilitate animals. I'm not even going to ask about the sweater." He followed the chicken's retreat across the yard until she scrambled around the side of the house.

"Uh…come inside." Skylar stepped back and allowed him to enter the log cabin where she'd been living for two years.

When her father passed, the family land had become her possession, as she was his only child. At least, it was hers according to a handwritten note Merlin Davis had written a week before his death. Skylar had lived in the house until she'd moved to Duluth for college. Eventually, she'd made her way back to the town of Checker Hill and set up shop as the resident veterinarian. She'd never gotten much business. The townspeople were leery of the name Davis. Now this home felt too big for one person, but it was a comfort to nestle onto the aged leather sofa in the evenings, blanket wrapped about her shoulders, and admire the photos of her and her dad that she kept on each and every wall.

"You want something to drink? I've got lemonade."

Joe grabbed her by the upper arm to stop her from fleeing across the open floor plan living area and into the kitchen.

"What is it?" She shrugged out of his grasp with a huff. He looked concerned now. Too much so. She didn't want any man's pity.

"Seriously? Skylar, I'm not here for lemonade. I'm here to make sure you're okay. And not bleeding." He looked from her head down to her shoulders and all the way to her feet, then back up again. "And—where did the shots come from? Do you know who it was? How long has it been? I should go outside and take a look around. It's this way, right?"

He headed through the living area and skirted the long quartz kitchen counter. Toward the back of the house sat the screened-in sunporch that stretched the width of the cabin and overlooked the lake. Once before, he'd been in this cabin. When her father had been dying, he'd come to pay his respects. But how dare he traipse on through—

Skylar stopped herself from reprimanding him. He was here on duty. And she had called the police for help, much as her better judgment had screamed for her not to. Would she hear about this from her uncle? On the other hand, maybe Malcolm Davis already knew about the incident. And, yes, that thought sickened Skylar.

"Just through the sliding doors," she called to Joe. "You can take the deck stairs down to the backyard."

After grabbing her cowboy hat, which rested on the back of the couch and which she wore like any other woman might wear earrings or a favorite necklace, she followed the man's bowlegged pace out to the deck.

Standing on the high wood deck, which was stilted ten feet up due to the slope of the ground below, Joe took in everything. The perimeter of the yard was round, echoing out from the firepit in the center. Surrounding the yard were striped hostas that grew thick and lush in the shade provided by the paper birch and sugar maple.

He took the stairs down to the ground. "Where were you? Were you burning a fire?"

He walked over to the fire pit and peered over it. Burnt cedar lingered in the air. As well, the grass was speckled with gray ash flakes from her hastily dowsing the flames with the garden hose after calling the sheriff.

Skylar cringed when she noticed the wedding dress was only half burned and melted among the charred logs. She hadn't thought to cover up what she'd been doing. It had been a personal moment. A much-needed ritual of release. A reclaiming of her power.

Joe scratched his head. Hands at his hips, head cocked downward, he stared at the remnants of the dress. Skylar didn't want to answer the question that must be lighting all the circuits in his brain right now.

"Tell me everything," he said. Then he stretched his gaze around the backyard and out toward the lake. "Did you get a look at the shooter? Were they on your property? Cruising by in a boat? Partyers out for a spin on the lake?"

"I don't know." Skylar walked over to the smoldering fire pit and stood beside the hitching post, which she utilized as a stand to hang roasting sticks and an emergency water bucket she always kept filled when she was burning.

"I was burning a few things. And… I was about here." She stepped to the right a few feet and Joe turned to eye her intently. Dark stubble shadowed his jaw. The golden evening light, beaming through the tree canopy, granted his eyes a rich emerald cast. Everything about the man was intense, dark and—waiting on her.

"Yes, here," she decided, stomping her boot toe into the grass. "I was talking to Stella—"

"There was someone else here?"

"Stella, my wolf."

"Your…wolf?" He hooked his hands in the back pockets of his pants and looked about. "What the—? You took in a wolf cub?"

"Stella has been with me a few years. I found her in a snare trap when she was a pup. I hate it when hunters call those things humane. They are anything but. I took her to the office in town and had to amputate her back leg. Since then, she's flourished. She's not around right now."

Skylar scanned the area. The wolf must be off with the half-dozen chickens—surprisingly, her best friends. Stella was protective of Skylar, but she always left the immediate area when visitors or company arrived. She was a little skittish until she could scent out the newcomer, and then she would eventually put in an appearance.

"I do rehabilitate animals," Skylar pointed out to Joe, who nodded.

"Right. I just thought keeping a wolf as a pet…"

"I have a permit."

"Sure. Still, they are a wild animal." He gave her a side glance that dripped with judgment.

"She had nowhere else to go. I tried to get her to return to the pack, but they wouldn't have it."

"Uh-huh." He wasn't having it, either.

Yes, wolves were wild and should never be kept as pets. Skylar agreed with that wholeheartedly. But when injured and abandoned by their pack, the wolf's only future was living as a loner. And for a pup living out in the wild populated with predators, the fate was most certainly a cruel death.

It didn't matter to her what Joe thought of her choice to keep Stella. Skylar loved her like a family member.

"So you were standing right there and…?" he prompted.

"I was watching the flames, talking to Stella and…at first I felt something on my ear. Thought it was a wicked mosquito bite."

She touched her ear and Joe stepped forward. It was well past the supper hour, and the forest edging her backyard filtered the setting sun, turning it into a hazy twilight. He dug out a small flashlight from a back pocket and shone it on her ear. The man stood so close she could smell his aftershave—something subtle yet masculine with a hint of lemony citronella.

He examined her ear, which had been nicked on the top and had bled minimally. Of course, she'd gasped at the sight of it in the bathroom mirror. She'd never been so close to being killed in her life. And that had angered more than frightened her. What would have become of Stella and the other animals she cared for if she had died? The thought of them being relocated, or worse, was heart wrenching.

As Joe looked her over, she studied his face. There were three Cash brothers, all born and raised in Crooked Creek, a sister town to Checker Hill. There wasn't a female in either of the two close towns who didn't know who they were, because those boys were genetic anomalies, fashion models roughed up by the wild. Sinuous and muscular. So sexy. And Joe's deep green eyes were a thing to behold.

"If that bullet had been half an inch closer…" The man suddenly bowed his head and winced.

Skylar was taken aback by his reaction. "Joe? What's wrong? I'm okay."

"Right." He lifted his head and his jaw pulsed with tension. "You always were able to take care of yourself."

He'd learned exactly what she'd hoped to teach him about her. Regrettably.

Skylar lifted her chin bravely. "Still can take care of myself."

"Being shot at is no way to go about it, Skylar. If anything would have happened to you…" He winced again and looked aside, toward the fire pit.

Skylar found herself leaning forward in hopes of him finishing that sentence. Then again, she suspected how he would finish it. He'd never hidden his interest in her. And she wasn't prepared for such a statement right now.

If only he'd said as much to her two months earlier. Of course, then he'd been avoiding her like the plague.

It was well deserved on her part.

He placed his hands akimbo and scanned the lake. "Do you know what direction the shot was fired from?"

She pointed out through the gap in the bowed birch trees that she'd always thought of as a sort of pulled-back curtain to the stage of the lake. "I feel like it came from that way."

"See anyone down by the shore?"

She shook her head. Then she remembered, and turned to point out the bullet holes that had splintered and pierced the hitching post.

"Two?" Joe bent to study the post with the flashlight. "These are clean, and one goes all the way through." He paused and glanced at her as if to temper his words for her tender ears.

"I'm a big girl, Joe. You can say the bad stuff without offending or scaring me."

"I guess so." He returned his attention to the holes and tapped the post with a finger. "I have some evidence bags in the truck. I'm going to grab them, but I should also call in someone to take some photos and—" His attention veered to the ground behind the post. "Here's a bullet."

He tugged out a black latex glove from his pocket, pulled it on and picked up the bullet from the ground. It was long, and Skylar leaned in to peer at it as he did.

Joe swore.

"What is it?" she asked.

"My dad collects guns, and he taught me and my brothers a lot about the different types and their ammunition. This is most definitely from a high-powered rifle, Skylar."

"I don't understand. Not the usual hunting rifle?"

"Nope. If that had been the case, that hitching post would be pocked with lead shot. As well as you."

Skylar sucked in a breath.

"Sorry. Didn't mean to say that."

She nodded, no longer feeling quite as strong as she wanted to.

Joe turned and again cast a glance across the lake. "I don't think the shooter was close. Could have been across the lake. Which means this is some serious business."

He turned to face her directly and asked, "What's going on? Why would someone be shooting at you? Skylar, is there something you need to tell me?"

Chapter Three

Joe had rushed to Skylar's home upon getting the call from Dispatch. Simply hearing her name had been all he'd needed to become immersed in those old familiar feelings he always got whenever he thought about the tall, sexy blonde. Feelings he wasn't prepared to let emerge right now, because then he'd have to struggle with what had once felt like heartache.

Hell, who was he kidding? It had been, and still was, heartache.

Save for occasionally spying her walking into the grocery store or out of the local café, he hadn't spoken to her for almost a year. That had been a purposeful avoidance.

Long, tawny blond hair spilled over her shoulders. And that cowboy hat she always wore shaded her blue eyes, but in the rich evening twilight, a flash of sun from across the lake created glints like sapphires in those irises. And when she parted her soft pink lips to speak, Joe's heart thundered.

"I don't know what you think I should know, Joe," she said. "How can I know who was shooting at me?"

Drawn back to the moment, he briefly met her gaze— and almost fell into that heartache again. But he managed to snag a grip on the present and pull himself up and into business mode.

"It's standard procedure to ask a lot of questions after an incident like this," he said. "Any details you can provide that might help me figure this out?" He cast his gaze across the lake again. "It had to have come from across the lake."

"Really? That far away? It's a good three-quarters of a mile to the other side."

"Sniper rifles can hit a target miles away. My brother, Jason, used to be one of the best when he was…well." Jason didn't like his family to talk about the fact he used to be a CIA agent. And most didn't know that he had been. "Not that it was such a rifle. Nothing's been confirmed yet. But whoever made that shot…"

It wasn't right to be impressed at a moment like this, but that was some distance to the other side of the lake. Had to have been a boat driving by.

Skylar blew out a breath, but it had a nervous vibration to it. She suddenly stepped to the side and wobbled. Joe caught her arm and shoulder against his chest and hugged her. The scent of pine and lemons teased his nose. He slid a hand down to her waist and across her back to offer her a sturdy hold.

"You okay?"

She nodded, but her expression indicated she was far from okay.

"Let's get you inside. I don't think it's wise to stand out here."

"You think they could still be out there? It's been over an hour."

"Unlikely." He helped her walk toward the deck. "But you could use a cup of tea or something."

"Brandy," she said, then laughed. "Oh, Joe, I guess it did throw me. I was fine after I called the police. But now…"

As they approached the deck stairs, a dog came padding out from the forest that edged the north side of the house.

But wait. That was no dog.

"Stella has finally decided you pass muster." Skylar gripped the deck railing and sat on the second step from the bottom. "Just give me a minute, will you?"

"Of course." While Skylar sat to settle her nerves, Joe whistled to the approaching animal. "A timber wolf."

"She's my rescue sweetie. Hey, Stella."

The beautiful wolf approached on light footsteps, her gold eyes and coal nose aimed for Joe. Her tail was held slightly erect, with a bit of a kink to it. Warning, but cautiously optimistic. He'd known that Skylar had found a wolf pup in a trap a few years ago, and thought she'd rehabilitated it and sent it off to its pack. But to keep it as a pet?

By instinct, he dropped to one knee and bowed his head as Stella neared. One thing a human should never do was look a wolf directly in the eye. It was a sign of challenge and authority that he dared not risk with this unfamiliar wolf. He noticed a slight hop to her step. She managed very well on three legs.

Raising his head, Joe held out his hand but did not stretch toward the curious animal. She would sniff him out, decide what she thought about him. As she had likely been doing when she'd been hiding in the woods. A wolf's sense of smell was far superior to that of a dog's. Stella had already decided whether he was friend or foe. Because of that, he felt honored that she'd come out to greet him.

The wolf approached on careful footsteps, stretching out her neck to sniff at Joe's fingers. Her tail unkinked and waggled slightly.

"I spent a lot of time with her in the early months," Skylar commented from the step. "Nearly twenty-four/ seven, sleeping with her on a mattress for weeks, acclimating her to my human self and letting her know I would not harm her."

She'd taken the right steps for a wolf to live with humans. But Joe always favored reintroducing the animal back into the wild before such drastic measures were taken. On the other hand, if her pack had abandoned her, as they may do to the sick or wounded, he could be thankful Skylar had been there for her.

"I suspect her mother was killed. Otherwise, I'm sure she would have stayed around her pup in the trap."

"Very possible. Wolves will never be pets," Joe said quietly. "They will always have the wild in them. Right, Stella?"

The wolf's tongue lashed his fingers, and he let out the breath he had been holding. Just one lick. She wasn't going to get overly enthusiastic about a new human, but she did seem to trust him. As proof, she allowed him to ruffle his hand over her fur and he went for the sweet spot behind her ear, giving it a light scratch. The wolf sat before him, reveling in the attention he gave her.

"She's beautiful. I'm honored to meet you, Stella. But where's your pack?"

"Pretty sure she was from the Boundary Edge pack," Skylar said. "I checked the records with the wolf center. They hadn't recorded any births, but they don't have twenty-four/seven watch, either. And only one of the pack males is tagged with a tracking device. They were able to tell me about a year after I'd had Stella that one of the females was missing. They hadn't found her body. So I'm sticking with the dead-mother theory. Stella was a long way from home. That pack travels about ten miles north from here."

"I'm familiar with that pack," Joe said. "Well, their territory. Never gotten close to any of them, but I have tracked them before. So Stella was found in a leg trap?"

"It was actually a snare. She was near death. Had been gnawing at her own leg. I waited and watched for other wolves, but there were none close. I figured she was about three months old at the time. It's been almost three years.

She'll never be mine, but I am her person. I did take her to the pack rendezvous point about a month after she'd been with me. Not a single wolf showed."

"They were watching," Joe guessed. "But by then Stella was marked by human scent." He combed his fingers through Stella's soft summer pelt. The brown, gray and black fur had likely received a good combing from Skylar, for he didn't notice any unpreened winter undercoat. She lifted her head, luxuriating in his touch. "That's too bad. She would thrive with others of her kind."

"She's not doing so terribly with me."

"No, she's not. Looks healthy and happy."

The wolf tilted her head against his head and he took a moment to relish the contact. It was rare he got to experience the wild so close. And, yes, she was still wild. He'd wager any man who came toward Skylar with intent to harm, or whom Stella hadn't properly sniffed out, would risk a bite or worse.

"You haven't started your own pack, have you, Skylar?"

"Of my own design. I rehabilitate all breeds here. Goats, chickens, cats and snakes. Even had a baby moose once, but thankfully, she went back to her mother. Stella was my first and so far only wolf. Which reminds me, I have to run into town tomorrow to pick up some red yarn."

"For rehabilitation purposes?"

"You met Becky. She wants a change of sweater. Very fashion forward, that chicken."

Somewhere on the edge of the yard, a goat bleated.

"Beyoncé knows we're talking about her," Skylar offered. "She's a dancer."

Joe didn't even know how to respond, so he let that one pass without comment.

Now Stella licked his face. So he sat on the ground and she stepped forward onto his legs. The wolf was big, perhaps eighty pounds, but not as big as some could get in the wild. Standing on their back legs, a wolf could rise well over a tall man's head. Their weight could range from seventy to one hundred fifty pounds, and they were strong and powerful. Stella seemed amiable, willing to accept him.

"This is the first time she's ever welcomed a stranger so freely," Skylar said. "There's always been something special about you, Joe. I think you're a wolf whisperer."

Joe shook his head. She'd never teasingly called him Nature Boy, as his older brothers were apt to, which he appreciated. It was a nickname that had stuck since that fateful weekend he'd gotten lost in the Boundary Waters. Just thinking about it brought up memories of Max Owen, and that forced Joe back to the present. Because he would not let Max's bizarre death be ignored without discovering the reason behind it.

"I just like animals," he offered. "All animals. And I respect them. They have souls and are more a part of this land than we will ever be. But enough of the greeting—we have to get your person inside," he said to Stella. "She's been through a lot. And I want to head across the lake to look around."

As Joe stood, the wolf followed, watching him guide Skylar up the stairs by her arm. She was reluctant to accept the assistance—he could sense her tug in resistance—but finally she relented and her body hugged his as he walked her across the deck toward the patio doors.

Skylar Davis possessed an independent streak deeper than his ability to express his true feelings toward her. They'd known one another since high school, and he'd pined over her from afar since then. They'd become friends as sophomores—biology class had paired them over a frog dissection—and following high school, college had separated them for years. But they'd both found their way back to Checker Hill, and one another. A few years ago, they had decided to take a chance at dating. Thing was, their schedules had never meshed, and each time Joe had asked Skylar if she was free, she had been seeing someone else. Vice versa, for one time she'd asked him out when he'd been dating a girl from Duluth.

There had been that time at a wedding reception for a mutual friend. They'd both been drunk. And, well, what had ensued that night—or rather, hadn't—had changed things between them.

And then Joe's best friend had stepped into the picture and had turned Skylar's head completely away from Joe. And that was the reason he hadn't spoken to her in a year.

Joe cast a glance down toward the extinguished fire pit. A wedding dress lay smoldering in bits and pieces. He'd like to ask about that, but he'd wait for a better time.

SKYLAR WATCHED AS Joe pulled onto the long, pine-bordered driveway that curled out to the county road. He intended to cruise to the other side of the lake and take a look around. All in a day's police work, she felt sure. Impressive, since she was aware he'd worked a full shift today and she'd thought conservation officers generally stuck to checking hunting licenses and beach patrol.

No, she knew that wasn't right. The conservation officers in the Boundary Waters had their hands full with poaching, theft of natural resources, search and rescue of lost hikers, and they were even called in to consult on murder cases when a body was found in the woods. They carried all the usual authority and powers a police officer would.

Much as she hadn't expected Joe to knock on her door this evening, she was thankful now that it had been him. Because she needed…something. Help? Support? This keeping her mouth shut about the minor indiscretions Davis Trucking employees committed and hoping her relationship with her uncle would improve was getting her nowhere.

Still, Malcolm had offered to buy a section of her land. Then she'd have seed money to build the shelter. But at what price was her alliance to her uncle? Would her dad have wanted that? He'd kept the land pristine. Had always refused to sell to his brother so he could fulfill plans to expand the business. Malcolm had no love for the environment, while Merlin, Skylar's dad, had been a certified tree hugger.

And now she'd been threatened. Seriously. She could have been killed. Had the threat come from Malcolm? That didn't make sense. If he wanted to buy her land he should be kissing up to her. And yet…

Two days ago, Skylar had stumbled onto something she shouldn't have seen. She wasn't sure what had been in those freezers in the Davis Trucking warehouse, but the man with a rifle in hand who'd discovered her had not been happy to see her.

What to do?

Because, much as Uncle Malcolm had stood for the opposite of everything her father had, he was still family. And family meant something to her.

But family didn't fire warning shots at one another.

Chapter Four

The drive around the lake did not bring Joe to the spot where he'd determined the shooter might have been standing. Calling for backup, he got an answer from a state patrol. An officer could be around in twenty minutes. Joe predicted a hike through the woods to get to the position across from the lake to the Davis home, so he waited for the patrol officer to arrive. Otherwise, they'd never find each other in the thick pine and birch forest that offered only narrow trails here and there.

As a conservation officer, he spent 90 percent of his time roaming the woods and lakes in his territory. He knew this area. But he hadn't spent much time on this lake. It was small and usually only boated by the residents living around it.

Antsy, and wishing he'd taken an hour in the gym this morning to work out, he bounced on his feet. His hiking boots were not the most comfortable for such movement, but he liked to stay limber. He snapped up his knee and kicked out in a Muay Thai move that could knock an opponent flat.

He'd developed an interest in martial arts from watching his mother practice her moves from the karate class she'd taken when her boys were younger. He'd started with karate, but after watching a few *National Geographic* specials and sports TV, he'd fallen in love with the ultrahigh kicks and swift elbow strikes Muay Thai offered. It was all about brute power. It worked his body in every way possible, and kept him limber and sharp. And a well-honed body only enhanced an ever-growing soul. He was constantly learning. His greatest teachers? Nature and the wildlife he had taken an oath to protect.

But honestly? It was a good means to get out his anger by kicking the sandbag now and then.

Pausing at the harsh, croaking call of a blue heron, Joe lifted his head and closed his eyes. He had to smile at that sound. Such utter peace here, away from the city and major highways. He opened his eyes, scanning the treetops in hopes of seeing the heron nest, but the canopy was thick. The last slivers of sunlight glinted like stars.

A car honked and Joe waved to the approaching patrol car. Brent Kofax was with the sheriff's department. In cases where someone had been shot, or threatened, they usually joined the investigation. He stepped out of the car and gave Joe a thumbs-up. Joe had worked with Brent on a few occasions when backup was necessary. Usually when he knew he'd be approaching a boat full of drunk fishermen, or that one time Joe had needed someone to help him sort out steel traps from a burned-out Quonset building.

"What do you have tonight, Cash?"

Joe shook Brent's hand and pointed over his shoulder toward the lake. "The Davis woman who lives across the lake was shot at earlier this evening. Judging by the trajectory of the hit, I'm guessing the shooter might have been in the woods about a quarter mile up. I need another set of eyes. You ready to do some hiking?"

"I always know you'll give me a workout when I answer your calls. Already changed into hiking boots. Let's do this!"

From his car Joe grabbed a backpack that contained ev-

idence-collection supplies, water and snacks, as well as a
compass and other survival equipment. He never ventured
into the woods without it. At his hip, he wore his pistol,
a Glock .40 caliber. Brent carried a 12-gauge pump shot-
gun, standard issue nowadays.

The two men picked carefully through the brush and
grasses, dodging roots and ducking low-hanging pine tree
branches. Brent was an avid hunter, unlike Joe, but he
wouldn't criticize the man's need to kill innocent animals
for food. The day he started doing that was the day he
volunteered to have his life held under a microscope and
examined for faults. He had many, but cruelty to animals
was not one of them. His anti-hunting stance got him some
razzing from his fellow conservation officers. They tended
to think that COs with wildlife management training let
their love for nature get in the way of their police work.
The opposite was true. Joe protected the citizens as well
as the animals.

They hiked half a mile through thick pine and aspen.
The sun had set, and he and Brent were now using flash-
lights, but the moon was three-quarters full and there was
still some ambient light glimmering off the calm lake
water. Thanks to Joe's sharp eye, they found a deer trail,
as well as scat droppings under some fallen maple leaves.
Their path kept them within a thirty-foot distance from the
lake shore. The shooter would have gotten close enough to
the edge of the forest for a good, clear shot, Joe decided.
Thankful for the beaten-down brush, he tracked until he
spotted shell casings. Ballistic evidence. Excellent.

They stood twenty feet in from the lakeshore, well camouflaged by tall brush and a frond of wild fern. With shell
casings just behind him, and the grass trampled down
around them, Joe figured this was where the shooter had
been positioned. He studied the ground, which was folded-
down marsh grass and moss. If it had been dirt, he might

have found impressions from a tripod the shooter would have surely utilized to hold steady aim and sight in the Davis property nearly a mile across the lake, as well as shoe tracks.

"You never cease to amaze me," Brent commented as he bent to shine his flashlight on the shell casings. "What? Did you grow up in the woods like Mowgli, or something?"

"I think Mowgli lived in the jungle," Joe commented. But there had been a time, in his family, when his brothers had referred to him as Mowgli, until they'd decided on the more annoying Nature Boy.

It wasn't often a boy found himself lost in the woods for three days, and was finally led out and home by a pack of wolves. That experience had changed Joe's life. First, his parents had hugged him and showered him with kisses. Then, they'd grounded him for wandering off by himself without taking a cell phone along, despite the fact that it wasn't easy to call home in the middle of the Boundary Waters where cell towers were few and far between. But Joe had taken the punishment and had used it to study up on wolves, and from that day forward his direction had been clear. He wanted to work with wildlife and protect them from the hazards of living so close to humans.

"You got an evidence kit in that backpack?" Brent asked. "I left mine in the car." He stood and flashed his beam around where they stood, hooking his rifle up on a shoulder.

"Always." Taking a pair of black latex gloves out of the backpack, Joe collected the two metal shell casings and put them in a plastic bag he usually used for collecting marine specimens from boats docked on lake shores. He'd seen the two bullet holes in the hitching post by the fire pit.

That the first bullet had nicked Skylar's ear told him someone did not want her dead. Whoever had pulled the trigger had skills similar to his brother Jason. To come so close without harming her? Such a shot required nerves of steel and perfect timing.

The second shot must have zinged within a foot of her body. Enough to scare the hell out of anyone. Any woman—or man—would have fainted or run screaming. He'd figured Skylar had taken it calmly, until he'd seen her falter beside the fire pit. He'd left her sipping brandy with Stella curled at her feet. She'd insisted she didn't want protection overnight, but Joe considered sending out a patrol officer to park down the long drive that led to her property.

Or he might do that himself. He'd been up since five, had hit the lake at six and had spent a hot day out on the water. It was late now, and he was exhausted, but he knew he wouldn't sleep if he left Skylar alone. He'd park at the end of the drive, and she'd never be the wiser. There were worse ways to spend a summer evening.

As he stood up from collecting the casings, his gaze caught something that was neither flora nor fauna. Brent took a step forward, his attention focused across the lake, and—

Joe swore and lunged into a kick that caught the officer on his hip, hitting none too gently and throwing him off course.

"What the hell, man?" Brent had dropped his flashlight and rifle, and splayed his hands in question before him.

The flashlight rolled and stopped with a clink. Both men looked to the spot where Brent had almost stepped. Joe cautiously approached the oak tree. His flashlight swept the ground, taking it all in, watching for a steel trap. But he knew he wouldn't find it, because the set snare wasn't usually used in tandem with such a trap.

The flashlight beam fell over the snare trap—a light wire cable anchored to the base of the oak. If any animal stepped on that, the loop would tighten about their leg. Or worse—if they sniffed the bait peeking out from under some wet aspen leaves, it would become a noose and string them up, likely breaking their neck. In a worst-case scenario, the noose would not snap and the animal would be suspended, alive, left to slowly suffocate until the poacher returned.

"Bastards," Joe muttered.

"I almost stepped on that." Brent eased a hand down his hip where Joe had kicked him. "You could have just called 'stop.'"

"I owed you one for that upper cut in the gym a few weeks ago."

Brent chuckled. "Yeah, that was a good one. Pretty rare I get the upper hand with you."

Joe picked up a branch and used it to nudge the snare. The trap sprang and released the snare in a flutter of leaves. Joe would disassemble the entire thing and take it in to the county forensics lab for a thorough study. With any luck, they'd find fingerprints.

"You got wire snips in that backpack?" Brent asked as Joe sorted through his pack. When he proudly displayed just that, Brent shook his head. "Never mind. Mowgli knows what he's doing."

Yeah, he didn't care for the moniker so much from people who weren't family. Joe snipped the cable and, latex gloves still on, untangled it from around the tree trunk. Brent gathered it into a loop.

The disturbance uncovered a few bits of bait meat. The smell was rancid, but Joe bagged it as well. The forensic lab could determine a lot from testing bait meat, such as the animal it had come from, and possibly even pick up some fingerprints. Briefly, he wondered if the meat was poisoned. It was an important detail that he wouldn't have proof of until tests had been run.

Stuffing the evidence bags into his backpack, Joe stood and looked out over the chrome-and-hematite-sheened lake. His investigation into the poaching hadn't taken him quite this far south. Now he'd expand that range. First, he needed to check whose land this was. He'd thought it was state owned, but he couldn't be sure until he checked a map.

The poachers weren't even sneaky; they seemed to be growing bolder every month, leaving traps everywhere. And the thing that had tipped Joe off initially had been an ad on Craigslist. Selling deer antlers and bear claws online? Blatant.

Yet he hadn't run into the poison that had been found in Max's system, even with the samples he'd sent in to the lab. He could be way off course in trying to connect the man's death with the local poachers, but Joe sensed he was on the right track. Every bone in his body pushed him to continue with the search for Max's killer. The man had not been accidentally poisoned. No one handled strychnine without taking precautions.

And now there was a new twist to the investigation. Could the one who had set this snare have been the one who'd shot at Skylar? It couldn't be coincidence that the shooting site was so close to a trap.

Joe narrowed his gaze across the calm dark waters. A small light showed from what was probably Skylar's living room. He hoped she would sleep well, with the wolf keeping guard outside. But he didn't guess Stella would provide protection, and he wouldn't expect it. The animal seemed skittish and hesitant to approach strangers, and that wasn't a bad thing. But that meant Skylar was not safe.

And yet, why would a poacher shoot at her? It had to have been some kind of warning. Did she know something that someone wanted her to keep silent about? And if it had been a warning, whoever had fired would have known his target would take it as a warning.

Which meant Skylar might know more than she was letting on.

"Lieutenant Brock said something about finding illegal guns in an Ely residence." Brent looped the coiled cable over his forearm.

"I found a cache of guns with the serial numbers filed off last week," Joe offered. "They were in a shed with a dozen illegal deer racks."

Brent shook his head. "You need help with any of it?"

Joe nodded. "Always. You can take this in to the county forensics van, for a start."

"I'm heading toward Ely. I think Elaine Hester is on shift tonight. Smart chick. What are you up to now?"

"Headed back across the lake."

He needn't tell Brent he had decided to stand vigil outside the target's home because he feared losing her more than his heart could stand.

STEPPING OUT OF the shower, Skylar dried off, then reached for the brandy goblet on the vanity. She downed the last two swallows. Whew! That burned. But she instantly felt the calming effects ease through her muscles, and the need to close her eyes and drop into a heavy sleep.

"Come on, Stella."

She padded naked down the hallway to her bedroom, followed by the three-legged wolf. Stella generally slept outside, but she would never ignore an invite to stay indoors. The security panel for the entire house was positioned at eye level in the bedroom, by the door. She turned on all the door locks and the perimeter alarm, which was set only for the weight of a vehicle since she had so many animals wandering around at any given time.

Stella jumped onto the end of her bed. Her spot. And let no man try to prove otherwise.

Pulling on a long T-shirt that hung past her thighs, Skylar crawled onto the bed and lay on top of the sheets across the middle of the mattress, so she could smooth her palm over Stella's fur.

She hadn't seen Joseph Cash in…must be a year. He got more handsome every time she saw him. He had the "tall, dark stranger" thing going on full force. Except he wasn't a stranger, and…she wanted to see him again.

Under better circumstances than getting shot at.

"It was a warning," she whispered, tracing the top of her ear, which felt tender from the bruise. She caught a swallow at the back of her throat, followed by a single teardrop slipping down the side of her face.

She'd walked into a warehouse on Davis Trucking land, and before calling out for her uncle, she'd glanced around. There were crates everywhere, marked with company names. Standard inventory for a trucking outfit, she figured. But the freezers, six of them, had stood out. They were the large white chest kind, probably close to twenty cubic feet in volume.

What had been in them? With a trucking business, it could be anything. And while she'd always assumed they didn't store goods on-site, she didn't know enough about the operation.

A man standing over one of the opened freezers hadn't noticed her, so she'd cleared her throat. He'd lifted his head and swung a look over his shoulder, focusing his gaze on her. She hadn't recognized him, and he'd immediately slammed down the freezer cover and grabbed a rifle. The feeling of utter dread had overcome her. Skylar had turned and run. As she had, he'd called after her, "Don't tell, bitch! This is none of your concern."

She'd run straight to her truck, past a few truckers who had called out to her and whistled. The stranger hadn't followed her. Forget talking to her uncle. She'd been creeped out, and had put her truck in gear and gotten the hell out of there.

She hadn't told anyone. Because she wasn't sure what she had seen. But it had been something. Because tonight they had warned her.

And yet, she'd dared to call the police. Because she would not be scared off by some idiot assholes who thought they had a right to threaten a woman. Hell, the shooter could have killed her.

Now, dare she ask Joseph Cash to protect her?

Chapter Five

Joe woke and winced. He was sitting at an angle—ah, hell. He'd fallen asleep in the truck parked at the end of Skylar's driveway.

The rapping noise that had woken him thumped again on his window. Sliding upright in the driver's seat, he moaned at the tug to his aching back muscles, then managed a blinking glance to his left. And then he opened his eyes wide and took in the view.

Could a woman look more beautiful in a cowboy hat, no makeup and plain denim shirt unbuttoned to just there? He voted no. She was like sunshine and all those pretty things guys liked to look at but were always afraid to touch for fear of smearing them with dirt or breaking something delicate.

Skylar Davis was not a delicate woman. She'd made that clear to him over the years he'd known her. And he expected some stern words to follow the admonishing look she was giving him now.

Turning the keys in the ignition, Joe pushed the window button, which slid down slowly. "Mornin', Skylar."

"Really, Joe? Did you sleep out here all night?"

"Most of the time? Nope. Wasn't sleeping. I was on watch. Must have fallen asleep a few hours ago." He wasn't sure what time it was and glanced at the dashboard. Seven o'clock. He may have gotten two hours' sleep at most. The night had been spent with the radio turned low to the '90s top hits, his eyes half-closed, as he'd kept an eye toward the Davis house.

"I told you I didn't need looking after."

"Just doing my job, Skylar. You were in danger last night. It's not clear that danger has passed. I wouldn't be a very good law enforcement officer if I'd walked away and left you vulnerable. How'd you sleep? Where's Stella?"

"She's playing with Becky. And I'm headed into town on errands."

"Right. Pink yarn, wasn't it?"

"Red. That, and groceries. Will you move your truck so I can drive through? Or are you now a permanent fixture that I have to learn to live with like some kind of skin growth?"

Someone was not a morning person. Still, her pretty eyes made up for that touch of rancor. "Listen, Skylar, I know you don't care for me—"

"My feelings for you have nothing to do with what's going on right now, so don't bring that into the situation."

She had *feelings* for him? Joe raked his fingers through his hair and sat up a little straighter.

"I appreciate you investigating the shooting," she said. "And I understand you'll have further questions for me. I'll cooperate as much as I can. But I already gave you my statement."

"As much as you can?" Joe opened the car door and stepped out. Another tug at his back muscles reminded him how little time he spent sitting all night in a car keeping a vigilant watch for intruders. "What's going on, Skylar? I feel like you know something you're not willing to tell me. Or are you afraid? Is that it? Is someone threatening you?"

"Of course I was threatened!"

"Yes, but why? If it was a threat, then generally the person being threatened has an idea about why."

She crossed her arms tightly over her chest, paced to the front of his truck and then swung out her arms in surrender. "It's not what you think, Joe. I just… Did you find the place where the shooter may have been positioned?"

"I did. As predicted, I found a couple shell casings. Sent them in to forensics for analysis."

Now she gave him her full attention. Sunlight flashed through the tree canopy, gleaming on her smooth skin. That someone had wanted to hurt her, or at the very least threaten her, tightened Joe's resolve to find the culprit. No woman, especially Skylar, should ever be put in such a position of fear.

"I found a snare, set and waiting to spring."

Skylar nodded subtly, taking it in. She didn't seem surprised. And for as rampant as poaching was in the Superior Forest, it wasn't as if most people ever encountered such a situation unless they went looking for it, as a conservation officer would.

"You ever catch poachers on your land, Skylar?"

"Catch them? No. I'd be a fool to go after an idiot with a gun and the mentality that animals are there for the taking, no matter the pain they cause the poor creatures."

Joe nodded. They were of the same mind regarding treatment of animals. All animals. Not just the ones society had designated as pets.

"Most of the land owners around here carry a gun," he said. "And while the majority are law-abiding and only hunt with a license, there are those idiots, as you call them, who think they can do as they please. I've been investigating a poaching ring close to this area for months."

"Is that so?"

He nodded. She was interested, but she was also holding back on the conversation. She knew something. He sensed it. Could she have information that might lead him to whoever had poisoned Max?

"You know it's your duty to report poaching activity, Skylar."

"I know that."

"Don't approach the culprit, just get a name or description, location of the trap or snare, and call it in."

"I can do that. And I will. If I ever happen upon something like that."

"You gotta be careful trekking through these woods."

"This *is* my property."

"Is it clearly marked? Fenced?"

"No." She hooked a hand at her hip and lifted her chin. "My father had a good relationship with all the area families. We all respect boundaries and will often allow one another to hunt on our land, with permission. I've never had a problem…"

Joe waited as her words seemed to hang. She wasn't saying something, and he really wanted to wrench it out of her, but he didn't want to play hardball and force their relationship into something uncomfortable for her.

Not that they had a relationship. Well, beyond that he'd considered her a friend up until a year ago.

"What about your uncle?" he prompted. He knew Malcolm Davis's land hugged Merlin Davis's—now Skylar's—land in some manner. It had all originally been owned by their father, Skylar's grandfather.

"What about him?" Skylar now studied the ground intently.

Joe shrugged. "I see Davis Trucking driving the highways all the time. In Duluth, too."

"They are the third biggest trucking company in northern Minnesota. I'm sure they have a loading dock on Superior."

"Been around forever, too. You have a good relationship with them?"

"Davis Trucking? I can't say it's good, bad or ugly."

"I mean your uncle Malcolm. Didn't I hear something about him and your dad having a feud of some sort? I think you mentioned that to me once."

"My dad has been gone for two years, Joe. Leave the past in the past."

"Sorry." He shoved his hands into his back pockets.

That had been a cruel means to try to get more about Malcolm Davis out of her. The patriarch of Davis Trucking was on Joe's suspect list. But he'd yet to get hard evidence on him, save a few random deer pelts and a couple bald eagle talons found in one of his truckers' glove compartments.

"I have to get to the store," Skylar said, interrupting his thoughts. "It's still early, and I have some mowing to do, plus I need to move the chicken house. I like to do that before the hot afternoon sun beats down. You going to move your truck?"

"I will. But I do have more questions. They can wait until after I've had a better look at the evidence. I'm not going to stand back and let you face alone whatever the hell is going on, Skylar. Just a warning. I'm here for you. Like it or not."

She nodded and looked aside. "Sure thing, Joe. Thanks," she said on a tight whisper. "Talk to you soon."

She turned and strode off toward the cabin. Her long legs moved her swiftly, as did her swinging arms. No-nonsense wrapped in a tease of femininity. Had Cole Pruitt really married her? Last Joe had heard, the date had been set. And that wedding dress. So many questions he'd like to have answered.

"She's hiding something," Joe muttered.

And that hurt him almost as much as losing his chance at dating her had. Was she involved with the poachers his investigations were centered around? It was a quick and harsh judgment, but it was something he'd have to consider. She was a member of the Davis family, after all.

"Don't do this to me, Skylar," he said as he slid back behind the wheel of his truck. "I have too much respect for you."

SKYLAR PAID FOR the two bags of groceries—pleased the small market offered sundries such as the red yarn—then grabbed the bags and headed out to her truck parked in the grassy lot in front of the store. The old Ford she drove had once been red, but the paint job had faded over the years to a rust-mottled pink. Cole had been good with the small fixes it had needed. That was about the only thing she missed about not having him around.

She set the paper bags on the passenger seat and closed the door to walk around to the back, where she paused and leaned against the tailgate to watch passing cars. She was no longer in an irritated mood caused by thoughts of Joseph Cash and his soulful green eyes. Because, mercy, that man had cornered the market on sexy.

Why had she never hooked up with him?

They almost had that one night. And then…

And then. The big rejection from him. That still hurt a little. Even though she could understand where he'd been coming from—she being drunker than a skunk. And he had been toasted, as well. That he'd had the mental fortitude to refuse her suggestion of sex was either because he was a strange beast or because he hadn't been as interested in her as she'd thought.

Either way, at the time, his refusal had humiliated her. After that, she'd thought pushing him away was the smart thing to do. Really, the idea of being happy and in love with any man had only driven her mad after losing her father. He'd been torn apart when her mom had left. Skylar had been twelve that morning she'd found a note from her mother placed directly on top of her bowl of shredded wheat. She'd missed the school bus after reading the two sentences: *I can't do this anymore. I love you, Skylar. Mom.*

And she hadn't seen or heard from her since. No check-in calls. No Christmas cards. Not even a "hey, I'm still alive, don't worry about me" message on the phone. Her teenage years had been depressing. Skylar had once been confident and self-assured in her schoolwork, but middle school had been merely going through the motions. By her sophomore year, Skylar had decided to put her anger into her schoolwork and had graduated a year early. As if that would show her mom.

It hadn't, but it was how she'd coped with the situation. If her mom didn't need her, then she certainly didn't need her, either.

But her father had not been the same after his wife left. He'd refused to even date after that, telling Skylar Dorothy had been his soul mate. On his deathbed he had smiled and whispered Dorothy's name before drifting away.

The woman had not deserved such reverence. Had she ever appreciated her husband's love for her? That was a question Skylar wanted an answer to, but she knew it would never come. So she'd moved forward, and was doing as well as she could now that her dad was gone. Life had felt empty for a while after his death, but her focus on the animals she rehabilitated had worked like a jolt of life infused into her system. She didn't need anyone to make her happy. Nor did she want to risk falling for someone and having them walk out of her life.

Yet now Joe was back in her life, bedroom eyes peering at her suspiciously. The man was investigating a poaching ring? Skylar had to think only one second to guess who might be on his suspect list.

"Damn it." She closed her eyes. "With Joe involved, this is not going to be easy."

She hadn't been surprised to learn Joe had found a live snare close to the shooter's position. She'd seen snares and traps while walking her property. If she'd confessed that to Joe, he would have battered her with questions, all of which would lead to her uncle.

"I don't need this craziness," she said. "I just want a peaceful, simple life. Is that too much to ask?"

Just her and her animals. The three-legged wolf and the naked chicken whose saving grace was a single white tail feather she preened scrupulously. The trio of piglets who had been born underweight were currently thriving. Add to that the occasional dancing goat or family of orphaned baby opossums, and her life had been going smoothly. All she wanted was to build the shelter barn for her menagerie and set up an office for her veterinary supplies, plus a small operating room, and help those animals that she could.

Her cell phone rang, and Skylar answered.

"Miss Davis? I was given your name as someone who might be able to help."

She got calls that began like this often. With no vet in Checker Hills proper, the DNR knew she was the one who took in animals in need of rehabilitation. The alternative was to transport the animal to Duluth, more than an hour away.

"What's up?"

"I've got a baby boa constrictor on my front stoop."

That wasn't exactly her area of expertise. And it wasn't a reptile native to Minnesota. Which meant it had to be some pet that had gotten loose or been abandoned after the owner realized how difficult it was to care for an exotic animal.

"Did you call Animal Control? They're the ones who can wrangle it and remove it from your property."

"Yes, and they're on their way. It's something else I thought you could help me with."

"And what is that?"

"The snake gave one of my old farm cats a good squeeze, and she's in a bad way. Broken ribs for sure. I'm not sentimental about animals. Generally might be inclined to put the poor thing out of her misery. But this one, well, she was my beloved wife's favorite. Olivia died two months ago, bless her heart. And I can't bear to see the cat go now."

"Give me your address," Skylar said. "I'll be right there."

She was a sucker for a sad tale. Also, the distraction would be just what she needed to keep her mind from Joseph Cash and the poaching that she knew was taking place on her land.

Tucking away her cell phone, she turned and walked right into Malcolm Davis. Stepping back, she assessed his cool smile, shaded by the Panama hat he always wore. His face was long and bony, much as her father's had been. In fact, the two men had often been mistaken as twins, despite their two-year age difference.

"Uncle Malcolm, I didn't see you there."

She glanced across the lot. She didn't see his big black diesel truck anywhere. The man drove ostentatious vehicles, but his simple clothing and ordinary manner tended to throw her off, because he was anything but unassuming. Rather caustic, truth be told.

"How have you been, Skylar? Haven't seen you for a while."

It had been days since she'd walked into the shed on the Davis land, thinking to confront Malcolm about the trap she'd found on her land. She hadn't seen him that day, and her welcome had been anything but friendly. It wasn't her fault the trucking section of the land was vast and had so many buildings. She never knew where the main office was located. Well, hell, she hadn't been on her uncle's turf since she'd been a teen and they'd had a family summer get-together. Better days, for sure.

She'd seen things a few days ago after wandering into the wrong building. And she suspected Malcolm knew that.

"I tried to find you the other day," she said, stepping back a bit. He used their proximity to his advantage, and she wasn't going to allow it. Shoving her fingers in her front pockets, she jutted out her elbows, enlarging her personal space. "I stopped by the place."

"I was told that. Reggie found you wandering around snooping."

"Nope. Wasn't snooping. I went there with a purpose. But that maze of buildings and parked trucks you've got over there will disorient anyone. I was looking for you, and I wasn't sure where the office was located. And I wasn't greeted very nicely, either."

"Reggie keeps a tight hand on security around the place."

"Not tight enough to allow me to wander for ten minutes and get lost. I'd appreciate it if you'd let Reggie know that family does not care to have a .32 caliber pointed at her. Nor…" Was she going there? She had to know. "Nor does family appreciate being shot at from across the lake."

Malcolm lifted his chin, looking down at her with her father's blue eyes. "What did you come by for, Skylar?"

No reply to her accusation? Probably because it was true. Damn it!

He sucked in the corner of his lower lip, a weird habit she'd noticed he did often. That is, when she saw him. Skylar made a point of not associating with Malcolm's bunch. Much as her father had tried to be kind to his brother, they'd struggled to the end.

"I almost stepped into a snare trap placed on my property. Thought it was one of yours."

"And why would you think something like that?"

Beating about the bush regarding the situation was not endearing him to her. And the hairs on the back of her neck were prickling more intensely the longer he studied her.

"Because I know you and your employees have a nasty habit of poaching. Cole told me."

"Did he?" Another suck at his lip. "Cole Pruitt. You know when I told you I'd hired him part-time, I hadn't expected you to break it off with him. You lost yourself a good one there, Skylar."

"If that's what you consider good, then I have to question your moral leanings."

"You've got that high-and-mighty streak like your father had, Skylar. It's not appealing."

"I'm not trying to appeal to you, other than to ask that you'll respect the property borders and not set traps on my land. I do a lot of hiking through the woods. My father made a point of ensuring the trails and off trails were safe."

"About that land…" Malcolm glanced over her shoulder, squinting at the sunlight. "You know my offer to buy that north parcel still stands. But not for much longer."

Skylar tilted her head. "I'm still considering it."

Was she? Dad wouldn't have wanted her to sell.

"It's just a quarter-mile section on the north end, Skylar."

"You've already got an access road to the highway."

"But cutting across through the end of my brother's land would reduce travel times measurably."

"It's my land now."

"What happens if you die?"

Skylar's jaw dropped open and she quickly snapped it shut. The audacity of such a terrible question should not surprise her, coming from her uncle, but it did.

"Someone shot at me last night, Malcolm. Nearly

missed boring a hole right through my brain. So I almost did die."

Malcolm was too fidgety right now, and he'd stopped sucking on his lip.

"That's a shame. It really is. But what about that shelter I understand you want to build? Some sort of wildlife sanctuary?" he asked.

The only one who could have told him about that was Cole. He had not been involved with Malcolm when they'd first started dating. Skylar wasn't sure at what point they'd hooked up and Cole had started doing things for him. Illegal things. And he'd been drinking, too. He'd never been a drinker before.

"Cole told me you'd lost your cosigner for the loan," Malcolm said.

Because Cole had been going to cosign on the half-million-dollar loan. It would take a frosty day in July now for Skylar to ever trust that man again.

"That's none of your concern," she said.

"It could be," he said quickly. "You sell me that land and I'll cosign for you. I'll go you one better, and put down earnest money that I'm sure you'll need."

The offer was not what she should want. But a flat-out refusal stuck in her throat and she had to swallow to keep from swearing at him. It was all that she wanted. A means to begin her dream.

"Think about it," he said. "And do be careful, Skylar. Calling the police on your family is unkind."

"I didn't—"

He sucked in his lip loudly.

"Only a fool *wouldn't* call the police after nearly being shot," she said.

"And you are certainly no fool."

"Never have been, never will be." She had to hold back

a wince, because she had been a fool in a wedding dress two months earlier. And he knew it. "We done here?"

Malcolm nodded.

Skylar had to walk around him to get to the driver's side of her truck. He didn't move, just watched her slide in behind the wheel, and when she was ready to back up, he still stood there, eyeing her in the side mirror. It was a cool yet malicious look, and it prickled her skin. He was not a man to mess with. As her father had well known.

And he had just given her another warning.

After shifting into Reverse, she waited as he slowly turned and walked away, straight behind her truck, which meant she wasn't able to leave until she could see that he was halfway across the lot.

"Bastard," she muttered.

She couldn't help but think her dad would want her to build the shelter. She'd told him about her dreams for it. He'd said she must do it.

But to surrender some of the land to do so?

She had to say no to Malcolm. Her dreams would be dashed, but at least she'd remain true to her dad.

Chapter Six

Joe watched Lucy Carnet, the forensic lab tech, work meticulously over the snare trap Brent had brought in earlier. He didn't often show up to wait for results, but today his focus had narrowed solely on this investigation. Because Skylar could have been hurt, or worse.

No more dallying with the poachers. He would track them down. And if they had been the ones to shoot at Skylar, a conviction would be secured.

The lab was a mobile van that traveled the county. Most forensic work could be done in this lab; they covered everything from bodily fluid identification to explosives and firearms examination.

"Any DNA?" Joe asked after about twenty minutes of watching Lucy pluck out bits of grass and other minutiae from the steel cable.

"Dude, I won't have that answer until I've examined these specimens. Could take a few hours or even a few days, because I still have to send it in to the crime lab in Duluth for analysis. Sorry."

"Right. I knew that. But the shell casings are definitely manufactured by Lapua."

Lucy had looked at those first and had, surprisingly, guessed the make because they were similar to a recent bullet casing she'd studied.

"I'd say so. Was an easy match. Italian-made bullets, which are often used with the Finnish-made sniper rifle by the same name. Surprisingly common in this county."

A sniper rifle was serious business. And it made the hairs on Joe's arms prickle to know someone had Skylar in his sights. Had a professional shot at her? Joe had to wonder who had such skill to sight in a target at that distance. And come close enough to merely deliver a warning skim across her ear and not accidentally kill her. Could the shooter be ex-military, like his brother Jason?

"You going to check the local gun registry?" Lucy asked.

"Of course, but I suspect we won't find any matches."

"You never know. There are all sorts of guns all over the state. Heard your brother was involved in a gun-running investigation in Duluth."

"Jason?" Joe shrugged. "He had a close encounter with the Minnesota mafia and a related foreign contact, but no guns were seized. It was a murder investigation, actually."

And Jason did like to brag about that case to Joe and their older brother, Justin. It had been a coup for Jason after he'd been removed from his CIA duty and placed in the small town of Frost Falls as their chief of police. A town of less than a thousand people, where the most interesting law enforcement activity involved an old man who liked to walk naked down Main Street whenever he got toasted. Which, according to his brother's wincing recounts, was often.

As a result of the murder investigation, Jason had hooked up with a pretty French Interpol agent who was still hanging around. Good for him. Joe suspected Jason would pop the question soon. They had plans to move to Ely, since Jason was considering taking a position with the county law enforcement, and his girlfriend had been selling her nature photographs at local events and doing quite well.

But Joe always picked up on his big brothers' subtle digs that Joe was just a fish and game officer who saw no real action. Despite his law enforcement training, he was a peace officer, with a further two-year degree in wildlife management. Joe just caught fishermen without licenses and talked to the trees and wolves, they said.

They would never know how much those teasing words—that he was a nature boy and was comfortable with his place in this world, and how it coincided with all things wild, wooly and winged—dug into Joe's soul. But his job was more than mere lake patrol and babysitting the trees. He not only protected the wildlife but the humans, as well. He may not be cruising the alleys looking for drug dealers or busting child trafficking rings, but he made a difference in a part of the world that needed protection and understanding. And this poaching investigation would hopefully not only cease the poaching of wolves and their dwindling population, but also lead him to Max's killer.

Max had to have stepped on someone's toes. He would never purposely approach a poacher. Max had been non-violent and believed that those who did wrong would answer to their greater power. But might he accidentally have stumbled upon some poachers? Seen something he shouldn't have?

Just like Joe suspected Skylar had. What had she seen—or what did she know—that someone needed to threaten her to keep silent about?

"Dude, do not lean on the exam table."

Joe straightened and lifted the heel of his palm from the steel table near the lab tech's elbow. "Sorry. I was thinking."

"Difficult to do more than two things at once? I get it."

"You are an annoying white coat," Joe jested, because he knew the lab techs hated that term.

"Touché. Now I'm going to run some boring machines for a few hours so…"

"I'm going to have a look at the gun registry," he told Lucy. "Call me as soon as you've got anything."

"Will do, Cash."

Joe left the van and wandered outside, where he inhaled the fresh air through his nose and pulled it deep into his lungs. So his job offered plenty of sunshine, clean air and outdoor activity. What was wrong with that? Nothing at all.

But he would show his brothers that he wasn't merely a nature boy. And he sensed Skylar had suddenly become the key to achieving that goal.

THE CAT HAD been beyond hope by the time Skylar arrived. There wasn't a rib that hadn't been broken, and she suspected a crushed skull, as well. Its breathing had been so slow, and five minutes after she'd arrived the cat had passed away. Poor kitty. She wouldn't have had much chance for survival even if Skylar had taken her home with her. She was in a better place now.

Skylar gave Becky a kiss on her bald head and set her on the ground. It had taken no more than forty-five minutes to knit a tiny sweater that slipped over her body. The red color really worked on her. She loved to scamper about, showing the other animals her new duds. She'd been born featherless—save the one straight white tail feather—and needed that extra coat to stay warm, even in the summer. Also, the sweater protected her from mosquitos and sunburn.

The purpose of a breed of featherless chicken that had been bred in a lab? To provide for easier and more efficient handling in factory farms. Skylar thought it inhumane, and just another means of man trying to play God. She was not a vegetarian, but when she did eat chicken, it was always one she had butchered herself. It wasn't right to eat something that had been tortured for the plate.

Becky was an anomaly, born of two feathered chickens. Her human owners, who lived on the farm just south of the Davis land, had almost killed her, but then had asked Skylar if she'd be interested in caring for her. Skylar had jumped at the opportunity. Just because an animal had been born different didn't mean it did not deserve a chance.

As for Stella, she had been born with four legs and had been a member of a pack, and, once again, man's cruelty had irrevocably altered an animal's life. She traveled well on three legs, but the loss of her pack had left her half the wolf she could have been. She remained cheerful and always by Skylar's side, but there seemed to be days the wolf moped. Skylar felt sure, when the distant howl of a wolf sounded on a clear night, that the look on Stella's face was sadness.

You could take the animal out of the wild, but you could never take the wild out of the animal. Still, Skylar had known that to even try to force Stella back into her pack would have resulted in her being ostracized, possibly even killed. She was marked by humans now.

Pulling a rawhide strip out of her back pocket, Skylar waggled it before the wolf, who, rather than moping, was rather curiously watching as Becky strutted off to show the others her new sweater.

"Treat?" Skylar asked.

Stella pawed the ground and sat. Skylar had not taught her that; she was simply a polite wolf.

She handed over the strip and ruffled Stella's fur behind her ear, where she loved a good scratch. "Have at it, sweetie. I'm going around back to keep an eye on the fire."

She'd lit the bonfire again this afternoon, and this time had poked the remains of her wedding dress farther into the stone circle. The flames were low, but the snaps and crackles lured Skylar closer. Sweet, smoky perfume curled enticingly about her. A few inches of hem remained on the dress. She grabbed the fire-poking stick and stabbed at the fabric, consigning the last traces of her stupidity to the flames.

Joe hadn't asked about the dress, but he had seen it. And if he was investigating poaching in the area, Skylar figured one of their future conversations might veer back around to the damned dress. It was inevitable. Because the information she had about Cole Pruitt placed him suspiciously in the poaching camp. She didn't want to go there with Joe, but how not to?

The trees on the distant shore across the lake were a deep green line, capped by softer jagged green, where they segued into the graying sky. Looked like rain. She loved the rain, especially sitting out on the deck and watching it scatter on the lake. Rain would keep poachers out of the woods.

And, hopefully, snipers.

Shrugging a hand up her opposite arm, she squinted to focus on where Joe had pointed when he'd been guessing the shooter's position. How long had the shooter stood there, sighting her in, waiting for the perfect moment to pull the trigger? And had it been merely a warning? Or had the shooter missed the target? *Her.*

Malcolm had avoided answering when she'd asked him about it.

Exhaling heavily through her nose, she shook her head. She'd done nothing to deserve such treatment. Even dumping an ex-boyfriend who thought he could tell her what to do, when to do it and how to do it didn't warrant being sniped at.

"Cole," she muttered. "I sure as hell hope you're not involved in this."

As Joe pulled up the driveway to his home, he received a call from Lucy. She'd gotten a DNA match from the snare. And it was startling.

Joe left his coat on a hook inside the foyer and wandered into the cool one-story house set at the corner of a tidy block in Checker Hill. He'd moved to the next town over from his parents' farm after his brother Justin had suggested the town had some nice real estate at good prices. Jason lived forty-five minutes away in Frost Falls. All the Cash boys lived in or around the Boundary Waters.

He would much prefer to live out in the country, and was working toward that goal. His savings were stacking up, and he kept an eye on the DNR land-release posts. Every so often they put up a parcel of land for sale, though it wasn't usually zoned for building. More often it was sold as hunting land, but with work, any chunk of forested land could be made livable. A real home smack in the middle of the nature he thrived upon.

He pushed the button on the coffee maker and placed a mug under it. He tugged off his work shirt and tossed it over the back of a kitchen chair. He hadn't gone out on the lake today, instead spending most of the day in the forensic lab and behind his desk checking databases. He did not go into an office each day. He had an office here at home. Most conservation officers worked out of their homes. He reported to the district lieutenant, who also made his schedule and assigned territories. Throw in a county-issued four-by-four truck, boat and Jet Ski? He felt sure his brothers would never admit their envy of that sweet arrangement.

What he needed was a shower and a good workout session to stretch out the kinks from sleeping in the car all night. Surveilling, that was. Keeping an eye out for Skylar. Because if he couldn't be near her, at the very least he could ensure her safety.

A call to Skylar was due. He needed to ask her a few more questions, because the DNA taken from the snare had turned up something too interesting to ignore. The shell casings had been clean. Joe suspected they may or may not have been touched by the same person who set the snare. Yet they definitely matched the Lapua rifle, and if they ever found another spent casing or bullet, that same rifle would leave familiar etchings, much like a finger-print. So that was a positive.

But the better lead had been the DNA. There had been a hair entwined in the snare that the lab had gotten a clean read off. And that hair had matched a person already on record in the database due to a few minor infractions a couple years ago. One bar fight that had resulted in busted ribs to the other guy and an assault charge. DNA extraction was now standard procedure during a booking if the offense the person was charged for could include jail time.

Joe was thankful whenever a match showed up because that made his job easier.

But this time around? Following up on this lead was going to try his soul. He hadn't seen his former best friend, Cole Pruitt, for over a year. Because he hadn't wanted to look in the man's eyes and know he had been the one to win Skylar.

Now, he'd look in those eyes and decide whether Cole was capable of shooting at Skylar. Or, worse, poisoning an old man.

Chapter Seven

Joe wandered across the front lawn before the house he knew belonged to Cole Pruitt. Or, at least, it had a year ago. Now the little two-bedroom rambler had a for-sale sign stuck in the overgrown lawn. A faded garden gnome with a broken red cap lay on its back in a patch of clover—a victim of neighborhood vandals, surely. A peek through the front window showed bare walls, hardwood floors and no sign of life inside.

When he'd decided not to pay attention to Cole and Skylar after they'd hooked up, Joe had no idea Cole would literally slip off his radar. Had he moved elsewhere in town? This town boasted four thousand people. Not small, and not large, either. Most people knew the majority of the citizens, and neighbors always looked after one another.

Speaking of which, the neighbor drove his Honda up the driveway next door. Joe waved and walked across the lawn, signaling for the driver to roll down his window, which he did.

"I'm looking for Cole Pruitt," Joe said. He was in uniform, so it wouldn't seem odd to a stranger that he was asking.

"Haven't seen that fellow in a couple months. Thought he was getting married. Must have packed up the wife and moved on," the man said. "Is there a problem, Officer?"

"No. Just checking in on an old friend. I've lost track of him over the last year."

The man shrugged. "Then you know him better than I do. He was never around much, and I didn't have a chance to get to know him because up until recently I've been working the night shift."

"You said he had a wife?"

"Oh, I don't know. I did see a woman going in once in a while. Just assumed. Like I said, didn't pay much attention to him. You might try his parents?"

Cole's parents lived a few miles out of town on a small alpaca ranch. "Thanks. Good idea. Have a great day."

Joe walked back to his vehicle and slid inside. He picked up the forensic report that detailed Cole Pruitt's DNA being found in the snare trap. That land where he'd found the snare must edge up against Skylar's land. Or could it belong to Davis Trucking? He knew the Davis families owned land plots next to one another. He'd have to take out a map and get a handle on the area. Maybe Cole had set the snare, thinking it was on Skylar's land? Which would then make Joe suspect Skylar had knowledge of that.

A wife? Joe's thoughts went to that burned wedding dress in the smoldering firepit.

Why wasn't Skylar being completely honest with him?

His heart sank to think of the possibility that she could be involved in the poaching he'd been trying to pin on the Davis family.

Malcolm Davis *was* her uncle. That family's tendency toward criminal activity was well-known in the area. Yet they covered their tracks well. Misdemeanors and the occasional overweight truckload were all that local law enforcement had ever been able to charge them with. Joe had to wonder if someone on his side of the law was helping Davis. Was a dirty cop in their midst? It wasn't out of the realm of possibility.

Just like it was possible that Skylar Davis could be working for her uncle.

Did Joe know her as well as he thought he did?

WIELDING IN ONE hand a wooden spoon dripping tomato sauce, Skylar opened the front door with her other, fully expecting the man standing there with his hands stuffed in his front pants pockets. Or rather, hoping it would be him.

"Joe. Just in time."

He checked over his shoulder, then quirked his brow at her. "I am?"

She licked the spoon. Hmm, it needed a touch more garlic. "I'm making supper. I always make too much pasta. Want to join me?"

"That's a no-brainer." He stepped inside and closed the door behind him.

Skylar sailed into the kitchen in time to turn off the stove buzzer that announced her roasted garlic was done. She took the small terra-cotta crock out from the oven and opened the lid. Inside, the garlic bulb had shriveled and browned, and smelled sweetly delicious.

Stella poked her nose against the patio screen door, and when she spied Joe her tail began to wag.

"Hey, Stella, good to see you again. Does she stay outside?"

"No, you can let her in. She'll want to taste the pasta, too."

He opened the screen door, knelt before the wolf, who stood as high as his head, and received a tongue lash across his jaw and hair.

It warmed Skylar's heart to see the two interact. Cole had always been afraid of the wolf and had shown it by trying to be the alpha, always ordering Stella to go lie down or go outside "where the wild things belong." Stella had not liked him, often showing her teeth and growling at him, but she'd never attacked, though Skylar feared she was capable of doing just that. Strangely, the wolf had tried to appeal to the obnoxious male by following him around, and once she'd even sat close to him outside on the deck— bless her loving but misdirected heart. She was as poor as Skylar at recognizing a good man.

"So did you stop by for a free meal or police business?" Skylar asked as she set another plate on the counter that stretched along the kitchen and served as the divider between it and the living area.

"Both?" Joe's smile was the sexiest thing this side of the Boundary Waters. "I got lucky with the meal. No man will ever turn down a home-cooked meal. It's in our genes to say yes to these things."

"Yeah? What if it's tofu on the menu?"

"Yes, yes and yes."

Skylar smirked. She remembered the one time she'd wanted him to say yes, and he had not. Her jaw tensed.

Realizing she was standing there thinking too hard, Skylar had to catch a drip that fell from the spoon before it landed on the floor. The man had to be aware of his stunning toothpaste-commercial smile and the effect it had on women. And combine that with the dark hair and stubble—devastatingly sexy. How to remain the strong, independent woman that she strove to be when all she wanted to do was snuggle up against him and see what developed between the two of them?

"I got some answers from the forensic lab this afternoon," he said as he slid onto a stool in front of the counter.

"You know who was shooting at me?"

"No. The lab is still running a trace on the shell casings to see it they match any recent findings. But I did get an ID on the make and model. They're from a foreign weapon. Italian-made."

"That's interesting. And weird. Is there a strange Italian wandering around the lake, taking shots at me?"

His chuckle didn't sound at all mirthful. "It was used in the Gulf War, which makes it a popular sell for gun enthusiasts here in the States. It's a sniper rifle. Whoever took that shot had to be a pro."

"Like a professional sniper? That's pretty far-fetched, don't you think?"

"Sharpshooting is a hobby and a profession. As well, there could be any number of ex-military personnel living in the area who may have specialized in sniping. My brother was a sniper."

"That's right. He's up in Frost Falls, isn't he?"

"You keep track of our family?"

"Hard not to with the annual charity calendar. You made a great Mr. February, by the way."

Did the man actually blush? Oh, sweet mercy. Skylar was in trouble with this one. She pulled a bottle of craft beer brewed by her favorite Minneapolis brewery from the fridge and handed it to him.

"Thanks." He screwed off the cap and tilted back a swallow. "I'm off duty, so I don't mind having a beer. But I do have some questions for you."

"Can they wait until after I've plied you with my famous tomato sauce?"

"Of course. I don't know that I've been plied before."

She smirked. "Stella and I will do our best."

With that, Joe winked at Stella, and the wolf eagerly wagged her tail. She had fallen for the guy, the poor girl. Was Skylar next in line?

THE MEAL WAS SUBLIME. And sitting next to Joe at the counter, sharing conversation, a couple cold double IPAs, and the creamy tomato sauce and pasta, Skylar had a stunning realization. She missed sharing meals with another person. And not just with her favorite wolf.

Or maybe it was that for the first time, she really enjoyed this man's company and couldn't imagine not enjoying it all the time. That threw her off course a little. Since when did she want a man around?

When Joe prompted her for possibly the second time, she startled. "Huh? Oh, sorry. Was just thinking."

"You've been distracted since I arrived. You okay, Skylar? How's your ear?"

Touching the tip of her ear, she glanced his way, then quickly averted her gaze. Due to their proximity, her body hummed with desire. Yes, she was distracted. By everything Joe Cash. It wasn't right. Was it? It could be. But no. He said he was here to ask her questions about the investigation. And she would be a fool to believe anything else could happen beyond polite police-citizen interaction.

"It's fine," she finally said. "Just a bruise, really. And I'm always okay." Because she could never admit when she was not. "You said you wanted to ask me stuff." She pushed her plate forward and leaned her elbows on the counter. "I still have no idea who could have shot at me. And now that you think it's a sniper...?" She shook her head, at a loss.

"I believe you. Do you have a map of your property and the surrounding area? I'm not sure if I was on DNR land last night when I found the snare. I know the property lines around here snake a lot."

"They do, and there are weird little arms that jut out from my land here and there that sort of mesh together like a puzzle piece with Malcolm's property. But there's also some DNR land around the lake. I have a map. It's in the office. Do you want me to get it right now?"

"Would you? I was going to look it up on the county

registry, but my laptop has been recharging out in the truck since I had that idea."

"No problem. Give me a few minutes. Stella, keep an eye on Joe."

She left them and veered down the hallway to the office, which was next to her bedroom. It was a relief to take a breather from sitting so close to the guy. But she wouldn't be so blatant as Stella, positioning herself right beside his chair and eyeing him constantly with tongue lolling out.

This had been her dad's office, and it was still furnished in dark brown leather, green-and-blue flannel curtains, and the enlarged photographs of insects he'd taken while on his daily hikes. She loved the dragonfly print, and felt sure the critter was smiling each time she looked at its big alien mug.

On the top shelf in the closet, she found the rolled map that her dad had given her just a month before his death. The lawyer held all the property papers and title. She hadn't had a chance to get her hands on those, and hadn't felt a need since losing the last good man she'd had in her life.

She clutched the map to her chest. It had been a sad day when he'd handed her this. Her dad had insisted she sit down and plan his funeral right then and there. He'd listed the songs he wanted sung and the bible verses spoken. It had torn Skylar's heart from her chest, but she had maintained a stiff visage and had gotten through it. Only later, when she'd found a few moments to walk along the lakeshore by herself, had she succumbed to wailing tears. No one should ever have to plan a funeral with the person for whom that solemn affair was to honor.

That first year after her father's death had been difficult. If she hadn't had Stella to hold and hug and cry to, Skylar wasn't sure she would have made it through at all. It wasn't as if she had a mother to hold her and tell her everything was going to be all right. She often wondered if Dorothy Davis was even aware of her husband's death. They'd never officially divorced following her mother literally fleeing the family. And when Skylar had asked her dad if he'd wanted her to find her mom to notify her of things, he'd simply shaken his head.

The past few years had tried her, yet Skylar was a survivor. She proudly stood upon the land her father had cherished as if it were a part of his very being. Because she knew exactly what it had meant to him. She'd grown up on this land, and felt as though the lake ran in her veins and the earth formed her bones. She had, as the best memories from summers, racing through the woods with a pet fox or climbing oak trees and hanging upside down from a maple branch with bent legs. Or swimming in the lake and diving for turtles nestled in the mud.

Skylar couldn't imagine living anywhere else in the world. This was home, where her roots had burrowed deep into the soil. And nothing could uproot her.

But was she safe now?

With the rolled map tucked under an arm, she wandered out to the kitchen to find Joe rinsing the dishes and placing them in the dishwasher.

"Oh, I can do that."

"No, problem," he said. "It's the least I can do for the free meal. See what your plying did to me?"

"I'll have to ply you more often." She set the map on the clean counter and rolled it open. "This is the detailed map of the Davis property—my property—and its boundaries. And this other one looks like the entire county." She pulled that map on top and perused it. Joe joined her on the opposite side of the counter. She pointed out her land on the bigger map of the county. "I'm here."

He turned the map around and studied it. "So I was right. That's DNR land across the lake. And looks like you're hugged on two sides by privately owned land for about three-quarters of your property."

"Right. The top part of it, which hugs the Boundary Waters, is not usable land. It's thick forest up there."

"But you're paralleled by two different land owners. Who owns this plot?"

"The Enersons," she said. "They're in their nineties. They've owned that land longer than my family has had this land. They don't have any children. I imagine their land will be auctioned off when they die. I should really save for that, but all my funds are going to my dream cache."

"Your dream cache?"

"The shelter I want to build."

"Oh, right. You'll do it. I know you will."

"I appreciate the confidence."

"What about these plots?" Joe pointed out the three plots that hugged her property on the west side.

"All three parcels are owned by the same person. That's an old access road," she said when Joe ran his finger along a red line that crossed over the very tip of her property. "I check the fence once a month. In the winter the snowmobiles try to plow through, and in the summer, I find truck tracks through there. I shouldn't mind, but it is my property and I do have it fenced."

"So the only way from this side of the lake to the other is to use this access road?" Joe asked.

"Or go the long way around. The only people who would need to use the access road would be people in a hurry."

"Who owns those three parcels?" he asked.

Skylar swallowed, then quickly said, "Malcolm Davis."

He met her gaze, and she knew what he was thinking. Most were aware of the trouble between the two Davis brothers. And since the townspeople were in the know, they knew to walk a wide circle around Malcolm Davis.

"Your uncle." He tapped the map. "The two of you… get along?"

The question felt heavy in her throat. An expected question from a police officer, especially a conservation officer, and she wasn't sure how to answer. Not this time.

"We don't invite each other to tea parties. Why do you ask?"

Joe shrugged. "I know there was some kind of family feud. I need to ask all the questions, Skylar."

"I understand. No, we're not friendly. I keep my distance and so does he." Except when she'd gone to talk to him. "Malcolm wants to buy some of my land."

"You going to sell?"

"It would help fund my dream cache. But my dad would never sell. That was the reason for their feud, among other things." Skylar had never gotten the details, but she suspected it had something to do with her mother and her alliance to the wrong brother. "So I'm struggling between keeping it for my dad's sake and selling it for the animals I could help."

"Tough decision."

"It is."

"Would your uncle stoop to threatening you, trying to coerce you to sell?"

"Oh, I don't think so." But as for keeping quiet about whatever she'd seen? With a confession on her tongue, Skylar was cut off by Joe's next move.

He pressed the heels of his palms to the counter and leaned forward, making direct eye contact with her. "Skylar, what's up with you and Cole Pruitt?"

She sucked in her lower lip. Now that was a question she wasn't prepared to answer.

Chapter Eight

"There's nothing up," Skylar said.

Feeling the need for distance from Joe's probing gaze, she pulled open the screen door and stepped onto the deck. Joe followed close on her heels. When she propped her elbows on the deck railing and looked down over the fire pit, the ashes showing no sign of white satin and pearls and lace, she breathed in the lingering scent of smoke and soot. The perfume of regret.

Joe put his elbows on the railing a foot away from her. Maybe she shouldn't have been so eager to invite him in for supper. Now she'd have to face some truths about her own miserable sense of want and trust issues.

Joe rubbed his jaw, taking in the evening quiet. The lake glittered and crickets chirped. The evening smelled liquid and green. When his gaze dropped downward, he asked, "Why was the wedding dress in the fire?"

Skylar straightened, gripping the railing with both hands. "I was taking care of something I should have done months ago. We didn't get married, Joe. And I don't want to talk about it other than to say I learned Cole wasn't the man I thought he was."

"I'm sorry."

"You and Cole used to be good friends," she prompted. "He'd talk about you."

"Yeah, well, I tried to avoid him after…"

"After?"

He shrugged. "He hooked up with you. Didn't want to stand in the way."

"You didn't think you could still be Cole's and my friend because we were dating?"

He smirked and shook his head. "Not really. Skylar, you were…are…" He huffed out a breath. "Screw it. I'm just going to put this out there, then you'll know."

Skylar turned to him, knowing what was coming. Because she felt the same? No, because Joe wore his heart on his sleeve, and that was one fine garment.

"I like you, Skylar. Have been attracted to you for a long time. You know that."

"I do. Or I did."

"I know our timing never seemed to work out. You were always seeing someone, or I was."

"Or you were refusing my proposition," she added quickly, then winced. Not the time for that one.

He turned, and eyed her steadily. "Are you still hung up on that night of the wedding, Skylar?"

She looked aside. *Petty* and *stupid* were two things that came to mind.

"If I could change that night, I would," he said. "We were both drunk. There was no way I was going to have sex with you—with any woman—when she wasn't clear in her head. That's just wrong. Though I sure wish you would have made that offer when we were sober."

She did, as well. Yes, he had done the right thing, but her needy self, desperate for attention from the right man, had taken it as an affront.

Time to move beyond that. Life had changed. She had changed. Mostly. Apparently, she was still trying to figure men out.

"I thought you avoided me after that because I'd said

something wrong," she managed. "It shouldn't matter anymore. It doesn't."

"No, it doesn't. Because two weeks after that party you and Cole hooked up. When the two of you got together?" He bowed his head and didn't say anything else. His whole body sank, shoulders bowing forward as he adjusted his weight against the railing.

He didn't need to say more. Skylar had felt the same sort of letdown. She'd chosen Cole over Joe. A man who had never measured up to Joe Cash. Quiet, gentle Joe with a good heart and, as she well knew, who possessed a well-honed physique from sparring at the gym. His physicality was the yang to his mental and emotional yin. She sensed he needed that physical punishment to his body to counter the softness within that strove to always do right.

And she'd known at the time what had occurred between the two men because she had chosen one over the other. Skylar had sensed, after a month or two of dating Cole, and not seeing Joe anymore, that Joe had tucked his head under like a scolded pup and hadn't wanted to deal with her or the idea that they hadn't worked out. And she'd blamed him for that drunken night fiasco when she should have let it go.

Cole had pursued her aggressively, and she'd fallen into his forceful charm. It had been a weird, false sense of security she'd felt when she was with him. He'd bought her things, told her she was beautiful and was always texting her innuendoes. To think on it now, it had been like a high school crush—the jock deeming to date the nerdy girl. A facade of desperation she hadn't seen through until it was too late and she'd donned white satin and lace.

Thank goodness she had learned his truth. Through Malcolm Davis, of all people.

"I haven't talked to him for a couple months. Cole's been

living off-the-grid," she offered. Joe lifted his head, curious now. "I believe he's trying to sell his house in town."

"I stopped by to talk to him. It's listed with a realtor.
Empty inside. Where did he go?"

"He's…north somewhere." She waved her hand in that
direction, unable to summon curiosity to the man's whereabouts. "Still comes in to Checker Hill once in a while to
pick up groceries and stuff." She had seen his truck but always turned the opposite direction to avoid actually making eye contact. "My guess is you'll find him most often
on Lake Seraphim. He likes to fish and…that's all I know
about the guy, Joe. Can we leave it at that?"

He nodded. "I need to find him. Ask him about the
snare trap Officer Kofax almost stepped in while we were
searching across the lake. Did you know Cole was poaching in the area?"

She nodded vaguely. She knew things about Cole. About
Malcolm Davis and his crew. And…a glance to the hitching post with the bullet holes in it silenced her.

"Really?" Joe noticed her focus. "Don't let anyone tell
you what to do, Skylar. You know I've got your back,
don't you?"

"You do?" Speaking the words loosened something in
her throat, and she sensed if she didn't lift her chin a tear
would also threaten. "Why? Why do I matter to you?"

"Skylar, you shouldn't even have to ask that."

No, she knew the answer. Joe cared about most everyone. And she had known she had broken his heart by
choosing Cole.

"If someone is threatening you or holding something
over on you," he said, "you know you can trust me enough
to tell me."

"Thanks, Joe, but right now I've got to trust myself and
sort things out alone regarding Cole Pruitt. The burned

dress was a beginning. I'm trying to stand on my own and be independent."

"You've always been independent. That's the reason we never—" He cleared his throat. "Right. Whatever you need to do. But just so you know, I'm not stopping until I learn who took a shot at you."

"I can take care of myself, Joe."

"Still not changing my mind about protecting you."

She put her palm on her forehead.

"You're stuck with me. Like it or not," he added firmly.

And all Skylar could do was smile a little. Because much as she wanted to push him away, she needed to pull him closer. She suspected he knew that and had probably known that far longer than she had. The man had been a part of her life for a long time. Why was she only now realizing just how important that part had been to her? He was like an anchoring post in a building she wished to erect. That shelter could not function without him.

Ah, hell. She'd made a huge mistake by getting engaged to Cole Pruitt. Much bigger than she'd realized.

Joe straightened to leave, but then leaned against the railing, his hands gripping the wood. "This is the wrong time to ask, but—"

"Ask," she said in a rush before she realized how desperate she sounded. "I mean, I think I know what you're going to ask about, and it's okay, Joe. *We're* okay. I've made some wrong choices in my life. But knowing you has never been wrong. I hope we can—"

He moved swiftly, dipping his head and meeting her mouth with his. It was a surprise kiss, but one that made her sigh all over. His hair dusted her brow, tickling it. The masculine warmth of him drew her closer, their bodies conforming. The stubble on his cheek glided under her fingertips as she stroked down his jaw and clung to his shirt to keep him close. Her breath caught.

Overwhelmed by him, yet not wanting to lose the heady feeling of lightness that swept over her, she tilted onto her tiptoes and deepened the kiss. She'd been kissed by many, but never had she lost herself so quickly and so freely as right now. The world slipped away.

When he pulled back, a small smile curled his mouth. "Had to do that."

"It was a long time coming," Skylar said.

Joe smiled more widely. "That answered a lot of questions."

"I'm glad that was how you chose to ask them."

"I'd better get going. Got some paperwork to do. Can I check in with you tomorrow?"

"I'll be here." She tapped her lips. "Waiting for another kiss."

He nodded and then wandered down the stairs to the ground and around the side of the cabin. Stella glanced to Skylar. *Should I follow him?* she seemed to ask.

Skylar patted her thigh, and the wolf skipped up the steps to her side. She wanted to race around the cabin and follow Joe to his truck, jump into his arms and kiss him deeply and for as long as she could, until her breath got lost in him.

But she stopped that impulsive need for connection with a man she hadn't realized she'd wanted so much until now.

Lucy had recorded her findings on the state database that went directly to the Bureau of Criminal Apprehension located in Saint Paul. Joe was on the phone with Harvey Logan, a BCA officer who had cross-referenced the data from the rifle shell casings and the bullet to other evidence collected from crime scenes across the state, as well as the entire United States.

"No matches," Officer Logan said, after keeping Joe on hold five minutes. "Which only means that if the same rifle was used to commit a crime previously, we just didn't find the evidence."

"Right." Joe scribbled down the officer's name and thanked him. The BCA would come out, process and investigate crime scenes, if needed. He didn't feel he needed the help yet. "You ever work with the Fond du Lac police department out in Cloquet?"

"Sure. You think this is tribal related?"

"No. I don't know. I've got another investigation. Native American man died from poisoning a few weeks ago. Not sure if it's related, but feels as though it might be. I contacted the tribal police, but his death was ruled accidental so they are not investigating."

"Then why are you?"

"Like I said, just doesn't feel right. Thanks, Harvey. I may be checking in with you again, depending on what turns up."

"Always here. Call anytime."

Joe hung up, then tapped the eagle talon hanging from the leather cord at his neck. The day after Max's death, after he'd woken up in Max's campsite, Joe had headed to Max's home along with Brent Kofax. The small one-bedroom house sat on the Fond du Lac reservation. Max had suggested it wasn't really his home, for it closed him in when his soul wanted nothing more than air and earth and water surrounding him. The man had lived a remarkably minimalist life. Almost Zen, save for some photos and old glass Coke bottles he'd collected over the years.

No clues. No family, save for his tribe. On the mantle, Joe had studied a few black-and-white photos from pow-wows in which Max had once danced hoops decades earlier. His costume had been amazing, decorated with eagle feathers that Max had told Joe he'd collected since he was a boy, finding them in the forest, tucked here and there, and once he'd even found a dead eagle roadside, had said rites for it and then buried it.

Joe had yet to speak with anyone from Max's tribe. What could they say about him beyond that he was a lone wolf? On the other hand, someone had to have known him. Who took care of his home when he camped in the summer?

Now he rubbed his jaw as he searched the tribal records on the computer. He found a tribal elders list, and he thought one of the names sounded familiar. Had Max mentioned him over the years?

He picked up the phone, and when the call went to voice mail, he said, "This is Officer Joseph Cash with the DNR. I'm investigating the death of Max Owen and would like to talk to you about him. Please call me back." He left his phone number, then glanced to the bookshelf opposite his desk.

On the shelf above his books sat a few tokens he had collected over the years. A fist-sized chunk of agate he'd found on the shore of Lake Superior, nearly round thanks to millennia of churning in the waters. An iron cross his parents had given him on his confirmation day, forged from iron taken from local taconite mines. A wolf claw that he'd found in the forest as a teen. And…an eagle feather.

Joe got up and went over to the shelf. He picked up the feather and turned it about. It was pure white, tipped with brown. The barbs were tight and the shaft strong.

What was it about eagles that seemed to gnaw at his instincts?

Chapter Nine

Joe navigated the boat along the southern edge of Lake Seraphim. The lake was shaped like an angel's wing, hence the name. He'd been told by a couple fishermen a quarter mile back that they'd seen Cole Pruitt cruise by and wave. This had always been his favorite spot for catching walleyes.

Joe had checked the fishing license database on his laptop. No current registry for Cole Pruitt. Nor was there a current address for Pruitt; it still listed the house in town that was for sale.

Spying the silver V-hull with the red blaze of flame across its stern, Joe moved in slowly, as he always did when approaching any fishermen in the area. He didn't want to scare off the fish or the people. And the DNR symbol emblazoned on the side of his boat let them know who he was. If someone were to suddenly fire up the engine and skid off, then he'd know something was up. He'd participated in a couple high-speed water chases in his service. He had to admit, the chase was a thrill.

He compared it to his brother Jason's love of snowmobiling. The guy should seriously consider professional racing. But Joe also added in Muay Thai fighting to get his physical adrenaline-rush thrills. He had to drive into Duluth to the gym to find opponents willing to match him, and when they did, the fight was on.

He used to spar with Cole. But that was then.

Pulling up alongside the boat, Joe waved to Cole, who nodded as he approached and put out his hand to catch the front of Joe's boat and steady it.

"Cash! I haven't seen you in a long time, buddy. Thought you were avoiding me for some strange reason."

Really? The man thought it was strange he'd avoid talking to a friend who had stolen the girl out from under him? Okay, that was unfair. He and Skylar had never officially dated.

"Been busy with work. I heard you were up this way so I wanted to talk to you. I have to do the official thing and ask to see your license."

Cole glanced to the cooler on the floor of the boat, which Joe guessed probably had a fish or five inside. The man had a fishing rod, not currently cast into the water, but it was propped aside the steering wheel, baited, and ready to cast. Near the driver's seat, a steel canteen wobbled on its side on the boat floor. It could contain anything from water to beer to—well, hell, Cole had never been much for hard liquor.

"You know walleyes are out of season right now?"

"Of course I do. Northerns and sturgeons right now. I'm sure I renewed my license this spring," Cole said. He made a show of patting his back pockets. "Never remember to carry my wallet with me from the car. Sorry, man. Just caught a few sunnies."

"Where are you parked?" Joe asked. The wake from a passing boat rocked his, and he gripped the edge of Cole's vessel tightly.

Cole nodded to the south. "Couple miles down. You going to make me go get my license to show you?"

Joe shook his head. "No, I trust you." He did not. And he knew the truth. But there was a bigger fish to fry this afternoon than an expired license. "There's actually a different reason I wanted to talk to you today."

"So this wasn't a coincidence, you running into me? Huh." The man crossed his arms over his chest. The wake wobbled them both, and Cole had to double step to keep his balance. In the process, he dipped forward too far. An odd move, Joe thought. "What's up? Still feeling sore over losing Skylar to me?"

The man's smirk had once made Joe laugh. They'd shared many a chuckle over beers and hockey games. Now it confused him.

"Doesn't appear as though you actually have her, does it?" Joe countered. Then he silently reprimanded himself for playing the one-up game. Skylar did not deserve such disrespect. "This isn't about Skylar. It's about the illegal snare trap I found across the lake from the Davis property."

Cole shrugged. "There are snares and traps all over the Superior Forest. It's what we hunters do. Oh, wait. I forgot. You're all into that save-the-wildlife thing. So what if I set a few traps?" A step backward had him losing his balance, and for the first time, Joe suspected Cole may have been drinking more than a beer or two.

"Depends on where and what you're hunting. Only thing in season right now is fish. And that snare looked like something set for a wolf."

"Thought it was illegal to trap wolves."

"It is." Joe lifted his jaw, meeting Cole's gaze defiantly. "A lab test found traces of your DNA on the snare. You set the trap, Cole. Which prompts my next question—just exactly what *are* you poaching and how long have you been doing it?"

Cole shook his head and chuckled. "Really? You're coming after me for that? Skylar told you, didn't she?"

"She didn't tell me anything. But it's true?"

"Did she tell you that I left her at the altar?"

"What?" Joe's jaw dropped open, but he caught himself and clamped his mouth shut. His fist curled as tight as his mouth.

"Yeah, she's a case, man. I couldn't go through with it. She was the one who talked me into doing some trapping for Malcolm. Oh. Oops." Cole's smirk had become obvious. Joe sensed he was either lying or, at the very least, stretching some weird truth. "Ah, hell, you're with fish and game. You know that family is dirty as crap. *All* of the Davis clan is. Including Skylar."

"Skylar would never—"

"They've been using her land. She hasn't said a word to anyone. Silence is the biggest yes in the world."

Resisting the urge to lash out at the man with a fist, Joe leaned forward, latching both hands onto the starboard side of Cole's boat. "You want me to believe Skylar forced you to set that trap?"

Cole shook his head. He swayed suddenly, and Joe caught a whiff of his breath. The scent was stronger than beer. "Nope. But she did get me involved with the family. She's not all innocent and as save-the-animals as you believe, man. That woman wants things. And she'll do what she needs to get 'em."

"What sort of things?"

Cole shrugged. "You know she's going to build some big old shed for broken-up animals. Wanted me to pay for it. Can you believe that?" he asked incredulously.

Joe did have a hard time believing Skylar would ask Cole for the money to build her shelter. That wouldn't make her much of an independent woman. On the other hand, he couldn't imagine how much a structure like that must cost. She might own a lot of land, but he'd never thought she was rich. Malcolm Davis, on the other hand, had money. And if Skylar were working for him…

"So what are you going to do?" Cole prompted. "Arrest me? Poaching is still a misdemeanor. I'll pay the fine right now. Only if you can show me the animal I snared."

"There was no animal in the snare." The police radio on the boat dashboard crackled with a call from Dispatch. Joe ignored it. "But we do have your DNA on the snare."

"Circumstantial evidence."

"You just admitted to poaching for the Davis family. I have a confession, yes?"

Cole shrugged.

"And you've been drinking."

"Oh, come on, man. Every fisherman out on a boat has a beer or two."

"You're not drinking beer. Smells like whiskey."

Cole waved a dismissive hand before him.

"Since when did you start drinking the hard stuff?"

"Since never!"

He was belligerent, and Joe was beginning to wonder if he was inebriated instead of merely tipsy. He stood well enough, his body only swaying with the wake of the boat.

Again the radio crackled, and this time Joe leaned over to grab the receiver. "What is it?"

"Got a crash on Lake Seraphim," Dispatch reported. "Jet Ski collided with a boat. Possible drowning. Isn't that where you said you were headed?"

"I'm here now. Send me the coordinates. I'll get there as quick as I can." Joe kicked against the side of Cole's boat to separate the vehicles. "You heard that."

"I did. Guess my ass is saved. For now."

"For now," Joe said curtly.

As he steered away from the smug idiot, Cole called, "She's not who you think she is!"

Tightening his jaw, Joe headed back in the direction he'd come.

Skylar was involved with Malcolm Davis? He didn't want to believe it. How could she possibly be? Cole had to be lying. It had been the booze talking. But *he* had left her at the altar? That was a good reason for a woman to burn her wedding dress. To dispose of bad memories.

And if a man like Cole Pruitt had deemed to leave her at the altar, that really made Joe question Skylar's ethics. Was she putting up a front for him? Using the worthy cause of an animal shelter as a means to cover for her support of Davis's poaching habits?

Max had once said something about seeing into a person's soul, how sometimes their exterior acted counter to what the universe had initially sent them to do. Joe knew that. People smiled on the outside, while inside they could be smirking. But Skylar? Really?

The radio crackled again, and Joe answered that he was on his way. Local lifeguards would also be called, but if he got there first, he might have to go for a swim.

All in a day's work.

SKYLAR CRUMPLED THE refusal papers from the bank for the loan she'd signed for herself. She needed collateral. Dare she risk putting up the land? It had been sacred to her father, which was why she should never sell to Malcolm. Even if his offer to cosign felt like the rescue rope she needed right now.

Besides, she had a suspicion that Malcolm's need to buy the land was not altruistic. Sure, it would make the drive for his trucks to the main highway a few miles shorter. But in the long run, did it really matter? Why was he so desperate to get that land?

She'd called her dad's lawyer and left a message for him to call back.

She hadn't been up that way in a while, so she decided now was as good a time as any to trek the length of her property and take a look around at the end. See if she could discover what it was that put the gleam in Malcolm Davis's eyes when he talked about that portion of land.

She prepared a backpack with water, protein bars and some snacks for Stella. There were no wolf packs within a good five-mile radius of the area, so she never worried that Stella would be singled out and attacked. But there were lynx and bears and all sorts of smaller animals that wouldn't mind threatening a wolf who was not accustomed to hunting bigger animals to survive. So Skylar also packed a Taser gun and a .30-06 rifle, for safety's sake.

"Come on, Stella," she called as she stepped out onto the deck and locked the patio door. "We're going for a hike."

Chapter Ten

Joe stood by as the emergency team pushed the stretcher into the back of the ambulance. One victim had been pulled out from the lake by a diver. He had been under water an estimated four minutes. He was unconscious, with a dangerously low heart rate, but they had hope and were in the process of resuscitating him even as the ambulance flashed its lights and took off out of the parking area before the boat landing.

Two patrol cars cordoned off the area, and three police officers were keeping onlookers from getting in the way. One officer talked to the boat driver with whom the Jet Ski had collided. He had abrasions on his arm and back—the Jet Ski had literally shaved across the side of his body as it had soared over his boat—but he was doing well otherwise.

Joe had helped the diving crew to secure the Jet Ski and get it on a tow truck. He also gave the sheriff's deputy, who had arrived after the victim had been pulled from the water, all the details. This accident would be their concern now.

When it was apparent his help was no longer needed, he lingered, watching, while the crowd of gawkers thinned and the deputy ensured the beach was closed off. They would investigate, and if the Jet Ski driver survived, would question him to learn if it had simply been a machine malfunction, if he had been drunk or—well, there could be myriad reasons the collision had occurred.

Backing up and turning, Joe almost walked right into a Native American man who immediately patted him on the shoulder and nodded. Weathered skin creped his face and hands, and Joe guessed him to be about eighty, near Max's age.

"I hope you find the truth behind Max Owen's demise," the old man said to him. His eyes darted toward where they were cordoning off the beach with yellow caution tape, then back to Joe. "I know it's important to you to learn the truth, Joseph Cash."

Joe lifted a brow. He had no idea who this man was. Max had never mentioned any friends, but then, they hadn't chatted about things like that. He had belonged to a tribe, had grown up on a reservation, yet hadn't been in close contact with them since his midforties.

"You have no idea what Max Owen meant to me," Joe said.

"No, no I don't. But I do know what you meant to him, boy."

That statement cut into his heart. This man knew he'd had a relationship with Max?

The man bowed his head and toed the pebbled parking area with a boot. "We were in the same tribe. Didn't get to see Max as often as I liked. He preferred the wild, while I like the comforts of a sofa and public television. But we talked. And I know how proud he was that you embraced the wild in your soul."

Joe swallowed. He'd never been aware of Max's friends. But, of course, a man could not completely seclude himself from the world, even if he managed to do so more than half the year. "What can you tell me about Max's death?"

"Nothing. Just that you and I both know it wasn't an accident."

Joe nodded. He hadn't told anyone he was investigating the death. The obituary in the newspaper had listed it as accidental. So how could this old man know anything?

"My daughter works for the county morgue in Duluth," he provided quietly. "She filled me in when Max was brought in. Told me about the officer who insisted on an autopsy. Figured it could only be the young man Max had told me about. The one he calls the wolf whisperer."

Joe tugged in his lower lip with his teeth. Max was the only one who called him that. And yet, Skylar had spoken the same words a few days ago. It was a moniker that lifted his head and shoulders, and filled him with pride. And respect.

"Check with Davis Trucking," the old man said. "Max knew something. Something dangerous."

"What did he tell you?"

"Nothing. It was that one time we were walking along the road and one of those big blue trucks drove by. I just saw it on Max's face."

That was vague, but then Max had been a remarkably serene man. Rarely showed emotion. For someone to pick up on his unease by an expression, they had to know him better than a passing stranger.

"Was probably the eagles," he muttered.

"The what? Did you say eagles?" There it was again: *eagles.* The word seemed to flutter around this case like the elusive bird itself.

The man nodded.

"Tell me, please?"

With a resolute sigh, the man bowed his head, folding his hands before his gut, then said quietly, "It was Max who was always trying to get us to stop buying—well, you know."

"I don't know. That's why I'm asking. Buying what?"

"Eagle parts." The old man rubbed a hand at the back

of his neck. "Feathers and talons. Our tribe is on the list to get the eagle parts the state confiscates."

Joe knew that any poached eagle remains were eventually turned over to the local tribes. They could apply for them. That prevented, or tended to prevent, poaching.

"But that list is long," the man said. "Sometimes takes years. And well, the contests pay big money."

"You just lost me. The contests?"

"The dance competitions at powwows. Fancy dance, grass, jingle. Traditional. Dancers can make a good living entering contests at the various powwows if they're willing to travel. If an eagle feather ever falls from a costume during a competition, the whole dance stops and a ceremony to pick it up is performed right then and there. The feather is treated as if it's a sacred, fallen warrior. It's a thing to see."

"And yet, you just insinuated those sacred feathers are obtained on the black market."

"Like I said, that waiting list is long. But Max finally talked some sense into the tribe elders. We don't do that anymore. Swear to it."

This was an angle of poaching Joe hadn't considered. He'd heard of it before, but hadn't put it into place during the investigation. Had Max known who was selling black market eagle parts and those people had, after losing the tribe as customers, shut Max up?

Joe needed to return to Max's campsite. To take it in again.

"Learn the truth," the old man said, and then with a nod, he wandered off toward a rusted pickup truck.

Joe's inner wild howled in defiance. He would learn the truth. Only then could he allow Max to rest peacefully.

"Davis Trucking," he repeated out loud.

It wasn't a surprise to hear that accusation. But how

to crack the barrier Malcolm Davis had erected about his business and family, and learn the truth?

Perhaps a family member was his best entry. And Joe did know a family member quite well.

SWATTING AT A MOSQUITO, Skylar stood ten feet from the ragged red plastic flag that had been planted in the ground by her father years ago to demarcate the edge of his property. Half a dozen of the same were within her eyesight. One was bent and lying on the ground. She was surprised any were still intact. The ones tied around trees tended to last longest, and she'd counted a few as she arrived here at the edge of her land.

Her land. It felt immense and also bittersweet to call it that. This had been her parents' land. No. Her father's land. Her mother didn't get to claim ownership since she had abandoned her family. It was as if she were dead to Skylar. She'd never wanted it to be that way, but the urge to seek out her mother had not been strong enough over the years.

Still, Skylar couldn't argue against a greater design and knew she was here in this world for a reason, and with a purpose. And that purpose was to be kind to animals and help those in need. Nothing else gave her such a feeling of completion. It wasn't even satisfaction or pride. She simply felt whole when helping a sick animal rise up to its healthy potential.

However, what with being shot at and her uncle's menace always looming close, it was difficult to concentrate on that which should garner her full attention.

Why was the end of the property such a golden goose to Malcolm? Sure, he could plow down the pine trees and clear the land to connect it to his property, which was only a quarter mile to the west. And if he laid down tarmac, paving a passage road, his trucks could pass through here instead of driving around the lake and out to County Road

7, a highway badly in need of reconstruction and paving due to incessant potholes. These old county highways were always the last on the list for repair.

To the east, the Enerson property nudged her land, so Malcolm would also have to buy a sliver of land from them to make his road work. And if completed, it would be a secluded passage, hugged on both sides by tall conifers.

"Almost…secret," she muttered, as she envisioned the road. And if Davis Trucking did take this way through to Duluth or from Duluth, then they wouldn't have to pass through the truck weigh station up the highway. "Hmm…"

There was only one reason a truck wouldn't want to stop for inspection.

What had been in those freezers in the Davis warehouse that had upset the man so much he'd yelled at her as if she'd caught him stealing gold bullion from Fort Knox? He'd threatened her with a rifle. Why would an employee of a trucking company carry a rifle while on duty? Sure, they were entitled to security, but…it hadn't felt right at the time. Actually, Skylar had been terrified and couldn't have gotten out of there fast enough.

The Davis family, Malcolm's side, had been poaching for decades with little worry of repercussion. And while it should be enough for Skylar to want to talk to Joe and get him to stop such poaching from happening, a weird niggle in her stomach held her back. Malcolm was family. And her father had never reported his brother for that very reason. Family didn't do that to one another. Even if family had ruined her father's life, draining the family inheritance to start a trucking company and leaving no funds for his brother.

Her father had been a good man. Too good.

Was it time Skylar brushed off her father's benevolent influence and started fighting that which should have been stopped long ago?

Squatting and brushing her palm over a growth of blue-berries, Skylar whistled. Stella, who had been wandering the woods nearby, hastened to her side.

"What do you think, Stella? Are we going to do it?"

If she did tell Joe everything she knew, then she could kiss Malcolm's offer to cosign and partially fund her shelter goodbye. She needed half-a-million dollars to get the shelter built and supplied. There was no way she could raise that herself, and she didn't have enough assets beyond the land to put down for a loan.

To fight her uncle and his empire would be like sacrificing her dream. But had the dream ever been possible in the first place?

She stood and started back toward the cabin, a good three-mile hike through the woods. Stella scampered ahead, always the leader.

She'd visit the lawyer today. There had to be some way to do this on her own.

Chapter Eleven

"You're not going to like hearing this. Your mother is still a legal owner of the property," the lawyer announced after he'd set the Merlin Davis file on the dark walnut table before him.

Hans Svendson offered Skylar ice water, which she sipped while wincing. She sat at the edge of the over-stuffed chair pulled up to the conference table, feeling the weight of the wealth that had furnished this small yet luxurious office. It was in the man's home. He didn't set up shop in town. He lived on a fifty-acre estate with security fences and cameras.

"How is that possible?" she asked, sliding the water glass aside to lean forward. "She—we don't even know where she is. She could be dead, for all I know."

"The will did give you ownership of the property," the lawyer said, "but that was dependent on both your parents' deaths. I'm sorry I didn't dig this out immediately after your father's death, Skylar."

"I just assumed, since he had given me that note saying I owned the land…"

"Yes, I remember that. Unfortunately, it's not legally binding. The original will holds precedence. As long as one of your parents is still alive—your mother—she holds half the property rights."

"That's crazy." Skylar sat back in the chair. "Again. How do we even know she is alive? Isn't there some sort of statute on how long that will can remain in effect if one of the parties is AWOL?"

"Until she is proven dead—and I did a quick search for Dorothy Davis online, no death certificate—then she is still considered a property holder. I'm sorry, Skylar. Merlin was such a good man. I wish he had made changes to the will before his death, but it dates back almost twenty years."

When she was ten and her mother hadn't yet abandoned them.

"What am I supposed to do about this? I was hoping to build a shelter, but if the land isn't even completely mine, I can't sell part of it." She closed her eyes. How could this be possible?

Then she opened them in a flash. "She can't be aware of ownership. She would have claimed it by now."

The lawyer shrugged. "That's possible. And remember, you do own half."

"Which half?"

Hans shrugged. "It's not so simple as drawing a line down the middle. Or it could be. It may be as simple as tracking Dorothy down and asking for her to hand complete ownership to you. Then I can help you see to using the land as collateral for a loan. Or maybe you should consider asking Malcolm—"

"Never," she cut him off. "You know my dad and his brother were at odds. If Malcolm ever found out I don't own all the land... You can't tell him."

"He's not a client of mine. And I have no reason to tell him anything. I don't much like the man myself. I remember the struggles your father went through when Malcolm was trying to buy half his land from him."

"My dad was dead set against forming any business that

might harm the environment. Farming, with all its chemicals, was out. And trucking, with all the diesel fuel, was a big no-no. He was an artist."

The lawyer nodded. "I actually bought one of his photographs. Still have it up in the living room. That man had an eye for beauty. Well. So now you know. Would you like me to put you in contact with someone who can locate your mother for you? I know a private investigator."

"Not right now. This is all new and shocking to me. I have to take a while to…" Skylar blew out a breath. "You know."

"Yes, I understand. But you will call me if you need anything, yes?"

She nodded and stood. He led her out to the front door and she headed to the truck.

The day could not get any worse.

JOE KNOCKED ON Skylar's front door and waited. The setting sunlight shimmered through the trees surrounding her house. This was a gorgeous, peaceful plot of land. Something he wouldn't mind owning himself. And he would have such a property someday. It would be a long yet fulfilling journey to make his dream come true.

He wanted to share that dream with someone. It was difficult to stand here now, on the doorstep of a woman with whom he could consider spending that future, because—well, because of what Cole Pruitt had told him.

The door opened and Joe noticed Skylar swiftly wipe a teardrop from her cheek. Her eyes were red.

"What is it?" He stepped across the threshold and slid his hands along her arms. She wobbled, and he steadied her.

"Stella," she said. "She's not doing well."

"Where is she? Are you okay, Skylar? What's happened?" He bent to study her face, and she nodded and managed a half wince, half smile.

"I'm fine. Heartbroken. Stella is out on the deck. I found her a few hours ago at the edge of the yard. She'd been vomiting and has a fever."

He slid a hand into hers and walked through the house toward the patio doors. Outside on the deck, lying on the big dog bed that was Stella's perch, he found the wolf. She didn't lift her head as Joe approached, and he could see her chest rising heavily.

He dropped Skylar's hand and knelt on the deck, cautious not to scare the wolf and sensing she was in her own world right now. Fighting something terrible within.

"How did this happen?"

Skylar settled next to him and stroked a hand over Stella's coat. "I found her struggling to stand and was able to get her up here. She's been whimpering, and her heartbeats are irregular. But I think the extreme effects are beginning to subside. I was able to give her an IV of fluids and activated charcoal to induce vomiting. I think she was poisoned."

"Poisoned?" Joe's heart thudded at the word. Why was every living being around him lately falling victim to poison? Of course, the forest was not the safest place; it was filled with poisonous plants. He met Skylar's gaze. "You got oleander or milkweed in the area?"

"She knows to stay away from the milkweed. I don't believe it was a plant. There were undigested chunks of animal meat on the ground near her. I think…"

Joe bit his lip and shook his head because he knew what had happened. "Someone did this purposely," he ground out tightly. "The bastards. Who would do this? What is going on, Skylar? First someone shoots at you and now they've sunk to the bottom rung by harming an animal? And Max…"

"Max?"

He shook his head. It couldn't be related. He was still out of sorts after talking with the man near the drowning incident about Max. He had to keep the investigations separate until there was good reason to pair them. "It's an investigation on the side. Not related to this. Maybe."

"Can we discuss the bad stuff later?" She bent and gave Stella a hug. "I just want to be here for her. She isn't seizing anymore, so I want to watch her for now."

Skylar curled up before the wolf and put her face right next to Stella's. The wolf's eyes were closed, but she nudged her nose against Skylar's cheek.

Joe blew out a breath. The anger in him wanted to rage and kick something. His better senses told him both Skylar and Stella needed him to be calm and reassuring. This was another puzzle in the case he'd stumbled onto, and he suspected it was all connected to the local poaching. Right now, however, all that mattered was seeing to Stella.

And securing evidence.

"Where did you find her?" he asked quietly. "I want to gather evidence. Have it analyzed by the lab. It could help in your treatment, as well."

"Yes, I can plan further treatment for her. Right down there, at the edge of the clearing by the lake. Thank you, Joe. I had no idea you were stopping by. Was there a reason?"

"Doesn't matter now." He kissed her on the crown of the head, and the moment felt bittersweet. He preferred such intimate contact under better circumstances. "I'm going to grab some evidence bags from my truck and take a look around in the woods. Call if you need me, okay?"

"I will." She clasped his hand and squeezed. "I'm glad you're here. I…needed someone to be with me."

Joe understood how difficult it was for her to say such a thing. Strong, independent and fierce, Skylar Davis had never needed anyone. It was sad that her armor was cracking because of outside forces.

He was glad he'd arrived when he did.

Chapter Twelve

Lying beside Stella on the deck, Skylar let her hand rest on the wolf's stomach. Her breathing was still shallower than normal, but she felt she was going to survive this. Strychnine, which had once been commonly used by poachers, usually worked quickly, within a few hours. Other poisons could take up to forty-eight hours and cause a slow, cruel death. Stella would need to be watched through the night.

From her vantage point, she'd watched Joe gather evidence from the shore where she'd found Stella. Then he'd wandered into the forest and disappeared into the thickness of maple, oak, birch and brush. Now and then the beam from his flashlight lit up the darkening woods. What luck that he had arrived when he had. She'd been frantic and worried over Stella, but had known she needed to gather evidence so she could later determine exactly what had happened to the wolf.

Her gut told her the poisoning had been a purposeful act. And she'd sensed Joe's entire body tense when she'd told him her suspicion. The man cared about wildlife and carried as strong a conviction about keeping animals safe as she did. She loved that about him. And she knew he probably felt the hurt as much as she did. That genuine kindness placed him a notch above all other men in her book. He was strong, smart and, by nature, a protector. And she had pushed that away in favor of what?

She'd thought she was in love with Cole. The man had been a high school track star, loved singing eighties hair band tunes at the top of his lungs, always had a cooler of Budweiser ready for a fishing adventure on the lake, and had told her she was beautiful and brought her flowers and made her eggs at midnight. He'd been hyper, and was never one to sit still. Opposite of her. He was different and new and everything she'd never thought she'd want in a man.

Cole had been a means to distance herself, really. He had not threatened her independence and had seemed like a good fit at the time.

How she could have ever thought she could be happy with someone like that was beyond her now. She'd been a fool. And it had been too close on the heels of her father's death. Grief had altered her perception of her real needs and wants. And because of her misdirected need for companionship—any sort of connection to a man—she had gotten caught in something bigger than her. And terrible.

She had to tell Joe what she knew. But would he trust her if she did so?

Becky popped up onto the deck and wandered over to peck at Stella's fur. The chicken sensed the wolf was not well, and she didn't pester her overmuch. Instead, she hopped up onto the low wood table and nestled down to roost next to Skylar's cowboy hat in her bright red sweater. She closed her eyes, keeping vigil.

Footsteps ascended the deck stairway and Skylar sat up. She patted the deck beside her and Joe sat down. Stella was sleeping erratically.

"I found a few chunks of meat down by the lake. Not sure what kind though. Could be fowl," he said. "Looks like someone might have pulled up to your dock in a boat and tossed it to shore. There were no footprints. I've bagged the evidence and will take it in to the forensic lab."

"Please make sure they forward that report to me. I'll be able to better treat Stella if I know what she's ingested."

"I will. How you holding up?"

"I'm better now that you're here."

He clasped her hand, and she reacted by tilting her head onto his shoulder. He smelled like pine and wet scrub that he must have stomped with his boots. Delicious. And he was...still. So unlike Cole. It was a difference she'd recognized easily when choosing Cole. But only now did she understand the implications of going against what her heart really needed.

And it hurt.

"She going to be okay?" His voice softened and cracked.

"I hope so. The best treatment is to watch her. She's a fighter. She survived the trap when most pups would have quickly perished or been eaten by a predator."

"Stella gets around well on three legs. She is a marvel. I'm here for you, sweetie," he said to the wolf. "You want me to get you something to drink?"

"That would be nice. I was thinking about camping out here by her tonight."

"I'll be right back. Tea good?"

"There's brandy in the cupboard above the fridge."

She caught his smile on his profile. "Brandy it is."

Ten minutes later Joe reappeared, boots off and padding in his socks, jeans hems scuffing the deck boards. He set a glass of brandy down before her, then began to lay out the blanket he had grabbed from the back of the couch. It was a quilt her grandmother had made for her when she was a teenager, fashioned from squares of fabric saved over the years from dresses her mother—Skylar's great-grandmother—had made for her. She loved this blanket and used it all the time.

"Okay if I put this here?" he asked. "It's a nice blanket. Maybe you don't want it out here?"

"No, that's good, thank you. And you even grabbed a pillow. Why are you so sweet?"

He shrugged. "Just doing what you need someone to do for you right now. You shouldn't have to struggle with this stuff yourself. You focus on Stella. But...is it okay if I hang around and hold watch with you?"

"Do you want to?"

"There's nothing I would rather be doing. The evidence won't be looked at until morning anyway, so I have no need to leave or report in. And I do need to punch the clock once in a while. Can't work twenty-four/seven. That is, if Becky doesn't mind."

The chicken cooed contentedly without opening her eyes. A sure sign of approval. Skylar patted the deck beside her.

He sat on the blanket before Stella, and Skylar moved in next to him, offering him a sip from her glass. He'd filled it half-full with the aromatic amber brandy. More than she'd ever drink. When he took a hearty swallow, she felt more grateful than shocked. A brandy buzz might be just the thing to soften her anxiety right now. *And* her nerves about sitting so close to Joe.

Below in the grass, crickets chirped, and the haunting call of a loon punctuated the still night. The tree canopy opened in the center of her yard to reveal stars speckling the sky.

Skylar pointed upward. "That's the best part about living away from a city."

"No doubt about it. I believe there are some city folk who have never seen a star in the night sky. Too bad for them."

She tilted her head against his shoulder and he took her hand and kissed the back of it. The moment felt intimate, private. Something more than two concerned adults holding vigil over a sick wolf.

Skylar looked up and Joe was already staring down at her. She smiled at his shadowed grin.

"What?" he asked, like the kid who had been caught sneaking something he wasn't supposed to.

"Have we ever made out? I mean, more than kissing?"

"I would remember doing something like that with you, Skylar. You know our timing was always off."

"Yes, and I regret that now."

"You do?"

She nodded. "But not even on that night…?" That dreaded night he'd refused her suggestion they have sex. And she'd been punishing herself, more than him, for it ever since.

"Not even." He winced. "When I make out with you, Skylar, I want to be fully present and not drunk."

"You get drunk all that often, Joseph Cash?" She knew the answer, but it was a gentle tease; she couldn't resist.

"Nope. I like to get drunk on nature."

Could the man be any more sexy than he was right now? Well, for sure his calendar spread, with the bared abs and wide shoulders, and oh, that come-get-me smile, had been the hottest month of the year. And she hadn't made out with him when she'd had the chance? Mercy.

She tilted up her head. Their gazes met. Skylar was pretty sure a couple stars twinkled in Joe's eyes. Without another thought, she said, "Kiss me."

Showing no reluctance, he bowed to her and his mouth met hers. The sigh she'd been holding in escaped in a sweet rush of desire. His lips played softly against hers, finding a moment to stay, to build up the heat, and then brushing here or there for a heartbeat of connection.

Sliding her hand up the front of his shirt, she glided it over the hard muscles beneath and landed on the warmth

of his skin just under his jaw. Stubble tickled her fingertips. Pushing her fingers around his neck and up through
his short hair, she clutched and held him to her for a longer kiss. A dive into a starry night that she never wanted
to end.

The faintest taste of brandy only teased her deeper.
And when his arm wrapped across her back, she thought
surely he was holding her to this earth, this moment, with
a sure and confident promise of safety. The spread of his
fingers against her side nudged just under her breast and
she wanted to ease into him, to feel him touching her, but
she cautioned herself that her eager need was probably a
reaction to her grief over Stella.

Her and grief. She didn't handle that well when it came
to getting her desires met. Keep it in the now and take it
slow, she thought. She didn't want to scare him away a
second time.

When they parted, he bowed his forehead to hers and
they breathed in each other's warmth. Her heartbeats thudded faster than Stella's, and Skylar cast a look to the wolf.
Her chest rose and fell at a more normal pace. She was
sleeping peacefully now.

"That," Joe said softly, "is a kiss I will never forget."

And at that moment Stella shifted and placed her paw
on Joe's thigh.

"I think she approves," Skylar offered.

"That means more to me than you can imagine."

"Animals are a good judge of people."

"That they are. She trusts you to take care of her. The
two of you together are good. You are her person."

"And she's my girl. You have any pets, Joe?"

"Nope. That's not my thing. Never home long enough to
care for one properly. Max always taught me…" He looked
aside and closed his eyes. "It's nothing."

"Who is Max? You mentioned him before."

"He's the Native American man they found lying road-side a few weeks ago. I'm sure you heard about it."

"Oh, right. News reports said he'd eaten some poison-ous berries or something and tried to walk for help but it was too late?"

"Max was smarter than that. He was poisoned," Joe said tightly. "But not by his own doing."

"You think so?"

"I know so. And now…" He spread his fingers through Stella's coat. "You said you didn't want to talk about this. Right now we need to focus on Stella. But you need to know, with her poisoning I'm more suspicious than ever. Something's going on, Skylar. And I will get to the bot-tom of it."

JOE WOKE TO bright sunlight. And an aching back. What was up with his strange sleeping situations of late that found him either in a car or on a deck?

Skylar had reentered his life, that was what was up. And he didn't regret one moment of it.

Shifting on the deck to his side, he saw Stella lying on her cushion. Head bowed and resting on her paws, her gold eyes held him steadily. And…her tail wagged.

"You feeling better, Stella?"

The wolf whined softly, which didn't sound so much painful as an agreement to her better state. He ruffled his palm over her coat behind her ears and the wolf rolled to her back, exposing her belly to him. Such an amazing sign of trust. Joe leaned on an elbow and gave her the belly rub she sought.

"You've stolen my heart, you know that, sweetie? What is it about you Davis females?" He lowered his voice to a whisper. "You do know I like your person, right? I've liked her for a long time. But… I'm worried about her. I know you've been taking care of her, just as well as she took care of you last night. But I sense something isn't right with her."

The wolf stretched out her paw and rested it over his wrist, as if to say *You're right*.

"You want to help me help your person?"

He bowed his head and Stella licked his hair. She had made it through the night, but she would still need some tender loving care until all the poison was purged from her system. No doubt Skylar was on it. Wherever she was.

He looked around the deck and down across the yard. Off toward the chicken coop, he spied Skylar's cowboy hat. Then he checked his watch—6:30 a.m.

"Too early." He lay back and eyed the wolf. "Let's catch a few more winks, what do you say?"

Stella laid her muzzle on his arm, and the twosome drifted off in shared slumber.

SKYLAR TOOK JOE'S coffee mug from him as he skipped down the front steps. Stella sat beside her, watching. She was still weak and would need a great deal of rest, but her tail wagged and she whined at Joe's leaving.

"Someone is going to miss you," Skylar said.

"I'll miss her, too, but I have to go. That evidence bag." He thumbed toward his truck. "That's not going to last much longer if the day gets any hotter."

"Thank you. Again." Skylar tilted up on her tiptoes and kissed him.

Joe pulled away from it and put his hands on her shoulders. He didn't want to kiss her again? What was up with that? Had last night been a fluke? Both of them had been tired and he'd reacted in a moment of silent weariness? What was it with the man and his refusal to encourage intimacy between the two of them?

"I, uh…" He bowed his head and then lifted it to look directly in her eyes. "You and me? This is something I've thought about for a long time. But you know, back then, when we were on different schedules? I've always known you were out of my league."

"Out of my—"

"It's just how I feel, Skylar. And I realized over this past year that you made your choice. And it wasn't me. So, I gotta go." He had turned to head to the truck when he paused suddenly. "What the hell?"

The goat was performing a dance on the hood of Joe's vehicle.

Skylar waved it off as usual goat antics. "She's playing. Just ask her politely and she'll get down."

Joe quirked a brow, as if considering how one goes about politely asking something of a goat. "Seriously?"

Skylar nodded and gestured for him to approach the goat. He did, slowly.

"What's her name?"

"Beyoncé!"

"Right. Of course. An obvious name for a goat. Beyoncé."

The goat stomped the hood playfully as Joe stood there, hands spread as if to catch her. Skylar winced, hoping she wouldn't dent it. The man finally gripped the goat carefully and set her on the ground. She bounced off, bleating happily.

Joe waved as he backed the truck away.

Skylar clutched her clasped hands over her freshly wounded heart. He thought she was too good for him? How ridiculous. And she hadn't made a choice between—

Though she could completely understand how he would feel that way. Fine. She had made a sort of choice. She knew it, just as he did.

She swore softly. How to tell the man she had been wrong? To make him understand that she simply needed him?

Chapter Thirteen

"Interesting." Lucy, the forensics analyst, set the slide before Joe and crossed her arms dramatically, pausing while he waited for her to continue.

"Yeah?" he finally prompted.

"That is eagle meat. Laced with strychnine."

"The same poison…" Joe's voice trailed off.

"That killed Max Owen." She nodded when he lifted his head abruptly. "I know about that case. Heard about the conservation officer who paid for the old man to have an autopsy because he didn't believe it was an accident. It was still ruled accidental."

"It wasn't," Joe said. "I knew Max. He wasn't that stupid."

"Some of those old Native Americans really know their flora and fauna, but everyone makes mistakes, Cash."

"Strychnine is not a natural substance, is it?"

"It's from the nux vomica tree, The seeds make the poison. It's not a plant native to Minnesota, but a person can get that stuff by bulk if they know the right people."

"And if they're looking to poison wildlife." Joe tightened his jaw. "And now, two weeks following Max's death, another strychnine poisoning? Don't you find that suspicious?"

Lucy shrugged. "In the overall scheme of things? No.

Like you said, hunters still use that nasty stuff to poison wildlife. Farmers use it to kill wolves. But if you narrow it down to the small area you've been investigating lately, then yes, I agree there's something fishy going on. The poison was definitely injected into those meat samples you brought in."

The satisfaction Joe felt at having Lucy corroborate his suspicion was short-lived. "Had Max Owen taken in the poison from surface contact or internally?"

"I don't know."

"Can you look it up?"

"Should be able to." Lucy tapped at her laptop on the short desk in the forensic lab van. She finally nodded and said, "It was contact. So he touched meat, or something with the poison on it. Think he was into poaching?"

"Definitely not."

"And now another incident of strychnine poisoning."

"Eagle meat," Joe repeated. "You know what kind of eagle?"

Lucy shook her head. "Hard to determine. But I do know eagle meat on sight. I've seen it more times in the lab than a person should have to. Poor birds. So someone was trying to poison the—did you say it was a wolf?"

"Yes, Stella. She's a rescue animal living with an animal rehab therapist right now."

"You think a poacher went after the wolf?"

Joe shook his head. "Not sure. I think someone was sending a threatening message to the woman who cares for the wolf. Now I just have to figure out if that someone also sent the same message to Max Owen."

Lucy leaned against the stainless steel lab table. "I get the occasional animal in here. I've seen this same poison in the bloodstream before. Maybe…recently?" She turned, jiggled the computer mouse and started clicking away.

"In this area?" Joe asked. "I've been investigating about a fifty-mile range with Checker Hill as the center point."

"Any leads yet?"

"I have my suspicions. Davis Trucking employs truckers from about the same radius."

"You mess with that company, they'll bring you down, Cash."

"Why do you say that? What do you know about them?"

"Same thing everyone knows. They own some of the law enforcement in this county. Can get away with virtually anything. Likely even murder."

And had they gotten away with Max Owen's murder? "They don't own me," Joe said.

"Here." Lucy turned the laptop so Joe could read the screen over her shoulder. "Last month, one of your fellow conservation officers, Robbie Anderson, brought in a burlap bag of bald eagles. Five of them. Taken down with strychnine-laced squirrel meat. We knew they'd been poached."

"Did Robbie find the source?"

Lucy shook her head. "I haven't heard from him. And he hasn't been in since then."

"Thanks, Lucy. I'll give him a call." Joe headed for the door but stopped when Lucy called to him.

"Be careful, Cash. I like it when you visit. I'd hate to see those visits stop. I'll see you soon," she said, and then gave him a wink.

It always startled Joe when women flirted with him.

He wandered out, sorting through the facts he'd just learned.

Max had touched something covered with strychnine. Could it have been an eagle? That made little sense; Max wouldn't have had reason to do such a thing.

This case was growing bigger. He pulled out his cell

phone, called Dispatch and asked them to patch him in to Robbie's phone. The call went to voice mail. He was probably out in the field. He left a message, asking him to call him about the poisoned bald eagles. "I've got a couple poisoning cases that are similar. We need to share notes."

THE CAMP WHERE Max had spent his summers had been cleared away by the crime-scene unit. It had been little more than a tent, a cookstove and a carved oak stump that the old man liked to sit on as he was whittling.

Joe inhaled a breath and wandered the area, determined to see what all the others had missed. There were so many footprints belonging to others who had no idea of the kindness of the old man. They'd remember him only as the victim or the dead man. The Native American living off the grid who had likely eaten something poisonous. Fool.

Squatting near where the fire ring remained, a circle of fist-sized rocks coated in soot, Joe took a branch and stirred the ashes. He wasn't looking for anything in particular. Or was he? Surely Forensics had poked and prodded with the same goal. All that remained was heavy white ash and chunks of charcoal.

Joe pressed his fingers over the eagle talon at his neck. It felt cool. His only token from a man who had taught him so much. He'd never told his parents about Max. Now it didn't feel necessary, though they should know their son had found a mentor in that great man.

Maybe he'd bring it up at the next family dinner. Mom called in the crew for those at least one Sunday a month. Of course, it might worry his mother that he was only mentioning his relationship with Max now. He didn't want to upset her. There was nothing to be upset about, but people went places in their imaginations when they heard things like a ten-year-old boy spending days in the wild with a stranger.

How might Max have gotten something laced with strychnine in hand? Someone had to have planted something in the campsite. Or had he found it while out wandering? If it had been an eagle, or animal meat of some sort, had it consumed the poison by feeding on a trapped animal? It was possible. Yet surely Max would have approached a dead bird or even bait cautiously, suspicious over its death until he could be sure it was a natural death and safe to handle.

Maybe.

Joe knew Max would sometimes eat a small animal he'd found if it was newly dead, and not sick or infested with insects. He didn't survive the summers on dandelion tea and blueberries.

After standing up, Joe wandered the grassy circumference that demarcated Max's little circle in the midst of the forest. A taconite slab with a sheered wall grew up ten feet on the west side. The rock was rusty red and black. He loved that stone, and Max had showed him how to chip off slices and hammer the edge to form a rudimentary blade. Fun stuff for a teenager. He still had one of those caveman blades, as he'd called it, somewhere in his office.

It was easy to see, from the footsteps of the crime team, when they had decided they'd searched far enough, so Joe crossed the crushed grass and wandered into the forest. He stopped before each tree trunk and pressed his boot down on the loamy earth. Max had a tendency to bury bones and organic matter such as compost. At the third birch tree, his foot crushed tender earth that had been previously disturbed.

Joe squatted and prodded the earth with his fingers. There was something buried there. He pulled out his knife and used it to dig, being careful not to point it, instead using the edge so he wouldn't damage any evidence. About six inches down, he uncovered something that made him swear.

"An eagle."

Chapter Fourteen

Skylar opened the front door and invited Joe in. She stepped back, lifting an arm to brace across her chest. He sensed a touch of coolness to her demeanor. He'd pulled away from her kiss this morning because he'd remembered what Cole Pruitt had said to him about Skylar knowing more than she was letting on.

Joe handed Skylar the forensic lab report. "The poison was strychnine. The meat was soaked in it. But you'll never guess what kind of meat it was."

Skylar glanced at the report then gave him a shocked look. "Bald eagle?"

"Bastards are poaching bald eagles. I knew they were taking wolves, deer and smaller animals without a license, but the eagle brings this to a new low."

"Is taking down a bald eagle still a federal offense?" Skylar asked. "Because I'd really like to see those guys go down. Especially since they went after Stella."

"Those guys?" Joe hooked his hands at his hips and faced her directly. "Would that be your family, Skylar?"

"My family? My dad is dead, Joe, and you know that. My mother up and left long ago. I'm on my own."

He did recall that Skylar's mom had left her when she'd been a young teenager. She certainly had her reasons to keep people at a distance.

"You know who I'm talking about. Malcolm Davis and the Davis Trucking empire. You don't consider them family?"

She gave a dismissive nod. "I suppose they are, but I don't talk to Malcolm unless I have to. And I generally don't have to."

Frustrated at her seeming ability to skirt around anything regarding the one person high on his suspects list, Joe pleaded, "Skylar, what aren't you telling me? How long have you been involved with what Malcolm is up to?"

"In-involved? Oh, no, Joe, you've got that wrong. I don't work for—you think *I'm* involved with the poaching?"

Her body language screamed *offense* as she shifted from foot to foot, stepping back, then forward, not sure what to do with her hands, which eventually formed fists.

"How dare you?" she finally blurted out. "I would never."

"But you know they are poachers."

"Everyone knows that. For heaven's sake—Joe, I *rescue* animals for a living. Do you think I'd be so heartless as to purposely take an animal's life?"

No, he did not. And yet. "I talked to Cole Pruitt yesterday. Found him out on Lake Seraphim. He told me that after learning what you were involved in, he was the one to leave you at the altar."

Her jaw dropped open.

"And he said you hooked him up with Malcolm's crew. That's the reason he left you, because apparently you were not the woman he thought you were."

She stared at him with an openmouthed glare. Growling, Skylar stomped out of the living room and into the kitchen. There she paced twice, hands to her hips, then headed to the back of the house. She stopped at the patio doors, turned and lifted a finger as if to punctuate a statement, then shook her head and spun away from him.

"Skylar, talk to me."

Her growl was laced with frustration, and she tossed up her hands in defeat. "Do you really believe all of that, Joe?"

To see her reaction, he didn't now. And he hadn't when Cole had said it to him out on the lake. Well, he'd had a moment of doubt, which was why he'd had to ask the questions. But, of course, Skylar could not be a part of the poaching going on in the area. He had only to look at Stella to know what a kind heart Skylar had.

And yet. "Malcolm has a lot of control over things in this county. Some say he might even have a hand in local law enforcement."

"He does, and I wouldn't put it past him to have a few dirty cops in his pocket." She slammed her hands to her hips, her head bowed. She wasn't about to look at him. Joe could feel anger radiate off her. Or was it fear?

"Does he control you, Skylar?"

"Never. He's tried, but—oh, hell."

Joe rushed over and took Skylar by the shoulders, turning her to face him. "He's tried? What? What has he done or said to you, Skylar? Please, you can tell me. I want to help."

"It's just…it's not what you think with the poaching, Joe."

"Then what should I think?"

Her expression showed she struggled with fear and anger and a pining sort of trust right now. She wanted to confide in him; he could sense it. He took her hands and held them and didn't say anything more. He wanted her to know he was there for her.

Finally Skylar said, "Malcolm has been after a parcel of land since my dad was alive. Dad refused to sell. Wanted to keep it pristine. You know what a tree hugger he was. But lately Malcolm has been putting pressure on me to sell. Even offered to cosign on a loan I can't seem to get for the shelter I want to build. At least, that was the plan. Until Cole and I, well…he was going to co-sign. But after I learned that he was involved with Malcolm I broke it off."

"Cole and Malcolm?" Joe nodded. That was not a big leap to take. Not after what he'd witnessed on the lake. Cole had been drinking hard liquor; that wasn't his MO. Something had changed with his former friend, and drastically.

"And then I learned that my mother actually owns half the land, and now I don't know what to think of anything."

"Your mother? I thought she was gone?"

"She is. Haven't heard a peep from her since I was twelve. Joe, I talked to my dad's former lawyer, thinking he might advise me on how to go about getting this shelter business begun without having to resort to taking Malcolm's assistance. Upon reviewing my father's will, we learned that my mother actually owns half the land. Dad hadn't rewritten the will after she left us."

"Oh man, that's tough."

"Right. But it has nothing to do with what you're investigating. I shouldn't have brought it up, I—"

Joe pulled her into a hug. "You can talk to me about anything, Skylar. I mean it."

"I know you do, and…" She pulled out of the hug and managed a brief smile. "I love you for that. Honestly. Ah! This whole thing is driving me crazy," Skylar said. "I just want peace. And I want to be able to walk out into my backyard without fear of being shot at because I may have seen something."

"You saw something? Where? At Malcolm's place? What did you see, Skylar?"

"I don't know. I was looking for Malcolm, going to give him a piece of my mind regarding finding yet another trapped animal on my property, and I walked into a warehouse full of crates. And…freezers. I was threatened with a rifle to leave and never tell a soul."

"Who threatened you?"

"I don't know. I rarely go on Davis Trucking property. One of the employees. He was tall. Had red hair. I ran. Fast. I'm sure that's why someone shot at me. They were sending me a warning to keep quiet. Of course, I don't know what I would talk to anyone about. Like I said, I don't know what was in those freezers."

"There's only one thing I can imagine that would be kept in a freezer. Animal parts. That bastard leaves carcasses all over the county, and hires his own truckers to set and monitor traps. I've learned that much. But I'm missing something. Something big. Something that has recently put you in harm's way. And… Max."

Skylar tilted her head. "You think the old man saw something, too? That he was silenced?"

"It's beginning to feel like it. I went back to Max's camp. Found a buried eagle carcass. I just dropped it off at the forensic lab, and I'm guessing it's laced with strychnine. It had to be what killed Max."

"He put poison on an eagle?"

"No. I think… Forensics said he had to have handled it quite a bit to absorb the poison through his skin and into his system. And Max had a reverence for all animals. I'm guessing he found the dead eagle, probably held it close, whispered to his people for it. Might have stroked its wings. Then he buried it. The whole time he would have never been aware of the poison."

"That's awful. But if he found it dead somewhere…"

"I think it was placed for him to find it. Probably by the one who would be most affected now that Max had convinced his tribe to stop buying black market eagle parts."

"Malcolm?"

Joe nodded and raked his fingers through his hair. "Still need a viable link. But I'll find it. I'm close. I can feel it."

"Malcolm told me Cole had taken down an eagle to show his alliance to him. That was the reason I called off the wedding."

"Why would Malcolm tell you that? You'd think he'd want to keep the illegal doings of all his employees as quiet as possible. Maybe he wanted to break the two of you up?"

Skylar shrugged. "I don't waste any time trying to put myself in the mind of that man. He was never kind to my dad."

"And yet, you avoided telling me all this until now. You could have said something that night I came over when I got the call."

Skylar exhaled heavily. "It's a family thing, Joe. I need to get beyond the whole 'don't rat on the family' mind-set. I have gotten beyond it. I'm tired of it all. And then to learn about my mother owning half the land? Like I said, I'm ready to end it all. So whatever you need to know about Malcolm, I'll tell you. But I've said all that I do know."

"I appreciate you finally trusting me enough to tell me. Is there anything I can do to make things better about the situation with your mom?"

She shook her head. "I've got to decide if I want a private investigator to track her down to see what she wants to do about the land. But if I just let it go, maybe she'll never return and I'll have the land. I mean, maybe she doesn't know she owns half. I have to think about it."

"Tough thoughts."

"Worthy of another few sips of brandy, for sure."

"You know Cole has been hitting the hard stuff?" Joe asked.

"I didn't. What do you mean?"

"I smelled whiskey on his breath when I talked to him on the lake."

"But he's a beer guy. I wonder if he's stressed-out? A guy can't work for Malcolm and retain his sanity. Or so I'd imagine."

"Yeah. I worry about him."

"Even after he stole the girl?"

Joe smirked. "Even after. You were never mine to steal."

"I wish I had been."

He tilted his head in wonder at that statement. And just when he thought now would be an appropriate time to kiss her, he remembered that something was missing. "Where is Stella? I expected a big ol' wolfie greeting."

"She's..." Skylar stepped away from him and poked her head out onto the deck to scan the yard. She called for the wolf a few times. "That's odd. She always comes when I call."

"Think she's out hunting?"

"She's too domesticated. She prefers her meat and kibble in a bowl. This is weird." She walked toward the forest edge. "I have to go look for her."

"I'm right behind you. Does she do this often? Wander off?"

"She usually stays close to home, and only goes out when I do. And she's still not feeling one hundred percent. So maybe... Stella!" Skylar stepped into the brushy woods.

Joe followed. If Skylar suspected something wasn't right, then he trusted her instincts. And if the Davis family was involved, he wouldn't stop until they paid dearly for their crimes.

"Let me," Joe said as he pushed ahead of Skylar. "I've been tracking wolves for a decade."

"Sure, but I know Stella." She moved aside for him on a narrow path that was tapering quickly and ended abruptly in a copse of birch.

Joe knelt and studied the ground. Here were patches of loam and mud and... He spied a very distinctive wolf track owing to the animal having only three paws to move on. The tracks led to the left, through a less grassy area and between two trees. He followed carefully, hunched over to keep his head low and nose closer to the ground. When tracking a wolf, it was wisest to breathe what they had breathed and see what they had seen. And from this vantage point, he spied the glimmer from the lake to the left.

The tracks paralleled the lake, so he followed.

Behind him Skylar suddenly let out a wolfie howl. Joe stopped and turned to her. She put a finger to her lips. Not three seconds later a wolf returned the howl. It sounded distant. Wolves could communicate miles away from one another. And it wasn't a surprise they had answered Skylar's call.

"It's not her," she said, and walked ahead of him, her head down, scanning the grass and branches and tree roots that would trip a person not paying attention.

He put out an arm to slow her and slipped in front of her. "Let me do this, please."

"She's *my* wolf," Skylar snapped.

"I know what I'm doing. I have a way with wolves."

"I know you do. But she'll scent me, so I need to be in front."

Ready to argue the ridiculousness of that statement, Joe forced himself to hold his tongue. Skylar was upset. Stella was missing, and she was still recovering from being poisoned. If they wanted to find her, they needed to work together.

"You know of any rendezvous points in the area? Does she often venture beyond your land?"

Skylar resumed walking, pushing aside branches and avoiding the pine boughs with ease. "There is an old rendezvous near the lake about half a mile ahead. You think she went there? She avoids that area because it's former pack territory. I think she can still scent them and maybe misses them."

"She might be trying to return home. Wolves are social animals."

"I know that. I don't need a basic wolf class from you."

She stomped ahead, and Joe fisted his hands. She was being obstinate. He wanted to give her some freedom, but who exactly was he dealing with here? Whatever she had seen in the Davis warehouse had to have been illegal if she'd been threatened. Twice. Could those freezers have contained eagle parts?

Crouching again, he eyed the ground and low grass, no longer picking out the tracks. Joe stopped and swung a look to the side, and then the other side. Stella had not gone this direction. She'd veered off…somewhere.

"Stop, Skylar," he whispered. "She's not that way. I've lost her tracks."

Skylar swung around, and the emotions playing on her face startled Joe. Was she near tears?

"I don't know what I'll do if I lose her, Joe."

"You won't," he said quickly, but wasn't as sure of the reply as he wanted to be. "Come here."

"I need to find her!"

"Just give me one minute. Come here, Skylar."

She wandered over and he pulled her into a hug, which she resisted at first, but then her body sank against his and she sniffled tears. He didn't know what to say, so he simply held her and allowed her to cry, to pour out the pain she must have been struggling with for longer than a woman should have to endure by herself. He tucked her hair over her ear and offered her a smile.

At that moment, he noticed the broken sedge grass and saw the low clearing where a wolf may have passed, venturing toward the lake. He gestured for Skylar to follow. "Give that howl one more try," he said as they walked.

Skylar let out a long howl. She was good at the vocalization.

A wolf answered almost immediately. Joe paused to study Skylar's face.

"That's her." She took off toward the lake, but she did not leave the woods, instead tracking along the edge parallel to the water. "Ahead!"

Joe followed as Skylar raced through the woods. Trees whipped at his face and shoulders, but he maintained a sure step. And then he scented the musty urine smell of wolves. It had to be the rendezvous point.

Skylar swore. He lost sight of her as she swung around a large, ancient oak. Something was wrong. Joe swiftly rounded the tree. When he saw the scene, he called out to Skylar. She stopped just short of Stella, who sat before the immobile body of a trapped wolf.

"Aw, hell." Joe marched up to Skylar. Resisting the urge to push her aside, it took all his control to squat and hold out a hand toward Stella. "Come here, sweetie. This is not a place for you to be."

The wolf whined and crawled forward a few paces on her front legs, but she didn't seem to want to leave the trapped wolf.

A dead wolf. Thank goodness. Because much as Joe hated to lose another wolf to a trapper or poacher, the worse result would be to find the wolf still alive, suffering a slow death from what would surely be a fatal bone break or injury.

"Stella." Skylar patted her thigh and the wolf lifted her head, eyeing her person with hope. "Come to me. Let Joe take care of her."

The trap had snapped the wolf's neck. A quick death?

He hoped so. And it couldn't have been in the trap long, for the insect activity was low. Just a few flies. This could have only happened within the past few hours.

"Damn poachers," Joe said curtly. "It's okay, Stella. You knew she was in trouble and you sought her out. Good girl. Now let me take care of her for you."

"Stella," Skylar said more softly.

Finally the wolf got up and approached Joe, sniffing cautiously at his outstretched fingers. He carefully slid a hand along her neck and patted her back gently. "Go to Skylar," he said. "She's worried about you."

The wolf did so, approaching Skylar with bowed head. When she got up to her and Skylar knelt, Stella bowed her head against Skylar's shoulder.

"I'm so sorry," Skylar said to the wolf. "What are we going to do about this?" she asked Joe.

"*We* are doing nothing. *You* are taking Stella home. Leave this to me."

"But I want to—"

"Go, Skylar!" The order came out with more vitriol than he intended, but it was too late to take it back, though it hurt his heart. Skylar was a member of the very family that had likely committed this atrocity. And much as he knew she was no accomplice, he couldn't move beyond that anger. "I'll carry her to my truck and turn her over to the wildlife division. They keep track of the trapped wolves in the area."

"I can help."

"You've done enough." With that, Joe rose and faced her down. Stella's ears folded back. He hated that he must appear a dominating alpha to the wolf, but he needed Skylar to just leave.

With a nod and a pat to Stella's head, Skylar rose and turned to walk away. Stella followed, glancing back frequently until the twosome landed on the lakeshore. They would follow that back to the cabin.

Joe blew out a breath. Another innocent creature's life taken for sport and profit. This had to stop. Anger coursed through his veins. He was just one man. He felt like he may never win this struggle.

Max's words echoed in his head: *You respect them, they respect you.*

He did respect them and would help them until he could do no more. Someone had to.

But was Skylar on his side or her own?

Chapter Fifteen

Joe's accusatory tone had been clear. He suspected her of involvement in the poaching. How dare he? Had he not listened to a word she'd said? She'd opened herself to him, had told him things she hadn't dared tell anyone.

Cole had told him she was the mastermind behind the poaching? Skylar would give that man a piece of her mind. And soon. He had no right to spread such lies about her.

Right now though, she wanted to get Stella home, and check her fluids and stats. She was still recovering. That she'd tracked all the way to the rendezvous site meant that she'd known about the trapped wolf. Wolves had such excellent senses of smell. Had she known Skylar would find her and rescue the wolf? Surely she had. Unfortunately, that wolf had been dead. Skylar prayed she had not suffered long after the steel trap jaws had snapped about her neck. There hadn't been noticeable signs of struggle in the dirt near where the wolf had lain. That could be a good sign.

After they reached the backyard, Stella trotted up the deck stairs and curled up in her bed.

"I'll get you something to eat," Skylar said. To Stella's sudden whine, she offered, "Without poison in it. And some fresh water, as well. No more wandering off, you got that?"

Stella lay down her head and wagged her tail.

THE TIMBER WOLF Joe had untangled from the trap and transported to the fish and game office had been tagged. He'd written down the tag ID before handing the wolf off for processing. They would check the body for its state of health, age and other important telling details that could be used in the wolf data for the state. Joe had also suggested they check for strychnine. Just an added precaution. He'd worn gloves and had been cautious to make sure the fur had not touched his skin when he'd tossed it over a shoulder to carry to the truck.

Now, back at home, after a shower to ensure no traces of contamination from the wolf might linger—he was overly cautious of poison lately—Joe slipped on some jeans and padded down to his office. He pulled up a chair behind his desk and powered up the computer. He rarely spent time in the office so it would take a few minutes for the computer to come alive. Meanwhile, he sipped his coffee and thought about how he'd left Skylar's place without a goodbye. He'd been too angry after hauling the hundred-pound dead wolf off her property. If she was involved in any way...

He didn't want to believe that. No woman who had rescued a wolf pup from a trap and made it a pet could be so cruel. And she had a naked chicken running around her property. And that crazy goat. Skylar was not inhumane.

Which meant everything she'd told him had been the truth. Cole Pruitt had lied to him. While he'd never known the man to lie, he had only known him a few years. They'd met in college and had become instant buddies. Whenever Cole had wanted to go out fishing, Joe had accompanied him. Of course, Joe did catch and release. He wasn't completely vegetarian, but he found it difficult to justify taking another being's life just to satisfy his palate. Cole had razzed him about it, going on about enjoying big steaks drowning in horseradish and butter. Joe took it all in stride. No man can change another; it was only himself he could change.

More of Max's wisdom that had crept into Joe's veins over the years.

"Max." He tapped his fingers on the desk as he thought about that buried eagle he'd found. Max had not been hiding evidence of his own foul play. "Was it the Davis family?"

Max had never mentioned anything about a run-in with Malcolm Davis or anyone else from Davis Trucking. Still, he obviously had said as much to the man Joe had spoken to on the beach. Who had found Max? Who had camped about six miles into the forest, following unmarked paths and using landmarks only experienced hikers and those who knew the land well could recognize?

Unless Max had found the bird close to the highway? No. He wouldn't have carried it all the way back to camp. Maybe?

Joe shook his head. He would never know what had gone on from the moment Max had found the bird—he needed to hear from Forensics to verify his guess it had been poisoned—until that terrible moment he had been found roadside and near death. The poor man. That was no way to die.

He checked his watch—7:30 p.m. The forensic lab might still be at it. He pressed the speed dial for them, and when it went to voice mail he clicked off. He'd call again in the morning.

The computer screen displayed a wildlife scene with a fish breaking the surface of Lake Vaillant. Joe had taken that photo himself on a cool September morning when the mosquitos had been buzzing over the water, a delicious treat for an industrious trout. He opened the state registry and typed in the wolf ID.

"The Red Seven pack," he muttered.

They were the closest pack to the area, yet still a good ten miles to the north, embedded within the Boundary Waters thick forest. If they had reason to travel south, that would land them on Skylar's property. The old rendezvous point, which was on her property, showed on a map, yet he decided it was no longer in use. Or wouldn't be, after the pack smelled the hunter and realized they'd lost one of their own. That reduced that pack to six. One alpha, two females, and he guessed the dead wolf was a lesser male. Perhaps even an omega, for the wolf had a scarred ear, showing it had either been torn in the woods or in a scrap within the pack.

Wolves showed their dominance by fighting and protecting the females. There was a definite hierarchy within the pack, and they all knew their places. But there were always the aggressive few who tried to challenge the alphas or take a female for themselves. Hell, they were constantly waiting, watching for the elders to show weakness and signs of needing to be replaced.

When he was nineteen, Joe had spent a whole year living in the Boundary Waters as part of a wildlife rescue program. It had been Max's suggestion he sign up, and despite his parents' concerns about him leaving the grid for a whole year, they'd backed him up, knowing it could help their son thrive. Joe had learned to track all kinds of animals, including cougar, elk, moose, badgers and wolves, and had learned everything he could about their ways and habitats.

A man had to abandon the industrial world, set aside his cell phone and dependence on microwaved food, and camp out in the wild to truly learn about the beautiful creatures on this earth. That summer, he'd canoed and camped through the entire Boundary Waters. And he'd been rewarded with the trust of those animals that no longer raced away when they sensed his presence. Joe knew how to tread the earth as if walking on clouds, and that silence was the only way to feel the heartbeat of the land and those animals around him.

It reminded him of another of Max's bits of wisdom. *You must hear the land. Walk upon it with reverence.* There was no way to do that with technology in hand.

Hunters—and worse, poachers—disrespected the wild-life with their entitled attitude that they had a right to take an animal for food. Some took the animals and sold them on the black market. Deer and moose antlers were sold to artisans for artwork. It was a crying shame that bald eagles were hunted for traditional Native American costumes. Even if the feathers and talons they used were treated with reverence and ritual, Joe wished it was a prac-tice that would stop. But, despite the threat of prison or fines well into many thousands of dollars, and losing vot-ing rights and the right to own or carry a gun, it was im-possible to stop those who wished to profit from the deaths of such beautiful creatures.

Wolves had been taken off the DNR's endangered spe-cies list a few years ago, allowing licensed hunters to snag them, but they'd recently been put back on. The usual ex-cuse for killing a wolf was that it had gone after a farm-er's valued livestock. Panic was the first reaction. Guns always won over compassion or a simple understanding of animal nature.

There were many better ways to steer a wolf away from cattle and chickens, ways that were more humane than buckshot. Putting up a fence of bright red flags around the property scared the wolves away. Also, motion sensor lights did the trick, especially at night. But Joe knew many a hunter or farmer liked to claim the victory of telling oth-ers that he'd got himself a wolf the other night. Stood up to that creature and taken him down with a powerful rifle.

Some even boasted about using AR rifles. The wolf didn't stand a chance against something so fast and powerful.

It broke Joe's heart. And his blood pressure always rose when he was in the presence of a poacher or when he happened upon what he'd found this afternoon. Which was why he'd taken his anger out on Skylar.

The wrong move.

His cell phone rang. It was Forensics.

"Saw your number on the missed calls," Lucy said. "I was just heading out, but decided this was important. That eagle you brought in was covered in strychnine. I was able to trace it to the poisoned eagle meat you brought in the other day. Same batch of poison."

"Really? You can determine that?"

"It was tainted with lead. Must have been stored improperly. But yes, I'm sure the source was the same. Which means somehow, the old man who handled that eagle came back from the dead to place those meat chunks you found on a lakeshore."

"You're being facetious, right?"

"I am. I think you've got a murder case on your hands, Joe."

Joe nodded. His suspicions about Max being poisoned were true. But knowing that did not make his heart whole; instead, it felt as if he'd been stabbed.

"Cash?"

"Got it. Thanks."

"I'm forwarding the toxicology report to the sheriff's department. They need this information about Max Owen's death."

"Do that. Send me a copy of it as well, please."

"Just clicked Send on your email. I'm sorry, Cash. The old man meant something to you?"

"He was a friend. Thanks, Lucy."

Joe hung up, then put his palm against his forehead. Someone had murdered Max Owen.

So the connection could be… "The sniper?" But the trap evidence they'd found near the sniping spot had not been contaminated with poison.

So far, the common thread was the eagles.

When his phone rang, Joe thought to let it go to voice mail until he noticed the name.

He answered. "Skylar."

"I thought you might stop in before you left. Did you get the wolf and the trap?"

"I did. I've got a lot of work on this right now—"

"Right. Sorry to bother you. I just…" Her sigh echoed heavily across the phone line. "I need to tell you about Cole and me. We were distracted by looking for Stella before I could explain. Are you willing to listen?"

"Cole used to be my friend," Joe said, "but I trust you more than him. And I honestly cannot conceive of you doing such a terrible thing to innocent animals."

"Sure felt like you were mad at me for something earlier."

Joe exhaled. "Sorry about that. I get angry when I find a dead animal in a trap. I took that anger out on you."

"I can understand, with the investigation."

"Tell me the real story about you and Cole. Please?"

"I can't believe he would say that it was me involved in the poaching. No, actually I do believe it. That man is a duplicitous charmer who hisses when he slides through the grass. I left him at the altar, Joe. I had just found out Cole was friends with Malcolm, and had been doing some work for him. That day I went to Cole's place and I found snares and traps in his shed. And there was a bag of eagle feathers tucked in a drawer in his bedroom. He lied to you.

And I don't know why he would want you to believe I'm involved, but I'm not. I could never."

She gasped. Was she fighting tears?

He wished he could pull her to him and tell her she was going to be all right. He hated knowing she had been hurt and that Cole was the reason for it. But right now he needed the distance. Because his heart hurt desperately for the loss of a good friend.

"You did the right thing," he said, "even though it might not feel like it. And you may feel alone and scared, but trust me, Skylar, I'm here for you."

"Are you really?"

"I am. Promise. I won't let Cole Pruitt come near you. Or Malcolm Davis. Is he the one you suspect shot at you? And the one who poisoned Stella?"

"I'm not sure it was Malcolm. He's got others who do his dirty work. Like the guy in the warehouse who threatened me."

"Think you could positively identify the man if I had you look through some mug shots?"

"I'm sure I could, but... I don't know."

"I might not even need a mug shot. I'm on the Davis Trucking website right now. There's an employee roster and some headshots. You said he was a redhead? There's a couple redheads," Joe said as he moved the mouse over the page. "Can you go online and take a look?"

"I can do that. But...will Malcolm find out?"

"If you can identify the man who threatened you, no one will need to know it was you. But catching them with evidence in hand is key. Have you ever seen them setting the traps on your property?"

"No. And I'm not sure they're aware of the property boundaries, because it's always close to the edge of where my land meets the DNR-owned land. They need a map."

Joe sighed. "They need to stop."

"Even better."

"You sure you saw eagle feathers in Cole's possession?"

"Yes."

Joe exhaled.

She sighed. "When will you stop by next?"

"How about in the morning? I have a lot of work to do right now. How's Stella doing?"

"She's good. Loping about this evening and playing with Becky. But she's suspicious of the chopped turkey I offered her. Might have to stick with kibble for a while until she trusts meat again."

"Poor girl. Can I...?" Joe rubbed his jaw. Dare he push it between the two of them? She'd confessed she wasn't involved, and he believed her 100 percent. Now, to make up to her for his harsh treatment earlier. "Can I bring lunch by tomorrow? Maybe we can have a picnic out on your deck?"

"That sounds wonderful. I'll make something sweet for dessert."

"Sounds like a plan. Don't forget to take a look at the trucking website."

"Will do. Talk to you tomorrow, Joe."

Joe hung up and smiled. That call had improved his mood. But only until he eyed the laptop screen again. Foremost on his agenda was learning who was poaching eagles and handling strychnine. He didn't have probable cause to search Davis Trucking. Not until he could place one of their employees at the scene of the sniper shooting.

There were two men with red hair shown on the roster. Could be many other employees who didn't have their photos on the site. And there were a couple shots in black-and-white, so no way to determine hair color. He'd wait and see if Skylar recognized one of them. Then he'd have grounds to bring him in for questioning. Because threatening a woman with a rifle? That was criminal assault.

With luck, he'd be able to secure an arrest warrant by tomorrow afternoon.

Chapter Sixteen

Skylar said goodbye to the owner of the farm-supply store. He'd sold her some clinical supplies and IV fluids that he ordered from a veterinary site. Stella was out of the woods medically, but Skylar wanted to replenish her stock. After leaving the store, she strolled down the sidewalk with the small box under an arm, nodding to a pair of elderly women who smiled bright, wrinkled grins.

Passing a big black four-by-four truck, she suddenly realized it was Malcolm's and paused just by the passenger door. She had no intention of talking to him. What was he in town for?

Across the street sat the café, and next to that a small office that rented to a variety of mobile businesses, including a tax accountant and a lawyer.

Skylar sucked in her lower lip. A lawyer. That made sense. Malcolm must have reason to employ all sorts of legal help. But a traveling lawyer? Good thing he'd never signed on with her dad's lawyer. Of course, she figured that could have been a conflict of interest on the solicitor's part.

Her mom owned half the land. She was still processing that information. And did she want to find her?

Part of her said, *Hell no*. But that part was the preteen girl who had wanted to run after Dorothy and beg her to explain herself.

Now she didn't want to think about it. She couldn't. Not with Malcolm and his crew breathing down her neck.

She glanced inside the truck. A brown file folder and some mail were strewn on the passenger seat. As well, a flyer for a local powwow. Why was Malcolm going to a powwow, or even interested in one?

And then it hit her. Hard.

She had to tell Joe.

SINGING ALONG TO Lynyrd Skynard's "Freebird," Joe navigated his way back toward Checker Hill. He'd just come off the lake. A group of five boats had been reported playing loud music, and girls were flipping up their T-shirts to expose themselves to passing boaters. Kids and booze and boats never mixed. Joe had been flashed three times in the process of issuing them tickets and following them inland to dock their boats. He hadn't made any arrests, but a stern warning, and the mention that he knew more than a few of their parents, had been taken seriously.

Now he intended to pick up some groceries for the meal he'd promised Skylar. He wasn't going to get prepared foods from the deli section. No, he had a few specialties he could make. She would get a taste of his macaroni special.

He checked his reflection in the rearview mirror. Should have shaved this morning. He was looking a little rough. Probably needed a haircut, too. His bangs hung in his eyes. He rubbed his stubble, thinking maybe he should try for a full beard like his brother Justin.

A beat-up Ford that had once been red and was now pushing for pink passed him in the other lane, going the opposite direction. Too late, Joe raised a hand to wave. That had been Skylar. She must be headed home from the errands she'd mentioned. They'd just passed, like two ships. The thought made him smile. He planned a docking this evening.

Man, did that sound corny.

Another car passed him, going well over the speed limit. A determined red sedan, which suddenly swerved out of its lane.

Joe touched the radio intercom to get through to county dispatch.

He didn't hear the sound of impact, but Joe saw the collision in his rearview mirror.

Chapter Seventeen

Joe slammed on the brakes, steering to the gravel road-side. Half a mile down the road, Skylar's truck sat in the ditch. The red car had continued driving.

He turned the truck around, switching on the police flashers as he did so. He waited for Dispatch to respond while he drove, keeping his eyes pinned on the red sedan, which quickly distanced itself from the scene of the accident. Damn it, he should have gotten a license plate.

Pulling up behind Skylar's truck, he saw motion behind the wheel. That meant she was alive. Looked like the driver of the red car had nudged her rear bumper, forcing her into the ditch.

Dispatch prompted him, and he realized she'd questioned him twice already.

"I've got a car run off the road on County Road 7. I'm getting out to investigate now. If there's a patrol in the area, the perp was driving a red two-door Monte Carlo. I didn't take note of the plates. I'll pursue after checking on the driver, who was run into the ditch."

"I'll send an ambulance," Dispatch said.

Joe knew Skylar would protest if she wasn't hurt too badly, but it was standard procedure.

"Thanks."

He got out of his truck and raced up to Skylar's vehicle.

The front end had hit a broken telephone pole. Long out of use and rotting, the foot-wide base was still intact. It had served to stop the truck from sinking into the water, which Joe estimated to be about a foot deep. The front of the engine was crushed in. The vehicle was totaled.

He pulled open the driver's door and Skylar blinked at him. Her forehead bled, and her lower lip wobbled.

"I'm here," he said. "I saw you pass me. Did you see who was driving the red car?"

She shook her head and held out her arms. He stepped up to help her down.

"How badly are you hurt?" he asked.

"Just shaken. My head hit the steering wheel because I was turning the radio dial when he slammed into me. I lost control, and the truck veered sharply." She clutched his arms and stepped onto the side runner.

Joe decided to sweep her into his arms. She didn't protest, which meant she had been shaken. He carried her back to his truck and gently set her down near the hood. Brushing aside her blond hair, he inspected the cut on her temple. It wasn't deep, more like a bruise. But she could have whiplash or other internal injuries.

"Dispatch called for an ambulance."

"Oh no, Joe. I'm fine."

She wobbled, and he caught her against him. He wrapped his arms around her and pressed his cheek to the crown of her head. She shook in his arms. He wasn't sure what he would have done if she'd been seriously injured, or worse.

More than anything, he wanted to go after the driver who had done this to her. It hadn't been an accident. The car had been swerving, which led Joe to believe the driver had been under the influence. Yet that driver had been clearheaded enough to have purposely gone after Skylar, accelerating until he'd been able to bump her into the ditch.

"Your ribs or anything else hurt?" he asked. Her body felt warm against his, but her shivers troubled him. She could go into shock if he didn't keep her calm and comfortable.

She shook her head. "I feel like you've been rescuing me a lot lately."

"I did tell you I'd be there for you. I just wish I could have stopped this before it happened. I wonder who that was. If I get going, I could probably track him down."

"Then you should go."

"I can't leave you alone."

"You said an ambulance was on the way. I'm going to be fine, Joe. I don't even want to go to the hospital."

"They'll take you to the clinic in town. Let me stay until the ambulance arrives, Skylar."

She shook her head. "No. Go. I want you to find whoever did this."

"You sure? Let me help you to the back of your truck to wait…"

An ambulance siren sounded miles away.

"The cavalry is on their way," Skylar said. "You take off. It's only been a few minutes. You can still catch him."

"You're sure it was a him?"

"I don't know. I wasn't paying attention to the car coming up behind me, then—crash!"

He pulled her close again and pressed his lips to her head. Her hair smelled sweet, and her body melded against his. He didn't want to let her go, but if he didn't, whoever had done this might get away with the crime.

"All right." He forced himself to walk away from the shaken woman. As he pulled out from the shoulder, the ambulance drove up.

The EMT driver rolled down his window. "Hit-and-run?"

"Yes. She's stable. I want to pursue."

"Go for it. We've got it from here."

IT TOOK FIVE minutes to catch up on the two-lane county road. It was normally a highly traveled road, but not so much at this time of day. That was one thing to be thankful for, because others might have gotten in the driver's way and the results could have been far worse. The red sedan led Joe all the way to the next town, fifteen miles east, and into the weedy lot of an empty fairgrounds. The driver parked at an angle in the big lot, then the door opened and out tumbled the driver. Cole Pruitt scrambled across the tarmac, slipping and stumbling as he landed on the grassy lawn.

Checking that the gun was holstered at his hip with a firm clasp, Joe ran after the man, seriously hoping he would not have to draw on him. The last thing he expected was to chase down a friend after he'd been involved in a hit-and-run.

"Cole!"

Cole stumbled again, and as he looked over his shoulder, his feet tangled and he went down, groaning, cursing and kicking at the air in his frustration.

Joe could smell the whiskey when he got close. Whatever the hell was going on with this man, he wanted to know. Because he had done a drastic one-eighty since he and Joe had been friends.

"You're under arrest, Cole," Joe said as he knelt. With a simple shove, he managed to get the grumbling drunk onto his stomach. He secured one wrist and slapped handcuffs onto him. "For driving under the influence, and the hit-and-run of Skylar Davis."

He turned Cole over and he muttered, "Screw you, Cash."

The man passed out, mouth open and legs sprawled.

Joe hated when the perp passed out. He'd need another officer to help him get Cole into the car and transported to the county jail. With a shake of his head, he wandered back to his truck and called Dispatch. Help would arrive in fifteen minutes.

All he could think about was that he'd had to leave Skylar, injured, by the side of the road. And that thought brought up the image of Max also lying roadside, obviously seeking help. What had his last moments been like, to have possibly known he'd been poisoned with nothing he could do about it? Whoever had left that eagle near his property was responsible. And while Forensics had not been able to get fingerprints or human DNA evidence from the bird, Joe knew all paths had to lead to Davis Trucking.

And if Cole Pruitt was working for Malcolm Davis, then Joe was not going to relent until Cole given him answers.

Chapter Eighteen

Joe pulled up to the county hospital and ran inside. He'd told Skylar they would take her to a clinic, but he'd known better. She probably had, too. The clinic closed early and didn't have emergency services. He veered down the hallway in the direction of the ER. It was nearing supper time, and the waiting room was packed with people, from babies to geriatrics. It had only been a few weeks since he'd last been here, looking for Max, hoping he was alive…

He stopped at the admissions desk. "Skylar Davis. She was brought in via ambulance. I'm with the DNR and was first on scene. And I'm a friend. Which room is she in?"

"Number eleven." The redhead behind the desk, with bespangled glasses perched at the end of her nose, pressed a button. To the right, a security door opened.

Joe ran for the door. Room eleven was around the corner. He soared in through the curtained divide to find Skylar sitting on the edge of the bed, her forehead bandaged, sipping juice from a tiny, brightly colored box.

"I tried to get here as fast as I could," Joe said. "What's the damage?"

"Just a cut and possible concussion. I'm supposed to have someone checking on me through the night, but I told them I'm okay to go home on my own."

"No, you're not. They give those orders for a reason. I'll take you home and watch you through the night."

Skylar's eyebrow lifted suggestively. "I think I can get behind that."

"You see? You're not thinking straight now, inviting strange men home with you."

"You do have your strange moments, Joe." She waggled the juice box. "Want a sip?"

"No, I'll let you have all that goofy grape for yourself. When will they release you?"

"The doctors are currently weighing my request to leave on my own, so I expect as soon as we can flag one down and tell them I now have a babysitter, I'll be good to go. I'm starving."

"Sorry, I was supposed to bring something to eat. And for lunch. We both got sidetracked. We can pick up something on the way home. Dairy Queen has a special."

"I'm in. As long as I can also get a chocolate malt. And not one of those impostor shakes. It's gotta have real malt in it."

"Deal." He sat on the bed beside her and studied the bandage. It was small, with no signs of blood seeping through. "Did they do a brain scan?"

"What for?"

"To make sure everything's still in there."

"Seriously?"

He let a smile escape. "I'm kidding. You're the smartest woman I know, and still could be."

"*Could* be?"

"Well, when you get your brains joggled…" He let that hang, hoping she'd take it for the joke he meant it to be.

"I may have lost an IQ point or two. I can deal with that. But more important, is my truck totaled?"

"I'd make a guess it is. The engine was crushed. You're

lucky you weren't seriously hurt. God, I'm so glad you're okay, Skylar."

He hugged her from the side. She was solid and real and not dead. It could have gone any way when she'd hit that telephone pole. A little to the left, and the pole could have sheered through the front of the vehicle and cut into the cab where she was sitting. Or had she not been wearing a seat belt, she could have flown through the windshield.

But she was safe. And mostly sound.

"Did you catch the guy?" she asked from within his arms.

"Yes, and uh…you sure you didn't recognize that car?"

"I didn't. I mean, I remember it was red, but everything happened so quickly. Why should I have recognized it? Who was it, Joe?"

"It was Cole Pruitt."

He felt her tense up in his arms and released his grip, allowing her to sit back. A deep exhale was followed by her shivery release of breath. "Cole? Really?"

"He was drunk. But that's no excuse. He knew exactly what he was doing. I arrested him and put him in the county jail. I plan to talk to him in the morning after he's sobered up. After all you've told me, there could be a lot of reasons he went after you, but I've never known the man to be the sort who would want to harm a person because they brushed him off or…left him at the altar."

"It's the poaching," Skylar said on a whisper. She glanced around. The ER was a hum of buzzers and alarms, and a baby wailed relentlessly a few rooms down. They were secluded in the little room, and no one paid them any mind. "I feel like there's something bigger going on, Joe. And Cole is involved. And whatever is going on, I think he's in over his head. He never drinks enough to get drunk. He likes his beer, but—"

"The breathalyzer showed he was well over the legal limit. He'd been drinking whiskey."

"That's his kryptonite. He usually walks a wide circle around that stuff. I know, because I have offered him brandy and he's refused that, as well, saying the hard stuff never agrees with him."

"I know the same about him. So why is he suddenly drinking and acting out of character? You talk to him about any of your suspicions?"

"Haven't talked to him for two months, since I walked— or rather, ran—away from the altar. Don't want to talk to him. But—" she winced, touching her forehead "—do you think I should?"

"Absolutely not. Let me handle this. I think you're right. There's something bigger going on, and I'm just starting to touch the edges of it all. The poaching is bad enough, but—did you ever hear Cole mention poison?"

"Never. You don't think he poisoned Stella? The two of them never got along, but I don't think…" Her shoulders slumped. "Though if he can bring himself to poach animals, then anything is possible. And if Malcolm ordered him to do so…" She sighed. "I really hate to believe that about him."

"Yeah, I'm not so sure he would do that to Stella." Or Max, for that matter. That would be premeditated murder. No, Joe wouldn't put Cole in that category. But— "What about those eagles you mentioned? You saw feathers in Cole's residence. Ever see anything else?"

"No. But if he's involved with my uncle, then I wouldn't put it past him. Those feathers though. He had a couple of them in a plastic baggie."

"They sell for big bucks on the black market. Tribes buy them for their costumes."

"That's it!"

"What's it?"

Skylar put a finger to her lips.

The doctor, a tall, thin woman with a swinging blond ponytail and pink running shoes to match her scrubs, breezed in. She flashed a penlight at both of Skylar's pupils.

"Looks good. I would prefer you remain here for the night, Miss Davis, if you don't have anyone to take you home—"

"I got that covered," Joe offered. "I'll be her watchdog."

The doctor's smile grew knowingly bright, but she didn't wink. Thank goodness. "Great. I'll put in for her release and send you home with instructions for her care through the night. I'll have a nurse come in and wheel you out, Miss Davis."

"Wheel me out?"

"Take advantage of it," Joe said. "How often is it you get the five-star treatment? I'll run out and pull the truck up to the door." He kissed her forehead. "Be right back."

THEY DIDN'T SPEAK until they'd gotten out of the Ford at the DQ and sat on the faded blue plastic benches at the far side of the outdoor court.

"So." Joe took a bite of his salad and then a sip of his Cherry Slush.

"So?"

"You had a eureka moment back in the ER."

"Right. Joe." She laid a hand over his. "It hit me when you mentioned Native Americans buying feathers for their costumes. I walked by Malcolm's truck today when I was in town."

"And?"

"I looked inside and saw a flyer, and couldn't figure why he'd be interested in something like that. I mean, he's the last man I'd even expect to care about Native American culture, let alone want to attend a powwow."

"A powwow?"

"That's what the flyer was for. There's one next month up at the Grand Portage Reservation."

"Interesting."

"You think he sells eagle parts to them?"

"Not out in the open. But that would certainly be the place to make connections. Build up a clientele. Thanks, Skylar."

"Guess my brain didn't get as joggled as we thought."

"You're still not getting rid of the babysitter."

"Wouldn't dream of trying."

NIGHT SOFTENED THE sky to a chrome gray with dashes of lilac edging the few clouds. Mosquitos buzzed about the lights on the deck. Chickens hushed out low, contented noises from the henhouse. Wet bark and moss perfumed the air. The day had been too long. Skylar should go immediately to bed. But where to put Joe? On the couch? In her bed?

Because despite what was going on in her life, she really needed to be held right now. To know that she was wanted, and yes, to feel sexy and attractive. She hadn't anticipated a moment like this—Joe having to spend the night—but a woman would be a fool not to entertain the notion of fooling around. Really, she did need to be checked on frequently. What better plan than to allow the man close access to her?

Joe closed the front door and called out to Stella, who came bounding through the pet door connected to the patio. The wolf bypassed Skylar and went straight for Joe, greeting him with a slobbery kiss and knocking him to the floor, where he let her shower him with all the love she could manage.

"I'm a little jealous," Skylar said. More than a little,

something she'd never admit to Joe. "But she is a smart wolf. She knows a good man when she sees one."

The behavior she exhibited with Joe was so un-wolf-like that Skylar almost felt embarrassed for her.

"I surrender!" Joe called out. The man stretched out his arms across the floor, and Stella stopped licking his face and sat alert beside him. "She's recovered one hundred percent," he announced.

"Yes, makes me glad."

"You going to shower and head to bed? The instructions the doctor gave me say I have to wake you up every two to three hours."

She was not going to stop a man from touching her every few hours. "I'll let you do what you gotta do. As for a shower…" She walked over to him and knelt on the floor. He still lay on his back. Stella looked to her curiously. The wolf's ears rotated, and she tilted her head. "You want to join me?"

Joe sat up abruptly, catching his elbows on the floor. He narrowed his gaze on her. "Is this the part where you have crazy thoughts because of the bump on your head?"

"Do you think taking a shower with me sounds crazy?"

"Hell, Skylar, that sounds like a dream, but…"

She bent down and kissed him. It was a firm and long kiss. Gliding her hand down his chest, she tucked a finger along the buttons and touched hot skin. She wanted him. Now.

No strings. She needed this.

"I want you, Joe," she said, and kissed his cheek, then moved her lips along his jaw and up to tongue at his earlobe. "Don't you want me?"

"I do. But I don't want to take advantage of a woman who's been injured and her brain—"

Another kiss was necessary to stop his ridiculous protest.

"Don't say no to me this time, Joe. Neither one of us has been drinking."

"I am completely sober. But you—"

She kissed him again to silence his protest. He settled into the kiss and soon spread a hand up her back to pull her closer.

"I am of sound mind and body right now," she said.

"You most certainly are."

"I'm going to fill Stella's water dish and make sure she's got kibble," she said as she sat up. "If I don't hear that shower running in a few minutes, I'm going to think you're not interested in me at all."

Joe stood and started toward the bathroom. "I can take an order!" he called.

Skylar laughed and ruffled Stella's fur. "Come on, Stella."

Chapter Nineteen

Water slicked over Skylar's skin and under Joe's palm as he glided it from her neck, down her chest and over her full breasts. He bowed to kiss each one and then lave the nipples. The night had taken an unexpected turn, but he was no man to argue. The two of them standing together, naked, in the shower, might be because of her head injury, but he didn't think so. Skylar was smart, and as she'd said, neither one of them were drunk. This time.

He'd regretted missing this opportunity years ago. He would never regret again when it came to her. This could very well be a one-night stand, which would challenge his wanting heart. But, right now, all that mattered was the two of them, skin against skin. Heartbeats racing. Moans mingling.

He kissed her mouth and pulled her in close. Her slick skin glided under his touch. His erection had achieved steel status, but they hadn't gone beyond kissing. He couldn't wait much longer and, to judge by her moans, neither could she.

"We're clean," he suddenly said. "Race you to the bed?"

"I get a head start."

"What?"

"I *am* injured."

"Fair enough." He switched off the shower, and Skylar

pulled down a towel and pressed it to her face. When she pulled it away, he kissed her forehead and then licked the water droplets.

"You sure you're up for this?" he asked.

"Oh, Joe, are you sure *you* are?" She teased her fingers down his wet abdomen and then gripped his cock.

He winced at the teasing squeeze, and nodded. The woman was in control, and he didn't mind that one bit. "You'd better get going," he said. "I'll be right behind you."

He toweled off after she left the bathroom. He heard her talk to Stella, and the wolf pattered down the hallway toward the back of the house. Had Skylar consigned the wolf to the deck? She must be really serious about this.

And he was no man to keep her waiting.

Wrapping the towel about his hips, Joe wandered down the hardwood-floored hallway and into the bedroom. He found Skylar lying on the white sheets on her stomach, her toes entwined with one another. She crooked a finger into a "come here" gesture. When he got to the end of the bed, she put up her palm and said, "Wait."

He held the towel and did as he was told.

"One night," she said. "No strings."

Every bone in his body tried to get Joe to protest that statement. He wanted strings. He wanted complications. He wanted Skylar. All the time, every time. And yet…she had just gotten out of a bad relationship. He was willing to play the game her way. Because he wasn't willing to lose her a second time.

"Agreed," he said. He dropped the towel and took some pride in the slow glide of Skylar's tongue along her lower lip as she took him in.

Joe sipped coffee while Stella lapped at water in her bowl, a noisy undertaking on her part. Skylar sat across the kitchen table from him, his green cotton shirt the only thing she wore—she hadn't buttoned it. Her long hair spilled like sun-toasted wheat over her shoulders. And the tiny mole that sat high on her left breast peeked out at him. She was gorgeous. And he would give everything he owned to go back to the bedroom and spend the rest of the day snuggling and making love with her.

But the very reason they had come together was because of a sinister evil that surrounded the Davis land and threatened Skylar's safety. He wasn't about to let that simmer reach a boil.

He set down his coffee mug and pulled out his cell phone from his back jeans pocket. He'd finish dressing when Skylar decided to hand over his shirt. Damn, it looked good on her.

"Business so soon?" she asked, catching her cheek against the heel of her palm as she leaned forward onto the table.

"Yes. I finally got a copy of the waiting list that tribes sign up for to receive eagle parts. Apparently, the wait is long."

"Thus, the black market."

"You know about that?"

"I know about a lot of things I'd rather be oblivious to. I remember years ago my dad found a dead eagle on our land. Hadn't been poached. Looked like it had a run-in with something with teeth. Anyway, he was going to bury it, but before he did, he carefully removed the feathers. Told me he had a friend on the Fond du Lac Reservation who could use them. That's when he told me about the illegal sale of those feathers, and all the other animal parts a person never imagines would bring in a price. Like bear gall bladders. They import those to Asia for medicines. It's nuts."

"Sometimes man can be ignorantly cruel." Joe scrolled through the list. Max's tribe was at the bottom. A long wait.

"So, Cole is stewing in the county jail right now?"

Joe set his phone on the table. "I wouldn't mind letting him sit there all day, but I've got to move while opportunity presents itself."

Joe wandered over, and when Skylar turned he pulled her into his arms. "But you *were* going to make the leap with Cole."

She looked aside. "I'd rather not discuss that."

"I know I don't have a right to ask. And I know you asked for the no-strings deal last night. But I'm hoping what's going on between us right now is going to become something much more…"

"Long lasting?" She bowed her head against his shoulder, then looked up, offering a shrug. "I'm *not* thinking about marriage."

"Don't worry. I haven't picked out a little pink house. Yet. But I do want to know about you and Cole. Why you decided that marriage was right between you two."

"I get that. And I'll tell you. Someday. But right now, things are too fresh, and we're only just getting to know one another again. Can we take it slow?"

"I can work with that. But with everything that's going on right now, I don't want you going near Cole or talking to him, understand?"

"I might be able to get some answers from him if you let me talk to him. Maybe I can accompany you on the interrogation?"

"That's my job, Skylar. A job that demands my attention right now. I'm heading in to town. That is, if I can get my shirt back."

She ran her palms across his bare chest. "You don't think the fish and game department will appreciate you in the buff? I know you were on the county calender a few years ago because it was right before Cole and I—"

Joe winced. Right before she and Cole got together. He didn't need the reminder.

Yeah, he'd posed for a local charity calendar. So had his brother Jason. They'd oiled up their abs and biceps, and had performed their best beefcake impressions. For a good cause. All proceeds were donated to a local camp for disabled children. Their mom had bought a hundred copies and was always giving them out to friends and bragging about her handsome sons.

"Yeah, but we were talking about Cole and you," he said. "Shirt?"

She started to shrug off his shirt, which revealed her bare shoulders and arms and then— Mercy, her breasts were high and full. Joe bowed to kiss each one as he caught the shirt when it slipped off her hands. She moaned sweetly and tilted her shoulders back.

"Sure you want to leave so fast?" she asked.

"Nope. But yes, I have to. Not going to be easy." He moved his kisses up along her neck and jaw and landed on her mouth for a warm, long, delving dive into her sweetness. "If I don't go now, I won't be able to walk into the office without advertising."

Skylar squeezed her palms over his hard-on. "I can take care of that problem."

"You tempt me." And he could make it a quickie…

From behind them, Stella yipped softly and then performed a playful pounce.

"She doesn't have the patience to watch her person get tangled with another person this morning," Joe said. He kissed Skylar once more, then slid his shirt on and buttoned it. "I'll give you a call this afternoon."

"I'll be waiting."

He smiled as he headed toward the door. A beautiful woman waiting on him? He could get used to this.

Chapter Twenty

Cole Pruitt had a manner about him that Joe had not previously found annoying. Was it his venture into hard alcohol? Something had changed the man from fun loving and a little goofy to…this. The man sat across a steel table from Joe, hands folded on it, gray eyes holding Joe's and a smirk crimping the corner of his mouth. Cole had no right to be cocky after what he'd done to Skylar yesterday.

"So you're telling me you didn't purposely run Skylar Davis off County Road 7 yesterday afternoon at 1:45 p.m.?" Joe stated for the recording.

Cole shook his head. "Nope. I was drunk, man. I admit that. You know it. Charge me with drunk driving. But I did not go after Skylar and force her into the ditch."

Joe sat back on the uncomfortable folding chair, spreading his legs and hitching his thumbs at his belt loops. Behind him, on the other side of the two-way glass, sat Brent Kofax. He hadn't insisted on sitting in on the interrogation. Wasn't necessary. Joe had all the qualifications of a police officer and had done many an interrogation before. But should he decide to charge Cole with anything it would be through the county, and the guy was already assisting with the investigation.

It was all he could do right now *not* to punch the smirk from Cole's face. They used to spar with each other, Muay

Thai style, so he knew the man could hold his own against him. Until Skylar had told him the truth about the wedding being off, and Cole's lie about her introducing him to Malcolm Davis, Joe had had no reason to hate the man. Dislike, sure. The man had won the girl. Though at the time, Joe had not pinned *purposeful stealing of the girl* on Cole. He'd known his friend had gotten lucky and asked Skylar out when she was available.

Not that Cole should have ever asked her out. He'd known how Joe had felt about her. But—hell, he was over giving the man a get-out-of-jail-free card. He was an asshole, through and through.

"Good thing you were there to rescue her, eh?" Cole shot across the table. He rapped the table. "When do you cut me loose? I suppose I gotta pay bail, show up in court—"

"You're not going anywhere until I learn everything about Malcolm Davis and your involvement with the family's criminal pursuits."

Cole snickered and gathered his hands in his lap. "I suppose Skylar wants you to believe she was the one to leave me at the altar?"

"Skylar has nothing to do with whatever it is you've been doing for Malcolm Davis. And you know it." Joe held the man's gaze until he finally glanced away, tilted his head and nodded, as if to say, *Very well.*

"They're a tough family," Cole said quietly. "And that's all I can say."

Because he knew that if he talked, he'd be punished by that tough family? Likely. The man had refused a lawyer sitting in on this interrogation. Probably shouldn't have.

Just the thought of what Malcolm Davis was involved in made Joe's skin crawl. And that was merely poaching and some minor assault arrests attributed to a few of his truckers. Could they possibly be connected to Max's murder?

"Do you want to be released?" Joe asked. "I can make

sure you spend some time in county jail for reckless endangerment and leaving the scene of an accident, in addition to the DUI."

"Might be safer here," Cole muttered. Then he lifted his chin and looked Joe straight on. "I'm not telling you anything. You're not a real cop."

"My badge says I am. I was trained as a peace officer before going on to train for the DNR. I have all the abilities and legal powers of any other law enforcement officer. And you know that."

Cole curled up his top lip in disgust and looked aside, before finally announcing, "I'll only talk to Skylar."

"Skylar doesn't work for the county. And I'm the one doing the interrogation. It's me or nothing."

Cole shrugged and crossed his arms over his chest. "Then I'll take nothing."

Joe lunged across the table and gripped the man's shirt, but just as quickly, he remembered he was being recorded. He released Cole and kicked aside the chair he'd been sitting on, then wandered along the back of the room where two-way glass was framed.

Joe ran through his options. He would not allow Cole within shouting distance of Skylar, that was for sure. He could lock him up for a while, but he'd have to charge him, and that risked sending out a smoke signal to the Davis family. If he were to get the sneak on Malcolm Davis, he needed to keep Cole's incarceration hush-hush right now. It was easy enough to hide illegal animal parts and to cover up any other crimes before a warrant could be drawn up to search the place.

"I'll tell Skylar everything," Cole offered. He nodded at Joe. "Nice talking to you, man. Now bring me back to my cell."

Joe knocked on the glass. Brent alerted the guard outside in the hallway. The door opened.

"Take him back to a cell," Joe said.

While Cole was escorted out by the guard, Joe rubbed his jaw and banged the table with a fist. Cole knew something. And the only way to get it out of him was by letting him talk to Skylar.

WHILE AT THE local police department, Joe commandeered a computer and tapped into their database. Through that he was able to view local businesses and check their employee rosters, if listed—companies were not required to release employee records. Privacy acts, and all that. But nowadays most employees signed a release protection form that allowed their information to be accessed by police and FBI if they were suspected of a crime. Only a few employees were listed on the Davis Trucking roster that had previously been released. From there, Joe cross-checked the names to police sheets, to see if they had arrests.

After an hour of work, he ended up with two employees listed as former military. One had served as a sniper with the army during the Gulf War: Reginald Marshall. And he was a redhead. His rap sheet was short, but it listed poaching and domestic violence. No DUIs, but Joe tended to assume alcohol was involved when a man beat his wife.

All of Reginald's vehicle registrations were up-to-date, and he'd applied for a building permit for a shed on his land last year. Joe couldn't come up with a reason to apply for a warrant, but he intended to find the guy and ask him some questions. Starting with where he had been the night Skylar had been shot at. If he couldn't offer an alibi, Joe would bring him in for further questioning.

His cell phone rang, and Joe sat back in the office chair to answer. His brother Jason announced he was calling from the back of a pickup truck filled with manure. He was helping a local family get an overturned truck out of the ditch before all their precious manure melded with the rain-soaked ground. He was literally up to his knees in bullshit. But between days like that and a rare moment he actually got to do real police work, his brother was happy as a camper surrounded by singing squirrels.

"Did she say yes?" Joe asked as he sorted through his notes in the notebook he always carried with him. He'd made a diagram of all the names of the Davis family and their petty crimes. Every single one had at least two poaching offenses. Malcolm was strangely clean.

He penciled in Reginald Marshall's name on the list.

"Of course she did," Jason said. "We're getting hitched in January."

"January?"

"I convinced her since we met in that brutal month, it was only fitting we seal the deal the same month. But she got to pick the location, so we're going to say 'I do' in France. She calls it a destination wedding."

Joe rubbed his temple. He'd never been out of the country, unlike his brother, who was former CIA and had spent years traveling the globe. The idea of visiting France appealed. Of course, Jason was overlooking one key issue.

"Mom will never get on a plane," he said. Indeed, their mother was deathly afraid of flying, and had not once in her fifty-eight years set foot off the ground for more than a leap or a rotation around the Ferris wheel.

"I know. You have to help me with that one, bro. You're the one she can't say no to."

That was true.

"I'll see what I can do." Joe rapped his notes with the end of a pen. "So tell me more about sniping for the military. Could a man hit a target three-quarters of a mile away?"

"With ease. I've made the hit three miles away."

"Nice."

"I am a talented man. What kind of rifle?"

"Shells are Lapua. Forensics guesses the gun is the same make."

"Nice weapon. If the perp had been overseas, he'd have opportunity to run into something like that and possibly use it in operations. Didn't you say you were looking at a specific family involved in the poaching?"

"Malcolm Davis, who heads Davis Trucking."

"I've heard of that guy. Runs a not-so-clean operation. But we can never pin anything on him directly. Couple of his guys have been arrested for assault."

"And poaching and drunk driving," Joe said. "I think they're selling eagle parts."

"Big business, that. All across the US. Would be easy to move around with a trucking company. They know how to hide things at border checks and weigh stations."

Joe sat back and squeezed his eyelids tight. "Malcolm has got two employees who are former military. One was a sniper. I need to start matching employees with arrest records and trucking schedules. I have to talk to Cole Pruitt again. He's working with Davis, but he's keeping his mouth shut."

"Isn't that the guy—"

"Yeah, whatever. She didn't marry him."

"Skylar was her name, wasn't it?"

Joe nodded, but smiled to himself. He had woken in Skylar's bed this morning. And if things went well, their relationship would only grow.

"Skylar Davis," Jason said firmly. "Is that the same family?"

"It's her uncle. She's not involved. But they're trying to make it look like she is. That is, when they're not threatening her. Or poisoning her wolf."

"Sounds like you've got your hands full, bro."

"This started out as simply tracking local poachers, and then when Max died…"

"Who's Max?"

Joe had never told his family about Max Owen. He'd let them believe that when their lost boy had found his way out of the forest after three days, it had been the wolves who'd led him home. As they had. But only by Max's direction. It was strange enough to see one's son being led home by wolves, but to know he'd spent days with a stranger alone in the forest? At the time, Joe had had the sense not to upset his parents even more. As well, he'd wanted to keep Max a secret because he had wanted him to have his freedom, and not be bothered by local reporters or even the police.

Max hadn't harmed him in any way. He'd only opened Joe's heart and mind to the world.

"Guy I used to know," Joe said. "He was poisoned a few weeks ago. Coroner ruled it accidental, but I think it's related to the poaching, and was purposeful. Been finding the same poison running through this whole investigation."

"Why would someone poison an old man?"

"Exactly."

"He had to have known something. You got help with this, Joseph?"

"Brent Kofax, with the sheriff's department, is my backup."

"He's a good cop. Well, give me a holler if you want me to drive up there. I'm only a half hour away."

"I will. But I wouldn't want to take you away from all that important bullshit."

Jason laughed.

"I'm good for now," Joe said. "But who's the brother who's doing actual police work now, eh?"

"I think that's Justin," Jason deadpanned.

Joe sighed. He knew it was a joke, but it still hurt that his brother could not accept that he was doing real police work.

"How's he doing with the private investigation work?" Joe asked. "I haven't talked to him for weeks."

"Ah, you know. He's adjusting. That brain injury did a number on him. He looks and acts normal, but I think some things give him trouble."

Joe knew Justin took medication, which any man who had been shot through the brain would. "He wants to be back in a patrol car."

"He wants that position with the FBI that he missed out on because of the damned bullet."

"Yeah, he's had a tough year. I'll make a point of visiting him soon."

"This weekend! See you at Mom and Dad's this Saturday?" Jason said. "Dad's birthday, remember?"

He had forgotten. That was four days away. "I'll try to be there."

"You have to be there, bro. Operation Get Mom off the Ground and Across the Ocean begins that night."

"If I can get away, I'll be there. And maybe with a date."

Jason whistled. "It's Skylar, isn't it? I know you've had a thing for her for a long time. Good for you, bro. She's a smart one."

"She is. Thanks again, Jason. If I see you this weekend, I see you. I can't make any promises."

"I understand. You've got an important case."

"Do you really understand?"

"I do. I know I razz you a lot. And I'm sorry. But you are the twerp of the family. Just comes with the territory. Talk to you later."

His brother hung up, and Joe picked up the notes he'd scribbled while talking: "Truckers transporting black market eagle parts across the US."

Most likely using the Indian reservations as contact points.

"Malcolm Davis is picking up customers at powwows," Joe muttered. "Has to be."

Now he remembered the freezers Skylar had mentioned seeing in the warehouse. Surely a trucking outfit stored product and had surplus. And yet, it wouldn't make good financial sense to store things. They transported goods from one location to the other. If they had something stored in those freezers, it had to be something that required being kept on ice.

Joe clicked the mouse and searched the database for shipping records connected to local businesses and the Duluth port. He needed to track all the pickups made by Davis Trucking.

And then determine how close they were to the local Indian reservations.

Chapter Twenty-One

Skylar set the chicken feed in the back of her truck. The farm-supply store carried everything from feed to tires to even some clothing and candy.

At the sound of a car horn, she turned. Joe Cash waved at her from his truck. Instantly her body warmed with a hot, liquid sensation from having lain next to him all night. That man knew how to kiss. And use his mouth on all the right places on her body. She waved and stepped around the side of the truck to lean against the back of it as he pulled into the empty parking lot and got out.

He hooked his hands in his front pockets and tilted his head. "Miss me?"

Skylar started to laugh, but then decided it wasn't funny. Hell, yes, she'd missed him standing close to her, close enough to smell his wild woods scent and to feel her skin tingle at memory of their lovemaking.

"Am I supposed to?" she asked with as much indifference as she could muster.

"Is that how it's going to work?" Joe rubbed his jaw and cast a glance down the main street. The Dairy Queen sported a queue of teenagers outside the walk-up window.

"No, it's not. I'd hug you, but…" Now Skylar glanced around.

"You don't want anyone to see? Wow." Joe dropped his

shoulders and whistled lowly. "You ashamed of being seen with me, Skylar?"

"No. I just—I don't know what's going on between us. I'd love to grab you right now and pull you in for a kiss, but is that real? I mean, was last night just a hookup?"

"I already told you how I feel about it." The man had a sweet way of looking down, which almost made him look shy. "Ball's in your court now."

Was she sure of what she'd thought it had been? It had been more than a night of sex. Right? Was it too soon to get involved with another man? Ending it with Cole had put her through the emotional wringer. And now with everything else…

"I'm sorry," Joe offered. "This thing between us is probably weird. There's an active investigation going on, and you're involved. I don't want to blur any lines between investigating officer and victim."

"I don't like being called a victim."

"You're not. You were a target. And so was Stella. But I like you, Skylar. Always have. Always will. And I'm not a one-night-stand kind of guy. But I don't want to freak you out, either. You might very well have thought it was just a one-time thing."

"I didn't, but I'm not sure…"

"You don't have to make any major life decisions right now. I'm ready whenever you are."

She nodded. "So you'll let me take a step back and figure out what I want and what I need?"

"I'm good with that."

"No, you're not." His body language screamed for her to embrace him. And hers was screaming much the same, though she held her arms over her chest to stop from flinging herself into those muscled arms.

He shrugged. "Have to be. I don't want to hurt you,

Skylar. Not like—" The man blew out a heavy breath and ran his fingers through that thick dark hair she could still feel brushing her skin.

"What is it?" She stepped up to him and studied his elusive gaze. When he finally did meet her eyes, his wince did not bode well. "Joe?"

"Ah, it's Cole Pruitt."

"We're not together anymore. I promise you that. I don't know how much more of a message I can send than a burned wedding dress."

"It's not that. I know the two of you are through. That comes across loud and clear to me. It's just, the interrogation this morning."

"Did you get what you needed from him? He wasn't the one who shot at me, was he?"

"I don't think so. Though I do suspect he's doing something underhanded for Malcolm. But he's not talking. And he insists he won't talk to anyone but you. Which is ridiculous. You're not the one investigating this case. And as far as I'm concerned, I intend to keep that man as far away from you—"

She gripped his shirt. "I'll talk to him."

"What? No, Skylar. He's doing this to manipulate. I can't let him have the upper hand."

"He's a stubborn asshole."

"He was never like that when I was friends with him. I think the drinking has changed him."

"I think so, too. I don't want to see him again, but if he'll tell me what's going on, I can do that for you."

"I don't want you to have to do anything for me, Skylar."

"Then how are you going to make him talk? Don't you want to solve this case? Protect me? What about Max Owen? Don't you want answers about him?"

"Max is first and foremost in my mind. But he's gone. There's nothing I can do to bring him back."

"Who was he to you, Joe? He must have been very special…"

He bowed his head and winced.

"If you don't want to tell me, I won't push."

Joe flipped his hair from his brow with a brush of his hand. The way the sunlight caught in his eyes shouldn't be so deliciously tantalizing.

When he turned back to her, he bowed his head and spoke quietly, as if imparting a secret. "Remember when I told you about getting lost in the woods for three days?"

"Of course. I even looked it up online. You were led out by wolves. That was amazing."

"Yeah, but there's a part I never told anyone about. I didn't want him to get in trouble."

"Him?"

"Max Owen camped in the woods every summer. He's the one who found me wandering, lost and hungry. He fed me and cared for me those three days. Taught me things."

Skylar narrowed her gaze on Joe. This didn't sound good.

"It's not like that," he quickly added. "He didn't do anything to me. He was a kind old Native American man who answered all the questions an eager ten-year-old boy had about how the wolves can understand one another when they howl. And why the moss only grows on one side of the trees. And how to make my own tepee. I wasn't scared, and I honestly didn't want to go home. In those few days Max taught me a lot. But he was the one who said I needed to go home. That my parents would be worried."

"I recall they organized a search party."

"Yes, but they didn't get far. Max sent me home with the wolves."

Skylar didn't know what to say to that. It was beautiful. And that experience must have been what set Joe on his path to work as a conservation officer.

"Max had an affinity for a pack that lived close to him. It was the same pack that had tracked me as I'd wandered deeper into the woods and gotten lost. I was never once scared or worried they might attack me. Weird, huh? If I'd known better at the time, I would have been freaked."

"Wolves do track humans, and if they are frail or the wolves are hungry…" Skylar hadn't heard of any humans being attacked by wolves lately, though on occasion, some stupid hiker who tried to approach the wild animal could get bitten. And a frightened, ten-year-old child alone in the woods could look like an easy meal to a pack.

"Max said they were keeping an eye on me. Protecting me. And they did lead me home. I started researching wolves and wildlife the moment I got home. Well, after Mom made me shower and made me my favorite macaroni and cheese. Guess I've been a nature boy ever since."

"And Max?" Skylar prompted. "You hadn't seen him since you were ten?"

"No, I uh…visited a lot after that. I'd tell my parents I was going on a scouting trip or staying with a friend, and then make my way to where Max stayed. It was about half a day's hike from the entrance to the Boundary Waters Canoe Wilderness. And two miles from where they found Max lying roadside, dying. He was poisoned, Skylar." He looked across the street, the sun again glinting in his eyes.

Skylar swallowed and nudged her shoulder against his. "I'm so sorry, Joe. I had no idea what the old man meant to you. Thank you for telling me that."

"I've never told anyone about Max. Didn't want him to get arrested or to lead the media closer to him. He didn't own the plot where he camped, but I'd be damned if I was going to turn him in for squatting."

"No, you protected him. Just as you're protecting me now. And I appreciate that, Joe, but you need to step back and allow me to help you. For Max."

She crossed her arms and waited for the man to accept her offer. Cole was personable and a charmer, and, yes, she'd fallen for him because of those attributes. But she'd quickly learned just how deep his stubborn streak ran. If the man wanted something—like to talk to her—then he could hold out for days, weeks even, until he got his way.

"Is there some kind of room where you can observe while I talk to the guy?" she asked. "Like on TV?"

"The interrogation room. Yes. But Skylar…"

"You know there's no other way. Cole will keep his mouth shut if he thinks that'll piss you off. And I'll be across the table from him, right? He won't be able to touch me?"

"He'd be in cuffs and chained to the table or floor. I still haven't agreed to allow you to do this."

"I'm offering my services as a citizen, Joe. It would be a pity if you didn't take advantage of my kindness, and if I had to go over your head to whoever is your superior…"

"You wouldn't do that."

"I can and I will. I want the poaching to stop as much as you do. And if I can help, I will."

Joe heaved out a breath. He rubbed his pinky finger along the side of her hand and hooked it with hers. Finally she slid her hand into his and squeezed, and she let him pull her into a hug. Right there, standing in the empty parking lot, which was clearly visible to all who drove by on Main Street. She didn't care because, right now, the only place she wanted to be was in Joe's arms.

"I'm charging him with drunk driving and reckless endangerment. But I'm sure, much as he denies it, he went after you with purpose."

"I hate to consider it, but you may be right."

He hugged her tighter. "I don't want him breathing the same air as you, but if this is what it takes…"

"I'll be fine as long as I know you're close."

"I'll be on the other side of the door. Promise."

"Okay." She tilted up on her toes and kissed him. But only a quick kiss. Much as her body had already decided it was all in for Joe Cash, her heart was still leery. And feeding the gossip mill was not what she needed right now. "Let's go there now."

"I have to coordinate with a fellow officer from the sheriff's department and verify some military records. Might take some time. How about you cruise over to the DQ and get yourself a treat, then I'll see you at the station in an hour?"

"I can do that."

She started to pull away, but Joe's clasp on her hand held firm. He lifted her hand and kissed it. "I wish it could have been different," he said. "I wish you'd never gotten involved with Cole."

Some days she wished for the same. "A person makes choices, whether good, bad or ugly, and learns from those choices. That's the way the world works, Joe. I don't dwell on mistakes, because some are meant for teaching."

He heaved out a sigh, and she disengaged from their clasped hands. "Think about it. You'll understand. I'll see you in a bit."

He watched her pull out of the parking lot and over to the main road. Yeah, she'd made a mistake with Cole. But she had learned a lesson. Follow her head and let her stupid heart take a pass. And now she was moving forward.

Next step? Figuring out what sort of pace she could manage.

Chapter Twenty-Two

Allowing Skylar to sit in the interrogation room alone with Cole Pruitt was trying every ounce of Joe's restraint. He'd cuffed Pruitt behind the back and through the chair so he couldn't move forward to try to touch Skylar. But he'd caught Cole's wink toward the two-way glass as he'd watched Skylar take a seat across the table from him.

The man was purposely trying to piss him off. And while he thought he could manipulate him by talking to Skylar, Joe was not going to take the bait. He could remain calm and listen without anger while the two talked.

Skylar took off her cowboy hat and set it on the table while Cole smirked at her. She glanced over her shoulder to the glass, which would not reveal Joe's position to them. Still, she gave him a small smile.

He wanted to rush in there and pull her out. To not allow Cole one more moment breathing the same air as her. He didn't deserve that time alone with her.

Joe turned to the clerk sitting before the recording console. "You recording?"

"Yes, sir."

He'd told Skylar to try to stick to the points: who Cole was working for and what, exactly, he was involved in. He'd warned her Cole would try to talk about anything other than those topics. He hadn't brought up his suspicions about the sniper. He could ask about that himself. She could handle this. He knew that she could.

"Long time no see," Cole drawled.

"Not exactly," Skylar said. She tucked her fingers under each thigh and sat straight on the chair, her back to Joe. "You waved to me in the Supply Mart parking lot last month as I was driving out."

"And you didn't wave back."

"I'm not here to reminisce, or to seek some sort of coming to terms between the two of us. We're over, and you know that. Joe needs answers from you, and apparently you're only willing to give those answers to me. So talk."

"You've become harsh, Skylar. You weren't like this when we started dating."

"Our dating history has no relevance to this conversation."

She was doing well, but still Joe winced. It could only get worse for her. And his heart.

"You lied to Joe," Skylar said. "You told him it was you who left me at the altar."

Cole shrugged. "You left me. I left you. Doesn't matter, does it? As you've said, it's over. For both of us."

"That it is. I could never remain in the life of someone involved in poaching. And what's this about the DUI? You never drank so much. It's beneath you, Cole. You're a better man than that."

Cole tilted his head and eyed the glass, as if he could see through to Joe. "Is Joe your better man?"

"I don't understand," Skylar said.

"I always wondered if it was him you wanted instead of me. Whenever his name would come up in conversation you'd get a big smile on your face. Guess I know the answer to that now. You've hooked up with him mighty fast."

"It's none of your business who I decide to have in my life."

Cole leaned forward. "Have you had sex with him?"

Joe gripped his fists tight. The clerk at his side shifted on his chair. He didn't want anyone else to hear this. Cole had become mean. It had to be the booze. Had working for Davis pushed him to drink?

"My sex life is also none of your business," Skylar said. She lifted her head. "Answers are what I came for. Who are you working for, Cole? It's Malcolm, isn't it?"

"You have," he said, ignoring her questions. "I can smell him on you."

Joe paced toward the door but stopped himself from gripping the handle. Just give her a moment, he told himself. She was so close.

"Tell me you loved me," Cole suddenly said.

Skylar leaned back in her chair.

"You did, didn't you?" Cole challenged.

She lifted her chin, unwilling to give him an answer.

"You don't give me answers, I don't give you answers."

"What do you want to hear?" she asked.

"The truth. You give me your truth, I'll give you mine." Again Cole cast a glance toward the glass, seeming to pinpoint Joe with precision.

"The truth?" Skylar blew out a breath.

Joe watched her shoulders slump. He didn't want to hear this. He should rush in there now and put a stop to this.

"I'm not even sure I know what love is, Cole. I thought I loved you. Maybe I did. More likely, it was some kind of lust. I was trying to fill a need, but it wasn't a real, honest need. Do *you* know what love is?"

The man straightened at the abrupt spin on the question. "Well, I don't know. I know you were the prettiest girl I'd ever met, and I was ready to make a life with you."

"Sure, but I heard no mention of love in that statement."

He sighed and bowed his head.

Joe's attention grew fierce.

"Fine," Cole said. "As long as Cash can promise me

there won't be any charges other than the DUI, I'll give him names."

Joe tapped the intercom and said, "As soon as bail is posted, you'll be released for the DUI until a summons is set, then the judge will likely revoke your license for a year. You'll be driving with whiskey plates for a year after that. No other charges. Promise."

Cole sneered. "Whiskey plates. Remember how we used to joke about those poor fellas who had to drive around with those flags on the tail end of their trucks, Joe?"

"It's a hell of a lot better than attempted murder," Skylar said bluntly.

"I didn't want to hurt you, Skylar. I was drunk. Angry. I…"

"Did you poison Stella?"

Cole looked up. "What? No. I would never. I loved that wolf. I mean, I tolerated her. But I would never harm an animal—" Cole tilted back his head and then surrendered. "Fine. I should have never gotten involved with that slimy bastard in the first place. You promise me some protection, Joe?"

Joe pressed the intercom. "If it's warranted, yes."

Cole nodded. "So I've been poaching for Malcolm. The old man's got me for a loan on my boat and I need to pay him off. But I won't be driving any trucks for him again."

Joe tapped the intercom once more. "Why would you be driving trucks?"

Cole squeezed his eyelids shut for a few moments. "They're running parts throughout the states and I believe they have a few routes going to the southern border of the United States. I almost got stopped at the Canadian border last week. I hate that subterfuge crap. I just want to fish and—hell, have a normal life."

Joe leaned forward and pressed the intercom again. "What parts?"

"Ah, hell. Bear organs. Deer antlers. Eagle talons, feathers and beaks. Davis goes to the powwows and finds buyers. He just lost a tribe in the area and was pissed about it. Some old man talked the tribe into waiting for the confiscated evidence the sheriff releases. That's all I know."

Joe tapped the button again. "Thanks, Cole. I'm going to come in and verify those statements, and we'll let Skylar take a break, okay?"

The man nodded, then bowed his head until his forehead rested on the table.

SKYLAR DECIDED NOT to wait for Joe to come out of the station. He could be a while longer with Cole. And much as she wanted to walk back into his arms and resume their hug, she suspected Joe might be a little twitchy about her after talking to Cole. She'd give him some space this afternoon. But she did plan on inviting him over for supper, so she drove to the grocery store.

Gathering lettuce, walnuts, dried cranberries and an interesting raspberry vinaigrette, she then picked up a bottle of wine.

"Wining and dining," she muttered as she walked out to the truck and put the grocery bags in the passenger side.

She stepped back and felt arms go around her waist. A hand clamped across her mouth. Kicking and struggling, Skylar was able to see only that no one was nearby in the parking lot to witness what was happening to her. Whoever had her carried her around the side of the grocery store and stuffed a cloth in her mouth before she could utter a scream. Her hands were wrenched behind her back and cuffed.

Lifted none too gently, she was tossed into the back of a black SUV that did not have license plates. Rolling onto her side, she only saw the torsos of a large man and another wearing an AC/DC T-shirt before the back hatch was shut. The windows were blackened, so she couldn't make out their faces.

The front and passenger doors slammed shut, and the vehicle took off. No one spoke. Skylar cursed her decision not to wait for Joe by the police station.

Chapter Twenty-Three

Cole signed the statement verifying his confession. He'd spend another few days in county jail, unless his bail was met. If the investigation was still active at that time, Joe would assess the man's need for police protection. And then the county judge would hear Cole's plea in a few weeks. Joe had given him the contact info for the local AA meetings. He hoped the man had the courage to go to one. But if he didn't get out from under Malcolm Davis's thumb, that would never happen.

With Cole's statement that Reginald Marshall was a sharpshooter, and owned some black market rifles, Joe could now get a warrant to search the man's property. Cole didn't know about his military history, but he said Reggie, as they called him, was Malcolm's right-hand man. Unfortunately, the judge was taking his time, said he needed to do some research. At the very least, Joe had a few hours to waste before he might hold the warrant in hand. He was suspicious of the judge's delay. The man was generally punctual. He certainly hoped he wasn't one of the men Malcolm had in his pocket.

He'd missed Skylar after the interrogation, so he planned to drive out to her place to thank her and to see how she was holding up. Cole had been malicious, but she had held her own. That didn't mean she hadn't been hurt by the experience, however.

First he stopped at home for a quick bite to eat. Joe locked the truck and wandered up the short sidewalk to his front stoop. There on the top step lay something under a sheet of newspaper. Joe's hackles immediately went up. He cast a glance around the yard, across the street and over the neighborhood. He took in all the house fronts, the shrubs, searching for anyone watching from behind a curtain or tree cover. The sun was setting, shadowing the opposite side of the street before the houses. But he didn't feel as though he was being watched.

Cautiously, Joe knelt and nudged aside the paper with the toe of his shoe. The bottom portion of an eagle body was revealed, talons curled under. Joe sucked in his breath. He immediately pulled out a pair of latex gloves from inside his jacket and tugged them on.

Carefully removing the paper, he then folded it and tucked it under the eagle's body. He didn't want to discard any evidence. The bird's wings were tucked in, as well as its head. It may have once been frozen, for it was still rigid; the head didn't joggle when he touched it. Yet it didn't feel cold. He didn't want to touch it too much, so he walked back to the truck to grab an evidence bag.

Again his eyes took in the neighborhood. Sunlight beamed low on his house, giving the lower portion that golden-hour glow. Someone may have seen who had been on his property. On the other hand, he hadn't been home since this morning. This could have been here all day.

Though he'd expect some insect activity if that was the case.

As he walked back to the step, he glanced toward the corner of the house and just under the soffit. The small green LED confirmed his security camera was still on. He'd know soon enough who had been on his property.

After bagging the eagle, he called the forensic lab van. They weren't anywhere near town, but would drive through in the morning. He'd have to wait until then to turn over the evidence.

Carrying it inside, he thought about placing it in the freezer, but if any poison was on it, that could contaminate the entire kitchen. Instead he set it out in an empty box in the garage. Then he peeled off the gloves and placed them in the box, as well. His next step was to shed his clothing and place that in a separate garbage bag. Forensics might want to test them, and he certainly didn't want them anywhere near his home.

Wondering who had decided he needed to be threatened, Joe stalked down the hallway to the bathroom to take a long shower.

JOE KNOCKED ON Skylar's door and waited. Within ten seconds of the knock, he sensed the curious wolf peeking around the corner of the cabin.

"Hey, Stella!"

The wolf wandered toward him, head down and eyes up. She held her tail low, as if she was afraid or perhaps cautious.

"What's up, sweetie?" Joe squatted, putting himself at her height. He held out his hand, which she sniffed, then nudged once with her muzzle. Stella then loped down the steps to the ground and waited for him. Still no tail wag.

"You want to play fetch or something? I need to see your person first. Make sure everything is cool with her." He glanced over his shoulder. "Is she home? It's been a couple hours since I spoke to her in town."

Stella yipped and walked toward the corner of the house. *Follow me.*

Joe stepped down and followed the wolf's slow steps. Perhaps Skylar was out back doing something and hadn't heard the doorbell. He rounded the side of the house to the backyard. A quick scan showed no sign of the sexy blonde with the slender curves and ever-present cowboy hat. Becky raced out of sight, but Joe just caught a flash of her new red sweater. Beyoncé was nowhere to be seen, thank goodness. He wondered if his vehicle insurance covered dents inflicted by a dancing goat.

His cell phone jangled in his front pocket, but Joe ignored it as he searched the glimmering lake beyond the tree line. The sun had almost set, yet dashed a tinsel of light across the water.

Stella yipped. Right at his side.

"What is it, Stella?"

The phone was still ringing so Joe answered it. "Officer Cash."

"Joe, just listen and let me talk."

It was Skylar and she sounded…not right. Opening his mouth to respond, he instead nodded, and then remembered she couldn't see him. "Go ahead."

"I'm okay," she said.

Those two abrupt words put up the hairs on the back of his neck. No one started a conversation with "I'm okay" unless they were not, or darn close to not.

"I'm with…people."

He heard a shuffle and Skylar's gasp. Had she been shoved?

"The Davises," she amended.

"What? Skylar—"

"No time for conversation, Joe. They picked me up outside the grocery store. They know Cole told you everything, and they're going to let me go free—"

"Go free?" Hell, Malcolm Davis had kidnapped Skylar? Joe gripped the gun handle in its holster.

"You have to drop all charges against Cole Pruitt and

drop the investigation," Skylar continued. "Please, Joe. I've never asked you for anything. I need this."

"Where are they holding you?"

"Not sure."

"At Davis Trucking?"

"Don't think so. It's dark in here."

"How are you talking—? Oh, they've got you on speaker. You bastards. You think leaving a poisoned eagle on my doorstep is going to scare me off, Davis?"

"Joe, please, they're going to hang up. As soon as the investigation is dropped and they know you won't bother them again—ever—they'll let me go."

"How the hell will I prove that?"

"I've been told to tell you they will know if you stop investigating."

Right. Because Joe's suspicion about Malcolm having the judge in his pocket was true. Could be the reason he was currently waiting for the warrant.

"Will you do me a favor?" Skylar made a painful noise.

Joe winced. They were hurting her.

"Check on Stella!" she quickly cried. "Talk to her!"

The phone clicked off. Joe punched the air with his phone, then kicked the ground with his heel. He swore. Once, then again. The blood rushed to his face and arms. Fists curled. He had to find Skylar. And he would not drop the investigation. He'd spent far too much time investigating the poaching, and with the poisoned eagle left on his doorstep he now had a link to Max Owen's death. Malcolm Davis knew his number was up.

So he'd kidnapped an innocent woman—his own niece—to hold up as his shield. The coward.

Joe swore again. He had to take a moment to think this through, plan his next move. He couldn't rush in, guns blazing, because Skylar didn't know where she was being held. It made sense that it was on Davis Trucking property.

Stalking back to his truck, he called up Dispatch.

They answered immediately. "I've got a situation at Davis Trucking," Joe said. "At least, it's a suspicion."

"Aren't you waiting on a warrant for that place?"

"I am. But I have reason to believe Skylar Davis is being held against her will there right now. I'm headed there."

When he turned, Stella sat waiting for him. She tilted her head, one ear cocked. Her whimper indicated she felt for him.

What had Skylar meant about *talking to Stella*? At a moment when she could be in danger and possibly be harmed, she had wanted him to talk to her wolf?

"I'll send out Brent Kofax," Dispatch said. "He's finishing up a domestic call right now. Shouldn't be too long."

"Thanks. I'm on my way there." He hung up and then ruffled Stella's fur behind her ears. "She loves you," he said to the wolf.

Stella scampered across the backyard toward the edge of the forest. She stopped and looked back at Joe. Never had an animal's expression spoken more loudly than it did in Stella's quiet gold eyes.

"You do want to tell me something, don't you?" he said.

The wolf was smart as hell. And Skylar's best friend. If Skylar wanted him to talk to Stella, then he would.

THE BLINDFOLD SMELLED like oil. And Skylar couldn't get a handle on where she was being held. They had traveled about half an hour after she'd been taken and thrown into the back of the SUV. She knew there were two men, and both had guns. Malcolm wasn't around. Or was he? He could be standing by, watching. In fact, she had the creepy feeling the men were being directed.

Was she at Davis Trucking? No way to know for sure, and she hadn't wanted to send Joe on a wrong path if it were not.

"I know you're here, Malcolm," she said. And to challenge him, she added, "And I know you had Max Owen killed."

A chair scraped on the cement floor. Someone gripped Skylar's hair and pulled back her head. The blindfold was roughly tugged away. Whoever held her from behind pushed her head forward.

Skylar gasped when she saw who stood before her.

Chapter Twenty-Four

The wolf tracked steadily through the woods from Skylar's place. Joe kept up with Stella, even when she veered from a path and wandered into brush and low seedlings and mossy ground. It was Stella's show, and he was thankful she seemed intent and focused on getting somewhere.

Where was she headed? Joe hoped she was leading him to Skylar, but they could be headed anywhere. The pack's abandoned rendezvous spot sat parallel to where they now passed. He could smell the lake and the cloying scents of animal.

He pulled out his cell phone. No service. With luck, Kofax's domestic call wouldn't keep him long, and he'd be on his way to Davis Trucking. Joe wore a pistol in his hip holster, and always carried a bowie knife that was useful for hacking through saplings and whittling off kindling from larger branches. It could be used for defense in a pinch. But he had no flashlight on him, and should have grabbed one out of his truck before leaving on this expedition.

Didn't matter. He felt more confident in the dark woods than a man might walking down a sunlit street in a dangerous part of Duluth. But he did need to be cautious for traps. Unfortunately, if they happened upon one, Stella would be the first to step into it, and that wolf could not spare another leg.

The *po-po-po* whistle of a boreal owl made Stella pause. Joe stopped roughly twenty feet behind the wolf's tread. Stella whined lowly and sniffed the ground. She cautiously stepped on the loamy earth, covered with rotting leaves and branches, and then leaped back and walked a half circle, drawing her once-straight path into an arc.

She looked to Joe, waiting for him to do the same. He did. And when he passed the brush where the wolf had spooked, he smelled the spoiled bait that sat on a steel trap.

"Thanks, Stella," he said quietly. "I imagine you've got a sixth sense about traps now, eh?" It was on Skylar's property. Damn Malcolm Davis. "Are you taking me to Skylar?"

The wolf turned and wandered forward, nose to the ground and tail bobbing side to side. Not talkative, but then it wasn't necessary.

After they'd tracked for what Joe estimated to be about two miles, they reached a clearing where the tree canopy opened to frame the waxing moon. As Stella kept walking, Joe cast his gaze upward and studied the stars. The Big Dipper was in view, and Arcturus beamed brightly. They were moving northwest of the property. If he recalled correctly the map he'd looked over, that meant they were either currently on DNR-owned property, passing over that small thumb of it, or already on someone else's land.

"Malcolm's land," he muttered.

He hadn't noticed any trespassing signs, and for sure that family would post. Then again, he wasn't on a trail.

Branches snapped, and he steadied his footsteps to land more lightly on the ground. He didn't want to alert anyone out patrolling or trip any security systems. There could be motion sensors. Hell, there could be booby traps, for all he knew. The family that poached would not risk intruders getting too close to their property.

Of course, they would not be prepared for a wolf's wily approach, or the man who could move like a wolf.

The scent of burning peat filtered into Joe's senses. A bonfire close by? He didn't see the flames, though the woods had thickened and Stella's steps had slowed. When he got closer to her, he crouched. The wolf turned to nudge his face with her head. A sign of affection, perhaps even trust.

"Is this where you wanted to lead me, sweetie?"

She pawed at the brush, and Joe realized it was matted up against a fence post. Higher up, strung around the post, a single wire was wrapped. Electrified, if his guess was correct. He tugged out the knife from his pocket. It had a wood handle, so if the fence was turned on, the handle would prevent the charge from shocking his hand. Rubbing quickly over the wire, Joe felt the tingle of current.

"Thanks for the warning, Stella. Let's take it easy from here on."

Because now they were encroaching on private property. Joe tugged out his phone again. One bar. He could make a call. He needed that warrant if this was a false lead and Skylar was being kept elsewhere.

When the sound of a rifle shot echoed through the night, he held the glowing phone close to his chest and ducked down next to the wolf, who stood rigid, and growled low and deep in her chest.

SKYLAR SAT STIFFLY on the chair. Her wrists burned from the rough rope they'd used to tie her, but the rope at her left ankle was loosening. She shifted her boot heel back and forth, firmly tugging while keeping an eye on the guy with the semiautomatic who stood guard beside her. The same redhead who had threatened her days earlier.

But he gave her much less worry than the other person

who stood before her—a woman she hadn't seen in seventeen years.

Her mother looked the same, save the weary lines under her eyes and around her mouth. Her blond hair was styled in a flipped bob, and the bright pink lipstick was still the same shade Skylar remembered.

Her heart raced. Every part of her wanted to scream and then cry and then shout her anger.

"I had to leave," her mother said dismissively. "I wasn't happy with my life, but that was my problem. Not yours. I wanted to contact you. But I thought it wiser to stay away. Let you and your dad have your peace. I've been catching up with old friends this past week."

Old friends? Meaning Skylar's uncle? Dorothy's brother-in-law?

Dorothy leaned forward and pouted her pink lips. "You should let Malcolm help you with the shelter."

"Help me? I'm tied up, Dorothy." It felt strange to say that name after so long. But she couldn't summon the word "mom." It felt dirty in her throat.

"The ties are just a precaution. And since when did you stop calling me Mom?"

"When you abandoned me and Dad."

"That was long ago, Skylar. We're both grown and wiser now. So just shush, and play along, okay? Malcolm needs to get the game warden off his back. He's not like the others."

"The others?" It was no secret her uncle had a cop or two in his pocket. Was he trying to recruit Joe to do his dirty work?

"No one will get hurt."

"Someone has been murdered, Dorothy."

Malcolm walked over to join them, hands in his pockets and cowboy boots clicking the concrete floor. "What's that about murder? You telling your mother lies, Skylar?"

When the rifle sounded outside the shed, all the men inside volleyed looks at one another. Skylar's guard moved closer to her and lifted his gun into position.

"What's up?" Malcolm asked the guard named Reggie. "You got the guard dog out there?"

"He croaked last week. I sent Steven out on post. Must have heard something or got spooked."

"Maybe it's Cash," Malcolm said.

"He's not stupid enough to come looking for me in the dark with a warehouse full of armed men waiting for him," Skylar said.

Malcolm rounded a look on her. "He isn't? Or is he? I figured you'd be the invite he required. Unless he's suddenly fallen ill."

Reggie smirked. "I hear that cop is a nature boy. Really likes his animals. He'd be real sad to see a dead eagle on his doorstep. Might hold it a bit too long."

"What's this about an eagle on Cash's doorstep?" Cole Pruitt crossed the warehouse, hands in his pockets. He didn't even glance at Skylar.

She hadn't realized he was in the building. How was he out of jail? Joe had said he'd be in— There were too many emotions wrenching at her heart right now; she couldn't think straight.

"None of your damn business, Cole," Malcolm said. "Go out and check on Steven."

"I'm not leaving this warehouse." Cole crossed his arms stubbornly, high over his chest.

"You are the only one available. And I did post your bail. Now go take a look!"

Skylar had never seen Cole so submissive. Head hanging, he turned and stalked toward the double barn doors at the end of the warehouse. That left her, Reggie and one other man, who also wielded a rifle, by the door. And her mother. Dorothy. Back from a seventeen-year absence, acting as if it had been a day. Telling Skylar to play along?

Had Dorothy ever loved her father? In those weeks before her mother had left them, Skylar had overheard her parents arguing. Malcolm's name had come up a lot. Her twelve-year-old self hadn't put two and two together. But years later, Skylar had wondered if her mother had a thing for the other brother. So why not simply divorce the one and take up with the other? Why abandon her family?

And now here she stood, siding with the one man who had tried his best over the years to make his brother's life hell. And had he done so by being the one who had prompted his wife to leave him?

Skylar expected nothing more from Malcolm. Or Dorothy.

By using her to call Joe and request he drop the investigation, Malcolm had known what he was doing. How he knew she and Joe had a relationship was beyond her.

They never should have kissed in that parking lot. Someone must have seen them.

On the other hand, Cole could have told him things. He'd picked up on her feelings for Joe when she'd spoken to him in the interrogation room. She should have never agreed to talk to him.

And why she was muddling over this stuff right now, when she needed to remain alert, was beyond her. She'd heard the howls earlier. Pack howls. Miles off, but in the direction of her land. They'd been disturbed, had seen something.

She just hoped the pack hadn't decided to stop that something.

Chapter Twenty-Five

Joe sat crouched in the brush, sure he was hidden from the dark figure who stalked along the birch tree line that paralleled a massive Quonset shed. This must be the back end of Davis Trucking. The shed was small compared to the vinyl-sided building next to it. That building must house the trucks and perhaps serve as a shop for the scents of oil and gasoline that filled the air.

A flicker of fire showed between the two buildings. Joe couldn't see anyone standing near the bonfire tending it, but it was a good three hundred yards off and the darkness hugged the amber flames.

He rested his hand at the back of Stella's neck, urging her to be silent, but the wolf was smart. She remained alert, her head lifted and sniffing the air.

Suddenly, he felt her entire body tense and she shifted to her feet.

Joe heard someone call out. "What the hell, Steven? You shooting at ghosts?"

It was Cole Pruitt. Stella recognized his scent.

Joe shushed her low growl and stroked down her neck. She kept on her feet and shifted, but didn't vocalize further, thank goodness.

How had Pruitt gotten out of jail? Had someone paid

his bail? Likely Malcolm Davis. Damn it, what had Cole gotten himself into? Had he taken Skylar?

"Thought I should fire off a warning shot," said the other man, who had been pacing alongside the birch trees. "Just in case. You think it was stupid for the old man to have the woman call a cop?"

"Maybe. But Malcolm generally knows what he's doing."

Joe watched the shadowed figures. They stood fifty feet from him and Stella, backs to them. Moonlight capped their heads and gleamed on Cole's nose when he turned to face the other man. "Not like the old man doesn't have half the cops in the county in his pocket. Probably time to bring another one in, don't you think?"

"I think it's stupid." The other guy spit on the ground.

Stella sat, still alert, listening. Joe rested his shoulder against her body. It reassured him of her movements and kept him close enough to grab for her in case she decided to take off, but he did not expect that from this wolf. She was too damn smart.

"We should just kill that woman and get on with things."

"You're talking about my ex-fiancée," Cole said.

"She must be ex for a reason. Don't you want to stick it to the woman who dumped you?"

"I dumped her," Cole said quickly. "And you don't get to talk about the Davis woman that way. She's not to be harmed."

"She'll talk."

"She won't. And that other woman is her mother. She'll make sure Skylar keeps her mouth shut."

"Is that so?"

Joe winced. Skylar's mom was here? But she had left her family long ago. What was going on?

"You check all the borders behind the building?" Cole asked.

"Was going to head around to the other side and take a piss."

"Didn't need to know about that. I'll let the old man know everything is clear."

"Don't worry, I got my eyes peeled. Nothing will get past me and this thirty-aught-six."

"I am completely reassured," Cole said.

Joe knew from his tone that he was anything but. The men parted, Cole heading toward the building and the other veering around the back of it.

Joe could wait for Kofax to arrive, but he had no idea how long that would take. And he couldn't stand knowing that Skylar was inside that building in God-knows-what condition with the asshole Cole Pruitt standing over her.

Pulling out his gun, he allowed Stella to sniff it. She whined lowly, but the sound was so soft he knew the man tromping around the back of the shed would not hear.

"You need to stay here, sweetie."

For as much as he was comfortable with wolves and could communicate his emotions and understand theirs, Joe knew she couldn't comprehend such a request. For her safety, he hoped she would remain hidden. The first thing a poacher would do on sighting a wolf was shoot. They had no conscience and always preferred a dead wolf to a live one that could attack.

Not that he suspected Stella had it in her to attack. She was a softy. And he wanted to keep her that way.

Rising slowing to a crouch, he said, "Stay," even though he figured Skylar hadn't taught her any commands.

The wolf sat and looked up at him, giving him that innocent, wondering gaze that most dogs had mastered and that could bring their owner to their knees for a hug and a tussle.

"I'm going to get your person," Joe said. "You keep watch for me out here. Don't make a noise." He shushed the wolf, then started toward the line of birch trees.

To her credit, Stella remained where she was sitting.

When he reached the edge of the white paper birch trees, Joe pressed his shoulder to one and scanned around the building. The lighting was dim, but there was a spotlight on the left side where he guessed the main doors were. The bonfire was too far off to provide illumination of more than a few feet. The guard had been around the other side for about three minutes. If he were pissing, he'd be done by now. But would he stay on that side? Joe wouldn't.

He had to move now.

Stepping lightly, he raced across the dirt and grass to the side of the building. Once tucked into the shadows, he hugged the corrugated metal wall and slinked toward the corner.

He heard a scuffle at the other end of the building. It was the guard. Joe pressed his back to the ridged wall, feeling the darkness cover him and knowing he was concealed, but essentially standing in the open, without protection.

The guard wandered to the birch trees. He moved his gaze upward. Stars littered the sky, and the moonlight would give him away if Joe moved so much as three inches forward. He waited for the stargazer to lose interest, but he kept his head tilted back for the longest time.

Joe began to inch to the right. The corner of the building was ten feet away. If he could get around to the other side—and into the spotlight—

Hell, was he crazy?

He should wait for backup. But by then it could be too late. What were they doing with Skylar in there? If they'd had her call him and stop the investigation, there was no need to keep her prisoner. He should have told them he'd agree. But would they really have released her? He didn't suspect so. The only way Skylar was walking away from Malcolm's grip alive was with help.

And her mother. Was she a hostage or an accomplice?

The guard suddenly glanced toward the woods. Had Stella alerted him?

If he wondered about the wolf's safety he could lose his own chance for movement, so Joe stepped faster until his shoulder felt nothing. He'd reached the corner.

He sensed the guard turn toward him, so Joe slipped around the side of the building and out of his sight. Taking in the area, he saw no one standing outside. There were three vehicles parked before the shed. That could mean anywhere from three men up to a dozen or more were inside, depending on how many they'd stuffed into each vehicle. Two buildings down, a diesel engine fired up. A truck heading out on a night route? Sure, truck drivers drove all hours of the day, but the timing was suspicious.

Joe needed backup to hurry.

Raising his pistol and gripping it with both hands, he approached the sliding doors, which were open. He didn't hear anyone speaking inside, which could mean they were onto him, waiting for his approach.

"It's a wolf!" he heard the guard call, followed by a gunshot.

Using the moment, Joe slipped inside through the open shed doors, keeping to the shadows. He saw an old man talking to a blonde older woman, who turned at the sound of the guard's voice. And seated on a chair, with her hands tied behind her, was Skylar. Beside her stood a thin man with a semiautomatic, which he lifted and pointed toward the wall that faced the birch trees.

They hadn't noticed him. Yet.

Using their sudden state of alert at the sound of the gunshot, Joe slipped to the left. But his motion turned the guard's head and he shouted, "That you, Steven?"

Joe aimed at the guard, and just before he could pull the trigger, he felt a pistol barrel butt up against his temple.

"We've got a visitor," Cole Pruitt said. "Move over there, Cash. Into the light."

Holding up his hands before him, Joe swore silently. Now that he had the opportunity to take in his surroundings, he saw the crates stacked everywhere. No telling what was in those, but the half-dozen freezers against the wall were enough to make him curse. He'd found the mother lode.

Chapter Twenty-Six

Joe stepped out of the shadows, arms raised. His pistol was in one hand. He could aim and fire in a second, if required. But he wanted to show that he was not here for violence or aggression. He could get this done by talking. And he stood a better chance of securing Skylar's safety—and not getting shot himself—if he played along.

"Davis!" he called.

The old man turned to him. The blonde woman standing beside him gripped his arm. A friend or lover? She had to be Skylar's mom. The man he recognized as Reginald Marshall from his mug shot aimed his rifle at Joe.

"We need to talk," Joe said, remaining in place. He stood thirty feet from where Skylar sat. Her body was tense, her gaze burning into him. He couldn't read her expression beyond that she was frightened. "Why do you have Skylar tied up? Is that any way to treat your own family?"

"How'd you find us, boy?" The old man held out his arm, staying his cohort with the rifle. He looked to Skylar. "You got some kind of GPS on you? Didn't you take her phone after she made the call?"

"I did. And I smashed it like you said," the gunner said. "All the frequency blockers on the property should have blocked any signals."

"It doesn't matter how I found this place," Joe said. "I figure you wanted to talk to me. Here I am. What do you want to say?"

"You got the message. You do as you're told and Skylar goes free."

"And if I don't?"

Malcolm stepped up to stand beside Skylar. "I figure you won't want any harm to come to your lady."

"I just want to take Skylar out of here, safe and unharmed. Will you let me do that?"

"Then what about us?" Davis asked. He cast his glance around. "You going to call in the cavalry?"

Backup should be on the way. But Joe hadn't received confirmation from Dispatch on that; nor did he have service while out in the woods.

"Poaching's not even a felony," Joe offered, trying to appeal to the man's sense of self-preservation. "You'll get a slap on the wrist."

Davis crossed his arms high over his chest and eyed him with that "you can't bullshit me" look. "Poaching is the least of my worries, boy."

Joe nodded. It was hard to dispute that fact. Malcolm had to know that the murder charge he intended to bring against Reginald Marshall was the elephant in the room.

"Now, I know you're an officer, and surrendering your weapon is not something that comes easily to you, but take in the scenario," Davis said. "You're outnumbered. Set down your gun, boy, nice and easy."

To keep Skylar safe, there seemed no other option. Joe nodded and crouched slowly, finally setting his gun on the hay-littered concrete floor. He eyed Skylar. She closed her eyes.

"Kick it over here," Malcolm said.

The last thing he wanted to do was disarm himself, but if Joe could keep them talking until Kofax arrived, he'd be fine. A gentle kick sent the gun across the hay. It stopped three feet away from Davis's boots.

"What the hell?" Cole Pruitt wandered into Joe's peripheral vision. "You fell faster than I expected, Nature Boy."

He'd told Cole how that moniker annoyed him.

"Someone has to look out for Skylar," Joe said, before he could caution himself against making the snide remark.

"And you're doing such a fine job at it," Cole volleyed. "Does it look like you have the upper hand, buddy?"

"I don't want any trouble, Cole. You talk to Mr. Davis and let him know that Skylar has nothing to do with any of this. She needs to walk out of here right now. I'll stay behind. We can talk about this then."

Cole chuckled. "Skylar will come around. Won't you, Sky?" He bent and winked at Skylar, who sneered at him.

"What are we going to do with them?" Reginald Marshall asked. Had he shot at Skylar from across the lake? "Where there's one cop, there's others not far behind."

Cole stepped up to Joe. "Did you call for backup?"

"Didn't have a chance, or cell service," he said. "Found this place by tracking through the forest."

"What?" Cole exchanged glances with Malcolm, then turned an annoyed sneer back on Joe. "I don't believe you. It's a good two-or three-mile trek from Skylar's place. Only one access road here, too, thanks to Skylar hoarding her land and not letting Malcolm pay her a handsome price for a small portion. Someone would have seen you drive up."

"Did you see my car on the road?" Joe asked.

"No." Cole flicked another look over his shoulder to the Davis elder. "We have to get rid of them. Both of them."

The woman stepped up, but Malcolm grabbed her by the wrist. "You said no one would get hurt," she said.

Joe squeezed his fingers into fists. "Murder is not something you want to add to your rap sheet, Cole. What in hell happened to you?"

Cole turned so swiftly Joe barely had time to register the punch aimed at his face. He dodged and took a hit to the shoulder.

A rifle shot echoed loudly in the building and thundered in Joe's ears. He stopped midpunch at Cole, and the first place he looked was the chair where Skylar sat. Tears ran down her cheeks. No one had been shot. Whoever had fired must have done so aiming out the open doorway. But he took the warning and again put up his hands.

This time, he saw the punch coming and had no choice but to let it happen. Cole's fist skimmed his jaw, and Joe twisted at the hip to follow through and take some of the brute power off the contact point. It was a wimpy punch that barely set Joe back a step, but he winced to make it look good.

"Walk away right now," Joe said. "Malcolm's already looking at murder charges. You don't want to be involved with that."

"I do believe you're right," Davis finally said. "This has gotten messy. No thanks to you, Pruitt." He nodded to the gunman. "Reggie, give him your rifle. He'll take care of matters."

"This is my gun," Reggie argued.

"The same gun you used to shoot at Skylar from across the lake?" Joe challenged.

Reggie lifted the gun and aimed it at Joe's head. "Not even close. That one was a real sniper rifle, but this one will serve its purpose—"

"Reggie!" Malcolm admonished. "You've said enough."

Enough for Joe to know he was the guilty party.

"Cole." Malcolm grabbed the gun from Reggie and handed it toward Cole.

"Oh man, I don't want to…" Cole lifted his chin, then

nodded. "Fine. Give me that gun. But you'll have to se-cure Cash's hands behind his back for me if I have to walk them out to the woods."

Davis nodded and his sidekick strode off, probably in search of rope to bind Joe's hands. Which was never going to happen if he wanted to walk out of here alive, and with Skylar at his side.

SKYLAR COULD NOT look Joe in the eyes. She'd glanced at him when Reggie had threatened him with the rifle, but seeing his stoic determination to help her cut into her heart. He was brave and strong, and she wasn't sure what she had done to deserve his kindness. Now he stood at gunpoint while some idiot looked for rope to tie him up—because he planned to kill him. And her.

To top it off, her mother was not arguing strongly for her release. Devastation struggled to reduce Skylar to a sobbing heap, but she had to stay sharp. And hope Joe had a plan.

The old man untied her at the ankles and shoved her shoulder. "Stand up. Cole will take care of you."

"Your brother never said a bad word about you," she said to her uncle. "Even knowing what you were involved in, he was always kind when talking about his family."

"My brother was a fool."

"Did you really murder someone?" Dorothy asked. The tremble in her voice wasn't false, as her proclaimed love for Skylar had been.

Malcolm sucked in his lower lip. "What someone would that be?"

"You know, that old Indian—" Reggie started.

"Reggie! You've got the widest mouth in the county. Now just keep back. My hands are blood-free." Malcolm shoved Skylar, and she stepped toward where Joe stood.

"You should have never trusted a cop, Skylar. He brought you down."

"If standing on the right side of the law is down," she said to Malcolm, "then I'll join Joseph Cash here on the down side."

She stepped up beside Joe. Feeling his warmth against her shoulder granted her a moment of relief, until she saw Cole wander over with a length of rope.

"Get them out of here." Malcolm turned and walked toward the freezers. He must be unwilling to witness the bloodshed, surely. His hands would never be clean.

Skylar felt Joe's hand clasp hers and squeeze. A teardrop slipped down her cheek. It wouldn't end this way, would it?

"I got you," he said in a low tone.

She wanted to believe that, but their immediate futures looked bleak.

"Turn around," Cole ordered Joe.

When Joe turned and slowly moved his hands behind his back, he looked at Skylar—yet his attention was diverted to the shed doors. Joe gaped, then grinned. And then he winked at Skylar.

She didn't know what was up. Suddenly a wolf's growl sounded. Joe used Cole's sudden distraction to lunge forward and shove Skylar to the side, wrapping an arm about her waist and tugging her out of the way.

Stella soared through the shed doorway and leaped, landing on Cole's chest.

Chapter Twenty-Seven

"Stay low and out of sight," Joe said to Skylar. She nodded, then shuffled over to a crate and knelt.

Joe turned just in time to see the butt of a rifle coming toward him. He kicked high, connecting his foot with Reggie's bicep. The hit was hard and direct. The man yelped in pain, dropping his rifle. Joe spun and landed another kick to the man's gut, and then a successive hit to his thigh, bringing him down, wincing and swearing.

Joe tossed the rifle to Skylar, which she caught and cocked. "Keep an eye on him."

Stella had her maw locked on Cole's bicep, but suddenly the wolf yelped and rolled off the man. A high-pitched whine indicated she'd been injured. Joe hadn't heard a gunshot, so that was one thing to be thankful for.

He charged toward Cole. His former best friend saw him coming, tossed his weapon aside and met Joe's approach with a high kick. "You sic your dog on me, Cash?"

"You're lucky to still be alive," Joe said. He ducked an oncoming punch and spun to swing up his leg.

Cole, despite being injured and bleeding on the arm, was still fast. He dodged, and Joe landed one foot on the ground. Out the corner of his eye he saw Reggie groan, but he was still on the floor, under Skylar's watch.

"There are better ways to get the girl." Cole delivered a kick to Joe's shin.

Bouncing on his feet to alleviate the pain of that hit, Joe worked Cole back toward the crates. Malcolm was nowhere in sight, but Skylar's mother clung to the chair where Skylar had been seated, watching them with fearful eyes.

"It's not about who lost the girl," Joe said. "It's about an old man who got in the way of another man's greed."

"That Indian guy? I had nothing to do with that. Reggie is Malcolm's hit man."

"Good to know." Joe kicked toward Cole's hip, but just as the man stepped aside, Joe transferred his weight to his swinging foot, landing on the floor and sweeping up a fist that clocked his former friend up under the jaw.

Cole landed on the ground, defeated.

The barrel of a gun connected with the back of Joe's neck.

"You've got some fancy fighting skills," old man Davis said. "But I've got all the power."

Joe slowly put up his hands. In the darkness, he couldn't place Skylar, but hoped she was still safe and armed. "Tell me what's in those freezers, Malcolm."

"Why? You hungry for some steak, boy? Move!" He walked Joe over to the freezer where Skylar's mom now stood. "Open it up, Dorothy," Malcolm demanded.

She did so. And revealed an empty freezer.

"The others, too."

All six of them were empty. So why did Joe feel the chilly air each time she opened another? No reason to have a freezer on unless it was in use, or had been in use recently. They'd moved the evidence. And that truck he'd seen before coming in had been refrigerated.

"Not hungry? I can make sure all your steak dinners are comped no matter where you eat," Malcolm offered. "All you have to do is keep your mouth shut."

"I'm a vegetarian. You had eagle parts in there, Davis. You thought Max Owen was a threat to your business, so you had him killed."

"The old man was a nuisance to my bottom dollar, but I'm not a killer, boy."

"No, but your hired gun lying on the floor over there is. He's the same one who left a gift for me on my front step, isn't he?"

Stella barked. Joe turned to find Cole's gun was aimed at the wolf.

"Don't you dare," Joe growled.

Cole's chuckle was followed by a spit of blood to the side. He cocked the rifle. Joe knew the wolf's fate was sealed.

But instead of Cole firing, another gun sounded from behind them both. Davis swore and the gun at Joe's head wobbled. Joe reacted, grabbing the old man's rifle.

Stella yelped and scampered out of the shed.

Joe twisted his gaze to find Skylar standing with her aim now on Cole, who bled from the thigh.

"You shot your fiancé!" Dorothy Davis screamed.

"Stay out of this, Dorothy," Malcolm said. "You've served no good to nobody since you suggested this cock-amamie plan to get the cop on our side."

"Just a flesh wound," Joe offered. "And she's not his fiancé." To Skylar he said, "Keep your aim on Cole while I cuff Malcolm, will you?"

Joe ordered Dorothy to step back, then cuffed Malcolm Davis. When he was finished he walked over to Reggie and punched him. He didn't have another set of cuffs on him, so it was the best way to detain him for now.

After picking up Cole's rifle, Joe pulled Skylar into his embrace. Keeping one eye on the fallen men in the building, he took a few moments to hug the woman.

"Stella saved us," Skylar said.

"That she did."

"Cole would have killed her." She turned to Cole. "You bastard!"

"She would have bitten my face," Cole growled. "I didn't want to hurt you, Skylar. I never would have."

"Tell it to the judge."

The sound of an approaching vehicle crunching across the drive was accompanied by the red flash of police lights on the shed interior.

"The cavalry is here," Joe said.

THREE PATROL CARS parked in the trucking lot, their flashers glowing in the night. Skylar stood back near a wall, arms crossed over her chest, and observed as Joe directed the officers to gather up Malcolm and his men. Calls were put in for more officers and a forensic team.

Joe sent a call to dispatch to stop a refrigerated truck on County Road 7. Within ten minutes the call came in that the vehicle had been apprehended. A stunning number of eagle carcasses were inside in cold storage.

As Malcolm was led out past Skylar, he sneered at her, then smiled. "This isn't finished," he said.

The hollowness in her gut rose to her throat. No, she imagined it was not. Would the sheriff's department have the guts to convict the man who had bribed some of their own? She certainly prayed for that. But a conviction could destroy Davis Trucking, bringing it all down like the house of cards it was. Skylar could only be thankful Malcolm didn't have a family who would suffer because of their father's dirty dealings.

On the other hand, she hadn't been aware of her mother's involvement with the man. Dorothy had suggested they kidnap Skylar to get Joe on Malcolm's side? Whatever was going on, Dorothy would get what she deserved.

Stella had hightailed it out of there before the first officer had arrived. Skylar had seen she was limping on her front leg, but she'd been determined to escape a scene where so many humans were around. Likely she was in the woods, not far off, licking her wounds. And hopefully those wounds would easily heal.

Dorothy stopped before her, wrists handcuffed behind her back. "I didn't do anything but love the wrong brother."

Skylar winced. "You didn't deserve Merlin Davis."

Her mom bowed her head. "I'm sorry, Skylar."

She didn't know what to say. Dorothy had been in love with Malcolm? She'd face her with all the questions when the time felt right. Now was not that time.

Rubbing her wrists where the rope had burned, Skylar watched with awe and relief as Joe stood, hands at his hips, observing the operation. He had it under control. Had been willing to sacrifice himself for her release. He'd rescued her.

And maybe she had been waiting for that rescue for a while. Years even. She needed that man in her life. She wanted him around her all the time.

And he was waiting for her to give him the signal.

At that moment, Joe turned, his eyes seeking hers even as officers walked between them, moving things about. A steady calmness lived in his gaze. He had her. Heart and soul.

When he winked, Skylar released the pent-up anxiety and felt a tear pool at the corner of her eye. She flashed a smile his way and nodded. They were good. And she was going home with him tonight.

Epilogue

A week later...

Malcolm Davis was arrested for kidnapping, assault, and poaching endangered species. He posted bail within four hours, but he let Dorothy sit in jail until the next day. She had been charged with collusion to sell animal parts. Apparently, she'd called Skylar after her release, but had left only voice mails.

Skylar had not listened to those messages, erasing them as soon as she'd seen the unknown number on her phone. Her heart wasn't ready for the talk she needed to have with her mother. Was it even necessary? She'd left her life so long ago. Skylar had moved on. She needed time to think and sort out whether reconciling with her mom would improve her life or just make it miserable.

There was the issue that she owned half of Skylar's land, so she would have to speak to her sooner rather than later. Suspicions were that Dorothy would not give up her half once she learned about it. Especially not if she was now seeing Malcolm. It would be his way to nab what he wanted.

Skylar would face that challenge. Somehow.

Cole Pruitt, charged with poaching, had paid a fine of eight thousand dollars and was allowed to enter rehab in a Minneapolis facility. He'd apologized to Joe but not to Skylar. Joe felt that had been backward, but Skylar had insisted he let it drop. She was just thankful the man was seeking help for his alcohol problem. One that had likely occurred because of the stresses of working for Malcolm Davis.

Reginald Marshall had been charged with murder. His fingerprints had been lifted from the newspaper that had covered the eagle left on Joe's front stoop. The same lead-tainted strychnine that had been on that eagle had also been on the one that had ended Max Owen's life. As well, he owned a Lapua rifle, and the ballistics forensic team had been able to match it to the bullets that Joe had collected from Skylar's yard. Currently sitting in jail, he awaited a trial.

Joe stood beside Stella under the shade of the paper birch trees that shivered in the wind. The two of them watched Skylar take measurements for the shelter building she planned to put up on the west side of her house. Now, more than ever, she was determined to raise the money to build the place. After Joe had suggested she try a Kickstarter program, Skylar had said she'd consider it. He knew she didn't like to take charity. That fierce, independent streak ran red in her veins. And he had offered to invest, which she'd also refused.

She would find a way to build her dreams. And that she'd allow him to stand beside her while it happened? There was nothing better in this world for him to do.

"Where's the goat section going?" Joe asked.

Skylar made a few leaps toward the center of the area she'd marked out. "Right here. And over there I want a nursery that I can keep stocked with an incubator. I've got big plans, Joe."

"That you do. You'll make it. I know you will."

"I love that you have such faith in me. But there's still

the issue of my mother owning half the land. You know Malcolm will pounce as soon as we reveal that to her."

"You talk to the lawyer about loopholes in the will? Maybe she forfeited rights by disappearing for so long."

Skylar shrugged. "Maybe. My lawyer is looking into it. It all depends on probate."

"It's something to explore. But whatever happens, I'm here for you."

"After all we've been through, you still give me the benefit of the doubt. Why do you do that, Joseph Cash?"

He pulled her into a hug and bowed to kiss her head. "Because I'm in love with you. And whatever makes you smile makes me smile, too."

"You know, you telling me you love me should freak me out."

"So does it?"

"Nope. I kind of like it. Might even get used to it."

"I mean it."

"I know you do." She pushed up on her tiptoes and kissed him. "Here's to a bright future."

"No more burned wedding dresses?"

"Not in the foreseeable future." She laughed. "Next time I decide to say 'I do,' it'll be because my heart wants me to, not because my brain thinks it needs something stupid."

"This heart is not stupid," he said, laying his palm over her breast where he could feel her heartbeats.

"No, it's not." She kissed him again, and said, "I'm falling in love with you, wolf whisperer. Or maybe I've loved you for a long time and have finally realized it."

"I'll take it either way."

She kissed him, then tapped the eagle talon at his throat. "I know it doesn't heal your heart, but did learning about Max's death answer some questions for you?"

"It did. I will mourn the man. He was a mentor. I think

he knows that I found the truth for him. Wherever he is right now, he's teaching and guiding."

"You're following in your mentor's footsteps."

"I hope so. This arrest didn't take out a key player like I had hoped, but it has called attention to the eagle poaching. Got a couple interviews with local news stations under my belt. I'm not going to stop talking about it until the laws and fines are so harsh that poachers will think twice before taking another animal life. I'm going to talk at a school next week about it."

"Really? You should bring along Stella. She'd make a great mascot for your cause."

"Yeah?" Joe patted his thigh and Stella tilted her head to look up at the twosome. "You cool with that, Stella?"

Stella yipped and then pounced playfully beside him, wagging her tail.

"I think she's challenging me to a race," Joe said. "Come on!" He grabbed Skylar's hand and the two of them raced to the house, with Stella loping along behind them.

* * * * *

COLTON 911: CAUGHT IN THE CROSSFIRE

LINDA O. JOHNSTON

To my wonderful husband, Fred. Of course.

Chapter One

Casey Colton dashed up the large stairway from the first floor of the sheriff's department building in Sur County, Arizona. As deputy sheriff, he was used to taking orders, but the curt phone call he'd just received from his boss, Jeremy Krester, was more of a command. Jeremy was usually fairly laid-back, so that worried Casey.

"Hi, Bob," he said as he entered Jeremy's outer office, not stopping behind the desk stacked with folders but swerving around toward the door behind it.

Apparently Bob Andrews, a fellow deputy, had been informed of his pending presence. "Go on in," said the young, wide-eyed guy, who was wearing a beige uniform that matched the one Casey wore. "Sheriff Krester's expecting you."

As Casey knew well.

He reached out, turned the doorknob and hurried inside. And stopped near the doorway. Sheriff Krester wasn't alone.

Of course, Casey had expected to see his tall, thin, gray-haired boss sitting at the desk facing the door of the sizable office. He wore a similar uniform to Casey's, too, but with a lot more decorations than the normal colorful shoulder patches of the Sur County Sheriff's Department. And his badge was even more prominently displayed on his chest.

But the other guy? That was a surprise.

So was the fact that he paced the wood floor and only stopped for an instant as Casey entered, barely maneuvering around him before continuing.

It was Clarence Edison, the town selectman of Cactus Creek. He was dressed in a suit, as he usually was, and was all business.

In his late sixties, Clarence hadn't gone completely gray but still had more darkness in his hair than Jeremy. He'd been a selectman for many years, but he was known just as much—maybe even more—for owning the successful OverHerd Ranch, outside of town, where he raised Angus cattle. Casey had only seen the large ranch when driving by it.

And, yes, its name—OverHerd—was intended to be a pun, he'd been informed. Not that he was surprised. The selectman was a kidder, someone who liked keeping things light. Casey had noted some of that, too, when he'd attended city meetings, where Clarence got people laughing at times—possibly to make other government officials or even local citizens lighten up. And, therefore, do things his way.

Casey had met Clarence now and then at various town events when the sheriff's department helped to keep things civil and in order. He seemed like a nice guy. He was smart and enjoyed being in charge and talking to large groups, even having fun with them.

But what was he doing here now? And why was he pacing that way?

"Sit down," Jeremy ordered Casey as he waved at one of the three chairs facing his cluttered desk. Jeremy also glanced at Clarence, but his expression toward the selectman appeared to be more of a suggestion than a command.

Casey obeyed as he eyed his boss without looking at the town elder. His curiosity increased even more but he couldn't push things. Not with these two men, who were both used to being in charge.

But it didn't take long for Clarence to start talking even as he did deign to take a seat, and then turned his chair to face Casey.

"Need your help, Deputy," Clarence growled in a low voice Casey hadn't heard before, his blue eyes intense. "I understand you helped catch a cattle rustler a couple months ago."

Was that what this was about? But what had Jeremy told him? "That's right, although it wasn't a big deal. There were only a few cattle involved—one bull and two cows. And it turned out it was a family-feud kind of situation."

Noting some movement from the corner of his eye, Casey turned and saw Jeremy making a slight throat-cutting gesture—in other words, he was telling Casey to shut up about that event.

"Ahh," Jeremy said with a clearly forced smile on his narrow face. "Our deputy there is being a bit modest. Yes, it did turn out to be a family problem, but the members whose cattle disappeared didn't know that at first, and neither did we. Casey figured it out—and found the missing cattle. There were some charges brought against the thieving relatives but they talked it through and paid for some of our time and…well, it's all resolved now, and they're back to being okay."

"Okay," Clarence repeated. He, too, had turned to face the sheriff. "You won't find anything similar in my situation, though."

"No," Jeremy said. "There's a lot more involved. Why don't you tell Deputy Colton about it?" He nodded to the selectman, then looked back at Casey.

He was right, Casey thought as Clarence filled him in. This situation didn't sound nearly as simple as the one Casey had helped with before. For one thing, it involved the disappearance of a dozen cows, not just three. And they were Angus cows being used to procreate, to increase the number of cattle at the ranch and for sale to other ranches.

Very valuable Angus cows. Each was worth thousands of dollars.

No wonder Clarence was upset.

"I want you to act quickly," he continued. "One good thing is that I've had all the cattle tagged with GPS, but the terrain doesn't work for cars, and helicopters or planes couldn't land there. Seeing anything like that could cause the rustlers to kill the cattle and run, anyway. Even drones could scare them into doing something bad. They seem to be on the move so we can't pinpoint where they are for you to send a whole team in to get them. Not yet, at least. And—"

Casey heard a buzzing sound. Clarence pulled a phone out of his pocket and looked at it, then listened.

After a minute he said, "Damn. I need to head back to my office right now for an important meeting. I want someone from here who knows what he's doing to get to my ranch right away. A couple of ranch hands are there and can show you around and explain what happened and when." He stood and began pacing between Casey and his superior's desk again. He looked at Casey. "Since you've solved one rustling case lately, even though it's not quite the same thing, I agree with Sheriff Krester that it makes sense for you to go and scope things out. Maybe even solve it on the spot." His grin toward Casey was wide, though his eyes narrowed and remained skeptical.

Casey asked, "Any people you think might be the rustlers—family members or not?"

"Not," Clarence said strongly. "I trust my family—but that didn't stop me from notifying the local members by phone and listening to their shock and sympathy. And analyzing it. I've no reason to suspect any of them. Besides…"

He paused, looked from Casey toward the sheriff, then back again.

"Besides what?" Jeremy prompted, as Casey believed was appropriate, considering the way Clarence had spoken and looked at him.

"Besides, the dozen cattle of mine that were stolen were all very valuable females. Cows." He paused. "So that tells me that whoever did it was one hell of a *cow*ard." All three of them laughed at the emphasis he

placed on the first syllable—briefly and not particularly hilariously.

"Well, let me at him. Or her." Casey stood directly
in front of the selectman. "I won't allow whoever it is
to cow me. I'll do my damnedest to figure this out soon
and get your cattle back."

MELODY HAYWORTH PULLED opened the front door of the
main house of OverHerd Ranch before the doorbell finished chiming.

She'd been waiting inside uncomfortably, along with
Pierce Tostig, one of the other ranch hands, since their
boss had called half an hour ago.

It was midafternoon. Earlier, a couple of the other
hands had headed out toward the pasture where one of
the herds of special, valuable Angus cattle had supposedly spent the night and morning, as usual…but they
hadn't found them there. Using the GPS apps on their
phones, they'd confirmed that the geotagged cows were
now far away, somewhere still on the ranch, but heading
toward its outer edges. It appeared that the fence had
been partly destroyed, apparently by rustlers, and the
cows had gotten out. Those hands had called Clarence,
who'd expressed concern not only about the missing
stock, but also about those that remained. He'd insisted
that all of the ranch hands—or at least most of them—
find and protect the rest.

He'd also said he'd get the authorities involved, and
then ordered that a couple of employees—Pierce Tostig
and Melody—should stick around to help and advise
the sheriff's department when someone from there ar-

rived at the ranch, then stay involved in finding those missing cattle.

Now, Melody said "Please come in" to the man in uniform who stood there—a deputy sheriff, according to the patch on his upper left sleeve.

"Thanks." He immediately held out his hand for a shake after she shut the door. "I'm Deputy Casey Colton," he said. "I was sent here by Selectman Clarence Edison because—"

"Because some of our—*his*—cattle have been rustled," Melody interrupted. She had no need to wait for any further introductions, but she noticed that his grip was strong and somehow sexy, which was irrelevant. Her boss had made it clear in his phone call that she and the others were to give the deputy who showed up all the information they had about the rustling situation. And to show him where the cattle had been located, and how they'd apparently gotten out…with help.

"Let's go in here first," she said to Deputy Colton, gesturing for him to follow her through the attractively decorated wooden entryway into the adjoining living room. Melody considered the decor a bit overdone, but it worked well for a ranch house owned by someone as revered—and rich—as her boss.

She watched the deputy's face as he looked around. The guy was good-looking, and not just because he wore that uniform. His hair was brown and cut relatively short. His matching eyebrows over dazzling blue eyes were nicely arched and his chin was slightly prominent. He had some light facial hair, maybe surprising because of his job. But it looked good on him.

In fact, every part of his appearance was eye-catching—and Melody could have kicked herself for even noticing.

The only thing important about this guy was whether he could find the missing cattle.

For now, his boots rapped on the portion of the wooden floor not covered by an antique gold-and-brown area rug. The deputy approached Pierce, who stood near one of the windows at the far side of the room beside the stone fireplace.

Heading toward them, Pierce was dressed even more casually than Melody's typical blue denim work shirt, jeans and black boots with tight laces. He wore an oversize, short-sleeved white T-shirt and overly faded jeans—fashionable, perhaps, but it seemed as if there were more holes than denim.

"Hi," the deputy said, stopping near the side of the ornate brown leather sofa set that dominated the room's seating arrangement. He introduced himself to Pierce, as he'd done with Melody, and was clearly taking charge of this meeting. "Can we sit down? I want to hear everything about the missing cattle—where they were, who discovered they were gone. Everything."

"Yeah, I figured." Pierce plopped down on one of the two-seater portions of the sofa set. Ears protruded from wavy hair clipped close on the sides of his head. He was around forty, like Melody, and was clean-shaven with blue eyes. Pierce was okay-looking and mostly genial, but perhaps not as hard a worker as he should be.

Melody took a seat on the similar sofa section, while the deputy sat on the larger one and leaned forward, his elbows on his knees. He looked toward her as if encouraging her to begin the description.

But Pierce took over. Pointing toward the rear of the house, he described the five-hundred-acre ranch and about how many cattle there were—quite a few more than those that were stolen, fortunately. "Our main range is out that way. It's divided into sections because of the terrain. Dry sand in some areas, grass and higher growth in others, lots of hillsides, small mountains, all that kind of thing."

"Interesting," the deputy said. "I'll want to see it soon, or as much of it as possible. Now, tell me more about who discovered the problem and how."

Again he looked toward Melody. Pierce attempted to answer, never mind that Deputy Colton seemed to be addressing her. But as much as she liked Pierce and the way he mostly helped her learn about this ranch, Melody disliked being ignored. She spoke up, talking over Pierce.

"As it turns out, I probably should have been the one to discover the problem, but I wasn't." She described how she and some ranch hands, including Pierce, resided in apartments in the bunkhouse behind this house and slightly west of the stables. The fenced-in ranch land began behind them, and the several herds of cattle ranged in different fenced areas within it.

Last night, she hadn't slept well, although she wasn't sure why. "Now, though, I believe I might have heard something in the distance while asleep that disturbed me, though I didn't fully awaken."

"I'll want to see the location of your residences, particularly yours," the lawman said.

"Of course, Deputy Colton." From what she'd learned, the name *Colton* was an important one in many areas. Whether or not he was a lawman, though, she didn't particularly like his knowing where she lived.

"Just call me Casey," the law-enforcement official said with a small grin on that good-looking face. As uncomfortable as she felt, she knew that getting along with him, including being on a first-name basis, was probably going to be helpful in the long run as they worked with him to find the missing cattle.

"Okay, Casey. And as you know, I'm Melody."

"And I'm Pierce," the other man said. "Are we all going to head to bed together now?"

Melody found herself laughing, even as the discomfort within her eased a bit. "Not I," she said.

"Only if the missing cattle are there," Casey retorted. "So, okay, tell me more about how you discovered that those cattle were missing." He smiled at Pierce first, then her. "And we'll keep our minds on the range, not in the bedroom."

"Fine with me," Melody said with a shake of her head. Although the idea of combining Casey and a bedroom… She forced the thought out of her head.

"Well, if that's the case," Pierce said, "I'm out of here. I'm supposed to be out in the east pasture with a couple of the other hands but thought I was needed here." He stood, nodded toward Casey and said, "Hope you find those missing cows soon. Real soon." And then he left.

So, no matter what Clarence said, apparently Pierce wasn't staying involved.

"I second what he said," Melody told Casey. "And though I can tell you a lot more about this place, I think it'll be more productive if we go outside and I show you around."

"Fine," Casey said. "I'll want to see everything you and the others have found so far before I really dig into the investigation."

"Sure," Melody said. "I've only worked here for about six months, but I've learned a lot about this great ranch. And although I haven't gone chasing those missing cattle yet, we can go to the place they got past the OverHerd fencing and start our real investigation there."

They both stood and she looked at Casey. He had an odd expression on his face. A scowl, she thought, and it seemed to mar his good looks.

What was he thinking? she wondered. Good thing he was scowling, though. He clearly wasn't having the same kinds of thoughts about her as she had about him.

Although… Well, not going to happen.

It was better that way.

Chapter Two

Our real investigation? Casey didn't want to contradict Melody, not when he needed her to show him what she and the others had found so far, but she wasn't going to be part of *his* investigation.

He was the deputy assigned here. This was his job.

And besides...well, he was finding it a bit uncomfortable to be around Melody, especially now, when they were alone.

Problem was, she seemed much too beautiful to be a ranch hand. Her long, dark hair was secured behind her head in a ponytail, and she had a gorgeous face, with deep brown eyes above high cheekbones and below attractively curved, dark eyebrows. Those eyes showed what she appeared to be feeling—sometimes infuriated by the rustling that had gone on here, sometimes amused, or irritated, by what Pierce had said, sometimes pleading with Casey to fix the problem...and always winsome and appealing.

Too appealing. Never mind that she appeared to be a little older than him.

And since he'd been left at the altar four years ago, he hadn't been interested in another woman.

Didn't want to be now.

But he needed information from her. So—

"Great," he said. "Let's go."

He glanced around again before beginning to follow her out the door. The sofa from which he'd risen, which matched the other seats, had been surprisingly comfortable considering how elaborate it was, with its leather seating punched evenly with deep matching buttons and back lined with attractive, carved wood. It looked expensive. Everything in this room—everything he'd seen at this ranch—looked expensive. But then, he didn't doubt that Clarence Edison could afford all that and more.

Though perhaps not as much if he didn't get back his valuable missing cattle.

Melody, hips swaying gently even as she hurried, led him in a different direction down the hallway they'd walked along before, and soon they passed through the large kitchen, which was also elaborately outfitted with expensive-looking equipment, though no one was working there now. Did Edison have a personal chef? He wouldn't be surprised.

Soon they were on the varnished wooden porch, having exited from the rear door. The yard beyond was mostly dirt decorated with desert plants, cacti and more. Straight ahead, past the elongated stables and an even larger barn with a peaked roof, a mountain range rose, not especially tall but broad. Another building, possibly a bunkhouse, was located near the back of the ranch house. Toward the south, beyond the substantial-looking fence, was land covered with grass, as far as he could see. He couldn't tell how large the vast rolling lawn was, but judging by what he understood of the ranch's success, it probably went on for many miles.

"I don't think you need to see the insides of the buildings, at least not now," Melody said. "The stable houses our horses, of course. We ranch hands usually ride them when we're heading out into the pastures to observe and take care of the grazing herds. The cattle don't spend much time in the barn, although the cows sometimes do when they're calving, or if there's any indication of illness. For now, we could ride out to the pastures on horseback, but I think you'll get a better sense of the pasture if we just walk this time. Okay?"

"Fine," Casey said. It would be a good idea for him to borrow a horse when he'd learned the basics and was ready to start his real investigation, but for now he would learn best if he took the time to walk around and look at everything he could from that perspective. As long as— "But you will take me to the fenced area where the cattle escaped, won't you?"

"Absolutely," Melody said. "All the hands are aware of it, and have seen the damage to the fence there, too. The other herds are now within different fenced areas so they can't disappear that way, too."

"Fine."

"And in case our boss didn't tell you, the cows are all branded with a logo that says 'OHR' for OverHerd Ranch. Even more important, they're all equipped with GPS trackers. But the terrain out there isn't appropriate for driving out to find them, so all we have so far is an accurate idea which way they went."

"Yes, he mentioned that. Thanks." Not surprising that the ranch hands were up-to-date—but it was a bit surprising that apparently no one had used the technology to go after the cattle yet.

Although it was a better thing that they hadn't, if rustlers were involved. Law enforcement was his job, not theirs.

For now, he found himself smiling slightly in amusement as the slender and clearly physically fit Melody hurried off in front of him, as she undoubtedly wanted to reach the pasture that usually contained the cattle— when they weren't missing. He hurried, too, to catch up with her and stay by her side. He began asking questions about the landscape, the types of plants and the topography, which was flat at first but he saw rolling ridges in the near background.

She climbed quickly over the portion of the long, substantial-looking fence that was chest-high to her, a bit less to him. The way she scaled it agilely made it appear as if she practiced daily. Maybe she did. And he told himself again to quit noticing such things.

His mind landed briefly on his ex-fiancée, Georgia. He and his fraternal twin brother, Everett, had known her from childhood And Everett's best friend had been Sean Dodd, Georgia's brother, but she'd dumped Casey.

But enough of that. He had important things to think about now. As he had to do too often, even now, he eliminated Georgia from his thoughts.

The weather was typical for this time of year—November—in this part of Arizona. It was sometimes warm but far from scorching, though it often grew cooler, especially at night. A nearly perfectly blue sky, no humidity. Nearly perfect.

Past the fence, as they both strode over the uneven, grassy ground, he asked what Melody knew about the ranch and its origins, just to make conversation until she got them to where she could show him something significant.

As Melody glanced sideways toward him, her long black ponytail swayed. "I can tell you what I heard, but I'm a relative newcomer here. The other hands have been here longer."

She wasn't looking at him now, but somehow her expression had hardened.

Where had she lived before? Why had she decided to become a ranch hand, and why here?

Was she unhappy about being the least experienced of the ranch hands here? He was highly curious all of a sudden, especially considering that oddly defensive look on her face. He asked, "So where did you come from? Is this your first job as a ranch hand?"

She again looked at him. Her brow creased and her mouth tightened. He assumed she was going to tell him where to go, to stop asking questions.

Maybe she didn't want to think of the past, either.

"Er… I'm sorry," he began, wanting to back off. "I didn't mean to be nosy."

But she responded…kind of. "I came from Texas. And, no, this isn't my first job as a ranch hand. I learned all about it there." She turned her attention toward where she was walking, as she should on this uneven area. "And one of the things I know well is that this kind of grass, this terrain, supports cattle well." She began a description of how she had studied different kinds of grasses and that these pastures seemed to incorporate several, although she wasn't certain. "Whatever they are, the grasses here seem to feed some pretty healthy cattle." She started talking about fescue and rye and stuff he really didn't care about, but she made it sound noteworthy.

"Interesting" was all he said. And in a way it was—considering the source.

He was finding Melody much too interesting... Which had to stop.

He started examining the topography more closely. It was flat in some areas, then rose to low hills and was flat again.

"Hey." Melody had suddenly stopped talking about grasses. "We're finally approaching where they got out."

She kept walking as she pointed out a spot in the distance...and then tripped. He instinctively reached out to grab her and hold her up, although he quickly realized she'd regained her balance on her own.

"Thanks," she said, anyway, her voice hoarse as she pulled her arm from his hand quickly. She immediately looked away from him and began to walk fast again.

He had an urge to hold her hand—to help her keep her balance. But that would be a bad idea.

A *very* bad idea.

He had a sense that if he tried it, he'd be the one to trip over his own feet and fall onto his knees.

And he'd be the one to look bad.

She was the ranch hand, not him. She could most likely wrangle a steer with her eyes closed. Even tie knots a lot better than him.

Instead of holding on to her, he'd take a different kind of advantage of her company now, since he'd be on his own for the actual investigation, at least initially, and possibly until another deputy or two was assigned to work with him. And being in Melody's presence... well, asking her questions related to what had happened here would be a whole lot easier for him than holding any other kind of conversation with her.

Like a flirtation? No way. There were no women in his life now. He didn't want any, despite how attractive she was. And especially not until he'd learned enough to be sure she wasn't involved in stealing the cattle.

So—who'd taken them, and why? They could certainly talk about that. It wasn't something he had much of a notion about on his own yet, not without investigating first—though he did have one potential suspect in mind that wasn't Melody.

According to local news, Edison's wife, Hilda, had left him last year and was no longer in town—or so Casey believed, but that didn't mean she was innocent. Hilda Edison was surely getting up in years, like her ex, so she probably couldn't have done this herself. But had she arranged for the rustling for her own financial gain, or revenge...or both?

Melody started responding to what he'd asked before, relaying her knowledge about the origins of OverHerd Ranch, which she had already admitted was limited since she'd moved here fairly recently. She understood that Clarence, who had grown up in Phoenix with a wealthy family, had moved to Cactus Creek after college and started the ranch. Then he'd married and he and his wife had a couple of kids, who were grown now and living elsewhere. She didn't know much about the ranch's development, which was fine since it probably had nothing to do with the current situation, although it might have been interesting to hear.

Casey could ask Clarence about that, if necessary, or maybe even look it up online. But for now, he interrupted gently and asked instead who she and the other ranch hands suspected in this, and why.

Unsurprisingly, she mentioned Hilda first. The other hands were already gossiping that their boss's ex might be involved. No one knew how much Hilda had gotten from the divorce, but if she didn't consider it enough, that could be a motive for her to steal some cattle.

Their kids? From what she'd gathered, Clarence had remained fairly generous with them, so while they were possible suspects, they didn't rank high on the others' lists.

Who else? Again, there were rumors, sometimes about political opponents or other townsfolk who didn't always agree with how Clarence ran things, but no one person stood out as having anything particularly against the man. No, the ranch hands seemed to think it was somewhat random.

"You might check in other areas around here to see if there've been other rustling situations lately, and if any of them seem at all similar," Melody said. A good idea, one he'd already thought of and would make sure Sheriff Krester had someone work on while Casey conducted his on-site investigation here.

"Will do" was all he said to Melody. And for the next few minutes both of them remained quiet. They were getting close to the clearly damaged fence, and Casey, at least, was studying the rolling hillside, mostly covered in grass and patches of other kinds of plant life, but with several other areas of bare soil. There were more pasture areas beyond the broken fence that seemed to stretch forever.

And no sign of cattle anywhere.

He glanced at his watch. It was nearing three o'clock. They'd been out for more than half an hour, and the walk back would also take that long. He wanted to spend some time at the broken-fence site first, too.

There would still be a few hours of daylight after their return, on this late fall day. Still, even if he found something around here, darkness might drop before he could deal with it. It would make more sense to return tomorrow. On horseback, maybe.

On his own, with whatever it took to track the cows' GPS signals.

Suddenly feeling the urge to stop wasting time and get to the fence already, Casey began sprinting forward. And he noticed that Melody was keeping up with him.

The fence consisted of oblong wooden stakes of moderate height, anchored into the ground, with three rows of straight metal piping connecting each pair of those stakes.

Here, though, four of the stakes had been knocked

from their anchors and damaged, with gouges in the splintered wood indicating that some kind of tool had been used. The piping had been removed and stacked in rows off to the side. And the grassy ground beneath the opening was tamped down unevenly, as if cattle had walked through it—not a surprise.

This was clearly not some kind of accident or natural phenomenon. Someone had done it. Probably several someones, since removing the stakes could not have been easy.

Casey emitted a low whistle. "Wow. What a mess." He kneeled and started examining some of the splintered wood and the pipes, looking at the ground, as well.

"With no tools left here, either, to show how it was done," Melody said.

"Yeah," he responded. "I'll request that my department send someone here to check for fingerprints, but I suspect they won't find anything."

Melody nodded her pretty head as she kneeled beside him. "Anyone skilled enough to do this most likely has done something similar before—and knew to use gloves."

"Could be." He, of course, carried plastic gloves in his pocket for situations in which he didn't want to mess up any evidence, as well as a gun in his role as a deputy sheriff. "Well," he said, "I guess I could start looking for any evidence right here, but—"

"But here's what we should do," Melody interrupted. "Let's find those cattle. We can go on a stakeout on horseback—follow the cows, thanks to the way Clarence has made sure all his animals are tagged. Keep following them until we find them, even if it takes a few days and nights. And—"

It was Casey's turn to interrupt. "Sounds like a great idea." Of course, he'd already been considering it— though not exactly the way she said. "And I appreciate your offer, but I'll do it on my own, starting early tomorrow."

"Well, of course, I'll come with you," Melody insisted. "How well do you know how to ride a horse? I'll have to pick out one for you that matches your skills, though I can handle any of them, the faster the better. I'm damn good at it, so—"

"Now, wait a minute." Casey stood up quickly and stared down at Melody. She, too, rose and met his gaze. "I'd appreciate your allowing me to borrow one of the ranch's horses tomorrow, and maybe longer," he said to appease her. He continued, "I'll have to see how things go before rushing back to town, so as you suggested I might camp out for a night or two, depending on what I find—or don't find. But that's me. I'm the deputy assigned to handle this investigation, and I'll do it. *Myself.*"

Her expression turned into a glare, even as she put her hands on her hips. He noticed then that her nails were short and plain. No polish on them. No lipstick on her, either. Not that she needed anything like that to look pretty. But this way she looked more like the ranch hand she was.

"Then maybe you'd better bring your own horse," she told him coldly.

They both continued to glare at each other as his

mind raced to try to figure out where he'd be able to get a horse on his own—and fast. Could he soothe her somehow in a way that ensured she'd still back off from interfering in his investigation?

She dropped her hands, even as she shook her head, a wry expression on that too-attractive face. "Look, Casey," she said—and for just then he'd have preferred her to refer to him as "Deputy Colton." "You're in charge of this investigation. I understand that. But I'll bet I can help you since I probably know this ranch, and cattle, better than you. Let's look around a little bit now and I'll try to convince you. But even if I don't, please let me join you tomorrow. I really give a damn about those missing cows, and I'll do everything I can to save them and bring them home."

He raised his head, just a little. "Look, Ms. Hayworth." He, at least, could return to formality. "It's one thing for me to be out there attempting to solve this apparent crime and to go after any perpetrators as well as the missing cattle. I'm trained to do such things. It's my job. But I don't want to have to worry about protecting you, too."

"Then don't worry about it. I'm volunteering. If anything happens to me, it's my own fault. And what if I really *can* help you?"

He recognized that this argument was going nowhere. "We'll see," he responded, then he moved forward to the broken fence and maneuvered his way to the property beyond, intentionally ignoring his difficult companion for the moment.

But he couldn't really ignore her, especially when,

a few feet away from him, she, too, edged her way to the far side beyond the broken fence. She started walking around, looking first into the distance, then glancing down to the ground. Then she did it again, even as Casey pretty much did the same thing.

And he saw some stuff that was interesting, like hoofprints in the grass, but unlikely to be any helpful evidence.

"Okay, Casey, look at this," Melody called to him. She gestured for him to join her, even as she continued studying the ground.

"Look at this," she repeated and pointed to an area right by her feet, where the grass had been tromped down and some dirt showed, similar to the ground he'd been examining, too. "See that? There are some hoofprints of cows, probably the missing ones since the prints are fairly new—sharp and prominent. They're heading in that direction." She pointed. "South. That's the way we should look for them."

Casey couldn't help himself. He laughed. "Guess what? Your cows left hoofprints over where I was standing, too, and I was studying them when you called me to come over."

Melody looked slightly abashed, but then her expression again became defiant. "Then, good. We're on the same page. We can compare and help each other and—"

"I understand you want to help and I appreciate it. But like I told you—"

"Look," she interrupted, "I know a lot more about cattle and hoofprints than you do. And more about the ranch and pastures, too." She was being a bit repetitious. He knew that, hadn't forgotten it. But still…

"I get all that," he told her. "And I've already told you why it's not a good idea for you to come."

"I'll prove otherwise," she insisted, contradicting him again. She began moving forward quickly, her head down.

But they weren't going to learn more now. Not here. Tomorrow he'd hurry in the same direction and hopefully find something helpful.

Maybe even those missing cattle…

"Hey. Look at that." Melody had stopped and was looking down to what was undoubtedly more cattle hoofprints. Only, she bent and reached for something, then stopped. She looked up at him again. "I doubt that any cow dropped that," she said.

"What?" he asked. He kneeled down beside her… and stared.

She was pointing to an area within a hoofprint, in dirt between fronds of tamped-down grass, and something small and shiny gleamed from it.

"What is that?" He resisted the urge to grab and examine it—and was glad she hadn't done that, either.

"It looks like some kind of silver charm," Melody responded in a somewhat hushed voice. "It could have been there before any cattle walked or stampeded around here through the fence during this rustling, but I've never seen anything like it in any of the pastures."

"I think," he mused, "and I may just be reaching for

something helpful to identify some suspects and get this thing resolved, but you just might have found our first piece of evidence."

Chapter Three

Melody was impressed, though not surprised, when Casey took a couple of pictures with his cell phone, then pulled vinyl gloves from his pocket, picked up the charm and stuck it into a small plastic bag he also carried.

Clearly, he was prepared to do his job, wherever it led him and whatever evidence he happened to find.

The charm was the kind worn on necklaces or bracelets, and appeared to be silver. It was in the shape of the letter *G*.

"Does this look familiar to you?" He held the bag containing the charm toward Melody.

She shook her head. "Not at all."

But that inspired her to continue studying the ground in that area, and Casey did, too. Neither of them found anything else other than more hoofprints.

"Do you think the charm was dropped by one of the rustlers?" Melody asked the deputy as they finally gave up.

"Anything's possible," he said with a shrug of his wide shoulders as he shot a wry look in her direction. A

frustrated look. She wished she could do something—
identify the charm, find something more helpful, to
ease that frustration.

But she was frustrated, too. And no solution came
to her.

"Let's head back now," he said, shoving the bag into
his pocket. "Maybe we'll figure things out better tomorrow."

"Absolutely," she said, hoping it was true.

The walk back to the ranch house was a lot faster
than the one to the damaged fence. But going in this
direction, they didn't need to check for any indication
of where the cattle were or who'd rustled them through
that fence.

Or whether there were any more charms on the
ground.

Not until tomorrow.

And, yes, she would be going along with Casey. It
was important to her to do the best job possible here.
This ranch had become her refuge after leaving her past
behind, and she adored its cattle. She intended to help
to save the stolen ones. Period.

She had to give Casey credit for not grumbling or
protesting when she said, as they started back, "So I assume that, as the first person to find evidence in your
crime investigation, I can come along tomorrow and
continue to help you."

"I assume so," he said resignedly. He shot her a
crooked sideways smile. "And, yeah, we can do the
kind of stakeout you described."

She couldn't help smiling back and was careful not

to make it appear she was gloating. Or at least not too much.

Besides, Casey was one good-looking guy, so it wasn't hard to smile at him.

Not that she had any intention of allowing her goal of helping to find the missing cattle by working with this guy turn into any kind of personal interest in him.

She'd learned her lesson not too long ago. It was why she had left her Texas home and found a job here, in Arizona, as a ranch hand, after her ugly, depressing divorce.

She knew now that it hadn't been the smartest thing to marry her high-school sweetheart, Travis Ellison, and follow him to Dallas. They'd only been married a couple of years before Travis, who'd become a big-city banker, had left her for a colleague, a much younger woman named Loretta Lane.

What had made it even more heartbreaking was that Travis had told Melody she was a "country girl," and he needed a "real woman."

Whatever that meant, it had hurt. A lot. She had sometimes suspected the worst about Travis before then, that he was cheating on her, but since she'd thought she loved him, she'd stayed with him, hoping they could work things out. At least she'd tried, but it had also hurt that he didn't seem to care.

That insult had finally led to the inevitable end of their relationship.

And, if being a skilled and happy ranch hand meant she was a country girl, then that was fine with her.

She realized she'd somehow sped up even more as

she allowed her thoughts to go—as they often did these days—in that painful direction.

"Hey, what's your hurry?" Casey called as he caught up with her again. "Got a hot date tonight?"

She slowed a bit and turned to look into his face. His expression was teasing, yet she read some curiosity there, too. "Yeah, sure. With some horses. I need to make sure they're taken care of, and also want to figure out which'll be best on our stakeout."

"Right. Good idea. But you do understand, don't you, that I'm planning to stay out there till I—we—find those missing cattle? You can return to your place at the ranch anytime, of course, but—"

"And you'll love it if I quit, won't you? Well, don't count on it. I'm in this to win, too. Those cows...well, they're kind of my wards now. They're mine, though I don't own them and just care for them. That's my job and my vocation. And I'll do anything to bring them home safely." Including argue with him, to save the cattle she cared for.

She was surprised that Casey stopped walking, but she did, too. She couldn't quite interpret his expression, but he appeared impressed, somehow.

Or maybe that was what she hoped he felt.

"Bringing them home safely is my job, too. And I'm glad to have someone like you helping me."

A warmth spread through her. He looked serious. But—

"But you didn't want me around and only gave in because I did something helpful."

He gave a brief laugh. "That's the point, isn't it?

Something helpful could grow into more. Or that's what I'm counting on. Do more of it!" He chuckled again.

"Count on it," she said, hoping she was capable of doing what she had just promised.

"And in case you're concerned, I understand that the stakeout you described involves sleeping outdoors for possibly several nights, camping out. I'm sure you understand that, too. But...well, if it makes you uncomfortable being alone with me that way, feel free to back out anytime and go home."

"Same goes for you," she said, liking his attitude... kind of. He wasn't meeting her eyes, as if he was embarrassed. But being alone with this man, sleeping alone with him out in the open...well, yeah, it made her uncomfortable, mostly with her own feelings. Damn if she didn't find this dedicated, uniformed sheriff's deputy too appealing. Too sexy.

But she wouldn't act on it, and wouldn't allow him to, either.

And, in fact, she reminded herself—as if she needed to—she had good reason not to become attracted to him or any other man. Not now, certainly. Not so soon.

And definitely not until she got to know someone well enough to feel sure he wasn't just playing games with this "country girl."

"If I get too suggestive with you," she continued, still trying to keep the conversation light, "or you become uncomfortable for any other reason, well, I'll keep looking for my cows and you can go home."

He laughed. "Sounds like a challenge to me. Who'll get most uncomfortable first?"

"Not me," Melody lied, already feeling as if, despite everything, she'd have to work hard to control her own attraction to this man.

CASEY WISHED JUST then that he could read minds. That way he would learn what Melody was thinking.

The idea of their sleeping out in the pasture together didn't seem to bother her. She'd sounded quite professional. She probably didn't feel the attraction he felt toward her, which was a good thing.

As they walked quickly, her expressions changed from light and humorous, to dark and apparently introspective and sad, and he was intrigued.

But he never asked her to explain. Figured she wouldn't answer, anyway. And now, he and the lithe, lovely ranch hand had reached the main house. The single-story, deep red structure had rich-looking wood and a beige roof.

Right now, his work vehicle, a black sedan with Sur County Sheriff's Department on the front doors and a light on top, was parked out front.

Beside it was a black luxury sedan. Clarence's? Casey asked Melody. "Yes, that's his." Melody looked down at the watch on her wrist. "He usually doesn't come home until around seven, but it's only five. I wonder if he's heard anything or—"

Before she finished, the front door to the house opened and the selectman stepped onto the porch. "Hey, you two. You're back. Did you find my cattle?" He had changed from the suit Casey had seen him in earlier into a long-sleeved charcoal T-shirt with the OverHerd

Ranch logo in white. He clumped down the steps in his
boots. Dressed this way, he looked a lot more rustic
and older than Casey was used to seeing him. He still
appeared relatively slender, but the skin at the corners
of his eyes sagged and lines on his forehead were appropriate for his age...or was it stress that caused them
to stand out?

"Not yet, sir," Casey said as the man reached them
and faced them on the paved driveway. "But—"

"Then why are you here?" Edison demanded. "Why
aren't you—?"

"I began showing Deputy Colton around, sir, and we
went out to the fence," Melody said. "Since we didn't
see anything helpful except for how the fence was destroyed in that area, we decided to come back for the
night and leave early in the morning on a stakeout of
the entire ranch and beyond, if necessary, on horseback.
We won't return then till we find the missing cattle."

"'We'?" Clarence demanded, glaring at Melody.

Odd that, after wondering the same thing, Casey
now felt he had to defend Melody and the fact he had
decided not to protest any longer. He understood her
rationale. And her presence might cost him time, since
he would have to protect her above all else. But she was
the ranch owner's employee. She had the kind of knowledge that could help him, as she'd mentioned. What she
was doing could definitely be of assistance.

He noticed she didn't mention the charm she had
found. Well, it might not mean anything, anyway. But
he'd take care of checking into it.

"Ms. Hayworth was kind enough to offer to come

along," Casey said. "We're going on horseback, and I'm sure, with her experience, she's a lot better rider than I am. Plus, she knows your land better than I do. I hope you'll allow her to come, sir. I think it will be to your advantage."

The selectman's expression changed from hard and angry to...well, resolved—and perhaps inquisitive. "And to yours, too, maybe, Deputy."

Casey saw the shock appear on Melody's face, even as he felt himself flush slightly. Had the selectman intended to be suggestive? Maybe not, but just in case, Casey said, "I intend to do my job and do it well, and I appreciate any assistance with it." He hoped he sounded strictly professional.

"Well, okay," Clarence said. "Hopefully that'll work. And I like what you said, Melody. You won't come back until you find my cattle. Right?"

"That's right." Melody looked relieved as she nodded vehemently.

"Right," Casey echoed. "So now I'll head back to town and return here early in the morning, around six thirty, okay?" He aimed his gaze at Melody.

But Clarence was the one to answer. "No, stay here tonight. We've got some apartments available in our bunkhouse, where our hands stay. And they're fairly nice, right, Melody?"

"Absolutely, Clarence," she responded, which made Casey tilt his head slightly in confusion. She'd called him "sir" before, and now she was using his name.

Informality might be in order at the moment.

"I appreciate your invitation to stay here," Casey

said to Clarence, "but I do need to go home. I'll need to bring the right clothing to wear on our stakeout, for one thing." And other appropriate things, as well, particularly since he didn't know how long they'd be out there.

"I get it," Clarence grumbled.

Good. But if Casey could have stayed, he would have; maybe he would have met more of the ranch hands. Gained more of their input about what had happened. But that wasn't in the cards right now.

He thanked the ranch owner and again said he'd be back bright and early the next day.

But Clarence wasn't buying that. "Nope, that's not happening. You can go home, get what you need and come on back as fast as you can—now. You're going to have dinner with Melody and me right here, just the three of us so we can talk, and then you'll stay here for the night."

The way he spoke allowed for no argument, but that was okay with Casey. He decided he liked this idea, since they'd be able to get an earlier start in the morning. He assumed that was also why Clarence was so insistent about his staying here overnight. Still, there were a couple of things he'd need to handle first.

"I'm still on duty," he told the older man. "And this is part of an assignment. I need to check with the sheriff first." Which he'd intended to do, anyway, although he had no doubt Jeremy would approve this intense way of tackling his investigation.

Staying at the ranch added another level to it, but that was likely to be all right, as well.

Especially if Casey—and Melody—actually found the cattle and the people who'd taken them.

But to do the stakeout as now planned, Casey would also need to pick up the camping gear he had at his home as well as some more supplies at a local store.

When he mentioned that, Clarence put up a hand and moved it as if he was erasing what Casey said. "No need. We've got it all here. You'll get it together tonight, Melody, right?"

"Of course," she said.

But Casey remained adamant that he needed to get some things. And so, a few minutes later, he found himself in his car driving along the rural ranch-surrounded roads toward town as the sky began to turn dark. There were a few other cars that were heading in the opposite direction, but no one was heading to town, like him.

He used the Bluetooth to call the sheriff. "Yeah, Casey?" Jeremy answered. "Did you find those missing cattle? And whoever stole them?"

"Not yet, for either of them." But Casey explained the situation to his superior officer, and how he was going to go on a stakeout with one of the ranch hands the next day.

"Would that ranch hand happen to be Melody Hayworth?" Casey could hear the suggestive tone in his boss's voice.

What was it with guys? Casey thought. Did they not believe in his professionalism?

Or did they find Melody as attractive as he did, and therefore let their imaginations run wild—their jealous imaginations?

Maybe he would change his mind and give it a try…

No. He was a professional. And clearly Melody was, too.

"It is Melody," Casey said in as formal a tone as he could muster. "She's good with horses, and she knows the ranch." Great reasons, even though talking about them was feeling a bit stale to Casey right now. "But looking for the cattle and the thieves—that's all we're up to. And I'll keep you informed."

But he realized as he hung up that he'd need to make a stop at the department to have one of the evidence guys check the charm for prints or origin, in case it could help lead to the perpetrator.

And there was something scratching at the back of his mind about it—but that was probably just because he hoped it would lead to something.

He still had a little ways to go before reaching the discount store he was heading to first, so he made another call, this time to Everett, who worked for the FBI in Phoenix. Everett was older by a couple of minutes, and they didn't look much alike. And for twins, their personalities weren't much the same, though they'd both gone into law enforcement.

"Hey, bro, what's up?" Everett said as he answered.

"On an interesting case," Casey replied, then described the cattle rustling and how he was attempting to find the missing animals and solve the situation.

He didn't mention that the ranch hand helping him was a woman, though. He'd never hear the end of it from Everett.

"I'll be out on a stakeout for as long as it takes," he informed his brother. "The ranch's owner has things set up so I should have power for my phone, but I haven't tried that yet."

"Well, better call the folks before you go, to let them know what you're up to in case you become unreachable."

Which Casey did next. He'd reached the store's parking lot, so he sat there as he talked to their parents, who both got on the phone.

Neither of them was in law enforcement. Dr. Ryker Colton, their dad, was an oncologist in town, and their mom, Maribelle Colton, ran the Cactus Creek post office.

As he finished and told them he was probably—but not absolutely—going to be reachable over the next few days, his father said in his aging scratchy voice, "Now, you be careful, son. Got it?"

"Got it, Dad."

"That won't keep you from coming for Thanksgiving dinner, or Christmas dinner?" his mom asked, her tone a sweet chirp, as always. "You know we'll want you to come. And…well, if you'd like to bring someone for Christmas, that's fine."

"Thanks, Mom," he said. "There shouldn't be any problem with my being there for either one." After all, Thanksgiving was a couple of weeks away, and Christmas even farther away. "And if I think of anyone to invite, I'll let you know." His mind had flown immediately to Melody, of course. But he didn't know if she had family here, or friends she'd want to spend the holiday with.

Besides, under these circumstances…well, he'd just have to see.

Chapter Four

Melody wasn't sure what she'd expected dinner to be
like with just the three of them—herself, Clarence and
Casey—that night, so she wasn't surprised. But this
felt unique.

And worrisome.

What if Casey and she didn't find the cattle and the
people who'd stolen them? What if the stock weren't
returned, especially after she'd sort of been singled out
like this to help handle the situation?

They sat in Clarence's posh dining room, with its
antique wooden table and chairs, a tall, matching buf-
fet against the wall and a glimmering chandelier hanging over the table. Melody felt she should have worn
something dressier, but the men with her also wore casual clothing. When Casey had gone home to grab what
he'd need while camping out, he had changed into jeans
and a deep blue long-sleeved T-shirt that hugged his
chest—and he looked hunky in it. She had to make
sure she didn't stare.

He was likely to wear that and similar clothes on
their stakeout, although he'd need to keep at least his ID

with him to show he was a deputy if—and when—they found the rustlers. Probably his gun, too. She would stay as remote as appropriate from him mentally, even though they would be physically near each other.

The large room was filled with the aroma of what was being cooked next door in the kitchen. Melody suspected she hadn't met everyone who worked here even now, after six months. Did Clarence have a special cook? Or was the person who prepared their food the same housekeeper who served it?

The housekeeper—Grace—was also dressed casually, in a long-sleeved black OverHerd Ranch T-shirt and jeans. She acted utterly friendly as she provided them each with a salad, a side of cheesy potatoes and, of course, a delicious steak. What else, at an Angus cattle ranch?

Melody had never dined in the main house before, had hardly spent any time here. There was a small kitchen and dining area in the bunkhouse where she lived and had numerous meals with her fellow ranch hands. That had seemed quite adequate since she'd begun working here. Clarence had always seemed nice enough, but she'd never felt close to her boss— nor should she.

"So how long have you been with the Sur County Sheriff's Department?" Clarence had started to quiz Casey from the moment they'd sat down.

"Five years," he said. "It's a good place to work. The sheriff's good at what he does, and—"

"Yeah, I know that. I help him keep his job."

Melody felt herself blink, though not in surprise.

Was that true? Or was it only Clarence's ego speaking? He had a big one.

"That's nice of you." She could hear the irony in Casey's voice and decided to change the subject.

"Clarence," she began, "you know we're going to start out early tomorrow. If there's anything you especially want us to do to find the missing cattle, we'd love to hear your suggestions."

"You'll be using the GPS, I trust."

She nodded, aiming a brief glance toward Casey, who looked amused somehow. "Yes. I've got the app on my phone like all the ranch hands, though I didn't use it when Deputy Colton and I were out there by the damaged fence. We did see a lot of hoofprints that indicated the direction the cattle had gone, so that's where we'll start out tomorrow."

"How about you, Casey?" Clarence asked. "Do you have the app on your phone? I made sure signals are available way out in all my pastures so cell phones work out there."

"I don't have the app," he said. "But I'd be happy to download it before we go."

"Right," Clarence said.

When Melody again glanced toward Casey, the deputy was looking at her, his expressive blue eyes making it clear he wanted to get out of there.

"Are you about finished with dinner?" the deputy asked as he glanced down at her nearly empty plate.

"I certainly am," she replied. "Because we need to get up early—really early, since I'll want to have a little time to make sure the horse we choose for you is the right one. I think we should head…" She hesitated for a moment, because she'd been planning on saying "head to bed," but that could sound suggestive. "Head to our rooms in the bunkhouse right away."

"Then I'll say good-night now," Clarence said. "Thanks to both of you, and keep me informed of your progress tomorrow."

IT WAS SIX O'CLOCK in the morning. Casey had awakened a while ago, showered, dressed and taken the things he had brought for their camping-and-stakeout expedition out to the bunkhouse lobby.

When they had arrived there last night, Melody had shown him to a small apartment on the second floor and given him a key. She'd let him know that her room was on the same floor but down the hall. He had gone out to his car—his own SUV—to retrieve the items he planned to take along.

When he'd come back in, he'd seen a couple of the guys including Pierce, whom he'd met before, and another fellow named Roger. They'd confirmed that the additional ranch hands had remained camping out in the pastures with the other cattle. Both of them indicated they'd be out in the pastures today, too. But Pierce seemed a bit displeased, hinting at his own desire to get out there and find the missing cattle. Casey thanked him but said that wasn't a great idea—particularly since he, a deputy sheriff, would be out there working on the situation, with help from another ranch hand. Pierce had agreed that was the better scenario.

Maybe Pierce and Roger had already headed out this

morning, since neither appeared when Casey brought out his things and waited for Melody, who'd apparently already been there. His equipment, which he'd packed in the burlap bags some of the stuff had come in, wasn't the only camping gear in the lobby. There were a couple of substantial-sized saddle packs right by the front door that he assumed were Melody's.

But where was she? Should he text her? Call her? Maybe he should go to the kitchen to see what he could grab for breakfast, or maybe that's what she was doing. He'd be happy to see her again before they headed out.

He'd be happy to be with her then, too—which concerned him. He shouldn't have to remind himself to remain professional.

He started down the first-floor hallway in the direction he believed the kitchen was located and saw Melody emerge from a door at the end, her hands full.

"Good morning," she called, not muffling her voice at all. He figured no one else was there. She would be the one to know it.

She strode down the hallway and entered the lobby. Her black hair was once again pulled back into a ponytail, although she'd worn it somewhat looser last night at dinner. She again wore a blue denim work shirt and jeans, though her shirt this time was darker in color and unbuttoned partway down the front to show a navy T-shirt below.

She looked damn pretty in it, despite how casual this outfit was, too.

He suspected she would look damn pretty in any outfit. Or none at all…

He immediately tamped down that thought. *Be professional*, he again reminded himself.

"I've got some stuff here for us to eat," she told him as she reached him. "Croissants and jelly. We can go wolf it down now with some coffee, if you'd like, before we go visit the horses. But we'll need to be fast."

"Sounds good. Is it okay to leave this stuff here?" He pointed to the small pile he had placed on the floor.

"It's fine. We'll be back soon."

Which they were. Their breakfast, unaccompanied by other ranch hands, took only about ten minutes.

He considered the kinds of food they'd eat out on the trail and figured she must have some items in her saddlebags.

Him? He'd picked up some dried fruit and beef jerky and energy bars—nothing that would go bad, and it could all be carried fairly easily.

Who knew how long they would be out in the pastures hunting cattle and people?

When they were finished, Melody helped Casey to download the GPS app onto his phone. She then told him to follow her to the stable. She picked up her saddlebags before he could grab them and she didn't seem inclined to allow him to be a gentleman and carry them along with his own stuff. She tossed him a slightly irritated look, which told him that any old-fashioned etiquette wouldn't be welcome around her.

He hid his smile. He liked that about her.

He was liking too many things about her.

For now, he closed the bunkhouse door behind him

and followed her along the paved pathway across this part of the ranch behind the main house.

Melody opened the stable door fairly easily, it appeared, despite how full her arms were. Once inside, she placed her saddlebags down on the hay-covered ground and closed the door again behind Casey.

There were seven horses in separate stalls, though a few stalls were empty and he figured that was because of the ranch hands who had ridden off to the pastures to protect the remaining cattle.

"We need to do this scientifically," Melody said, standing beside him. There was a humorous catch to her voice. "Let's start with this. Have you ever ridden a horse before?"

"Well, yes, sort of." Smiling wryly down at her, he described the few times he had ridden at commercial riding areas in parks, and at family friends' farms as a child, along with his brother, and also occasionally at county fairs and the like. "No real riding on trails out in the countryside, though."

"Got it. And I also know who's best for you. Witchy's the horse here who's the least challenge to newbie riders." She led him over to a red-and-white horse a few stalls down.

"Really? A horse named Witchy is fairly tame?"

"Yes. We'll try her. Me, I'll take my favorite—Cal." She looked back toward Casey and grinned at him in a way that made him anticipate what she'd say next. "That's short for Calamity."

Casey couldn't help it. He laughed. "Sounds like we're headed for some wild riding. Witchy and Calamity."

"You got it," Melody said. "Now, let me get them saddled up and we'll try them out in the paddock outside. I'll also show you a bit of grooming and other things you'll need to know when we're out on the trail. Still, if all goes as I anticipate, we should be good to start our expedition in twenty minutes."

"YOU'RE DOING GREAT!" Melody called to Casey a few minutes later, meaning it.

She was seated on top of Cal, a sleek brown quarter horse and her favorite mount, while watching Casey trot around the perimeter of the corral on top of Witchy, a gentle and friendly pinto. The deputy sat tall in the saddle and appeared perfectly at home as he gently pulled the reins now and then to get Witchy to turn around and head in the other direction.

He'd seemed to have gotten the hang of it from the moment he had put his left foot into the stirrup and lifted himself into the saddle. Witchy's head had turned just a bit to see who her rider would be. The mare seemed fine with it, and Melody had only given Casey a few cues about how to remain seated comfortably and maneuver the reins to direct the mare.

She also told Casey how to gently squeeze with his heels to tell Witchy to speed up, and showed him how to click a bit with his tongue if he wanted her to go even faster.

As always, Melody appreciated being outdoors, listening to the clomping of hoofbeats at different speeds on the hard corral turf. She smiled, closing her eyes for a moment as she lifted her chin toward the sky. She felt alive here, and free.

This part, at least, was fun. And when she opened her eyes she saw that Casey had slowed Witchy down and was staring at her…and smiling, too. She looked down and shook her head, and directed Cal, with her heels, to start walking.

After a short while, Melody asked Cal to begin trotting as she directed him to get in front of Witchy. Then she urged him even further, and Cal began galloping around the corral, his mane blowing as he moved.

Melody glanced behind her. Yes, Witchy and Casey were keeping up. Not surprising, but it confirmed what she was thinking: it was time for them to head off to that critical pasture.

Chapter Five

They had almost returned to the site of the mutilated fence. It had taken much less time today, thanks to the horses and their speedier gaits.

Casey was happy to be on horseback. He liked Witchy and felt he was doing an okay job playing cowboy, as he rode this calm, obedient and enjoyable steed along the uneven, mostly grassy terrain.

Even more, he was enjoying watching his companion on this ride, Melody, on her somewhat more energetic equine, Cal.

She seemed more at home here, somehow, intensely watching their surroundings and handling her reins, gently guiding her mount in the direction she wanted. She wore a cap now, a blue denim one that matched her shirt, a lighter color than her jeans. He, too, wore a cap, with his sheriff's department logo on it—the only current indication of his status as a deputy. But he needed the shading of his face from the sun, which was bound to become even more intense as the day grew later.

It was still early in the morning, around nine, and the air was clear and a bit cool for Arizona, not surprising in

November. An airplane flew high overhead in the blue sky, and Casey wondered for a moment which airport it had come from and where it was going. It appeared to be flying north, so maybe it had just taken off from Tucson International.

Reflexively, as he'd done often during this ride, he glanced behind himself at one of the two very large, but not particularly heavy, saddlebags Melody and he had filled. The other was attached to her saddle, similarly behind her. With her instruction, they'd fastened them on their mounts before leaving the stable. His contained a small tent in case they had to sleep outside for a night or two, which wasn't beyond the realm of possibility. Each of them also contained lightweight, closely folded sleeping bags.

The most bulky and necessary items they'd included were water bottles, although Melody had assured him that she knew where some creeks—perhaps including the one the town of Cactus Creek had been named for—were located. They could utilize these creeks for water, which they could purify with her portable water filter. That way, they should be able to keep their own water bottles filled, as well as making sure the horses had drinkable water.

And possibly the most important thing? His duty belt was hidden inside that saddlebag. It contained items he hoped he wouldn't need, but would be crucial if he did, including his gun. He'd also stuck his wallet and badge inside in case he needed money or to identify himself, though he kept his phone in his pocket since he figured he might need it quicker than the rest.

He'd fortunately had time to take that charm Melody had found to the sheriff's department to examine it and determine its likely source, as well as check it for fingerprints. They'd be passing the area where she found it soon, which he thought about now. If it turned out that the charm belonged to one of the perpetrators, it might be useful as evidence, but that remained to be determined.

And something about the charm was still tugging at his mind, though he remained unsure why.

"How are you doing?" Melody's voice came from beside him. She looked great on that horse, sitting tall, the reins held in her right hand, her jeans-clad legs hugging Cal's sides and her black boots in the stirrups. Her ponytail waved beneath her cap in the breeze as they moved forward.

Of course, Casey recognized that she looked great when not on horseback, too.

And despite knowing full well and even vocalizing that they were both there on business and would remain professional, he knew he'd have to be careful if they spent nights out here together to keep it that way.

"I'm fine," he said. "Wish I'd learned to ride a horse this way before."

"So you're having fun." Her words were a statement, and her smile was one of the biggest Casey had ever seen.

One of the prettiest, too.

Okay, he told himself sternly. *You like this woman. You like her appearance—and more. But keep it all to yourself.*

"Yeah," he responded. "Definitely fun."

"So here we are," Melody said as they arrived at the fence. "Our starting point, sort of. We'll head in the direction those hoofprints lead us."

"Let's check the GPS app."

Just before they'd headed out to the pasture, she had helped Casey download the GPS app, then shown him what the GPS portion of the tags attached to the cattle had looked like on her phone's map—a group of small, overlaid dots in one location. But without streets or even an indication as to what part of the open land the dots were located in, other than a rough idea of the terrain if the right part of the app was on, it didn't seem to Casey as if the GPS would be of much help except maybe to provide a general direction. But as with a lot around here, Melody was much more experienced and skilled in such things than he. He'd looked on his own phone and found the map, too.

"Good idea," she responded. "Let's do it before we head any further."

She'd apparently put her phone in her pocket, too, and pulled it out now. As she did, something else fell from her pocket—her wallet.

"Damn." She started to dismount.

"Here, let me," Casey said. "I'll pick it up while you check the GPS."

"Thanks." She nodded at him. "That'll save us a small bit of time. I assume you're skilled enough now to get on and off Witchy without my guidance."

"I assume so, too." He pulled his right foot from the stirrup, then lifted his right leg to move it around to the same side of the horse as his left one. Mounting and dismounting hadn't been that hard to start with, but he did feel as if the little bit of practice he'd been getting made him somewhat of a pro, like Melody.

Her wallet was in some grass just off to Cal's right side, and Melody's horse stomped a little as if he was uneasy to have Casey walking around. "It's okay." Casey stroked the brown quarter horse's side in front of Melody's leg, enjoying the feel of the soft coat. Cal seemed to quiet down immediately, and Casey bent to pick up the beige leather case.

As he did so, he noticed that the strap that normally held the two sides together was unsnapped, and before he could get it back together he saw Melody's driver's license inside. He barely glanced at it at first, but did a double take when he saw that it was a Texas license— the address wasn't in Cactus Creek, it was in Dallas. Understandable. Though she'd been here for six months, she must not have gotten herself a new one yet since moving here for this job.

But the more startling thing was…well, did this belong to this Melody'? The picture was hers, and so was the first name, but the last name wasn't Hayworth, it was Ellison. Was she married? Using an alias for some reason? What was going on?

And how was he going to ask her?

He wouldn't. Not now. Whoever she was, and whatever her name, she clearly worked for OverHerd Ranch. The name situation was personal, since he'd no reason to suspect her of any crime—

None of his business, despite his curiosity.

"Here we are," he said brightly, holding out the now-fastened wallet to her.

"Thanks," she said. "And better get back up on Witchy. We're going to have a long day still, out here following the missing herd."

"Why? Are they on the move?"

"Looks that way," Melody affirmed. "And they're heading even farther from this area. The ranch is five hundred acres, a lot of it in that direction." She waved in front of them as he mounted Witchy once more. "But my suspicion is that those missing cattle are beyond that far end already or will get there soon."

MELODY FOUND HERSELF looking away immediately as Casey handed back her wallet. Had he opened it? Was he that nosy?

Of course, it could have opened by itself when it fell from her pocket.

Maybe she should have shoved it into her saddlebag back at the stable, but she liked having a couple of things on her—her phone and her wallet.

She hadn't noticed whether he'd snooped into it or not, of course. She'd been studying the GPS map on her phone app, as much as she could, at least. The map sort of indicated major differences in the terrain such as deep ravines, moderate hills and high mountains, but not minor things like the usual rolling hillsides, waterways like streams, or any landmarks, although she wasn't aware of any out here. But it did provide the general direction of where the cattle were heading, and the distance of maybe fifteen or more miles from her current location with Casey.

Now she knew the cattle were farther away than they'd been, as well as the direction they'd gone, but whether Casey and she could follow directly would depend on that unfamiliar terrain. And if she was correct in her interpretation, they'd at least come to steep hills on the way that they'd navigate.

Melody now felt certain they would be spending at least this night out in a pasture on the way to catching up with the missing herd. She'd ridden out this way several times before since beginning work here, just to get the lay of the land, with one or more of the other hands with her. But she was far from knowledgeable with regard to the actual topography.

"I'm not really sure how difficult our route will be," she told Casey when he was back in the saddle and they were moving again. "Although the direction we're taking still looks right."

"Guess we'll just have to figure the rest out as it comes." His tone was somewhat curt, and she wondered why.

If he had been nosy enough to look in her wallet, he might have questions he wasn't asking aloud. Just as well. Since she had just finalized her divorce six months ago, her old Texas license still had her married name—Ellison. Thanks to the nasty, cheating jerk she'd been married to.

Which was dumb on her part, in many ways. She never should have married him in the first place. And once she had, she should have ended it faster. She'd had a sense sometimes that Travis was cheating on her, and it had hurt.

Well, at least being called a "country girl" had helped her make that final decision, and now she appreciated that, as a ranch hand here, she really was a country girl.

But one of the first things she should have done upon moving to Arizona was to at least get a new driver's license, so she'd never have to look at that old, unwanted name again.

At least Clarence had accepted her official divorce documents and hired her under her real name, which she'd returned to using, Melody Hayworth.

But she'd become so involved in her new job, so busy...well, that was her excuse, anyway.

And now, with this reminder, true or not, she knew she would do something about it soon.

Should she bring up the subject, explain it now to Casey?

No. If he'd been snooping, that was his problem. And she hadn't talked about her prior life much since she'd moved here, didn't necessarily want to do so now. Wanted to keep that difficult time behind her. She had definitely moved on.

If Casey asked about it, she'd answer. But right now, he just seemed to be quiet and didn't interrogate her as a sheriff's deputy might.

Not that her prior ID should have made him suspicious of anything. She was a good, law-abiding citizen who was now trying to find whoever had stolen her employer's valuable cattle, get those cattle back to the ranch where she worked and then go about her usual life once more. She hadn't been involved in the theft, and to her knowledge no one had even considered the remote possibility that she was.

Except, perhaps, for Casey. He was a law-enforcement officer and he might have seen something that didn't quite fit with what he'd previously been told.

Whether or not that was the case, it now felt uncomfortable just riding beside Casey so quietly. They'd at least chatted before about the pasture and where the other cattle were currently ranging and what it was like to work on a ranch.

Working on a ranch. She had an idea how to start a potentially lighthearted conversation.

"Okay." She glanced over at Casey. His handsome face, which looked as if it had been chiseled from stone, was expressionless as he stared forward. Then he turned his head to look at her.

"'Okay' what?" he asked, still straight-faced.

"I like how you're now doing on horseback out here. Let's see how you do when we find the cattle. Of course, you're the law-enforcement guy and I know you'll need to take the thieves into custody."

"I intend to," he said, remaining solemn. "If there are a lot of them, I'll call for backup, assuming I get phone service out here as Clarence said we would, and if not we'll just follow carefully behind them until I can get a team to join us and arrest them."

"Right. But meantime, I'm now considering that you should have an alternate career. You're doing great riding. I'll have to see how you do with the cattle when we find them, but you look good up there, sitting on the horse and scouring the pasture with your gaze. I think you should consider becoming a ranch hand. Maybe even a cowboy yourself someday."

He pulled slightly on Witchy's reins, stopping her.

"You're kidding." He stared at Melody, and she stopped Cal. Casey's brown eyebrows arched even higher over his attractive blue eyes, a quizzical expression on his face—a good change from before, when he had no expression at all.

"Could be." She grinned widely at him. Then she attempted to grow more serious. "But what do you think of being here on the ranch? I mean, if you weren't trying to find stolen cattle, would you like riding here? Not just riding a horse, but riding one in this kind of environment? You don't necessarily have to herd cattle to be here, either."

"So you think I should become a ranch hand? You don't think I'm a good sheriff's deputy?"

She laughed and gently kicked Cal to get him moving again. Casey also gave Witchy a slight nudge so she started walking again, too.

Melody then looked at Casey. "I'm still sizing you up, Deputy. As far as I know, you're good at what you do. I think you'd be good at this, too. Could be that you can handle anything that life throws your way, right?"

"That's what I believe. In fact, I'm sure of it, but—"

"Great. I wanted to be sure that the man accompanying me on this potentially dangerous outing is smart and brave enough to handle it."

"I assumed you already thought so or we wouldn't be out here like this."

"As I said, I wanted to be sure." With that, she again gently kicked her horse and Cal's speed increased.

So did Witchy's, beside them.

Oh, yes, she'd already accepted that Casey was one good deputy, or his boss wouldn't have allowed him to be the one to take on this chase out here in the kind-of wilderness. To be the one to find the bad guys in this situation and either take them down himself—with her limited help—or get some colleagues to sneak in wherever they happened to be and help him out.

But all she'd wanted to do now was get them talking again. In a friendly manner.

Maybe also get him to reveal what was on his mind, although she believed she knew that part.

Why not just ask him? She might, if he continued to remain less friendly than he'd been before. It didn't make sense to be out here with someone who perhaps had some suspicions or concerns about her and didn't reveal them.

And…well, heck. She didn't really know much about him, either. Only that he was an officer of the law who'd been given this difficult assignment, including working with an unknown: her. She'd liked him before, and he'd seemed to like her.

And now? Well, who knew? But did she want to spend more time with this man out here without them getting along well?

Should she attempt to fix it by telling him all about her prior life?

Maybe so. But she wouldn't unless he asked.

Though she could find out more about him by asking some questions of her own—eventually.

But not now. Not until she could think this through.

WHAT HAD THAT been all about? Casey wondered. Although he thought he might know.

She might have seen him peek into her wallet after all, even though she appeared to be engrossed in checking out the cattle GPS.

But why hadn't she just asked him?

Or should he have been the one to bring it up first?

Maybe so. And maybe he would bring it up sometime. For now, though…

Their horses were walking fairly fast, but the ground below them had started to become rougher, and he felt it in the way the saddle bumped his butt harder now as his horse's hooves hit the uneven surface. He pulled slightly on Witchy's reins. "Slow down, girl," he said, then looked ahead as Melody, on Cal, passed them. "Yeah, you, too," he called to his favorite—and somewhat difficult, at least right now—ranch hand. "Slow down." *And you, too. Call "whoa" on your attraction to Melody.*

Chapter Six

The warming Arizona day seemed to progress quickly as they continued to track the cattle.

They remained on horseback and though they were still in grassy pastures, they headed in the direction of some canyon areas filled with bushes and trees, which Melody considered a good thing. If they found the right spot, there might be some cover for where they'd ultimately sleep that night. And if she remembered correctly, there was also a small stream in that area, where they and the horses could get more to drink than they'd found earlier today, once it was filtered. Plus, she and Casey could also wash themselves.

They'd already come across other spots today where the terrain was irregular or the plant life was more vibrant—a good thing for when they needed breaks way out here in the middle of nowhere.

Melody had enjoyed the conversations they'd been holding; at her urging, they discussed things in their lives—some of the time, at least—that had brought them to where they were today.

"Do you like to see wildlife in the outdoors?" was one of the questions Melody asked Casey.

"I'm always after people who live a wild life," he said, making her laugh. "But if you mean do I like to see birds and animals and all out here, the answer is yes."

"Me, too," Melody told him, and they talked a while about visiting areas like this and various sanctuaries and zoos in their childhoods.

And Casey's enjoyment of animals upped him even farther in Melody's already climbing opinion of him.

Melody didn't bring up her divorce. She didn't even want to think about it.

Mostly, she peppered Casey with additional questions. Somewhat to her surprise, he didn't want to talk much about anything personal, either. His attitude might be forthcoming and professional, but he seemed almost shy as he responded in few words at first to her repeated questions about why he'd become a peace officer. Because he wanted to. Because it was a childhood dream. She considered that sweet. In fact, she was finding him *much* too sweet and appealing.

But that didn't keep her from pushing for more detailed answers when he attempted to change the subject. Besides, she was curious.

"Okay," he finally said. "It's no big deal, but if you really want to know…"

"I do."

"I grew up here in Cactus Creek," he told her, somewhat softly. He didn't meet her eyes as he spoke, and instead looked into the distance, as if viewing the area he spoke of. Maybe he was, in his head. "It's a great town, but like everywhere else there are good people and bad people. And I wanted to be out there helping to bring justice to my town. I got a degree in criminal justice from Arizona State and visited home as often as I could during the school years. I returned here full-time as quickly as I could and was hired as a deputy sheriff right away."

She had no doubt that he'd done well in school. He seemed highly intelligent as well as dedicated.

He was the right deputy to be out here with her on this assignment.

And he'd mentioned his twin brother. "Everett wanted to get into law enforcement, too, and he did, though a different way. He's with the FBI in Phoenix."

Was Casey close with his brother and the rest of his family? It certainly sounded that way as they talked. His parents lived in Cactus Creek, too, and it sounded as if Casey saw a lot of them. In fact, he was planning on spending the upcoming holidays with his family, and he said, "They're always happy to have guests join us at Christmas. Why don't you come, too?"

The idea had surprised, even shocked her. And made her feel all fuzzy inside.

For a minute. But then she began to have qualms. "That's so nice of you. And your family. But…well, I might have other plans. Is it okay if I let you know?"

Any other plans would be simply to find a way to back out of this.

"Sure. Just give us a few days' notice if you're coming, and I'll let my folks know I invited you. I'll check with you again when the time gets closer."

"Sounds good," she said, feeling a bit relieved. He didn't sound upset or hurt. In fact, the invitation might just be a kindness to a near stranger, not because they were becoming friends.

He then turned around the conversation, pushing her to explain why she became a ranch hand.

"I come from Texas," she reminded him, as if that explained everything. And, in fact, it kind of did.

"I can tell," he said drily, which startled her. She glanced at him. She appreciated the Southern way of speaking, but her usual speech didn't include an accent. "Gotcha," said Casey as she looked at him quizzically. "Actually, I'm sort of surprised that you don't have more of a drawl. You sure you come from Texas?"

"Of course." She'd actually been born in New York State, but her parents had moved to Texas shortly thereafter. She'd learned to talk the way they did first and generally kept that up in her speech.

But just because her accent wasn't particularly Texan, that didn't mean the rest of her wasn't. She'd come to love ranching at a very early age, partly because her dad had become a ranch hand after they'd moved. Even when she was a child, she had loved accompanying him on horseback into the fields and pastures. He had taught her a lot.

Including how to love what he did for a living— enough that it was also what she decided to do.

Even these days, there weren't as many women who were ranch hands. But the owners of the place where her dad worked seemed to appreciate her take on watching and caring for their livestock, which also included mostly cattle and horses.

She told Casey all of this as they were riding, but not how she'd fallen for and become engaged to her high-school sweetheart, who'd convinced her to quit her job on the ranch outside Fort Worth and find another position in Dallas.

Then dumped her—and that hurt enough that she'd decided to leave the entire state of Texas, yet keep the career that she loved.

As much as their discussion reminded Melody of some of the bad things in her life, she realized she enjoyed talking to Casey about the good things from her past, especially because he seemed to enjoy hearing about them. Opening up to him about herself that way felt surprisingly wonderful.

She checked the GPS app on her phone now and then. Initially, the cattle kept moving but eventually stopped.

Of course, sunset was nearly upon this area. It didn't make sense for the rustlers to continue going forward in the dark. They apparently knew it and were likely settling down for the night.

And although Casey and she continued for a while, it certainly wouldn't make sense for them to go on with no daylight at all.

So, as sunset grew closer, Melody had Casey join her while she investigated some of the land around them in search of shelter. There were, as she'd hoped, areas of greater vegetation.

And as darkness began settling around them, they settled down, too, in a spot both of them agreed would be a good one for the night, with a small stream nearby where they could collect water and use the filter on it.

There were even some pecan trees for cover for them and the horses—not that any rain was expected anytime soon, but there was less likelihood of being seen here, should any of the rustlers be snooping around to determine if they were being followed, than if they and their horses were on fully open ground.

Plus, they could tie the horses to a couple of the more barren bushes.

And camping out with Casey overnight? Melody wasn't sure how she should feel about that. The warmth at the idea that flooded her was highly inappropriate, but since nothing would happen anyway, she would just allow herself to enjoy it.

"How about you?" Melody asked Cal as she dismounted. "Are you ready to stop for the day?"

As if the horse understood, he made a snorting sound, looked down to the ground and nodded his head.

Melody had to laugh, and she heard Casey's deep laughter, too. "Let's see if Witchy feels the same way." Casey also dismounted, and though Witchy didn't express how she felt, the mare didn't appear to want to continue on.

"Good. Let's assume this is our lodging for the night, shall we?" Not waiting for an answer from anyone, human or horse, Melody began to unhook the saddlebag from Cal's back. Casey came over to help, and they placed it on the ground that was covered with dry leaves. They did the same with Witchy's saddlebag.

Then, also together, they removed each horse's saddle so they'd be more comfortable for the night.

Next, each walked their mount in a small circle, talking to them softly, just to settle them down. They removed the bits from the horses' mouths, though they left their headstalls on.

They soon collected water from a nearby creek, filtered it and carried it in metal containers to the horses.

Then, after returning to the spot where their saddlebags were, it was time to tie the horses' reins to the nearby bushes for the night.

Unlike the humans, the horses didn't have to wait for dinner. During the journey here, they'd been eating some of the grass in the pasture, which, of course, was of high quality. Melody liked the way her boss treated his livestock—and now she was happy there was good food out here for the horses, too.

Even so, as a healthy supplement, Melody also gave them some of the hay and grain she carried in the saddlebags.

And in actuality, the humans didn't have to wait for their dinner, either. This wasn't like a real camping trip, where they would light a fire and cook meats or anything else they had brought along. No, the dried jerky and fruits, as well as carrots and celery they had stuck in their saddlebags would have to do.

First, though, while there was still a small bit of fading daylight, they worked quickly together to raise the small tent. Melody was well aware that they hadn't had room to bring two. But, heck, they both were professional.

Although staying so close to Casey overnight…

She'd deal with it.

"You doing okay?" Casey asked her as she helped to stretch out the canvas and attach it to the small poles.

"Just fine," she said sweetly. "And you?" Surely he didn't think of her as some wimp—not out here. Not when she was the skilled ranch hand, not him.

"Absolutely." And he was the one to finish the unrolling and attaching. That was fine. She was using his masculine skills, that was all. And admiring them...

After they put the saddlebags inside and unrolled their sleeping bags, it was time to head down to the nearby creek again. Melody made certain to bring along some of the paper towels and sanitizer liquid she had packed so they could achieve some semblance of bathing without leaving chemicals in the water. Neither undressed completely, but they did unbutton shirts and pull up T-shirts and unfasten slacks, leaving underwear intact and also doing their ablutions with their backs to one another.

There. That wasn't too uncomfortable. At least Melody didn't think so.

And she avoided turning to peek at Casey's muscular physique while it was somewhat bared.

Or at least she didn't peek *much*. But she did manage to maneuver her own cleansing so she had to turn just a little here and there. And, heavens, this deputy sheriff really was one highly fit, highly toned—and extremely sexy—dude.

Was he doing the same with her? She managed not to look at his face.

If he was, she didn't want to know. Especially if he found her even a fraction as attractive as she found him.

Not when they were about to spend the night in such close quarters.

She was done with men, at least for now. She was still hurting some, even though her divorce had been six months ago. She no longer trusted most men. And she didn't have any interest in just having sex with one for fun.

Well, not much interest…and that was the problem.

Finally, both of them were done washing. Melody collected the few paper towels they'd used, then they walked back up the small slope together to the tent. There, they each said good-night to their horses. Casey opened the flap and Melody slipped inside first. Casey turned on the two small battery-operated lanterns so they wouldn't be totally in the dark.

"You ready to get your phone charged?" he asked after he pulled another battery-operated gadget from his backpack—yes, a phone charger.

"Sounds good, but I need to let people at the ranch know my progress first." Fortunately, the phone worked as she knelt by the edge of the tent. There was, in fact, service out here, at least for now. Unfortunately, when she tried Clarence's personal line he didn't answer, so she left a message that Casey and she had made some progress but hadn't caught up with the herd.

She called the general line for the ranch hands next, hoping she'd get one of the senior hands, preferably Pierce, but instead one of her fellow newbies, Roger, was the one to answer. She gave him the same info as in the message to Clarence.

"Are most of the hands still out with the safe parts of the herd?" Melody asked.

"Yeah. I'm pretty much the only one around here tonight," Roger replied.

"So Pierce is out in the pastures, too?" Melody wondered which direction he'd gone, and which of the cattle he was helping to protect.

"Yeah. Don't know exactly where, though."

"Okay. Well, I'll keep in touch as much as I can." Not with Roger, though, unless he was the only one she could reach. And this way at least one person would be aware that she was still available by phone.

As she ended her call, she noticed that Casey was on his phone as well. He soon ended his call, too. "Just giving a status update to the sheriff, like you did with the ranch," he said. He'd obviously been eavesdropping, but that was fine. "So now is it okay to charge your phone?"

"One more thing," she said. "Let me check my GPS again first."

No difference in where the cattle appeared to be, judging by the multiple dots all in the same area as before. And they must have been on the move about the same speed during the day, since Casey and she didn't seem to be any closer.

As Casey connected their phones, Melody removed several of their meal items and two bottles of filtered water from their saddlebags, slipped his share to Casey, then sat down on top of her sleeping bag.

The ground felt solid beneath her butt, and she folded

her legs to become as comfortable as she could. She noticed that Casey took a similar position.

Ah. Something else they had in common—among the few things she'd noticed, like attempting to save and return rustled cattle. And enjoying riding horses out in the wilderness while talking sometimes and staying quiet other times… Okay, maybe she was stretching things, since nothing she'd thought of was unusual. She didn't want to think about what else they might have in common—and hoped she wouldn't have to worry about finding out more that night when they attempted to go to sleep, *attempted* being the operative word.

But, no. She would go to sleep, or at least pretend to, without thinking—much—about the person across the tent from her.

For a while, neither of them spoke as they ate, though they did manage to glance at each other and smile a bit.

But Melody felt uncomfortable, knowing that their pseudo-meal wouldn't last long and they'd soon wind up just sitting there, or lying in their sleeping bags.

Would they talk? Stay silent? That remained to be seen. But talking would be okay, as long as it didn't lead to anything else.

"I like these fruit bars," Casey finally said, waving one of the items Melody had brought in the air. "I've had a lot of other kinds, of course, but there's something special about these."

"I like them, too," Melody said. "That's why I keep a supply at home and chose to bring them along on this trek." She went on to describe how she had found them online when searching for healthy and wholesome snacks. Good. This was a nice, safe subject for them to discuss.

They also talked about the pros and cons of bringing water with them. "Sure, there are quite a few creeks around," Casey said, "so I really like your portable filter. We don't have to carry many bottles this way. Once it's filtered, the water is clean enough to drink—but I don't particularly want to think about what else was in it before, what fish or bugs or whatever live there, what dirt it flows through or bacteria grows in it or—"

"Ah, but you definitely are thinking about it," Melody said with a laugh. This conversation didn't mean anything, but she felt happy they were talking, even if it was about nothing.

Although, seeing him in the shadows across the tent from her—even though he was currently fully dressed, as was she—she couldn't help thinking about how they'd been a while ago in that potentially nasty water that was okay to bathe in but not to drink without filtering.

Damn, but Casey had looked good only partially dressed.

"What about when you were a kid?" Melody asked, to change the subject within her thoughts. "Did you ever go camping then? Drink the water?"

In the shadows, she saw him nod. "I did attend camps for a couple of weeks each summer when I was a kid. Even then, fifteen years ago or so, they were talking about some of the not-so-pleasant stuff that could be in the ponds or lakes or rivers we were near. In most cases, the camp counselors showed us how to boil what we'd drink."

Fifteen years ago, he'd been a kid going camping? Melody had figured he was in his late twenties, early thirties, so that worked.

But she... Well, for her to even think of dashing across the room and pulling off the guy's clothes—which, yes, the thought had crossed her mind—turned her into a cougar. Which would be fine with her. In fact, she rather liked the idea. But him?

Had he guessed their probable age difference? If he happened to feel any attraction to her, her being upfront about it could end any such thoughts on his part, depending on how he thought about such things.

But maybe it would be a good idea to mention it, partly to make sure any unwelcome thoughts on his part never fully materialized—and partly to make sure she wanted nothing to do with him, assuming he made it clear he had no interest in an older woman.

Although if age didn't matter... Or he did like older women...?

Well, it wouldn't hurt to find out. "I went camping a couple of times when I was a teenager, which was more than twenty years ago, not fifteen," she said. "When, I gather, you were just a little kid too young to go to summer camps."

She watched his body stiffen just a bit in the scant light—or was she just imagining it?

"Interesting," he said. "How old are you? Me, I'm thirty."

Thirty. A ten-year age gap.

That could make a big difference as to whether they were attracted to one another.

Or at least whether he felt attracted to her, since his age was irrelevant to her.

"Oh, you're just a kid," she said with a hollow laugh. "I'm forty."

"Really?" He did sound surprised, which gave her an unwanted sense of pleasure. So did his following words. "You look so good and seem so physically fit—I thought you might be a little older than me, but not that much."

"Well, thanks," she said. "And now this old lady's going to lie down and, even though it's not especially late, try to fall asleep so I can wake up early in the morning and get on the trail again."

"Good idea," Casey said. "I'll do the same thing. Only—"

Before she could think about what he was up to, Casey had crawled the short distance between their sleeping bags and was suddenly right in front of her, on his knees.

He bent toward her, reached out and touched her arm, drawing her closer, then placed his hand behind her head. In moments, his mouth was on hers.

His kiss was hot, intense, amazing—and very short. His lips explored hers, and he thrust his tongue into her mouth just a bit, only a hint of what other parts of them could do together...

It felt incredible, and it enticed her body to want a lot more.

He pulled away, though, looked down at her and grinned. "Hey, you kiss pretty well. Now with a bedtime kiss like that, I think I'll be able to sleep well. Good night, sweet senior citizen." He laughed, and in moments he was lying inside his sleeping bag with his back toward her.

Chapter Seven

Now why had he done that? Because the lovely Melody, whatever her age, had appeared sad and somehow vulnerable, as if she expected him to say he'd never be attracted to someone that much older than him?

Or had he just been acting on that very unwanted attraction on his part? For, yes, she was clearly fit and smart and skilled at what she did, no matter how much older than him she was.

And after that kiss, despite its brevity and his attempt to be humorous, he knew he wanted her. Only for a night, or perhaps for several nights. He didn't want any relationship, though, especially not now. Not ever. It had nothing to do with their age difference and everything to do with the fact he'd been dumped by someone he'd thought he cared about and he never wanted to deal with anything like that again.

Dear Georgia. Leaving him at the altar like that, shattering his expectations for the future. Damn, but it had hurt.

Still, sex now with Melody? Oh, yes.

Not now, though. Not under these circumstances.

Now, he just lay there in the faint light of the lanterns, feeling the hardness of the ground beneath his sleeping bag digging into his shoulder and the rest of him, warmed maybe too much by the bag's enveloping cover…and the lust he was tamping down. Fast.

He listened to the silence across the tent from him.

He also listened for any sounds outside. He wasn't certain but thought he might have heard some clomps of hooves, just stomping down but not disappearing into the distance.

A snort, perhaps, also from a horse?

Nothing at all from Melody. What was she thinking? She surely couldn't have fallen asleep that fast.

Especially considering that kiss.

That kiss. Again, why had he done it?

And why had it seemed so appropriate, despite their being mere colleagues now, most likely for a while?

Yet, who was she really? He recalled again the name on her driver's license that he'd seen: Ellison, and not Hayworth. What did that mean? He was the one in law enforcement, and if he'd been in town he'd have attempted to check it out. Was she using an alias on this job? If so, why?

Or was she simply married without telling anyone about it?

And why did it make a difference to him?

But out here, Melody and he were the only humans in sight, for now just seeking stolen cattle. They might need to work even more closely together to get the cattle back and take down the thieves on their own, if there was insufficient time to bring in backup. He had to rely on her. On her integrity. And did an inconsistency in her name mean there were other inconsistencies in her life that he should be concerned about?

Or—

Well, despite the brevity of their acquaintanceship, the fact they were working together and the inappropriateness of any feeling for her other than as colleagues, he'd come to like the woman, in addition to wanting her.

She seemed nice. She liked animals. She had a job she liked and was dedicated to it and her employer.

Enough of this. He was overthinking the entire situation.

It was time to go to sleep. After all, they needed to awaken at dawn to continue their mission.

Sleep, he commanded himself.

And eventually, maybe an hour later, his body complied.

MELODY WOKE UP EARLY, as she'd intended, the next morning.

Or maybe she hadn't slept at all. She thought she'd dropped off now and then but couldn't be certain. She hoped so, though. She needed to be wide-awake to continue their journey to find the missing cattle.

And falling asleep in the saddle was simply not an option.

She lay there for a short while, listening. Yes, she believed the soft, regular sound she was hearing was Casey's deep breathing, while he was still asleep. He wasn't snoring, though. That was a good thing.

She thought again, for maybe the millionth time,

about his kiss last night. He'd been joking, right? Only it had turned her on even more than her attraction to him that she'd been fighting somewhat successfully— *somewhat* being the operative word.

And now?

Now she simply couldn't, wouldn't, let it happen again—no matter how much she yearned to be the one to start the next kiss…

Enough of this. It was time to get up. Get going.

For now, though, she remained as quiet as she could, as she unwrapped herself from her sleeping bag, slipped her shoes back on and glided out of the tent.

And stopped. It was gorgeous out here! She'd seen lovely Arizona sunrises before from around the ranch house, but this was spectacular. The sky was multiple shades of bright orange, a beautiful coverlet that lit up everywhere, showing the distant hillsides and mountains in silhouette. Some clouds in the sky gleamed white, streaking through the vivid color.

It was startling. Stunning. Incredible.

Okay, she had to share this. She hurried back inside and found Casey sitting up in his sleeping bag.

"You've got to come and see this!" she exclaimed.

Before she could explain what *this* was, he was on his feet. He was still dressed in the clothes he'd been wearing yesterday, as was she. This wasn't a place to stick on, or even carry, PJs. "Are the rustlers out there? Should I grab my gun?"

She laughed, but what did she expect from a deputy sheriff on the job?

"No, I want you to come see something good that has nothing to do with our cattle quest."

He looked puzzled. "What—?"

"Get your shoes on and I'll show you."

Like her, that was one thing he hadn't had on when ensconced in the sleeping bag. His boots, the same as he'd worn while in uniform, were beside him, and he immediately pulled them on.

Melody didn't wait any longer. She pushed open the tent flap once more, stooped down and straightened when she got outside.

It hadn't changed. That beautiful sunrise was still there. If anything it was even more breathtaking since the few white clouds interrupting the color had disappeared. The orange gleamed brighter, but Melody knew that it all could disappear fast as the sun rose even more.

"Wow," Casey said, stopping short. "I've seen great sunrises before, even out in open areas like this, but I've never seen any as amazing as this one." His tone sounded awed, even reverent, and Melody was surprised—no, shocked—when suddenly he reached out beside him and grabbed her hand.

His was somewhat cool and definitely strong as he tightened his grip—not too tightly, but she had no doubt that he was there and hanging on, sharing with her, united in this special moment.

And her? She tightened her own hold as well. They were sharing a lot of experiences these days, and this one was definitely the most spectacular so far.

She found herself taking a step sideways, closer to him. Feeling his arm, in its long-sleeved blue T-shirt, against her own arm. Without thinking about it—much—she leaned her head against his arm as she continued to observe the universe around them, still holding Casey's hand for another minute. Longer.

Off to the side, she heard a couple of equine snorts, and that brought her back to her senses. So did the fact that the incredible orange of the sky had started to fade just a bit in some places to a softer peach.

"Wow," she echoed. "But I think it's time for us to start getting ready to go again."

"Yeah, you're right." He let go of her hand, and she looked up, smiling at him—and his eyes caught hers. He stared down at her, and she felt her face nearly freeze, then melt as his mouth moved downward and met hers.

This kiss was softer, more tender, than the one they'd shared before, but it still got to her. She reveled in the feel of his growing facial hair. She wrapped her arms around his neck and pressed herself against him there.

And felt regret when they both pulled away, as well as a bit of shock.

"I think we'd better stay away from sunrises," she gasped as she backed even farther away from him. "This one must have somehow mesmerized us." She shook her head slightly, then turned to look beyond Casey to the other side of their tent, where the horses were still tethered to the bushes, stomping a bit as if demanding attention. "Let's get ready right now, and get on our way." She said that even more firmly this time, figuring he wouldn't object, anyway, but made it clear she wouldn't tolerate an objection or delay.

Especially because her mind returned to reality. They

had a job to do. An important job. Finding and saving those cattle. And who knew what kinds of danger that might involve, even later today?

"Absolutely," Casey said, sounding all business, and when she looked back she saw that his expression had changed from the softer look he'd aimed at her after their kiss to one that appeared much more serious. He must be thinking about reality now, too.

Without looking back toward Casey, Melody hurried over to untie Cal's tether from the bush and started leading him once more to the nearby creek, hearing the crunching of dried leaves beneath her feet and Cal's hooves in the cool morning air. She expected Casey to follow, and he didn't disappoint her.

In fact, the guy seemed never to disappoint her in anything since she'd met him—was it only a day or so ago?

She would definitely have to be careful. When all this was over, they'd have no reason even to stay in touch, let alone camp out together and observe stunning sunrises.

And she knew only too well what it was like to have a real relationship end with a horrible jolt. She didn't need to let herself get so involved with Casey that she'd feel even a little upset when they stopped seeing each other.

They were business associates. *Period.*

For the next twenty minutes, Melody worked on ensuring that the horses, and their own gear, were ready to go.

After Casey and she performed some quick morning ablutions by the creek, they handed each other more of the snacks like those they'd eaten for dinner. She still had a bit of water left in her current bottle and added some water she filtered to refill it, then did the same for Casey and the horses.

Casey handed her back her phone after detaching it from the charger, which he returned to his saddlebag. She used that opportunity to check the GPS.

Damn. It appeared that the herd of cattle was on the move again. Most of them, anyway, increasing the distance from Casey and her, heading south. Was there something wrong with the system? One dot appeared still and not particularly near where the others had spent the night. Strange. But she'd had the GPS system act oddly at other times now and then.

Of course, she'd been able at those times to tell one of the more senior ranch hands, usually Pierce Tostig. He took her to a tech store in Cactus Creek and had her phone checked and, when it needed it, fixed.

That wasn't going to happen out here. She just hoped it continued to work adequately for them to locate the herd, even if it had occasional glitches. And they could always check Casey's phone, too.

"You ready?" she asked Casey, sticking her phone into her pocket and mounting Cal. She studiously avoided casting a look toward her male companion with whom she'd shared such an amazing few moments earlier beneath the incomparable sky.

"Yep." Casey mounted Witchy as he spoke, then just sat there watching her, but only for a few seconds. "Let's go."

Which they did.

They were silent for a while. Melody couldn't help seeing that sunrise in her mind over and over—and reliving its aftermath somewhat.

Her hand enfolded in Casey's.

That kiss.

And her regrets about it. Sure, it had felt wonderful at the time, but she didn't want to feel that way about any man: *close*. She wanted to be with him. Wanted to touch him.

But that could lead to more touching...more feeling.

She felt a bit uncomfortable now and wanted to put those thoughts behind her and talk to Casey again like the professional colleagues they actually were and would continue to be, at least for a while.

He was the one to ultimately break the silence as the horses kept walking at a swift pace through the grass and along the irregular meadow turf in the cool November morning. "I assume we're headed the right way, according to your GPS, right?"

"Right," Melody agreed. "The cattle seem on the move toward the south, and that's the direction we're going. We need to speed up a bit since they're continuing to move at the same rate as before, and it would take us a full day to catch up with them if they were standing still. There might have been a glitch, too." She mentioned seeing the lone dot by itself. "Nothing major, fortunately. Even so, I just hope that's not the case now."

"I hope so, too."

They were both silent again for maybe a minute. Melody didn't like it. She looked at the vast green pasture in the direction they were heading. It was also broken up here and there by patches of trees or bushes and was a very pretty outdoor venue with a purpose: feeding grazing cattle.

And horses, since, as they weren't traveling extremely quickly, Cal and Witchy occasionally stopped to bite into a patch of grass, and she and Casey let them.

Getting to their destination a few minutes later would be fine if their mounts remained healthy and well-fed.

But— "What are we going to do if your GPS is entirely wrong?" Casey asked, aiming a troubled frown toward her. "Is that possible? I assume the one I downloaded would be the same."

"Yes, it would. And it's possible for the GPS to be wrong, but very unlikely, fortunately. I've talked to other ranch hands about that kind of possibility, and also the tech guy in downtown Cactus Creek who takes care of the ranch's system as well as the apps on our phones, and I never got the sense that there could be that kind of a major problem."

"But is the system obvious on the cattle? Are the rustlers likely to know about it and try to find a way to turn it off or, worse, somehow aim us in the wrong direction?"

"Again, yes, that's possible. But our Angus cows are all black, of course. Their tags that contain their ID numbers and GPS chips are dark and purposely attached to their ears, where they're not particularly visible to people, even those who are specifically looking for them. But even so…"

She had just remembered her own concerns about cattle security when she had started working at Over-

Herd Ranch and had mentioned them to Clarence and the other hands.

Clarence had scoffed at her worries. He was the one in the business and he had done his research—or at least he'd hired and spent a lot of money for people who really knew what they were doing to install these kinds of location systems. Or supposedly knew.

Even so, she'd had a suggestion. "What about bringing on some herding dogs and a trainer or two?" she'd asked him. "There are several different breeds that are popular and apparently quite skilled. They can help to gather and keep track of the cattle and find them if any go missing."

"Yeah, right, I've considered that," Clarence had responded. "But that's an added expense and, worse, having dogs around sniffing and circling them and barking might only make the cattle nervous. Our cows need to be able to procreate without getting all anxious and edgy because there are dogs around giving them a hard time."

Melody had considered doing some research and providing Clarence with evidence that having herding dogs around would be a big plus rather than a problem, but she'd decided against it. Sure, she'd had a lot of those kinds of dogs around at the ranches she'd worked at in Texas, but right now she needed to be sure to keep *this* job.

And criticizing the ranch owner, who also happened to be a town bigwig, wasn't a great idea.

So she'd shut up about it.

And wondered now if she should have tried again.

She mentioned the idea to Casey. "Not that I'm an expert, but I've had good luck at past ranches where I worked, but Clarence wasn't interested in giving it a try."

"Too bad. I like the idea. And if there were dogs at OverHerd now we could have appropriated them to help us out here."

Melody felt a small surge of warmth inside that she quickly tamped down. He liked her idea. But so what? Clarence hadn't, and that had been what was important then.

And now?

Now it was just Casey and her—alone.

Chapter Eight

The slightly cloudy sky was mostly blue now, though it was still fairly early in the morning. Casey was glad that Melody, who now rode quietly beside him, had awakened him for that amazing sunrise.

And had held his hand—well, let him hold hers—while they watched it. And shared a kiss…

Okay. He was overthinking this, as he tended to do about Melody. Sure, he enjoyed being with her. Sharing things like the sunrise…and their kiss. But so what?

He could admire her as a ranch hand, one who apparently felt comfortable instructing him in what he needed to know to survive and to do a good job out here chasing cattle and suspects. Even admire her looks. She appeared to be one heck of a woman.

That didn't mean he should allow his admiration for her to get out of hand, not only now, but also as their assignment continued.

For now, he looked down at his horse's neck and mane. Witchy was a nice, calm girl who walked steadily enough to keep Casey comfortable on the hard saddle he'd put back on with Melody's help, along with the

saddlebag. Today it had seemed pretty much routine.
A stakeout with a beautiful cowgirl wasn't really something he'd imagined while thinking of his career with
the sheriff's department, but it was enjoyable for now,
partly thanks to Melody's tutelage.

When they actually found the missing cattle, things
would change. He'd be in charge of handling that and
making sure his department sent whatever backup was
needed to bring down the perpetrators.

He recognized that he was thinking a lot as he rode
this morning. Melody and he had been quiet for a while,
after she'd described how she had suggested to her
boss, Clarence, that having dogs around would help
with herding and locating lost steer. He'd thought that
was a good idea, too. Another thing to admire about
her, and maybe to talk about as they continued riding
along the turf in the direction where the main herd of
cattle appeared to still be heading.

First, though, Casey did wonder about, and considered asking more about, the lone GPS dot Melody had
shown him. A cow who'd wandered away from the herd,
or a problem with the GPS? Melody didn't seem certain
and, in fact, had mentioned some of the app's quirks—
which could spell disaster if there was a glitch taking
them in the wrong direction somehow.

But he was just speculating, worrying for nothing,
hopefully. Time to ask those questions.

"I like how you suggested those dogs to Clarence,"
he began. "Not that I know much about ranching, but
that sounded like a good addition for a ranch owner to
help ensure that he always knows where his cattle are.

And yes, I know it's not as technologically advanced to have a dog or two compared with a satellite-assisted GPS system, but it still sounds good and potentially useful. You said that you came from Texas and worked on a ranch there. Did they have dogs?"

"The first one did. That was partly because of my father's suggestions back then, and the owner liked the idea and started always keeping trained dogs to help."

Ah. He was getting some of her background. Interesting.

"So you began working at the same ranch your dad did? He was also a ranch hand?"

"That's right. He taught me a lot—and I liked it."

Then why had she moved here? he wondered. He wanted to ask, to learn everything, but if she'd left because her dad was no longer around, no longer alive, did he really want to remind her? That might be cruel and also might end any chance at a nice, friendly, neutral conversation as they continued.

Was she close to her family? Did she have siblings? Did she want to have kids someday herself?

Well, that wasn't going to be a topic of their conversation.

He began talking anyway. "I'll bet your father's really proud that you decided to follow in his footsteps." He aimed a smile at her.

And now he did see some emotion written in her expression. But it didn't appear to be grief—only pride.

"Yeah, he was. Still is."

"Then why aren't you still working with him?" Casey

blurted. Maybe it wasn't his business, but he was curious nevertheless.

He watched as the emotion on Melody's face changed to— What was it? If he had to guess, it was fury.

Wow. Maybe this wasn't a good idea, after all. But his curiosity increased exponentially.

"This isn't something I like to talk about," she finally said, hissing out the words between her teeth. "Or even think about. But I quit working for the ranch where my father was a few years ago. I married a guy I'd known for a long time who wanted to move from Fort Worth to Dallas, which we did. And then—"

"And then?" Casey repeated, encouraging her to continue when she stopped talking.

"And then I got a divorce and decided to leave."

No, MELODY DIDN'T want to think about her past, let alone talk about it. But Casey seemed nice enough in his attempt to make conversation and learn how she'd wound up here, and the only way to prevent telling him would be to lie or to shut up.

She didn't want to do either. And now she'd opened the door to describe the rest of it.

She shook her head as she continued to look forward and not toward her riding companion, concentrating for a moment on the feel of Cal walking beneath her.

Why had Casey decided to be so nosy? And now, her mind was back on her divorce, at least a bit. She had to think of something else.

At the moment, Casey seemed to be struggling to find something to say, and she almost smiled at that.

"Oh, sorry to hear that," he said finally.

Oh, what the heck. The subject had been broached.

She didn't want Casey's sympathy or anything else, but she could be frank about it, anyway, now that she was thinking about it, then make things clear, when she was done, that the subject was now off-limits.

She manipulated the thin, cool leather of the reins in her fingers without communicating any changes in direction to Cal, needing something else to do besides think of what she was talking about.

"Look, here's what happened. It doesn't hurt for you to know about it, and it doesn't hurt for me to talk about it." Not much, at least.

Thinking about it—how she'd been used, how she'd been insulted, then dumped—well, that still hurt.

She didn't mention Travis's name but figured she didn't have to. If nothing else, Casey might recognize that her married name was Ellison, presuming he had seen her driver's license as she believed.

Nor did she have to explain the horrible, hurtful details.

So she kept it light and somewhat brief, even though she knew she could have talked for hours about what a jerk Travis was.

"The guy I married I'd known from high school in Fort Worth. He was a smart guy, attended college, even got an MBA. Me? I was happy working alongside my dad as a ranch hand, but my then fiancé didn't seem to mind. In fact, we married soon after he got his degree. He'd told me by then he wanted to move to Dallas, which was okay with me. I even found a good job there. But...well, things only worked out for about two years. It was a mutual decision to divorce."

Yeah. Travis wanted to marry Loretta, whom he considered a "real woman." He had no interest any longer in the *unreal* woman, a mere "country girl."

And Melody didn't want to stay married to an SOB like him who insulted her over and over again. And also had an affair that he'd denied, of course—at first. Plus, if he didn't like being with a "country girl," why had he married a ranch hand in the first place?

Not that she'd made a lot of money, but Travis had seemed happy that she was out there doing something productive.

The thing was, after they were divorced, she just couldn't see heading back to Fort Worth in shame to work on the ranch with her dad again, around so many people who'd known Travis and her in school. Instead, she looked around and found the job here, in small but enjoyable Cactus Creek, Arizona.

But she didn't go into detail about it with Casey. She simply said, "Things just didn't work out between my ex and me, but I wasn't about to let my divorce get me down. I decided to use it as an opportunity to try something new, still doing what I loved but finding a new place to do it—right here."

"You sound as if you did the right thing," Casey said. She'd been looking straight ahead, then down at her hands again as she spoke, trying to keep her feelings to herself. But now she glanced at him and saw what appeared to be relief—and was that admiration, too?—on his face. "Exes can be hell, can't they? You one-upped me, though. I wasn't married, but mine dumped me at the altar four years ago."

"Really?" Melody said. "Wow. That sounds pretty bad, too. What happened?" Poor guy. That must have hurt.

Maybe she and Casey did have something else in common.

And they both were single now...

In any case, she now felt curious. Was what had happened to him as bad as what she'd experienced with that louse Travis? And did he finally feel ready to move on with another woman?

OKAY, HE DIDN'T have to talk about being dumped. He definitely didn't want to think about it—although his thinking about it happened too often.

Like right now, partly thanks to Melody's story.

She was obviously emotionally stressed from having told him about her ex. And he needed to continue riding with her, working with her, conversing with her.

Maybe if he shared the most miserable part of his life with her, as she'd just done with him...

He'd just keep it short. And light. Or at least as light as possible.

"Well, the thing is," he began, "I met my ex, Georgia, and first became close to her, because her brother Sean was my twin's best friend when they were kids."

"So what happened?" Melody asked.

"Georgia never really explained except to say she'd made a mistake. I gathered from Everett that Sean hadn't been thrilled about our engagement. Didn't think

I was good enough for his sister, and best I could tell he finally convinced her, when we were about to be married, that he was right."

"Did you ever talk to Sean about it? Did Everett?"

"Sean wouldn't talk to me," he said. Casey had tried, though. Wanted to know whether what he'd come to understand was true.

He had even tried talking to Sean's wife, Delilah, an accountant who seemed to be fairly levelheaded, to see what he could learn from her, but she'd avoided him, too.

And Georgia? She'd been pretty, though not as pretty as Melody—at least not the way he remembered her. She'd been closer to his age than Melody.

Not that it mattered. He'd been dating Georgia for a while before they got engaged and were nearly married. He'd loved her. A lot. Which had turned out to be a big mistake.

He had no romantic interest in Melody, so her age didn't matter.

But he had no intention, after what had gone on with Georgia, in getting romantically involved with a woman anytime soon. Probably ever.

He'd seldom seen Georgia after she dumped him so nastily, which was probably a good thing. They'd both actually shown up for the ceremony, but she wasn't wearing her wedding gown. Instead, she told him then that she wasn't going through with it.

Her excuse? She had decided she didn't love him after all and had no interest in being married to a deputy sheriff.

He didn't even know what she did for a living now. She hadn't had a lot of ambition when they were together, so it was probably for the best that she'd dumped him, or maybe he'd have been their sole breadwinner.

He did have the impression, though, that Sean, too, wasn't wild about him partly because he was in law enforcement. That made Casey wonder if Sean had been interested in some kind of criminal activities— or maybe he'd already started back then.

Casey never tried to find out. None of the cases he'd dealt with had ever involved either Sean or Georgia, or even Delilah. Too bad, in a way. He'd have liked a bit of revenge for the misery he had gone through. Love? Yeah, he'd felt it. Too much.

But that was then. Now—well, it wasn't worth going through that hurt ever again.

"So how did you feel? How do you feel now?" Melody's tone sounded curious.

Really? They were going to have a longer conversation about it?

He should have hated the idea, but somehow, talking with someone he was now working with, someone he liked—and someone who'd suffered through something similar and could most likely understand if he snarled as he spoke about it more—didn't seem so bad.

He looked over at Melody to find her watching him. She seemed to be staring at him intensely—just as he'd done to her—in an attempt to read him.

"It was hard at first," he admitted, looking away to study the pasture in front of them as if he was concerned about where they were going. Which he was. He took a deep breath and continued. "I'd imagine you, if anyone, can identify with what it's like to have had expectations and hopes for the future—the long-term future—and believe that it'll be good, enhanced by a relationship that seems long-term. Forever, even. Fulfilling. Sharing dreams. And…heck, I must be sounding like some kind of oddball idealist. That's not me. But even so…"

He heard a small laugh and again glanced toward Melody. She was shaking her head a little, causing her pretty ponytail to sway back and forth. He felt his heart shrink. She didn't get it. She did consider him an optimistic weirdo or something. And—

"Oh, yes, I know what you're talking about," she said. "In fact— Well, with you, you might have had some wonderful hopes and wishes for the future. Me? I was already married, for more than a year, in fact, before I let myself recognize any problems in the relationship. And at first I imagined I was dreaming it. Maybe even having stupid thoughts of my own that this wasn't working and that I needed some new guy in my life already." She stopped for a moment, then blurted out, "But I finally realized, when it was over, that I didn't. I didn't need the jerk I was married to, and I didn't need anyone. *Don't* need anyone else." She went silent for a moment. Casey glanced toward her briefly and saw she was staring at the back of Cal's head with an expression he couldn't read. "But it was still damn hard," she said.

"Yeah," Casey agreed. "It was still damn hard."

They rode along in silence for the next few minutes. Casey's mind kept mulling over what Melody had said, and how, though their circumstances were definitely different, they'd both suffered some pretty rough times thanks to relationships gone bad.

Really bad.

He had an odd desire to get off his horse and give Melody a hug in understanding, but that would be inappropriate.

Plus, it might give her the wrong idea. He'd definitely made it clear that he didn't want another relationship after what had happened before. Not now, certainly, and maybe not ever.

And he'd understood that Melody had the same opinion of getting too close to another person of the opposite sex.

Sex. That was not the same thing, even though romantic relationships usually led to it.

Did he want to sleep with Melody? He certainly wasn't against it, but it would definitely be a bad idea—even worse now after he'd learned they weren't just associates with the same assignment from their respective employers.

They were both smart individuals who'd learned a lot from what being with the wrong person could do to you.

So for now—

"I appreciate your understanding of that miserable mess," he finally said. "And I definitely understand that you went through something similar. We're comrades in arms in many ways." He laughed and was delighted to hear laughter from Melody, too. Somehow his recollections seemed to hurt a bit less now after he'd shared them. He was glad she'd shared hers, too.

"We definitely are," she said. "Empathy's the thing

between us, for good reason." She hesitated, then went on. "But let's leave it alone now, okay?"

"Unless I think of a way we can each help the other get revenge," Casey said, keeping his face straight as he looked toward her yet again.

"Hey, I like that idea," Melody said, her expression thoughtful as she nodded her head up and down.

Then they both smiled at one another, and Casey felt the heat of attraction pulse through him even as he told himself that wasn't what this was about.

Camaraderie was.

"Okay," he finally said. "Let's think on it. Meanwhile, tell me if you're aware of anyplace it'd be good to stop for a while and grab our huge, delicious lunch."

More laughter. And that made him feel really good.

Chapter Nine

Melody enjoyed their ride for the rest of the day. Not that she hadn't before, but they actually now seemed like friends. They'd each experienced a difficult aspect of life in different ways and survived, and shared it.

Would this new bond survive after they achieved their goals of locating the missing cattle and bringing down the thieves? That remained to be seen. But right now, she hoped so.

They continued to chat a lot as they rode forward, picking up the pace a bit. No more discussion of their horrible exes, at least not for now.

But they did see wildlife here and there, which made for some interesting conversation. There were lots of lizards out here, for one thing, and she was the one to win their contest of seeing and identifying the deadliest. She saw a Gila monster and pointed it out, and they were both very careful to guide their horses way off to the side. Gila monsters were dangerous and had some pretty nasty venom.

But reptiles weren't the only wildlife around. They

saw more birds flying by. "They look like small hawks," Casey said, pointing at one that came relatively close.

"They're kestrels," Melody informed him.

Melody also pointed out some brown-headed cowbirds, which seemed appropriate for their quest—although she also mentioned they were a type of blackbird. They saw a few jackrabbits, a couple of different kinds of rodents that Melody believed were Arizona cotton rats and quite a few mice. There appeared to be more wildlife out here than they'd seen yesterday. Of course, they were a bit farther from civilization—assuming that the ranch house and related buildings were considered civilization.

Or maybe they were just paying more attention.

They turned it into a game. "Whoever sees the next animal out here gets to have first choice of which energy and fruit bars to have for dinner tonight," Melody announced at one point.

"Hey, that'll be me," Casey responded, his tone full of good humor, too.

As it turned out, Melody was the next one to see a creature. It was another kind of lizard, one not nearly as scary as the Gila monster. She didn't directly point it out to Casey, but she waved her arm generally in that direction.

"Hey, I see a lizard," Casey said, pointing directly toward where Melody had indicated.

"Oh, yeah," she said, pretending to be surprised. "Looks like it might be a fence lizard to me, though they don't really need fences to survive, fortunately."

"But you saw it first, right?" Casey sounded amused,

and when she looked at him, he arched his brown eyebrows and cocked his head to the side.

"Who, me?" She smiled and batted her eyelashes, and his laughter seemed loud enough to scare that lizard—and it did run off, which caused Melody to chuckle, too.

"Maybe we should write down all we see," Casey suggested.

"Maybe so—especially if we start seeing any signs of cattle besides their hoofprints."

There were more grassy areas than dirt or mud where hoofprints would show up. But there were also areas where that greenery had been tamped down, most likely by cattle walking through it. That, even more than the GPS, told them in which direction to continue.

And so they kept going, with occasional breaks so they could walk around a little themselves, especially in areas with bushes around, and the horses could get a short breather without people on their backs.

They also discussed their pasts a bit more, though Melody was glad that neither of them brought up their exes or their respective breakups again.

Instead, she really had a question. "You mentioned that you have a twin, right?" she asked a short while after they'd seen and pointed out another rabbit. Cal walked right by it without paying attention, but the rabbit certainly noted their presence and leaped away.

"That's right—my brother, Everett. He was born only two minutes before me. That makes him my older brother, right? He certainly thinks so and has sometimes rubbed it in if he wants to get me irritated."

"That's silly," Melody said, unable to help herself as she stared toward the horizon, which was starting to take on some color. Soon it would be sunset. She began looking ahead of them for a place to stop for the night, even as her mind continued to swirl around what they'd been briefly discussing.

Two minutes? Why would that make a difference?

But as they continued forward, she enjoyed the amusement Casey imparted to her about how he and his brother had behaved in classes as kids, from elementary through high school. Sometimes they were in the same class and often not, but either way they enjoyed goading each other about it.

And sometimes they gave teachers or fellow classmates a hard time, pretending that they weren't twins or even brothers.

His description made her a bit envious. She'd always been close to her parents, but she had no siblings.

But she'd wanted to add to her family by having kids someday. Not going to happen now, though. Not while she had no interest in remarrying.

"We drove our parents nuts at times," Casey admitted. "Silly, of course, but it was fun. When we tried it in school we sometimes got called into the principals' offices so we tried to be somewhat cautious about where and when."

"I'll bet," Melody said, picturing such mischief in her mind. And she also imagined how annoyed she would feel if any twins tried that around her.

Yet working as a ranch hand, she'd seen plenty of bovine siblings around who looked similar, or even identical, that she needed to tell apart. Angus cattle, in fact, were generally all black in color and closely resembled each other; their personalities, too, were often similar.

The first cattle she'd dealt with, on the Fort Worth ranch and then in Dallas, were generally Hereford or Holstein, and though there were similarities they didn't necessarily look alike.

Good thing, thanks to Clarence and his rules, that the Angus cattle she now worked with had tags that contained their names and ID numbers, as well as GPS microchips.

Eventually, Melody started leading them off to the east despite their general need to continue mostly south, but she noticed some hillsides with more plant life that way and she hoped for another creek, too.

Which, after a bit of hunting, they found, along with another good place to tether the horses on a couple of trees before the hillside they chose sloped down to the creek.

They now had a hint of a routine. They both dismounted, and Melody was pleased to have Casey help remove the saddles and saddlebags once more before they both led their horses down the hill to get water to be filtered to provide them with a drink.

As they'd done yesterday, both Witchy and Cal had eaten grass and extra feed along their route. And after grooming and checking over the horses, they tied up the animals for the night. Then Melody helped Casey raise and secure the tent and they put their saddlebags inside.

After they conducted their bathing ritual, they called their respective bosses after Casey turned on the lanterns.

Melody, sitting on top of her sleeping bag, wasn't particularly pleased that the reception wasn't great where they were. She was happy, though, that she reached Clarence on the first ring this time.

"Sorry about that static," he grumbled. "I'll have to get one of my tech advisors to check it out tomorrow. So—have you located my missing cattle yet?"

"Unfortunately, no. They seem to be continuing to head farther away, according to the GPS. It may still take another day or two."

"Great." She heard the sarcasm dripping from her boss and winced, but what could she do? "Just so you know, I've had the hands who were watching the other herds lead them back closer to the ranch rather than fanning out the way they were. It's easier for them to help each other take care of the other herds that way."

"I'd imagine so," Melody agreed. She looked across the tent at Casey, who seemed to be talking animatedly to someone. Was he having a better time with the sheriff than she was with her employer? For his sake, she hoped so. But she also knew they'd all be a lot happier once they'd found and rescued the stolen animals.

She couldn't help noticing, in any case, that Casey looked relaxed in his jeans and the sweatshirt he'd put on over his T-shirt. Very relaxed.

Very sexy, especially since they were here for the night, alone once more…

And Melody had to keep her mind on what was important. That included not becoming attracted to this man who also would have no interest, after what had happened to his love life, in getting involved with her, any more than she wanted a relationship with him.

"And...damn it all." Clarence was suddenly yelling into her ear, bringing back her focus. "One of the hands who's supposed to be back here helping out isn't around. I gather he told a couple of the others that he'd go out and find the missing cattle and report back. Never mind that you're already spending—and I hope not wasting—your time out there and you've got a deputy sheriff with you."

"That's right," Melody agreed, and wondered who the disobedient hand was. If she had to guess, it would be Pierce; he'd seemed particularly concerned and interested in the case, and like their boss he enjoyed being in charge.

"Well, if you happen to run into Pierce out there, tell him to get back here where he belongs. Unless, of course, he's actually located the cattle." So she'd guessed correctly.

"Of course, sir," Melody said, rolling her eyes but glad he couldn't see that. "And I'll report back to you again tomorrow, one way or the other, assuming I still have phone service."

"Good. You do that." Clarence ended the call.

Casey wasn't talking any more, either. "I just let the sheriff know we're still out here trying," he told her. "No news wasn't good news, though." He tried to make that sound like a quip, but he clearly wasn't happy.

"Same goes for me and our town selectman," Melody said with a sigh. "I think maybe it's time for us to grab something to eat."

"Yeah, maybe that'll make us feel better," Casey agreed, and they both dug into their saddlebags for food.

When they were done eating, Melody decided to go back outside to check on the horses. "It's colder outside than it's been since we started out," she said to Casey. "I want to be sure they're okay and not bothered by the increased chilliness."

"Good idea," Casey said, and stood to accompany her. She liked that about him. He was always there for her, willing to help. He even swept the tent's exit flap out of her way.

She needed to ignore that—despite the way his eyes caught hers for a moment, too. She made herself keep going.

The horses still stood where their reins were attached to nearby bushes, and they both appeared relaxed, even sleepy. They looked up when Casey and she approached and Witchy even nodded, but neither appeared to need any further attention.

"You're the expert," Casey said, "but they both look okay to me."

"Me, too." She patted both of them nevertheless and got some curious but apparently neutral looks from their mounts, who didn't attempt to move, at last not at that moment.

Suddenly, Casey grabbed her cold hand, tugging her along until they were back inside the tent. She was even more amused—maybe—when, after helping her to get down on her opened sleeping bag, he joined her there, sitting closely beside her with his arm around her.

Which felt good. Much too good. And not just because it helped to warm her a bit.

She was even more aware of him than usual. Of his body, touching hers. Not in any sexual way, and yet she couldn't help thinking about how his hip met hers, how his warm side also pressed against her, somehow turning her on. How his hand, which latched on to the outside of her leg to pull her closer as they sat there, increased her awareness of his fingers and where they might go if they moved, rather than simply holding her loosely.

And yet, she just sat there, as he did. They talked more about their respective pasts and what had brought them to this point in their lives.

Eventually, Melody felt herself relax as they continued their light conversation.

This was fine, she told herself. Two professional colleagues keeping each other comfortable.

That was all it was…right?

KEEP TALKING, CASEY told himself. That way, he could just hang out there with Melody snuggled beside him as he sat up.

Her light, feminine scent, maybe due to whatever she put on after their attempt at washing, intrigued him.

So did the feel of her. The sweet, humorous tone of her voice…

Plus, Casey enjoyed, maybe too much, her responses to his questions about what her dad had taught her—and not taught her—about being a ranch hand.

Her father had taught her to love animals, although

that might have happened, anyway. To want to take care of them. To love the outdoors and work there to achieve everything necessary to ensure that the cattle, horses—and sometimes dogs—were well cared for and also worked well with each other.

Would she be as caring with a husband? Kids? Somehow Casey thought so. But he wouldn't be the one to find out, if anyone did—although the idea of her possibly being so loving? Well, it intrigued him.

He cast his thoughts aside.

"What was your favorite lesson?" Casey finally asked.

"When my dad showed me how to ride horseback and cull a cow from the herd without scaring either of them, or myself. And then he had me practice it. It was sort of the initial lesson of how to become the best ranch hand I could."

She'd moved even closer beside him, if that was possible, as she spoke. Even laid her head against his shoulder, moving it so she talked upward, toward his ear.

He wanted to pull her even closer, maybe on top of him.

Better if he was on top, though…

No. He had to keep his mind under as much control as his body. "Sounds great," he said. "Everett and I didn't become interested in law enforcement thanks to our parents, though. Our dad is a doctor, an oncologist, and he loves what he does, but neither Everett nor I ever aspired to become an MD. Our mom's the local postmistress. She's a great lady—didn't want us to follow in her footsteps but did want us to give back to our community. So, in our ways, we have—even though Everett's not living here now."

"Then I assume your mom's fond of Cactus Creek, too," Melody said.

"Yes, she's lived here all her life as well. But though our folks were nice and encouraging, they didn't particularly inspire us with how to spend our lives."

"So how did you choose law enforcement?" Melody asked. Her voice was starting to slow down and sound sleepy.

But Casey wanted to answer her question. "Well, somewhere along the line we heard of some distant relatives, more Coltons, who didn't live around here but were cops. Everett and I both became fascinated, looked into it more, watched long-distance, to the extent we could, what those relatives were doing…and here we are."

"Yes, here we are," Melody repeated, her tone soft.

"You sound tired," Casey told her. "Ready for some sleep?"

"Sure," she said.

He started to move away from her, to cross the small expanse of the tent to get to his own sleeping bag, but she grabbed his left hand until he turned back toward her.

"It'd keep us both warmer if we slept together," she said, and then her pretty eyes widened beneath the light of the lantern. "And I do mean *sleep* together," she clarified.

"I figured," he responded with a laugh. "Sounds good to me, as long as we actually get some sleep that way."

They were in Arizona, not Antarctica. But it was chilly, and staying warm would help them sleep to prepare for the next day.

Melody replied to his comment. "What, do you think staying that close will cause us to lose the professionalism we've been so good at so far?"

"I guess we can find out." He winked at her.

But in the next few minutes, they did lie down together, both of them on top of Melody's opened sleeping bag, with Casey's spread over them.

They started out lying side by side, and he gathered that Melody actually fell asleep that way.

Not him. Not at first.

He was too conscious of her presence.

Of her sexiness, even as they worked at being professional despite her being so close, pressed up against him just slightly, yet emphasizing how wonderful her nearness was, causing his body to notice…

Not that he'd do anything about it.

Even though he found her sweet, clean scent tempting. Very tempting.

He worried whether he'd keep that promise to himself as Melody shifted in her sleep, turning so she lay with her back against him.

Oh, yeah, he was warmer that way. Much warmer.

And sleep? With Melody so near him?

With her butt touching his most sensitive area, which reacted by doing anything but sleep thanks to that arousing contact?

With, in turn, his right arm under her head, his left

arm over her shoulder…and his hand so very close to her full breasts?

Okay, he told himself after feeling he'd been awake for hours, but it had probably only been for half an hour. *Enough of this. Time to sleep.*

And somehow he managed to nod off.

Chapter Ten

Was she the first to awaken? Melody believed so, just as she had yesterday morning.

Only then, they'd been in this same tent together, sure, but across from one another.

Now she was snuggled up against Casey on top of one of the sleeping bags, with the other one covering them. It felt good and warm and friendly, but nothing else, right?

And maybe her recollections of snuggling tighter against him, feeling his seeming arousal pressed tautly against her throughout most of the night, especially when she was just falling asleep, had been her imagination.

A dream.

A much too exciting dream…

Casey moved behind her…and she once again noticed what felt like an erection pushing into her back. She sucked in her breath, wondering if she should slide forward. Get up. At least move away…although she realized she liked that sensual pressure.

"Hey, Melody, are you awake?" Casey's deep, raspy voice startled her.

"Yes," she said, finally sliding forward because it seemed appropriate now. "I was wondering if you were."

"Yep. And I think it's still early enough for us to slip outside and see how the sunrise looks this morning."

He stood up first and held out his hand to help her stand. She could have gotten up just fine but appreciated his gentlemanliness, so she grasped his warm hand and was soon standing, though bent over in the tent, facing him.

They'd just spent the night together. Close. So close. But nothing untoward had happened—at least not on purpose.

Damn, but she appreciated the guy and his attitude.

Even as she found herself much too attracted to him and, as much as she disliked the idea under these circumstances, sexually frustrated.

Not that she'd let him know it. "First one out of this tent gets to choose what they'll eat for breakfast first."

"You're on." She was amused as, still in their heavy shirts, they both put on their shoes, then pretended to scramble for the flap. She got to push it open and recognized that Casey had held back so she'd be the winner. She considered doing something to let him out first, but then decided, what the heck? She got to see the sunrise first yesterday, so why not today?

Which she did. It wasn't quite as vivid as the prior morning's bright orange, but it seemed to be peach, striped with the white clouds. "Lovely," she breathed as she stood there, turning slightly to take it all in.

"Yes, lovely," Casey said beside her, but his throaty tone made her glance at him.

He was staring at her, but only until their eyes met. He looked away then and began studying the sky.

Was she just imagining that? Did he feel attracted to her the way she felt attracted to him?

Well, they had spent the night together. Very closely together. And he was a man. Definitely. Which meant his sexual instincts might even be more active than hers. Although hers...

Okay. Enough, she told herself. Without saying anything else to Casey she headed toward where Cal and Witchy were tethered, both of them now watching the humans. She unhitched Cal from the bush, while Casey did the same with Witchy, and they walked the horses to the nearby stream for a drink.

Yes, oddly, they seemed to be in somewhat of a routine out here on the ranch's extensive grounds. But they hadn't accomplished any of their goals yet.

They hadn't caught up with the stolen cattle even after two days.

That had to change. Somehow.

Did the rustlers know they were being followed?

Were they doing something to ultimately prevent it besides continuing forward?

Casey knew more about such things than she did, but she realized they needed to be careful. And do more to catch the criminals fast.

And Melody knew that she, as the experienced ranch hand in charge of this part of their expedition, had to decide what to do next to accomplish it.

Sure, that would eventually mean no more nights with Casey. But they needed to achieve their goal. And no longer being together?

Things would be better that way.

Although she truly would miss it.

THEY WERE OUT on the trail once more. As always— well, at least since this assignment had begun—Casey had first checked out the hoofprints they were following, which were a little more visible today in the drier grass of this area of the ranch's land.

Yes, Melody and he seemed to be heading in the right direction. Only this time, they weren't just following those hoofprints.

"Let me check the GPS," Melody had said a while back, before they'd had that day's breakfast.

She'd shown the map on her phone to him after they stopped. Yes, the cattle seemed to be on the move again. Still.

So they had a long way to go to catch up, even though Melody had suggested that they get the horses to go at a faster pace today, allowing for only brief rest stops. Her call, of course, since she knew the horses and the terrain best. But would that actually wind up in their going farther over the course of the day?

Casey wasn't sure. But somehow, they needed to get closer. Catch up.

Save those cattle a lot faster than things appeared to be going.

It felt like more than just his job now. It had also become his own personal goal.

"Our current routine hasn't gotten us far enough," Melody had told him, and that seemed true to him, too.

And now? Well, they'd also decided to take a slight detour—to check out the single separate dot showing on the GPS map, since they'd be passing it that day.

Had one of the cows lost her tag? It could still be sending a GPS signal even if it had been dropped onto the ground.

But they'd decided it was better to check it out, in case there was something at that site they needed to know—like an indication the thieves had discovered the sensors and were somehow allowing the others to send signals about false locations. Or maybe this was a test, where the rustlers had purposely left this one, along with someone observing it, to see if they were being followed.

They would have to be careful.

And in addition to everything else, it was Casey's job to ensure that Melody wouldn't come to any harm. Which felt as important to him—more so—than saving the cattle.

It wouldn't be surprising, after all, for the rustlers to know about the GPS. Many farms and ranches used it these days, according to Melody. "But if these rustlers know about it," Melody had said, "and if they have any smartness at all, they'd have done something to prevent the signal from showing us how they're progressing and the direction they're going."

Casey agreed but added, "If they can figure out how," and Melody had nodded.

"So if you weren't out here trying to catch cattle

rustlers," Melody said a short while after they started off, possibly to break the silence, "what would you be doing?" She kept Cal walking right beside Witchy, and she looked witchingly good, tall in the saddle with her jeans and hoodie hugging her body…as he'd hugged her last night. And would like to continue doing even now.

Instead… "Not sure," he replied. "Guess it would depend on what kinds of crimes were going on in town, or at least what was suspected—or reported, rightly or wrongly. I'd most likely be sent to a location where a citizen reported a theft or even an assault, with or without a weapon. That seems to be my most usual assignment. Crime in Cactus Creek is fairly minimal, mostly thefts. Very few robberies or worse."

"And I assume you'd help the person who called as well as you could, depending on the crime and its status then, right?"

"Exactly."

"Which is your favorite kind of crime to investigate?" Melody asked. Judging by her expression as he looked at her again, she was actually interested in his answer, and he had to think quickly to come up with something that would amuse them both.

Maybe even something that was true.

"Battery," he said after a few seconds of pondering, well aware of Witchy's clomping steps on the ground beneath them. "That's when someone—"

"Not only threatens to hit someone but actually does it, right?"

"Yes," he said, somewhat impressed. Many citizens didn't know the difference between battery and assault, which consisted of pretty much only the threat but no actual touching.

"But why do you like battery?" She sounded upset by the idea.

"I didn't mean that I *like* it," he clarified, "and even at that there are some kinds I prefer investigating over others. Not anything life-threatening, but I find it a tiny bit enjoyable to have to follow up on a call where someone complains of being hit by someone else, but it's sometimes because a kid used some kind of flexible toy these days—often a tube like they sometimes bring into in swimming pools, or a plastic bat."

When he looked over at Melody next, unsurprisingly still riding tall—and sexily, somehow—on Cal's back, she was staring at him skeptically. "Really?" she asked.

"No, not really." He grinned and used his heels to encourage Witchy to pick up her pace a little more.

They continued to converse as they rode, which Casey found himself enjoying, probably too much. He considered what he'd do when this assignment was complete and they didn't need to see each other professionally any more. Would he find a way to keep Melody in his life? No matter how much he was attracted to her out here, he hadn't changed his opinion about having any kind of romantic relationship, no matter who the woman was and how much he enjoyed her company.

And he did enjoy Melody's company. A lot. And getting to a point where he'd no longer see her?

Well, he didn't really want to think about that.

Just in case, he kept reminding himself of Georgia. Of her dumping him, and not just doing it any random time. No, she'd waited until the last moment, when they were just about to get married. When it would hurt him the worst.

No, he didn't need to risk anything like that ever again.

And besides, Melody was a new divorcée.

So she would be a good choice to continue developing a friendship with. Less risk with someone who'd also been there, done that, and come away with a similar attitude to his.

He realized his musing had caused a silence between them—one he needed to end. "Sorry," he said. "Just thinking of some of the battery cases I've looked into—and fortunately most of the perpetrators were arrested and found guilty at trial."

"The kids, too?" Melody asked, in a tone that told him she was joking.

"Oh, absolutely," he lied, then laughed. "No, I haven't tried prosecuting any kids."

And so their conversation went as they continued forward, sometimes discussing Melody's life as a ranch hand and her favorite part of it.

"Cleaning up a pasture after some members of the herd have been moved," she told him, her expression sincere…until he started laughing. Then she started laughing, too. "Or not," she said. "Instead, that could be my least favorite part."

"Got it," Casey acknowledged. As he did often, he scanned the mostly green pasture they were traversing at a quicker pace than they had over the last couple of days. This part seemed more irregular than some of the locations, with its deeply rolling hillsides and even more areas with bushes. Plus the grass was pretty long except where it had been worn down right around them by the cattle who'd been driven through here. He doubted that many cattle were brought out here to graze.

It shouldn't be too long, he figured, until they reached the area where that one lone red dot appeared on the GPS app.

That was Melody's take, too, he assumed when she slowed Cal down a bit and pulled her cell phone from her pocket. Holding the reins more loosely, she looked at the screen and swiped it.

"We're almost there," she said. "Let's head a little to our right. Whatever's causing the dot to appear in my GPS tracker is just over that hill." She pointed ahead, but unsurprisingly toward their right.

"No further indication of what it is?" he asked, even knowing that greater detail, even close by, was highly unlikely on a GPS map.

"Nope, though it's likely to be a cow—or just the GPS tag that's somehow been taken off. We'll find out soon."

And they did. The result clearly upset Melody. A lot.

For as soon as their horses walked over the small ridge nearest the dot's location and they could see the grass-covered part of the hillside beyond, the cow that was wearing the tag was visible.

Lying there, on the ground.

Clearly dead.

"No!" MELODY QUICKLY urged Cal to get closer, then slid off the saddle from her horse's back. There were bushes close by, so she quickly tied Cal to the nearest one and kneeled near where the black Angus cow was lying on the ground, unmoving, a mat of darkness against the otherwise green-and-brown surface below her.

And yes, it was a her, undoubtedly one of the female cattle they were chasing.

What had happened to her?

And what were they going to do about her?

Melody would definitely have to notify Clarence, and soon—but not until she had more answers for him.

She moved around on her jeans-clad knees on the roughness of the dirt and the little bit of grass above it until she reached the cow's head. Wincing, she nevertheless reached forward until she had the poor creature's ear in her hand. It felt cold, despite the warm air surrounding her. No warmth of life. And, fortunately, no smell of death—at least not yet.

With a sigh, Melody gently massaged that ear, anyway, not because the cow could feel anything but because Melody needed the information from the tag concealed at the back of her ear. She knew it still had to be there, for why else would the GPS have picked up this location?

She noticed then that she wasn't alone kneeling on the ground beside the dead member of the herd she'd been seeking. Casey was beside her, one arm around her back as she continued to lean forward and caress the cow's closest ear, her left one. The other ear was beneath her head, against the ground. Fortunately, the OverHerd cattle's tags were always attached to the left ear. Otherwise, they'd have had to find a way to lift that heavy head and maybe even the front part of the body.

And, oddly, the brand at the back of the poor cow's side, near her tail, looked off. This had to be one of the OverHerd stock, yet instead of displaying OHR, some of the hair around it had been singed differently, and somehow so had the skin beneath. It now said SG.

What ranch was that?

"Can you tell yet what happened?" Casey asked.

"No. I'll do what I can here to check, but I'm no expert in anything medical." But she did finally feel the small tag by the cow's ear and, though she hated to move away from the comforting feel of Casey beside her, she edged closer and looked down.

It was well camouflaged, so it was entirely possible that the rustlers weren't aware of it. But Melody could read it. The poor cow was Addie. Melody had worked with her before. Now, Melody stopped herself from giving her a hug while she attempted to study the tag.

She also tried to remove it before Casey said, "Don't do that. It's potential evidence in this crime. In fact, don't touch it."

"Of course," she agreed. She took a picture of it with her phone, although the tag's text was hard to read that way. She would grab some paper and a pen from her saddlebag soon and jot down the number on the tag that confirmed the cow's identity.

She could notify Clarence of both, let him know that they'd found one of the stolen cattle—and what condition she was in.

But Melody really wanted to know why. And so, before rising again, she started crawling around on her knees, examining all she could of poor Addie—

And then, as she moved a bit more, looking at the cow's head from a different angle, she saw it: the hole in the middle of her forehead, above the closed eyes. It was a little difficult to see in the cow's black fur. Only the tiniest bit of blood had seeped from it.

She pointed it out to Casey, who also remained on the ground but not right at her side. Instead, he was nearer the cow's still legs and hooves.

"There," Melody said, hearing the hoarseness in her own tone. Not surprising, considering her sorrow. And anger. "That may be what caused her death. Is it…do you think it's a bullet hole?"

She held her breath, hardly wanting to look toward that hole and not choosing to see the expression on the face of the deputy who was with her. He had a lot more experience, she presumed, with recognizing bullet holes.

"Yeah," he said. "I just noticed that myself and… well, I wasn't sure I should point it out to you."

"Of course you should." Melody felt affronted. She needed to know all she could about what had happened, all the details possible.

Even the most horrible ones.

"Then, yes. Best I could tell, that's a bullet hole. And would you like my take on why someone shot that cow?"

"Yes." Melody had an urge to shout at Casey. Tell him off for treating her like some fragile little woman and not revealing all he knew or suspected to her.

She needed to know it all.

Casey turned to point somewhat behind him…and Melody saw at once what he was pointing at.

One of the cow's limbs seemed extended in the wrong direction. Had she broken her leg?

That would have given the rustlers reason to leave her here, since she couldn't have kept up with them.

Was slaying her somehow an act of kindness to prevent her suffering? Melody shuddered. Nothing about this was kind. It was horrible that the cattle had been stolen and herded along out here—

And that this one had somehow been injured and therefore killed.

"I—I see," she said softly to Casey. "I think you're right. I need to let Clarence know what we found, right away. I doubt he'll send a team here immediately but he might want to. First, though, I want to look around here a little more. I doubt there are any more dead cattle, with just the one GPS dot showing up, but I'd like to see if I can tell how this one got hurt in the first place and if there's anything else I need to tell Clarence."

"Fine. I'll stay with you."

Which she appreciated. She pulled herself up to a standing position, and Casey did the same. Then she looked down again at Addie.

Melody felt terribly sad for her. She'd suffered an injury and then been killed because of it.

"You poor thing," she whispered, then looked around.

Casey had started walking away—he was heading toward a row of uneven bushes at the edges. She was unsure why he pursued that track. Had the cow somehow slipped there? But how had Addie wound up back here, at the top?

Maybe they'd never find out exactly what had happened. Melody pulled her phone from her pocket again and took some pictures of the poor, dead cow.

Then she followed Casey toward the slope.

He waited for her there, holding out his hand. "This does look a bit treacherous, though that cow must somehow have been injured up there since the rustlers probably couldn't have gotten her back to the top otherwise. But we can go down to check it out." It was, in fact, a fairly steep slope, one that a cow probably could not walk down safely without assistance, Melody believed.

"Fine," she said, then took another couple of pictures from this angle, before they started down.

And then—

Casey must have seen what Melody did at the same time. "Damn!" he exclaimed, still holding her hand as they began to hurry as much as they could on this dangerous incline.

"No!" Melody shouted, pulling ahead of Casey as much as she could without falling. She shoved her phone back into her pocket—for now.

In moments, she bent down over the horrible thing in front of her.

"Pierce?" Melody called out as she kneeled beside the body of the kind, smart ranch hand who'd pretty much been her mentor. Her friend. She felt as if she had been punched in the gut. She had felt sorry about the dead cow—but Pierce? Surely he would be okay, right?

She grabbed his wrist to try to find a pulse, but with

his pallor, his lack of breathing or any other movement, and what she saw, she knew the answer.

There was a similar hole in the middle of his forehead, but much more noticeable than the one on the cow. Blood had flowed from it…and was visible on his ashen face.

Pierce Tostig was dead.

Chapter Eleven

Casey immediately dove into deputy mode. He kneeled down to check for any indication the victim was still alive and found nothing. Even so, just in case, he quickly started CPR, but when chest compressions still had no effect, he noted in his mind the location and the hour— one in the afternoon—though he wouldn't be the one to determine the time of death.

Now he realized Melody had begun sobbing beside him. How well had she known the guy? No matter. They'd clearly at least been coworkers and probably friends.

Would she cry so much if he was injured…or worse? Casey didn't want to find out, yet on one level he hoped she cared enough about him to do so.

Ridiculous.

He kept performing CPR a short while longer, then stopped and decided it was time to make a call.

He stood up and Melody stood beside him, not looking down toward the body. Her eyes were red, her cheeks damp, but she was no longer crying.

"What—what should we do now?" she asked him.

"I need to phone this in. My department will undoubtedly send a team out here as fast as possible to deal with the situation."

She nodded. "I understand…though getting out here will be a challenge." She pulled her own phone out of her pocket but just held it against her chest for a moment. Then, clearly tense and upset, she looked down and took a picture before turning away again and putting back her phone. "I'll wait to hear what's happening before I call Clarence and let him know."

"Good idea."

Still watching her, he pulled his own phone from his pocket. He hoped it still had reception this far out, though since Melody's did, at least enough for her GPS to work, surely his would, too—right?

Fortunately, the answer was yes. He immediately called Sheriff Krester directly. Also fortunately, he answered right away.

Casey put the call on speaker, since he thought Melody might be able to contribute to it as far as how to find them.

"Hi, Casey," his boss said. "I didn't expect to hear from you till tonight, since—"

"We've just come across a dead body, sir," Casey interrupted.

"What? Who. And where?"

Casey explained the circumstances as quickly and succinctly as he could, including that he was still with Melody, and they continued to search for the missing herd of cattle.

"So you think the cow's death and that ranch hand's are related?" the sheriff asked.

"They must be, since they died so close together and so similarly, but I have no idea why, at least regarding Pierce."

"Well, we obviously need to bring Pierce's body back here to have it checked out first by medical personnel, then by the coroner. How do you propose we do that?"

Good question, Casey thought. "We're out here on horseback, as you know. And we'd already determined that anything in the air like a plane or helicopter would give away our location and let the thieves know we're chasing them. But—"

"Under these circumstances," Melody interrupted, "I'd like to suggest that you use a helicopter. If you send it from around the ranch and in the same direction we've been going, and keep it relatively low, the rustlers aren't likely to see it. I gather they're still some distance ahead of us and the terrain between them and us rolls a lot. And maybe if you use a helicopter that isn't marked as part of the sheriff's department, they won't worry as much if they see it, anyway—assuming they could see any markings on it."

"Good idea," Casey said, admiring his partner in this search, though that was nothing new. He'd had a similar thought but didn't know the terrain as well as she did. "Of course, if they see any indication of a chopper they'll probably figure that the body they left here has been found."

"But they won't know how or by who, or that the people who found it are following them," Melody said.

"Although…well, we really need to be careful. If they get too suspicious, they may kill the remaining cattle and disappear before we catch them."

That wasn't a new concern, but voicing it again to Jeremy couldn't hurt. Another reason for Casey to admire Melody.

And he felt certain that she wanted no further harm to come to the missing herd—or any other person.

"Okay," Jeremy said. "We'll send a chopper right away. It wouldn't do to leave a body out there, plus you need to stay with it till it's been picked up rather than continuing on your trail. I'll get something going and call you back."

"Yes, sir," Casey said, and then, after a few more brief comments and questions, they hung up.

"Guess we'll see a helicopter soon," Melody said. He noticed that her beautiful and sad brown eyes had seemed glued to him during the whole conversation. Surely it was because she didn't want to look down at her fallen comrade rather than for any other reason.

"Guess so." Because it was the right thing to do— and because it might help Melody cope a little better with their discovery of her friend's body—Casey kneeled, pulled off Pierce's black sweatshirt and put it over his face.

She wasn't watching, he noticed. Though she'd taken a picture of Pierce lying there, she now seemed disinclined to look down at all. In fact, she had taken her phone from her pocket again. She pressed a button and Casey figured she must feel it was time to notify her boss about what had happened out here.

Bad stuff. He'd been assigned to find missing cattle, not deal with a murder. Oh, but he definitely would help to solve it. But this shouldn't happen anywhere, let alone around Cactus Creek.

MELODY FELT HER eyes tear up again as she pressed the button on her phone to call Clarence.

A small portion of her distress was because of having to make this call. Her boss was more than the owner of the important, lucrative ranch that she worked for. He was also a big man in town, its selectman, and he expected everyone to recognize his importance and do what was necessary to comply with promises made to him—and she was about to deliver bad news.

At the moment, though, she'd been handed a particularly important job. But all she'd done so far was help locate a cow who'd been injured and killed. And worse, much worse, she had also helped to find the body of another ranch hand, one more important than she was, who'd probably come out here on his own, intending to be a lot more successful than she'd been in bringing down the rustlers. Well, he'd apparently found them first.

Enough. If Clarence wanted to fire her for being ineffective—and finding Pierce—so be it. She glanced toward Casey, who was watching her, probably reading, in the expression on her face, her sorrow at her failure—and, worse, in finding poor Pierce's body. Pierce, who'd always been so kind to her, who'd helped her learn what she needed to about this ranch and its livestock.

Surely he'd been out here attempting, like her, to find

the missing cattle—and hadn't been involved in their disappearance. She refused to believe that.

She made herself take one deep breath, then another. Casey had allowed her to participate in his conversation with his boss, and she believed she'd actually been of some use.

Following his example, she made herself give him a small smile as they continued to stand there, their backs toward the area where poor Pierce was lying, and pushed the buttons on her phone to call Clarence and put the conversation on the speaker.

She half hoped this would be one of those times when Clarence didn't answer first thing…but he did.

"Okay, Melody," he began, "I'm surprised to hear from you in the middle of the day. Does this mean you've actually made some progress?"

She winced at the criticism in his voice and his tone, allowing herself to glance slightly sideways to see Casey's reaction.

"Hello, Selectman Edison," Casey intoned in a chilly voice. "This is Deputy Sheriff Casey Colton. I'm here with Melody, and we have a couple of matters you should be informed about."

A slight pause, then Clarence said, "What matters?"

Melody suspected that their finding the body of one of his precious cows would be of greater importance to him than the fact they'd also discovered Pierce's body, even though he'd been one of Clarence's employees. Nevertheless, she said, "Sir, we have unfortunately discovered the body of one of your senior ranch hands, Pierce Tostig. We're not sure why he was here—prob-

ably trying to help by looking for the missing herd,
too—but we found him near the dead body of one of
the cows."

"What! Tell me more about this—the cow and
Pierce."

Melody wasn't surprised at the order in which he
asked about them. She shot a glance toward Casey,
whose expression appeared full of irony as he shook
his head slightly. He'd caught that Clarence had put the
animal before the man.

Melody opened her mouth to begin relating what
they'd been through but Casey beat her to it. He described how they had first come upon the corpse of
the poor cow, how its leg had been broken and that it
apparently had been shot as a result. They had started
looking around the area for any ideas about who'd done
it and when—and that was when they had discovered
Pierce's corpse.

"Was he the one who shot the cow?" Clarence demanded, his tone suggesting he'd have gladly shot his
employee, too, if he'd discovered the dead cow first.

"I don't know," Melody said. "It's possible that he
found the poor, injured cow and decided to prevent her
from suffering anymore."

"And someone decided to prevent him from suffering any more, too," Clarence said almost pleasantly, as
if he was nodding his head back in the town at the ap-
propriateness of the act.

Again Melody met Casey's gaze, and she cringed
at the anger she saw there. "Anyway," she said hastily,
"the sheriff's department is going to come here to pick

up poor Pierce's body. We'll need to leave the cow here for now because there's no good way to take her back to the ranch, especially since we're still hoping the rustlers won't realize we're out here and chasing them."

"Then hurry up and catch them already," Clarence shouted, making Melody move the phone farther from her ear. "I don't want you to wind up finding any more of my valuable stock out there dead, you hear me?"

"Yes, sir." Melody did her best to keep the annoyance she felt out of her tone. But she couldn't joke, either. "And I'll keep you informed as we continue, though not tonight. 'Bye."

And then she hung up—and felt those damn tears return to her eyes again.

She was grieving—for Pierce, of course, and the cow...as well as the peacefulness of her own life.

She again caught Casey's gaze, even as he took several steps toward her. Neither of them was looking down.

In a moment, she was in his arms as he gave her a hug. She hugged him back. She knew they were sharing sympathy and empathy and sorrow. She needed that.

And wondered how she was going to survive this assignment with her sanity in place.

CASEY DIDN'T KNOW the helicopter pilot or the EMTs—a man and a woman—who appeared at the site not much more than half an hour later, landing on the nearby pasture. He did appreciate the quick arrival and how they immediately got to work checking out Pierce and confirming that he was deceased—no question in Casey's mind about that, either, as unfortunate as it was. This was definitely a homicide, and a full investigation would need to be commenced. Casey could only hope it would be solved fast and the perpetrator prosecuted quickly. A couple members of the sheriff's department were along, too, and Casey knew them. He was surprised that one of them was Deputy Bob Andrews, the young guy who mostly hung out at the department answering the phone and greeting people who came in, then sending the more experienced deputies out on calls. Maybe this was to be a learning experience for him, since he was unlikely to accomplish much.

But Casey wasn't surprised that he was accompanied by Captain Walter Forman, who had a lot more seniority than Casey, and was even nearing retirement. Most important, he was one of the most experienced investigators in the department.

Well, Walter might have more experience, but Casey was already involved in this situation. He intended to remain a primary investigator out here, even while continuing to hunt for the missing cattle.

He hoped to be the one to find the answers.

As the EMTs got busy checking Pierce, Walter had Bob take a lot of pictures. He then began asking both Casey and Melody questions about how they'd gotten here, what they'd seen, how they'd found Pierce's body and more. Casey knew how to respond efficiently and did so, and was glad to hear Melody do so as well. Bob asked a few questions, too, furthering Casey's assumption that he was along partly to help but probably also to learn more of what an investigation was like.

On Walter's request, they took Bob and him up the rise to look at the dead cow while they left the EMTs and helicopter pilot near the site where they'd discovered Pierce's body. Melody led the group, and Casey enjoyed watching her athletic body, in her hoodie and jeans, navigate along the rise. Casey assumed she wanted to spend as much time with what was left of the cow that she could—or at least point out what she could about the poor animal's condition.

Their horses, fortunately, were still tethered close by, which prompted Casey to ask Walter some questions of his own. "Do you have any knowledge about how Mr. Tostig got out here? Are you aware whether he also rode a horse here from the ranch? Ours are here, but we didn't see any others."

"No, we're not aware yet how he got here," Walter said. "Or even why, although we gather he may have gone after the missing cattle on his own, without approval from anyone at the ranch. We already have a team at the ranch asking questions, and I'll make sure they check to see if Mr. Tostig was out here on horseback, which seems logical. Maybe while you're out on the range, you can keep an eye out for his missing horse as well as the cattle. And once Bob and I complete what investigation we can out here we'll head back to the ranch, too, after Mr. Tostig's body has been taken to the morgue."

They'd reached the cow's corpse, and flies buzzed around it now. Melody swiped at them with her hand, then said, "I know Clarence will want to see this cow himself or at least send someone out here from the ranch to deal with her body. Is there some way we can cover her up for now, keep her as clean as possible?"

"We've got some blankets in the helicopter and could use those," Bob said.

"Thank you." Melody looked down again at the cow and shook her head slightly. Casey assumed she was crying again, or at least fighting not to, so he approached and put his arm around her. He doubted he'd be much comfort, but at least he could try.

She looked at him. Sure enough, her eyes were shimmering, but she took a deep breath and smiled at him. "This is hard. I don't know how you can hang out at crime scenes helping people or doing what else you do and keep your sanity."

"Who says I'm sane?" he quipped, and her smile grew even larger.

After answering a few more of Walter's—and Bob's—questions, they returned to the area below. Pierce's body had been removed, and Casey assumed he was inside the helicopter. Walter told Bob to go inside and get the blankets to cover the cow.

Casey figured Melody and he had helped around here all they could, answering questions and showing the other members of his department around.

They were through here, as far as he was concerned, although he didn't know how long the others intended to stay.

No matter. Melody and he had their own assignment to resume.

He approached Walter, who was taking more pictures with his phone of the barren area where Pierce's body had been. "Melody and I are going to get on our way now," Casey told him. "There's even more reason now to locate the missing cattle and the people who stole them."

"Very true," Walter said. "Only…well, we'll do the same thing with the chopper when we leave as when we arrived here. I'll make sure our pilot heads the same direction we came from and keeps it low and hopefully not too noticeable. But who knows where the killers are? You'll need to be careful. And once I've done my report, it's entirely possible that Sheriff Krester will want to send a whole unit out in the direction you're heading, maybe in another chopper, even if it's seen by the thieves. We definitely need to apprehend them now, since the only evidence we have points to them as the probable murderers."

"I understand," Melody said. She'd been speaking with Bob, who now held some blankets off to the side of where Casey stood with Walter, but she must have been listening. "But, please, give us another day or two and keep in touch with us. I'm just afraid that when the rustlers realize Pierce has been found and people are definitely after them, they'll kill the remaining cattle, too."

"Let's hope not," Walter said, sending Melody a sympathetic look. "But I'm sure you realize that catching a perpetrator after a murder investigation will have to take precedence."

"I understand," she repeated, "and I appreciate your covering that cow up with those." She looked first at Bob, who nodded as he moved the blankets around. She then turned to look Casey straight in the eye. "Please, please, let's get going now."

Being here, finding first the cow, then poor Pierce, had been hard. Very hard. But also motivating.

Melody had obviously wanted to find the rustlers before. Now, Casey believed she felt it was even more important.

Well, so did he. Oh, yeah. It was time to get going.

Chapter Twelve

Bouncing a bit as her horse navigated the rougher grass-and-dirt terrain, Melody had an urge to press her heels harder against Cal's sides and get him to gallop. And if Cal sped forward, Witchy would, too.

But for now, she continued at their current pace, which was the fastest they had traveled so far on this fiasco of a search.

Why? Why had nice, helpful Pierce been killed? And why had he even been out there?

What did his death have to do with the poor cow being killed?

And where was Pierce's horse…assuming he'd had one? How else would he have gotten there, in the middle of nowhere? Perhaps the rustlers had another helicopter that Casey and she hadn't seen?

All the more reason to catch up with those horrible thieves…and most likely murderers, since who else would have killed Pierce?

At least she believed they were still going the right way. She'd checked the GPS on her phone before they got back on their horses and headed in the same direction they'd been going before the horrible interruption they'd just experienced. Sure enough, the cluster of small red dots was ahead of them—still way ahead of them and continuing to move, but maybe not as fast as before if Melody was interpreting correctly. And they didn't seem to have changed course. No further small dots on their own, fortunately.

But who knew what would happen next? More animal killings?

More murders?

That had now been several hours ago. After their delay, they only had another hour or so before they'd have to stop because of darkness.

"You doing okay?" Casey asked from beside her.

"Yes," she said, then felt herself grimace. "And no. I'm getting really tired of this outing." Well, not entirely. She was enjoying his company. But still— "I want answers. Results. Saving those poor cattle out there and letting you arrest the damn people who—who killed…"

She knew she was about to cry again, and so she forced her gaze to go forward without finishing her sentence.

"I'm so sorry, Melody," Casey said, his tone bleak enough that she had to look at him. "I should have insisted from the first that only people from my department should be out here doing this. We'd have found a way to deal with crossing the land even without knowing much about the terrain. The GPS signal should have been enough."

"No!" Melody exclaimed, then repeated more softly, "No. That's not what I'm trying to say. You didn't know

Pierce was coming. None of us did. And having one of the hands from OverHerd officially along with you was the best way to do this. I'm glad I was the one chosen. It's just that…well, I understood the possibility of finding some of the cattle injured or even killed under these circumstances. But another one of the ranch hands? I hadn't considered that. And what if Pierce had been the one to accompany you instead? He certainly knew this terrain as well as I do, probably better. I know he had lots more responsibilities at the ranch he needed to tend to, so in some ways it made sense for me to go along, but maybe he'd still be alive if—"

"I understand why you're doing this," Casey interrupted. "You're trying to figure out how to deal with what happened, but coming up with a way to blame yourself won't work. It won't bring Pierce back, or even Addie the cow. Best thing we can do is to continue along here, get to the herd and deal with the bad guys, and the cattle, in the best way possible once we recognize what that is."

"You're right." Melody looked across the short distance between their mounts, appreciating Casey's attempt to make her feel better. It actually helped, at least a little.

And she was determined to ensure, in whatever way she could, that they were successful in catching the rustlers. And bringing them to justice for killing Pierce. That would also make them pay for what they did to Addie.

"Come on," she said. "Let's step up the pace a bit more, okay? I'm beginning to see some color on the clouds at the horizon and the sky's not as bright as it was before. Sunset's getting close."

"You're right, as I gather you usually are. So—" He suddenly pressed his heels against Witchy's side, and his horse sped up.

"Let's go, Cal," she said and did the same thing.

But she would only allow it for about twenty minutes. She didn't want the horses to get too tired or injure themselves.

They'd have an even bigger day tomorrow, she figured. Their pace would be like this, on and off, for much more of the day.

Would they finally catch up with the rustlers?

Oh, yes, she told herself, realizing she might not be realistic. But she'd do all she could to ensure that came true. It was certainly about time.

When she finally started slowing down Cal and calling to Casey to do the same with Witchy, they'd fortunately reached another area where the vast, rolling pasture was broken up with patches of underbrush as well as thick, tall bushes. Plus there was a pond nearby with a small creek flowing through it, which would be great for the horses and for their own preparations and ablutions that night.

The main problem would be the same anywhere around here. The air was already growing chilly and would only get colder.

But things could be worse. The clouds in the sky were few and did not appear dark. That was one thing that had worked in their favor these days and nights— no rain.

"How's this?" she asked Casey, waving her arm to encompass the area she was contemplating.

"Looks good to me," he said. "It'll be only a short while 'til the sun's completely down. Let's get ready... and plan to leave here as early in the morning as possible."

"Great," Melody said and directed Cal, who was now just walking, toward an open spot that was clear in the middle of some areas decorated with underbrush. It was large enough that they could attach the horses right there and also put up their tent for some semblance of cover.

Hard to think it was nearly time for bed, getting their tent—their single tent—set up so they would rest together again that night, but yes, they needed to get to sleep fast so they could get as early a start as possible in the morning.

They began what Melody now considered their routine. Would this be the last night for it? She hoped so, despite how she had come to enjoy it—performing silly, small chores alongside her comrade in this chase.

And she forced herself not to consider how much she would miss it—and him—when they were finally successful.

In a short while, they'd dismounted from their horses, unsaddled them, removed the bits from their mouths, and walked them to the pond, tying them there. Then Casey and she set up their small tent nearby.

By the time they'd taken care of themselves, filtered some water for drinking by the horses and them and made paltry attempts at bathing—clothes on, of course, although with lifting and unbuttoning and replacing a lot of the time—the sky was nearly dark. And despite herself, Melody had tried peeking at Casey but hadn't seen anything exciting.

Melody checked again on the horses and figured that where they were currently tethered should work for the night and would allow them to drink from the containers of filtered water at their leisure. She again gave them some of the grain she had brought, although they shouldn't be hungry considering the amount of time they'd been tied up at the grassy area where... Melody moved her mind away from that as much as she could and let herself dwell on the other times Casey and she had slowed down or stopped to allow the horses to rest—and eat—a bit.

She looked around and, not seeing Casey, figured he was inside the tent. Glancing at it, she saw the fabric on the top moving a little, confirming her presumption.

Another night was coming up when she'd be alone with Casey. Would they snuggle together to stay warm as they had last night? She hoped so.

She could use a little human contact for other reasons, too, after this very difficult day.

Particularly with this man, who was becoming an important part of her life.

For now, she assured herself. Just for now.

In a moment she, too, had bent over and made her way inside the tent. She kneeled on the dirt floor, although one of the sleeping bags was already spread out on the ground not far away.

Casey had also turned on the lanterns.

"Ready to eat?" she asked, walking forward on her knees to where the saddlebags rested on the ground to her left.

"Always," Casey said. "I'll be glad when I can take you to a nice restaurant for a salad and a real meal."

"Or I'll take you," Melody said. And how enjoyable would that be? Going on a date with this man might not be appropriate, but she felt sure it would be fun. "After all, your assignment now may be to chase bad guys, but it's also to help out our town selectman. We can let him treat."

She watched a shadowed grin appear on Casey's handsome, somewhat bearded face and had to smile back.

"Sounds good to me," he said. "I guess we can order some pretty tasty steaks at his expense, right?"

"Right."

She wasn't sure what Clarence would think of something like that, but figured that if—when—Casey and she returned to Cactus Creek after successfully tracking down and apprehending the bad guys and, even more importantly, bringing back the remaining valuable cattle, her boss wouldn't blink an eye at granting them some kind of reward. A good dinner should surely be on the agenda.

But for the time being, they again pulled out the bottles of filtered water for that evening as well as the standard fare of dried fruit, carrots and celery, trail mix, energy bars and some beef jerky, which they hadn't snacked on much since they hadn't brought a lot of it.

They both sat on opposite ends of the sleeping bag

that was stretched out beneath them. Melody reached for something to say. They'd probably exhausted talking about their pasts. Maybe their hopes for the future… besides capturing the rustlers and saving the cattle?

Actually, she was willing to talk about nearly anything, wanted to talk about nearly anything—except what had happened that day.

"So," Casey said, waving a half-eaten energy bar in the air. "Once we're finally through with all this, I'll visit you on your ranch again, but even more important, I'd like you to come see me at the sheriff's department. I'll want to show my fellow deputies who they could have been helping if they'd been the ones to volunteer for this little task."

Interesting. Casey assumed they would see one another again after they'd completed their task together. Melody had begun to hope for it but doubted it would happen. But if Casey wanted it, too?

"Did you volunteer for 'this little task'?" Melody asked, to keep the conversation going appropriately. She had gotten the impression that the sheriff had pressed him into service for this assignment, without any choice. But right now, she figured that Casey was searching for a noncontroversial, nonemotional topic for them to talk about, and she appreciated it.

"Well, no," he replied, "but I would have, if I'd known someone like you would be my contact out here. And, hey, we're about to spend our third night together."

Which made Melody laugh…just a little. She also, unsurprisingly, thought about what he'd said, what he'd reminded her about unnecessarily.

She was about to spend yet another night with Casey, one where they hopefully would snuggle again for warmth.

But she had a feeling it wouldn't be easy to stay remote from him again. Still. Not after everything that had occurred that day.

Having someone to hold her had never sounded better. But more? She recognized that having his hard body against her tonight might be enough to get her to try to forget all the bad things in exchange for something special.

Which she recognized was impossible. Touching him, making love with him, was absolutely prohibited. She couldn't let her sorrow toss her into something she definitely didn't want.

Or maybe, if she acknowledged it to herself, she did want…too much. But she definitely didn't want a relationship with another man. Not so soon after her divorce. So why even consider getting physical?

Except…well, maybe it would in some way help her deal with that sorrow.

"Look, Melody." Casey inched closer and took her hands into his. "I just want to…well, apologize in a way, even though there was nothing I could do to prevent what happened today. But I assume you and Pierce were pretty close. And—"

She glanced into Casey's wonderful, sympathetic blue eyes, and didn't—couldn't—look away. "In a way, yes—as mentor-protégée, I guess, though I already knew a lot about ranching before I came here. But

Pierce was the main hand here to teach me about this particular ranch. We became good buddies."

"So I'm sure what happened to him was even harder for you than if he'd simply been a fellow ranch hand you worked with now and then."

Casey's gaze changed slightly—was it hardening? Questioning? Was he making the wrong assumption? Maybe he was allowing himself to believe that she and Pierce had some kind of romantic relationship, which would stop anything from potentially occurring between them.

But she wouldn't imply a relationship that didn't exist. Casey and she had to have only truth between them, she told herself.

Especially if the untruth somehow flipped their rapport into distance.

Her voice, when she responded, was soft and raspy, but she continued to look straight into Casey's eyes. "To me, Pierce was just another ranch hand—a special one, sure, and one whose help I appreciated. But I'd have felt this bad if the same thing happened to any of my coworkers. Our connection is always special, but it's all wrapped up in making sure the cattle are treated as well as possible."

"Which is why you were so upset about finding that dead cow," Casey acknowledged.

"Exactly. It's kind of a strange bond among all of the ranch hands and to some degree the animals we care for. I don't know what it's like for you as a sheriff's deputy, but maybe you can relate what I feel to losing another peace officer you knew, or maybe a victim you tried to help." She couldn't help hesitating. "That could be an exaggeration, I know. But—"

The expression on his face changed again, this time to what appeared to be even greater sympathy. "Exaggeration or not, I get it," he said, and suddenly he moved closer so there was no longer any gap between them.

They sat for an instant facing each other, close up. And then…well, Melody wasn't sure which of them reached out first, but suddenly they were kneeling again, in each other's arms, tightly, sensually, as their lips met in a kiss that was far more than any sympathetic gesture between friends who'd suffered difficult circumstances together.

Casey's mouth was hot and searching on hers, and Melody couldn't help responding in kind, wanting to experience all she could by this wonderful kiss.

But their position on the sleeping bag, as they pushed up against one another, felt awkward.

And Melody knew just what to do about it.

Gently but firmly, keeping her arms around Casey, she pulled him down so they were both lying on top of that sleeping bag, still kissing heatedly.

She enjoyed the feel of his growing beard against her skin. And in moments their tongues were playing an exploratory touching game that made Melody's insides begin to sizzle, then burn when one of Casey's hands moved down her back and grasped her butt.

"Oh," she gasped, even as her own hands began to move, partly by design and partly because, instinctively, she wanted—needed—to touch him as sensuously as he was touching her.

And that desire was triggered even more when, as they drew closer, she felt a hardness press into her stomach, a sexual stimulus sparked by her recognizing his erection but wanting to feel it more.

Maybe even see it.

But before she could pull away to reach between them, she felt Casey tugging gently at the back of her jeans. "Don't worry, I'll keep you warm," he said, barely moving his mouth away from hers.

She couldn't help smiling a little. "And I'll keep you warm," she said. "No—*hot*."

For she realized then, appropriate or not, what they were about to do.

In moments, they were both nude. The air was chilly around them, but at least there was no breeze inside the tent. And they remained so close to one another, first touching bared skin, then reaching for the other's most sensitive parts.

Hardly aware of where they were or anything else except that she was with Casey, and what she'd been wanting without allowing herself to acknowledge it seemed about to occur.

Casey caressed Melody's breasts first and her nipples hardened beneath his fingers. She gasped and used the stimulus to move her own hands to his most sexy places, first his now-nude butt, then around to his erection.

She inhaled with more than a gasp at the feel of its length, its hardness, beneath her fingers. As he made a noise that sounded like the most sensuous moan she had ever heard, she stroked him with a pumping motion that imitated what she wanted him to do…within her.

Instead, she almost shouted in frustration as he pulled away, rolling over so his back was to her and he faced his saddlebag. What? He was hungry for food again now rather than—

But he soon turned back, something in his hand.

A condom.

He'd anticipated this? Or was it just another way this accomplished deputy sheriff stayed prepared for anything?

Instead of shouting, she smiled again. "Let me," she said as she reached for it, then pulled away the wrapping. Unrolling the condom upon his amazingly hard length turned her on as much as anything she had ever experienced.

Until, moments later, he was on top of her, kissing, sucking her breasts…and then he reached below to caress her most sensitive parts. "Oh, Casey," she moaned, then gasped again as he moved again and carefully but insistently pressed himself inside her.

She could hardly think during the next…how long was it? Hours? Moments? She felt no sense of time, only touching and heat and desire as Casey's movements increased in speed and intensity…until his body stopped moving and he moaned.

Even as she felt herself come, too.

And as Melody soon lay there beside Casey, still enjoying his closeness, she wondered how their working together would be over the next day or two.

She felt certain nothing between them would ever be the same again.

Chapter Thirteen

Casey felt invigorated as he lay there beside Melody, breathing hard, holding her tightly against his bare skin. He wondered whether they could enjoy each other even more tonight, just in case this was their last night together. Or even if it wasn't.

Melody had attracted him before. She definitely did now. But he realized this was a bad idea, in many ways. So what? It had been one of the most amazing experiences in his life, here in the dim light of the lanterns, where he could see Melody's body, full of curves in all the right places, which had felt even better as he caressed them. And then he'd made love with her.

"I take it you're still awake," Melody said against his shoulder. She felt warm. Very warm, which was more than welcome in the coolness of the tent.

"Yes, and I guess you are, too." He began moving his hands along her bare back, then down, where he could grasp the globes of her small, tight buttocks.

Which made his erection start thickening and hardening once more…

"That was…wonderful," Melody breathed. "But I'm not quite tired enough to sleep, so—"

She didn't have to say any more, especially since her hand moved down between them and touched him and made him want to do anything—everything—but sleep.

He could only breathe heavily and smile as they made love once more.

And then again…

Afterward, Casey just lay there, still—again—holding Melody closely against him, but only after, this time, unfolding the other sleeping bag on top of them for warmth. He figured that was exactly what they would do at last: sleep.

He felt sated…for now, at least. How would he feel in the morning?

In the future?

Well, he'd find out—

He finally felt himself relaxing enough to fall asleep.

HE WOKE UP early the next morning, or at least there was a small bit of light seeping into the tent.

Melody was still sleeping. She was naked beside him beneath their thick cover and he tamped down the urge to start something new. As enjoyable as it might be, it would take time.

And they had to start once more on their mission out here on this vast ranch as soon as possible.

But… Melody's breathing was still deep, the sound of it—what else?—a melody in his ears, soft and even and very, very sweet.

He'd particularly noticed her scent before, when

they'd merely slept together. Now he wondered how she could continue to smell so wonderful after their ride. She must have brought along some kind of body wash with that addictive floral scent. Although maybe that was her natural aroma. He wouldn't put anything past this determined, self-reliant, skilled—and sexy— woman.

He reveled quietly in how close they were, how her body heat warmed him. He wanted to remember every moment of it, knowing how unlikely it was ever to happen again…except, perhaps, if they did wind up sleeping outside again in this tent for another night or two.

But once they returned to reality, after this difficult adventure was over, that would be that.

He'd hope to see Melody now and then, of course, but despite how much he had enjoyed being with her— especially last night—he still distrusted the idea of any relationship.

Not after what he'd gone through with Georgia.

He startled as Melody moved slightly in his arms, as if she was reading his thoughts. But she only murmured slightly and moved more closely against him, if that was possible.

It was certainly enjoyable…and turned him on once more. Not that he'd do anything about that now.

He gritted his teeth, once more in the throes of recollections he wanted to somehow erase from his mind, but realized he never would.

Georgia. Strange that he'd think about her now— or not so strange. They'd had sex, of course, but never like this. But—

Georgia. He suddenly thought of that charm that they'd found where the fence had been destroyed. A silver charm with a *G* on it. His thoughts had touched on it occasionally since he'd picked it up and taken it to the sheriff's department for analysis, and not just because it was an obscure clue of some kind.

He finally recognized why.

At some point during their planning, he'd heard that Georgia's parents had given her a charm to wear in celebration on their wedding day. The charm he'd found had her initial on it. Could it be the same one?

Not hardly…right?

That would be too much of a coincidence. How could Georgia be involved in this rustling situation?

She couldn't. He must still be asleep somehow for all of this to barge into his mind.

He was clearly thinking too much right now. He had to stop.

Or if he was going to think, he'd rather muse over what he'd done with Melody last night.

And…well, if he couldn't just wake up Melody and share again the wonders of what they'd done—and he couldn't, because of their need for speed that day—it was nevertheless time to wake her up anyway. To get going.

And to stop thinking, especially about what they'd done last night. It couldn't continue, after all. He wouldn't want it to, and neither would Melody .

So…the best way to awaken her, and to start their day? He moved even closer and kissed her on her full, enticing lips.

Foolish? Maybe. But it had the result he wanted.

Her eyes popped open immediately and her arms moved enough to draw him closer, until their kiss deepened enough to stimulate other parts of his body.

But no matter how he felt, or what he wanted, they needed to get on the move right away.

Pulling slightly away, he said, "It's morning. Ready to get back on the trail?"

He felt her stiffen a bit in his arms. Had he hurt her feelings? But they had the same goal in mind, their jobs to perform, and she immediately said, "Absolutely."

Her response, to his dismay and surprise, hurt his feelings a bit. But he just said, "Last one up and dressed has to pass out our water and breakfast treats."

She rolled over quickly and soon stood away from their sleeping-bag bed. He rose as well but couldn't help observing her luscious body in the nude once more, before she could pull on her underwear, jeans, T-shirt and hoodie, then comb her hair and arrange it again into a ponytail.

Which only made him feel worse that they hadn't engaged, just this once more, in a tiny, short bout of sex.

But this was the right thing to do. In moments he would get dressed in his warm clothes for the day, including his sweatshirt…though not before Melody had turned slightly and also observed his bare body, which, of course, reacted to her gaze. He ignored it. They had to get on their way.

"HEY, CAL KEEPS trying to slow down," Melody called to Casey. It was nine o'clock in the morning, and they'd been riding once more over the grassy, rolling pasture toward the red dots on her GPS that indicated where the cattle were. They set a quicker pace than they had before, as planned. As always, before they'd started out she had checked her GPS app. The cattle would soon reach the hill they'd need to get down, in the direction of a long rural road, or turn sideways. It appeared that Casey and she were making progress in catching up with them, but not a lot.

Whichever route the rustlers decided to take, she and Casey would follow. And, hopefully, catch them soon.

Right now, she was enjoying the bumps and movements of being on horseback, even if it wasn't as fast as she wanted. She continued, "Do you think my horse wants us to spend another night in the tent before we catch up to the cattle?"

She was kidding, of course. Last night had been fantastic. And though sex was a wonderful experience in a relationship, what she had with Casey was *not* a relationship.

"Well, I didn't get the impression that Cal and Witchy did anything different last night from what they'd done before, and I doubt they care what their riders were up to, either." Casey's voice was loud enough to be heard over the sound of hoofbeats on the ground.

"Guess you're right." Melody shot a positive expression toward her fellow cattle seeker—well, criminal hunter—and nodded her head, then laughed. "Oh, well."

"Yep—oh, well," Casey returned.

And that should have been the end of it. Melody wasn't going to say any more on that subject that gripped her mind—and her body—even now. Unless she figured out another way to joke about it. Make it clear that, in her opinion, Casey and she would just remain buddies, as well as professional colleagues.

Still, despite their prior conversations and her own thoughts about it, Melody felt a bit hurt. What they'd had clearly meant little or nothing to the man she was with.

Well, she knew better than to wish otherwise. And she knew far better than to expect anything more, no matter how wonderful she had found it.

Something occurred to her that she could ask about in a casual manner…kind of. At least it might indicate whether Casey, too, thought they could remain friends. "So what should I expect if I'm able to join you and your family for Christmas dinner? I think you said your brother lives in Phoenix, right? Will he be joining us here?" And was he coming here to join his family for Thanksgiving? Melody didn't know what they were doing then. Her invitation was for Christmas, an extra month away.

"Probably. He'll want to see our parents, and maybe even me." Casey's expression looked light when she glanced at him. She gathered his relationship with his twin brother remained close, even though they didn't live in the same town.

"You're sure your parents will be okay with me coming, too?" She gritted her teeth slightly, half expecting him to rescind the invitation.

"Oh, they're always fine when we ask friends and acquaintances to join us for Christmas."

She looked away, feeling ridiculously hurt. She was just a friend or an acquaintance, in his estimation.

That was true, but it still felt painful after what they'd shared. Even so, she wanted to continue the friendly conversation. "So what do your parents think about their sons both being in law enforcement, though different types?" she asked. "I gathered from what you said before that your mother might be happier about it than your father." As she recalled, Casey had said his mother had hoped her sons would also give back to the community.

"Oh, she worries about us. They both do. They're always telling us to be careful."

And so would she, Melody realized, if she was part of their family. Which she wasn't, of course. "So *are* you?"

"How careful can I be out here in the middle of nowhere with you chasing bad guys?"

"I wondered about that," Melody responded. "At least your parents' jobs both sound fairly responsible. I don't envy your dad, though, trying to cure people of cancer. At least there's not much danger involved for either of them—unlike working for the sheriff's department or FBI."

"Yeah, and Everett and I have the same likelihood of running into bloody situations as our dad does, since he performs surgery sometimes. Or at least I occasionally deal with bloodshed in my job—not that I dig into people intentionally, of course, though I sometimes get involved in contentious situations. Or I find...well, you know."

She did know what he meant, but she refused to mention Pierce, either, or how they'd found him. Instead, she said, "Glad I'm a ranch hand. Sure, there's occasionally blood involved, especially when one of our cows gives birth, but fortunately things tend to be fairly calm and blood-free."

She did find it interesting that both twin brothers had wound up in law enforcement, though, with their parents in such different careers.

For the next half hour, they talked often but about neutral topics, not generally their families but sometimes about their education and what they liked, or didn't like, about Cactus Creek.

Melody didn't get into her thoughts about the future, though. She liked Cactus Creek, intended to stay here, but she didn't want to marry again.

Although she would regret not starting a family.

Well, maybe someday, if the right man happened to show up in her life…

Not Casey, though. Not anyone, this soon after what had happened to her.

For now, she was glad when they urged their horses to a faster gait, then had them slow for a short while.

Melody then decided they should stop so the horses could rest and nibble some grass, while she pulled her phone out to check its GPS once more.

Were they getting closer to those red dots? She certainly hoped so—although if the rustlers continued to drive the cattle forward at the same pace as they'd been doing, she and Casey might be somewhat closer but possibly not near enough to catch up with them today after all.

But when she looked at the app, the number of miles between the cattle and them had shrunk.

"Hey!" she said. "I don't think our quarry is moving much at all today."

"Really?" Casey's eyes widened. "How close are we?"

"A lot closer than before. And if we keep our mounts at the speeds we've been going and the cattle don't go any faster, I think we're going to do it."

"Do what? Catch up with them?"

"Exactly."

HE HOPED SO. Damn, how he hoped so.

He wanted to apprehend those thieves—and murderers—more than nearly any other perpetrator he'd ever gone after. Get this situation resolved. Find out if Georgia did have anything to do with it, since he couldn't help suspecting her thanks to the charm. Although it could, of course, be someone else who had the same initial, or had a friend or relative who did.

After they'd remounted and set out again, he dug his heels into Witchy's side just a little to speed up her pace a bit more. And, of course, Cal—and Melody—kept up with him.

But even as he did that, he considered again that resolving these crimes, hopefully in an appropriate way, would end this closeness with Melody.

At least with her joining his family for Christmas dinner, he would see her again. Plus, as he'd already considered, he could stop in and see her at OverHerd Ranch sometimes.

But…well, he'd only been with her for a few days. And nights.

And then there was the closeness they had shared last night…

"Hey," she called from slightly behind him. "Hey, Deputy Sheriff Colton. Looks like you really want to catch those missing cattle fast now." She—rather, Cal—caught up with him and he glanced at the beautiful ranch hand beside him. Her hair, in its ponytail, bounced as she rode this quickly. She looked as excited as he felt.

Okay, it would be a good thing to get this criminal activity dealt with at last.

And after?

After, they'd hopefully wind up being friends, at Christmas and otherwise.

"It's about time we made more progress," he said. "Although—well, I don't want to delay anything, but if we happen to get close late, we won't want to start our capture of the bad guys and saving the cattle till daylight again. Maybe we'll spend another night together." He turned and aimed a quick wink at her.

"Sounds good to me. But only if that's how things work out."

Chapter Fourteen

As Melody rode—silently now, as she wanted to concentrate on their task at hand, which might actually come to an end soon—she checked the GPS on her phone screen again. And again. She was continuing to use its special terrain-depiction feature—though they were far enough out that her reception had become bad at times, and things often blurred. That both annoyed and worried her.

Even at this more-than-moderate speed on horseback, she was aware that Casey kept glancing over toward her. She glanced back, managing to give him a grin now and then before looking back at the phone.

She had already recognized before they took off that morning that the cattle were nearing the end of Over-Herd Ranch, where the rustlers would need to decide whether to head down the hillside toward the road a bit beyond it, or get the herd to veer to one side or the other.

Which would they do?

In her visits to many parts of the ranch property, Melody had never come this far. She didn't believe there was a fence all the way out here to indicate the end of the ranch property, but she wasn't sure.

But for all she knew, there was a fence out here, too, that was slowing the cattle they were chasing. The GPS map did show a line that could just have been the edge of the property, but it might also be a fence. It also indicated rises and drops in the topography, including rocks and, to some degree, bushes and trees.

And not too far in the distance, she could see more underbrush growing, which indicated this part of the pasture either hadn't initially been cleared and replanted as well as the rest, or simply wasn't cared for as well.

Melody still assumed the rustlers would veer off to one side or the other. It was the practical way to go, although where would they head next? Staying somewhere on OverHerd Ranch didn't seem like a good option. Were they neighbors of this property? Maybe that was the answer. They'd drive the stolen cattle onto their property and sell them.

Although if their herd suddenly increased in size thanks to some valuable Angus cows, wouldn't someone notice?

Someone with clout, and money, like Clarence—or someone who'd want to make a good impression on their rich neighbor who happened to be the town selectman?

Or the rustlers, neighbors or not, might just go ahead and drive the cattle toward that public road, assuming they'd get down the upcoming hillside easily and safely enough. Rather than keep the stolen cattle around here, wasn't it more likely they'd take them somewhere else to care for, or sell?

Had they already changed the brands on all the cows to SG, as they had with poor, dead Addie? And what did it mean?

And speaking of safety, why endanger the valuable stock they'd stolen by potentially getting them hit by cars on the road?

Of course, that assumed there would be vehicles out here in the middle of nowhere on this mild November day.

If that was the decision, surely even the rustlers would want to slow and stop the cattle. Herd them somewhere away from the road. The animals wouldn't be worth anything dead.

And people in vehicles would be at risk, too—not that the rustlers were likely to give a damn about that. They already had one animal death and a human murder on their shoulders.

She was not just OverHerding, she was overthinking this situation, Melody realized. Even so, she continued to view the map on her phone, which she held with one hand while the reins remained in the other. At the moment, that map was fairly clear.

"Hey, it's one thing to keep track of those cattle," Casey called over to her. "But you look like you're going to get bounced right out of the saddle since you're going this speed and not really hanging on. Haven't you checked the location enough?" Cal was keeping up with Witchy, and Casey looked damn good as a cowboy in the saddle even at that speed, his posture straight and his shoulders back. Melody wasn't exactly happy about his criticism, but the idea that Casey was concerned about her safety sent a little pulse of pleasure through her.

And she was, of course, going forward swiftly. Even Cal's long, deep brown mane was blowing erratically in the wind around them, something like her own ponytail.

"Just trying to determine which way they're going." She described the hillside, the road and the possible fence, as well as mentioning the likelihood the rustlers might instead take a sideways route. "I'm not sure which would be best for us, but I'm sure that's not a factor for them." Melody almost laughed at the sound of her own voice as it became sometimes garbled and uneven as she bounced.

Casey didn't complain, though. He did, however, call to her. "Okay, then. Let's slow down a little. We need to come up with a plan to get right up on where they are and bring down the rustlers, whichever way they go."

Sure enough, Witchy started slowing down as Casey pulled slightly at her reins. What else could Melody do but slow Cal as well? She was kind of the law-enforcement assistant here. She couldn't save the cattle and bring down the bad guys herself.

That was more smart and skilled—and good-looking and sexy—Deputy Sheriff Casey's job.

Casey pointed toward what appeared to be a gully off to their side, surrounded by bushes. "Let's let the horses get a drink, okay? We can hopefully purify some water there. I wouldn't mind a drink, too, so I need to get my bottle out of my saddlebag."

What? Actually stop here when they were getting close?

But Melody realized she was thirsty, too.

Besides, not knowing what the rustlers were up to, if she and Casey got too close without a plan, they might somehow be outmaneuvered.

Or even attacked.

Okay, a rest. A drink.

Some discussion.

Hopefully, when they continued forward again they would have more of a plan.

But first…what was that? Something on her screen was changing, and she needed to understand why. Was it because of poor reception? It didn't seem that way. In fact, the reception appeared fairly good here.

Would what had changed at last provide her with the answers they needed?

CASEY LIKED HOW Melody seemed so dedicated to their task, which he hoped—believed—would come to an end soon. But as much as he wanted to capture the murdering rustlers and bring in the missing cattle, he wanted to do it safely, with Melody at his side, not falling off her horse and getting hurt because she was trying so hard.

And if it wound up taking an extra night, as they'd mentioned before? Well, his body reacted slightly at the very idea, though that wasn't the point.

No, they needed to do things safely and well.

Hence, their break right now. It should be good for their horses, too. And he wouldn't allow it to slow them for long.

He slid off his saddle and helped Melody down—not that she, a skilled ranch hand, couldn't have done it herself. But once again, he was concerned for her safety, partly because she'd just begun really staring at and manipulating the screen on the phone in her hand like some careless teenager glued to something on social media or whatever.

He had seen several situations at the Sur County Sheriff's Department where young people had done something similar while driving and caused accidents. Hurt themselves, and sometimes other people.

Out here, Melody probably couldn't harm anyone but herself, but she wasn't going to do even that if he could help it. And he could.

Besides, touching her even so neutrally felt good.

"Everything okay?" he asked, but she didn't respond. Not yet. But he'd get her to talk to him and let him know what was on her mind.

Soon.

Once she was standing by Cal, still swiping at things on the screen in front of her, Casey returned to Witchy and took his horse's reins, directing her toward the slope down to the small creek running through the middle of some bushes near them. When he'd gotten some water ready for her and his horse seemed happy, he returned to get Cal and make sure Melody knew what he was doing.

She didn't even spare him a glance at first, though she looked up immediately when he joined her after taking Cal to Witchy's side. "You've got to look at this," she said, gesturing with her phone.

At last. He'd get some answers. "What's going on?" He spoke more firmly this time and fought back an amused urge to inquire whether she'd discovered a new YouTube video. But he had come to know her well enough over the past few days to feel certain that whatever she'd found, it had something to do with their quest for the cattle and the thieves.

Maybe even, considering Melody's apparent excitement, something that would help them end their search at last.

She looked so gorgeous standing there, her dark hair framing just one side of her pretty face since her head was tilted, her deep brown eyes agog with what appeared to be excitement. Although was there just a bit of puzzlement there, too?

Was he coming to know her well enough to read her expressions and know what she was thinking?

He hoped so, but still, he wanted to know what was causing her to apparently nearly bounce up and down on her toes as she continued to stare at her phone, then back at him as she waved it in invitation for him to see, too. She looked so cute behaving like this.

So appealing. Even so, the reason he drew closer was because of what she said.

"I've got to show you this," she told him. "I've been trying to figure it out and have at least a clue, though no real answers yet. Take a look."

She still held the phone, but this time it was in front of both of them. He bent to touch his shoulder to hers as he looked.

The map he saw this time appeared fairly detailed, with more ups and downs and trees and rocks and bushier plants. It seemed to indicate they were heading into a slightly different environment.

But that wasn't the only thing that was changed. Except for that same poor, dead cow, the rest of the red dots indicating the whereabouts of the missing cattle had previously been clumped together.

Not now.

"I've been watching this for a while," Melody said. "Some of those dots are moving individually. At first, it was just a couple, and then they stopped. And then those couple were joined by one more that had left the first group, which still remained a group. More are apparently being led away the same way, and I think we need to figure out where…and why."

"I agree." Casey looked up and stared in the direction they'd been moving, since that was also where the cows were previously being led, together, in a group.

What did it mean that it appeared they were now being led individually, at least for a short distance? Did that have to do with the topography?

He asked Melody her opinion as he held out his hand to look more closely at her phone. She was better skilled in manipulating the screen and figuring out locations using the GPS, so for the next few minutes he did what he could to look more closely at the dots and the cattle's surroundings—and Melody helped by reclaiming her phone, swiping or otherwise changing it now and then, and handing it back to him.

"So what do you think?" she asked him finally.

"I think we need to get back on the trail, but not as quickly since our quarry seems to be slowing down, whatever it is they're doing."

"That could work out well for us, right?" Melody was looking up at him now, and not at her phone.

Her dark eyebrows were lifted and her expression appeared hopeful.

"Guess we'll find out," he told her, nodding as if he fully agreed with her.

He only hoped she was right.

So how were they going to deal with this? It was Casey's call, of course, but Melody wanted to know in advance what they would try.

Best she could tell from her GPS map and those individual, sometimes moving dots, that hill at the end of the ranch property could be steeper than she'd figured, and she explained that to Casey. It did seem to be shrouded in plants, and it overlooked the road that showed up on her map, in the distance.

Whatever it meant, the rustlers had apparently reached that location. Instead of veering right or left, it seemed that they had decided to lead the stock forward, one at a time—possibly down that hillside she speculated about, rather than herd them forward as they'd been doing previously.

"I'd really like to see that area close up, before we reach the rustlers and cattle," she told Casey. "I don't know what we should expect, at least not exactly."

"Nope, but you're right about needing to get closer to observe and make a rational decision what to do next," Casey said. "And surprisingly, we may be in a good situation for that."

"What do you mean?"

He pointed at the gully where they still stood with the horses and the bushes around them. "Since it's November, some of the plants have lost their leaves but kept their branches, even little twigs, so there's still some substance to them." Then he said, "Let me see your phone, please."

She handed it to him, watching both him and the phone closely to try to determine what was on his mind.

"If you're right about the meaning of the dots in clumps and individually here, about half the cattle have been led down the hill. That means we should get closer soon. We're less likely to be seen if we're on a different level from the rustlers, but we don't know that."

"So what are you thinking?" Judging by the intense expression on his face, she had no doubt he had something on his mind.

"We should probably go just a little farther through these bushes." He waved around them. "Then hitch the horses someplace where they can stay a while. You and I can hurry, under cover as much as possible, to the hilltop and figure out which cattle—and rustlers—are where. Then we can at last go after them."

Chapter Fifteen

This could be interesting, Casey thought as he walked Witchy along. But they were definitely approaching the place where the rustlers were apparently still leading the cows down the hill one by one.

He found himself thinking a lot about what had already happened and what was going on now, rehashing it all in his mind and therefore not talking much, at this point, with Melody.

Pretty Melody. Determined Melody…

He glanced at her and saw that she was studying the terrain ahead of them and off to the right, where hills rose and fell, and bushes abounded. She appeared to be thinking, too.

One of the main things he thought of was the extent of his wondering from the beginning how this entire situation was finally going to end. He'd made himself not dwell much on how to bring the murderous rustlers to justice once they caught up to them, but he intended to improvise strategically and wisely once any opportunity arose. He was generally a planner, but there had been too many unknowns out here to try to zero in on a plan of attack that might be impossible to undertake.

Sure, he had a gun with him, but he didn't know how many people they might be up against. His improvisation might involve Melody, as long as he could keep her safe. Or maybe he would determine it was time to get some backup from the sheriff's department here. A lot was still to be decided, depending on what they found.

Plus he'd remained concerned, out in the vast open-pasture areas, whether Melody and he would be seen on their horses long before they caught up with the cattle and rustlers, and the bad guys would slaughter the cattle and escape themselves. That had always been a major worry, even from the first, when they'd decided to conduct the chase on horseback rather than by all-terrain vehicles or helicopters overhead, and his concern had grown even more intense after they found Pierce's body.

Why had he been killed? Because he'd simply gotten too close? As a warning to others? Both? Or had Pierce actually been involved with the rustlers?

Casey had figured Melody and he would be okay as long as the criminals couldn't actually see their pursuers. And Melody and he weren't wearing GPS trackers, although if the bad guys had the phone information of either of them, they might be vulnerable that way. But surely they didn't have that, especially if they didn't know they were being followed—though they might suspect it, of course.

Still… His life, and Melody's, could be at risk. Probably were. Best he could do was to stay aware and alert and be prepared to do anything necessary to deal with the situation. They would continue following from a distance, finding some kind of cover before they got too close. He'd always intended to observe the rustlers and gather information before calling his department in for backup to help end the situation. But he had to see more of what was going on before that became feasible. And his number-one priority then would be to protect Melody.

One good thing was that he felt sure she'd be glad to wrangle the cattle away and protect them no matter what he was doing. He, as the armed deputy sheriff, could take care of himself. Or call in that backup.

But one way or another, this had to come to an end. A good end for them and their mission.

Most particularly if they could do more than simply point at the rustlers. They would need to prove that the bad guys they found were the thieves and killers.

Would determination of the changed brand on the cattle, SG, help with that, assuming that the dead cow, Addie, wasn't the only one that had been done to?

And that charm that was now being analyzed. Would it help somehow in identifying the killer?

Sure, it was interesting being out here, chasing the stolen cattle. But he was a sheriff's deputy. He needed to ensure as much as possible that there was evidence to bring down the bad guys.

"Are you okay?" Melody said from off to his left. When he glanced over yet again, she wasn't glued to their surroundings or her telephone screen as she rode on Cal's back, but was looking at him.

"Yeah," he said, relieved in a way to move his

thoughts to her and engage in a conversation. "I'm just trying to think this through better than before, when we were just following but didn't have a plan in place for stopping the rustlers."

"You have one now?" She sounded excited. "I'd been thinking about that more now, too. A lot more. But I hadn't come up with anything besides continuing to follow, nothing that guaranteed us to come up with the perfect outcome."

"Hey, I want a guarantee," he said facetiously. Then he grew more serious. "And it's kind of you not to give me a hard time for not having it all planned out."

"Of course I wouldn't. We're comrades out here in all ways. I'll help you and expect you to help me, too, depending on how things go. But the main thing…well, I just want this to come out right. No more dead cows." She paused, and Casey looked at her. There were tears on her lovely cheeks as she said, "Or people."

Casey wanted to get them both down off their horses and hug Melody, and not just out of sympathy for her. He hated that another ranch hand had lost his life on his watch. And it had been someone who'd been known by and liked by Melody, which only made the situation worse.

For now, though, he figured they needed to more fully develop and implement his plan, now that the end was conceivably in sight.

"You're right," he said. "There's been enough blood shed already. Our first priority will be to prevent any more." Okay, he fibbed a little. If he had to shoot or otherwise harm the bad guys to end this, of course he

would. And the fact they had already murdered someone suggested they wouldn't be averse to attempting to
physically harm Melody or him, either.

He wouldn't allow that.

"Absolutely." The look she shot at him suggested she
admired and trusted him, believed in him, figured he'd
do his job perfectly as a deputy. He might be reading
too much into it, of course, and hoped he did, since the
whole idea made him squirm in the saddle.

He was far from perfect. But he would do anything,
even give his own life if necessary, to protect her.

Once more, he was overthinking. Sure, he now had
a plan. Was it a great one? Probably not, but he would
succeed—he had to.

So what was the plan Casey had in mind? Melody really wanted to know.

She'd figured, judging from his expression during
the past mile or so as they rode, that he was deep in
thought. His thick, light brown eyebrows were furrowed
into a pensive frown, even as he continued to look ahead
of them and around, as if studying their surroundings
for the answers he sought.

No clues out here to help him figure out who the
people were that they were after. Since he was an officer of the law, that was probably on his mind.

Hers, too, in a way. Whoever they were, they'd killed
Pierce. Why? Would they try to kill her, too?

And Casey?

Well, she'd been looking around and searching for
answers, too, and after a while of not sharing anything

but, in effect, their environment, she'd thought it was finally time for her to say something. And so she did.

And, of course, the brief conversation she'd initiated had morphed into something emotional, at least for her.

But she could turn it now into something a lot more useful and, hopefully, more effective.

"So," she said, "it's time. Let's discuss your plan and see how we can best get it implemented." Or possibly not, if she didn't think it made sense.

But she had come to know the man beside her— this deputy sheriff with a conscience and a heart—well enough to believe that, whatever he'd been pondering, it could potentially finish this long, lengthy stakeout in the best way possible. Successfully. It had to be.

"First, can you check your GPS? I could do it, but you're better at it out here than I am. I want to confirm that the cattle still seem to be beneath that hill they were apparently being walked down."

Melody quickly took her phone from her pocket and looked. Again. And she was able to confirm the information for Casey. "It appears that eight of the cattle are in a herd together at the bottom now. Two more may still be at the top of that hill, and another's on the way down, if I'm interpreting this right."

"I'm sure you are."

She glowed a bit under Casey's smile and nod toward her, but stayed quiet, waiting for him to continue.

"Okay. Here's what I'm thinking now." He described a scenario where they'd go a bit farther, getting closer to where the topography dipped downhill, then dismount.

Next, the two of them would advance farther on foot,

using more underbrush and the rolling land as their cover while they got nearer to the edge of that hillside, where they should be able to see the rustlers.

"We'll observe them then and figure out the best way of bringing them down…and saving the cattle, of course," he explained. "Does that work for you? Do you have any suggestions? Of course, we can modify anything as we go along, if it seems appropriate."

Fine, Melody thought. But he'd better take good care of himself, too. "It sounds really good in generalities," Melody said. "And, yes, as long as it's all subject to change I'm fine with it. Only—"

"Only you're concerned about our excellent mounts here, aren't you?" Casey leaned forward and stroked Witchy's neck.

"How did you guess I was going to address their welfare further?" Melody was both amused and impressed. It wasn't a surprise, though, that Casey had come to know her well enough to understand how much she liked the livestock in her life.

"A little bird told me. Oh, no, wait. It had to have been a little horsefly." Casey smiled, and Melody couldn't help laughing. "Well, what I figured is that once we get into range of where I think it's time to leave our horses, I'll let you check it out and make the decision as to when and where to tie them up. Securely and safely and with grass and water around, since we're not sure how long they'll have to stay there without us."

Like, would they ever return? Melody wondered that immediately. If all went well, of course they would. But if it didn't, would there be time and opportunity to contact other ranch hands or some of the deputies Casey worked with to ask for their help in saving the horses, too?

Well, the two of them had to do things right so this wouldn't become an issue. Melody knew that and she trusted Casey well enough to believe he'd do everything in his power to make sure not only the cattle, but also these wonderful horses, came out of this situation healthy and happy.

And he'd said he would let her make the decision. "Thanks," she said. "I'm not sure I'll be able to figure out the best locale for the horses so I'll want your input, too, but I appreciate that you'll let me make the decision."

"Oh, I've got a feeling that if I attempted to do it all on my own I'd hear something from you, like it or not."

"You've got me," Melody said with a laugh, and then realized that her words could be interpreted as a bit suggestive.

Well, they'd not get that opportunity now, while finally at the stage of finishing this vital assignment together.

"So after we secure the horses, we'll hike toward where the cattle are, or at least approach the hillside they're being led down?" Melody was fairly certain that was what he'd said and what he intended, but she needed to keep talking now, so she would know what he was thinking. She also wanted to keep her own thoughts in line with what they would need to do, and not be distracted by any unwanted, though much-too-tempting, ideas.

"That's what I think will be best. I'm just hoping there'll be enough bushes or other cover around there so we can continue on foot without being seen. And since we need to do it today, hopefully the cattle won't be too far ahead of us by then."

"There's that road parallel to the base of the slope that's not far away," she reminded him. "I'm hoping the rustlers are smart enough not to attempt to drive the cattle to the other side, at least not if there are any cars at all using it."

"So far, we don't really know how intelligent the criminals are," Casey said. "They can't be too smart since they stole some pretty valuable cows from one of the town's most powerful people. No way would your boss back down and allow them to keep going with any part of his herd."

"And no way would I stop now without making sure those cattle are nice and safe and back with the rest of the herd." She hadn't needed to say that, of course. He knew that.

"Right. And no way would I stop and give up and let those felons escape without my arresting them."

"So we're together on this," Melody said, as if there'd been any doubt before. But she was enjoying their teasing fellowship at the moment.

"We're together on this," Casey agreed, and the grin he shot her way...well, did he really intend it to look as sexy as it did?

Not that it mattered. Not now, when they were still out chasing their quarry, and not later, even after all had been resolved—favorably to them, she reminded herself. There could be no other result. Period.

"So let's find that right spot for our buddies here," Melody said. She scrutinized the area in front of them.

"Absolutely."

They only continued for about another twenty minutes before Melody said, "Let's stop here and take a look at this place." It was an area where there were lots of bushes with thick branches, as well as a few trees that appeared to be firs. At the far side, the narrow brook they had seen before ran by. There were patches of tall grass, as well.

To Melody, it appeared ideal. "I vote for this location," she told Casey while still seated on Cal's saddle. "If you want to look farther, we can give it a try, but I suspect we'll return here. What do you think?"

He looked ahead of them. From Melody's perspective, the route to the hill dropoff was getting close. She saw no cattle at the top, nor any people to watch them or spot the horses. The last of the cattle must have been accompanied down.

She waited, though, to hear Casey's opinion. He was the law-enforcement agent, after all. In some ways, he was in charge—as long as she didn't disagree with him.

"Let's get down and have a look," he said.

"Good idea."

Melody edged herself out of the saddle and eased down to the ground. She tied the end of Cal's reins to a nearby bush just to make sure he didn't start walking away, and noticed Casey do the same with Witchy.

For the next few minutes, they wandered around

the area. It still looked appropriate to Melody but she wanted to hear Casey's opinion.

"I think you're right," he said, and she enjoyed his appreciative smile. "You ready to do a little hiking?"

She considered his question for a moment. "Soon," she said.

She was glad her boots were comfortable and made for walking and more, with their laces tied nice and firmly. Her work shirt and jeans felt just fine in this warm temperature. She'd get warmer, anyway, as they proceeded.

To make sure Cal felt comfortable after they attached him here for his safety, she removed his saddle and saddlebag and placed them on the ground, and also removed the bit from his mouth and loosened his girth. She was happy that Casey did the same with Witchy. Fortunately, the brook appeared fairly clean and they left the horses near enough that they could drink from it. But Melody also left filtered water in containers near both of them.

She then reached inside her saddlebag and removed her fanny pack, making sure it contained her wallet and personal information, which she wouldn't want anyone else to pilfer, as well as some tissues and other things for comfort. She fastened it around her waist.

"I'm ready," she finally said to Casey, who had also been checking his saddlebag on the ground and removing a few things, which he stuck in his pockets.

The last thing she noticed was that he took out his gun and stuck it into the back part of his belt. He wore a long black shirt outside his white T-shirt, with the gun hidden beneath it.

He turned and walked over to her then. To her surprise, he got close. Very close. Close enough that he pulled her into his arms for a tight hug, and, of course, she reciprocated before even considering whether it was a good idea.

And when she looked up at his face, she saw his heated glance back down at her. In moments, their mouths met in a hot kiss. A very passionate kiss. Appropriate out here? Well, why not? She threw herself into it. But it was too brief.

Casey pulled away more quickly than she was ready for, but it was for the best. "I'm ready, too," he said.

Chapter Sixteen

Casey wasn't sure how best to approach the hilltop. Thanks to Melody's GPS, he believed the bad guys had gathered the cattle just beyond the foot of it. Hopefully, they were with the cows now. In any case, there was no sense in being too obvious in his approach to the edge, especially with Melody. He asked her to walk close to the plant life beside them and sometimes even close to the cover of the bushes, where there was room, just in case one of the rustlers sneaked back and checked out the direction from which they'd come for anyone who might be following.

Like them.

If anyone ahead had exceptional hearing, perhaps they'd even be able to make out the crunching of his and Melody's feet on the dead leaves on the ground. He looked back at his companion often, glad they were both wearing long sleeves since bushes along their route scraped at them constantly. He was also glad they were both dressed in dark colors, to help limit their visibility.

At least the air temperature remained tolerably warm, even though it was now midafternoon.

Melody tapped his shoulder, so he stopped and turned toward her. "Is it okay to talk in a normal voice now?" she asked softly. "Otherwise, you probably won't know I'm saying anything."

He started walking again slowly, beside her. "Should be fine for now, but not when we get much closer. I'm not sure when we're likely to run into anyone, or if they'll be able to hear us from down the hill."

"Our footsteps in the dried leaves of these bushes make a lot of noise, too." She'd noticed that as well, which wasn't surprising.

She was frowning in apparent concern, and he wanted to reassure her all would be well. But he couldn't do that. Not without taking the chance he'd be lying. Instead, he found something to ask her. "Do you know what kinds of plants these are?" He gestured toward the low bushes beside them, then raised his hands to where tree branches stuck out overhead. A few times he'd caught a sweet aroma that originated from the nearby growing things.

"Not really. My thing is livestock, not plant life. But if you wanted me to guess, I think some of these bushes are honeysuckle, or barberry…maybe. And the trees? We've already decided some, those tall ones, are likely to be firs of some kind, and the ones that aren't evergreens might be a type of mesquite, and maybe a type of buckeye."

"Who says you don't know your flora? Don't know if you're right, but that certainly sounds good."

They continued to walk beside each other. Casey had

an urge to grab Melody's hand—just to help stabilize her, he told himself.

But she clearly didn't need any assistance to stay upright and move quickly and steadily alongside him. Still, he kept her closest to the cover of the bushes, so she did occasionally reach out to push some greenery, or bare branches, out of her way.

As they inched closer to the top of the hill, Casey developed his plan further. One that would keep Melody safest. He would take all the chances, although he wasn't yet certain how much cover there would be to keep him from being obvious to the bad guys. He couldn't yet see the actual slope beyond the wide summit, although it shouldn't be too bad if the rustlers had managed to get the cows down it, one at a time.

That probably indicated someone standing at the base could see someone leaning over the top, though, or slipping down it some way. But he would nevertheless figure out a way once he was closer to get to the level of the cattle, without being seen.

Depending on what he observed, if he believed it was too dangerous he'd tell Melody to remain in hiding up here.

And somehow find a way to get her to agree. That woman definitely had a mind of her own.

If he could find a way to convince her it was in the cattle's best interest for her to wait on top of the hill, that might work.

But he preferred not to get killed or captured, either. His gun remained easily reachable, stuck into his belt.

And once he saw the actual layout, he would determine the best way to close in on the rustlers.

He would then perfect his plan.

He kept checking the area around them. There did appear to be paths leading sideways into the cover of the bushes and trees, which could be okay. If he found a way to head in that direction and get down the hill beyond the point the rustlers did, he might be able to draw nearer without them seeing him, especially since these bushes and other growth appeared to be fairly thick off to their right.

"Are you trying to figure out how to get down that hill without being seen?" Melody asked even more quietly than before, remaining at his side as he slowed just a bit.

Damn, but she was perceptive. And smart. And... well, attractive. Too attractive, even in her casual clothes out here in the middle of nowhere. Ranch-hand clothes. Not that he hadn't noticed that before. He had to get himself to stop thinking about it, and her, though, and what was beneath those clothes...

Now, especially, when they were reaching the end of their journey, and the possible meeting with the bad guys they were chasing, was a bad time for distractions like that.

Those thoughts were irrelevant to where they were, what they were doing. He had to think deputy-sheriff thoughts only—to accomplish his mission out here, where Melody was simply his colleague.

Or not so simply.

"Yeah," he responded. "I've got some ideas, and I'll welcome any suggestions you have, too."

They talked about it briefly. Melody had some thoughts about going in the other direction from the way he'd been considering, toward the left, maybe until the area at the top of the hill grew level, assuming it eventually did as she'd learned from the GPS, then hurrying to the roadway and walking back that way.

"But I doubt that would work well even if the hill does end in that direction, the way it appears," she said, gazing straight into Casey's eyes. She looked to be even more worried than she had on most of their expedition. "For one thing, I'm not sure what the road shoulder's like. We wouldn't want to walk down the middle of the road, of course. We'd not only probably be seen, but we'd be more likely to get hit by a car."

"My thought was going the other way." Casey pointed off to their right side, into the bushes that were their current cover. "I'd like to head that way before we get too close to the hilltop."

"Will we be able to see what's going on below from there?"

"Don't know yet," he admitted. "We'll just have to check it out. And if that doesn't work, maybe something that will work will become obvious."

"Or not," Melody said glumly. "If not…well, I've been thinking about contacting Clarence and maybe getting him to send a van or two down the road to hopefully collect the cattle there."

"And I'm telling you not to do that," Casey said abruptly. "I don't want any more of your ranch hands put into the line of fire, not till we have some control over what's going on. Besides—" he looked her straight in her beautiful face with an expression he hoped appeared concerned—as well as reminding her who the leader of the two of them was "—your cattle will be endangered more that way, too. If the rustlers see any indication that their prey is about to be collected, they'll most likely start killing all of them, the way we've been afraid of all along. And us, too, if we're close enough and they've noticed us."

Melody shook her head and looked down, walking forward once more. "You're right. But I just don't envision anything coming out the way we want now. I'm glad we've been following and are about to catch up with them, but… Look, I don't want to be critical of you or what you've been doing, but—"

He laughed harshly, feeling as if she'd kicked him where it hurt. Nevertheless, he understood, and acknowledged it.

"You're right," he said. "Our just following was a good idea, before. Now we need to do something to end it. *I* need to do something," he amended. "And…well, I understand why you don't trust me. But I'm damn good at my job." And he was—though he'd never been in this kind of situation before. Even so, he continued, "You need to follow my instructions as we go ahead. We'll save your cattle and bring down the murderous thieves. I promise. Got it?"

She'd stopped walking again at his outburst, which was a good thing. She seemed to study his face, as if hoping the truth was there.

And then she nodded. "I trust you, Casey," she finally said. As if to punctuate and underscore her words, she stood on her toes, pulled down his neck and gave him a big, hot kiss right on the mouth.

Which made him want to swear he'd do anything she wanted.

"Good" was his somewhat strangled response. "Now, let's go."

SHE NEEDED TO trust Casey, Melody thought. And she did. He seemed sure of himself, at least in some ways. He might not have all the answers yet, but he seemed certain they'd—he'd—figure out a way to end this appropriately: cattle saved, rustlers arrested.

But…well, he kept going, and so did she. He led her not to the edge of the hill, but into the bushes off to the side where a path had been cleared. His muscles flexed beneath his shirt as he moved small branches out of her way.

"Hey, you know, if nothing else maybe we can locate some interesting birds or other animals here in the forest," he said, clearly joking. "And then you can herd them, keep them together right around here while I go ahead and grab the bad guys. Okay?"

"Yeah, sure," she said, enjoying the slight respite. "Maybe some more kestrels, or spotted owls, if you like birds, but I doubt I'll be able to manage their flocks. Maybe rabbits or rats, though. They might have some interest if I find food for them."

But then she turned back to flash a grin at him and gesture for him to follow—as if he wouldn't. It was her own stab at a joke, sort of. This might be a fun exchange, but she was worried.

What was he really thinking? Was he hoping she'd stay out of his way while he performed his job? Was he thinking about how to protect her?

"Right," he said, catching up with her. "You can go look for some rabbit or rat food, and—"

Stopping again, she glared at him. "Cut it out," she said, nearly exploding. "I know what you're doing. And I appreciate it, if I'm right—that you want to protect me while you go finish this. But I'm doing my job, too. You can go get those evil rustlers, and I'll be delighted when you do. But I'll be right with you, taking care of the cattle. Got it?"

"Yeah," he said, his deep, throaty voice a grumble as he glared at her. "But—"

"No *buts*. Let's do it." Yet again, she hurried ahead of him.

When they'd gone maybe a quarter of a mile farther, Melody noticed that the path they were on had another section, one that didn't parallel that hilltop but connected with their path perpendicularly. Since she was the one ahead at the moment, without even asking his opinion, she headed that way. Plenty of plants appeared at the edges—places they could hide as they looked down.

She felt Casey's hand grasp her shoulder. "Hey, wait a minute. Good idea to go that way, but bad idea to do it like this."

"So tell me how."

"I'll show you," he said. "And, yes, you can join

me, as long as you're careful and follow my instructions. Got it?"

They'd stopped walking at the edge of that side portion of the path, and Casey looked down at her sternly. In his face, Melody believed she saw that he was not only taking charge, but there was also concern.

"Got it," she said and grabbed his hand. She gazed up earnestly into his handsome but clearly worried face. Okay. Much as she hated to keep admitting it to herself, he was in charge. She knew it and appreciated what appeared to be his caring nature.

She'd go along with his instructions as long as he didn't shut her out, tie her to a tree like the horses or whatever to end her participation.

His hand felt warm and strong in hers. His expression softened somewhat, and she had to prevent herself from reaching up to bring his head down for another kiss.

"Fine, then," he said. "Here's what I'm planning. For both of us."

HE EXPECTED SOME argument when he told her he would do it all from now on.

"I'll head toward the end of this part of the path," he said, "then hide and look down at the area below, and, if possible, make my way down this part of the hillside, preferably totally surrounded by brush so I can't be seen." When Melody nodded, he continued, "You'll stay near the top and watch and, if necessary, you can call out the troops."

Casey informed her he would even exchange phones with her so all she'd need to do would be to push a button to call the sheriff's department, request backup and explain why. He knew the number so, if necessary, he could call them, too, on her phone.

Simple enough.

And he was pleased that, though she stared hard at his face in the shadows as he told her his plan, she didn't argue, despite her increasingly angry frown. Would she yell at him when he finished?

Nothing. Silence when he stopped talking. He sighed inside in relief. He'd go ahead. She'd stay safe. End of story, assuming he did apprehend the rustlers and was able to do that before they could injure any more of the cattle.

"Great," he said after a few moments of silence. "So give me your phone, and here's mine." He pulled it from his pocket, allowing himself to once more feel the hardness of the gun stuck into the back of his belt as further reassurance all would be well.

"That sounds reasonable," she said as she exchanged her phone for his, though she checked the GPS first and showed him that the group of red dots below them was not moving. "Or at least this part of it sounds reasonable."

Uh-oh. "What do you mean?"

Surprise, surprise. She didn't like being left behind, even when he again attempted to make it appear that what he was doing was best for the cattle, not just her safety. But he did remind her about what had happened to Pierce, and that the rustlers clearly would have no compunction about killing Casey and her, too. Coming after them both, if they knew there were two of them.

Beyond saying she would do what seemed right, she didn't argue with him. She just glared into his eyes, her expressive, deep brown eyes hardening beneath her long, dark lashes. Her gaze was much icier than he believed he'd ever seen it before.

Which hurt, damn it, even though he shouldn't care what she thought.

He did.

So he pulled her into his arms and held her close. "It'll work out fine this way," he promised her, hoping it wasn't a lie. "You'll see. And you can call my department if there's any sign of trouble. You'll be in charge."

"Right," she said, speaking against his chest. And then she moved back just a little.

Just enough to pull down his head to hers, where they engaged in what was probably the hottest, most emotional kiss they'd shared. Her use of her tongue reminded him of their night of sex, and her holding him tightly against her seemed a hug of utmost caring. And desire.

Which made his body react. Made him want more. A lot more.

That wouldn't happen, though. Not now, and not later when this was all over. Successfully.

And when the kiss was ended, she pulled back again beneath the tall bushes where they stood and looked at him, those gorgeous eyes of hers moist but intense.

"Now go for it," she said. "Be careful, okay? I'll be watching. If I see anything that looks like trouble, I'll make that call. And if you want me to call, just put your hand up and wave as if you're waving to the cows. That'll be our signal, okay?"

"Okay," he said, grabbing her for another kiss before heading forward.

Sure enough, she stayed behind him.

He kneeled on the ground as he reached the area where this part of the hill finally sloped downward. He looked where the cattle were.

He could make out three people there at the edge of the herd, though they were far enough away he couldn't tell much about them.

There was one of him. And he had one gun.

Hell. He was glad he had Melody as backup and they had a plan for him signaling her.

It was time for him to ease his way through the bushes and head down the hill.

Chapter Seventeen

Melody sat on the hard, leaf-covered ground beneath a healthy-looking bush that gave her plenty of cover. But back here, within the shrubbery, and still a distance from the end of the path that led down the hill, she hardly needed any cover.

She needed finality. A successful close to their stake-out.

Victory by Casey in what he had just set out to do. Safely. With neither of them harmed, certainly not like poor Pierce. And hopefully they would learn why the murderers killed Pierce.

She hadn't needed Casey's reminder about Pierce. She wondered yet again if her fellow ranch hand had worked with the rustlers, which she didn't want to believe, or, more likely, attempted unsuccessfully to face them down.

And as Casey had mentioned, she couldn't help feeling worried that he, or even she, could be hurt, or worse, too.

She had fought any kind of emotion deep inside her—and not so deep—as he had set off away from her, partly bent over, through the underbrush. She'd watched him head away on the bush-shrouded path ahead of her, finding herself staring at his wide-shouldered back in the dark blue shirt, his jeans-covered butt and legs, and his boot-clad feet until he disappeared. She forced herself to stay put. Not follow.

But did she feel comfortable he'd handle it completely successfully on his own? Of course, she hoped so—but she wasn't going to make the assumption he would and could.

And so she kept his phone clutched in her hand as she made herself remain seated, wanting to count the seconds since he'd left her there. She intended to head after him, no matter what he'd told her, once she'd reached a minute. At the most, two.

But to be as safe as possible that she wouldn't catch up with him, she waited maybe five. Even so, she worried that he'd hear her. Sense her presence some other way.

They didn't need to take the time to argue now. And arguing would definitely make noise, perhaps even enough to let their quarry know they were on their way.

Why follow him? Because she intended to protect him, at least somewhat. She would stay way back, just watch, stay safe herself. And call for help immediately if he needed it. Soon, though, it was time for her to get on the move. She stayed alert, listening and watching to the extent she could under this cover of leaves and undergrowth as she moved quickly forward.

Where was Casey now? Had he hurried his way to the bottom of this part of the hill, or had he stopped to try to observe where the people below were and the best way he could approach them without being noticed, until he was close and aimed his gun at them to bring them down?

Or was there something else a skilled deputy like him would do, some other way to capture the criminals with as little risk to himself as possible?

Heck, she thought as she continued to head in the direction he'd gone. If his main goal was to minimize risk to himself, he'd have had her go with him, from the first, to help. Though she wasn't armed, she could make that call to his real backup immediately when he said to.

But he'd still wanted to protect her. Sweet, but impractical. And more dangerous to him. After all, there were also other ways besides aiming a gun that she might have been able to get the bad guys under control.

That thought made her sweep her gaze around for any sign of a nice, large branch she could use as a weapon if she needed to.

Well, she saw nothing in this confined area, and even if there was something she'd hardly be able to drag a big, heavy branch with her. But she'd keep watching for something compact and potentially usable as she continued forward.

Rationally, though, she realized she would be doing this without a weapon.

At least she didn't see any of the rodents she'd teased Casey about before. Insects, though, and worms…but she worked outdoors. She might not love them but she was used to them.

She had recognized that this part of the downward-sloping hillside was long, but she hadn't considered the amount of time it might take for her to reach the bottom, particularly since, though she attempted to be fast, she tried to move as little visible plant life and make as little noise as she could.

Was Casey going even more quickly than she was? She hoped not. She didn't want to catch up with him, but she wanted to be there for him if he needed any assistance, as soon as she could, once he reached the base of the hill.

Casey. They were partners in this challenging enterprise. They had different skills that should meld well together for finally dealing with the killers and retrieving the stolen cattle. Or so Melody believed, although Casey and she hadn't really discussed it. But she trusted that wonderful deputy sheriff.

And they'd been working on at least finding the cattle for days. Nights.

Night. No more nights together with Casey now. She ought to be glad. Oh, she'd enjoyed their time together—their amazing encounter last night. But there were many reasons for their closeness then—partly to distract and support her after the murder of her coworker.

But she didn't want to think about Pierce now. She wanted to think about Casey.

It had been fun. It had been memorable.

And it had been a one-time wonder.

Still, maybe they'd remain friends and potential colleagues in other ways. She hated the idea of never seeing Casey again after what they'd been through…and what they were likely to go through soon.

She was thinking too much again. She realized it. And yet how could she keep her mind primarily on sneaking down the hill and remaining off Casey's radar and certainly that of the horrible rustlers?

For the next few minutes, she tried to think of something besides Casey. As a ranch hand, she was outside a lot, anyway. Not creeping down hillsides decked with foliage, but out there wrangling cattle.

She hoped she would be doing that again soon. Very soon. With the remaining eleven of the stolen cattle.

Hey. What was that? She stopped moving and just remained where she was, listening.

Cattle, somewhere far ahead of her. Their sweet, soft lowing. She had to be getting close, and fortunately they didn't sound in distress.

But with them, Melody heard voices, too. Must be the thieves. Assuming she heard what she believed she did. It all seemed so hushed at this distance.

Was one of the voices Casey's? Was he with the rustlers now? Had he already arrested them, gotten possession back of the missing cows?

Or…was it something else? *Someone* else? Who was talking?

Was Casey just listening, too?

Or was he participating?

She just stayed still…for now. Trying to decide what to do.

When to move forward.

She couldn't see Casey yet. Wouldn't be able to view his hand signal, even if he gave it.

Not sure where he was, she figured she might not

have been able to see a signal from him even if she'd listened and remained at the top of the hill.

Well, she was going to help him, like it or not. At least she would be there to call in his real backup if he got into trouble.

THEIR BACKS WERE toward him—all three of them. They all wore jeans and thick, full hoodies, as well as tennis shoes, and somehow they appeared nearly the same height that way, though maybe that was because where they stood was somewhat rough.

They were still too far away for him to hear what they were saying, even though it was loud enough that Casey knew they were having a conversation. About the lowing cattle, whose moos helped to obliterate the people's words, that they stood near?

He gathered that was the case, since the few words he made out included "forward" and "keep going."

He had nearly reached the end of the foliage-strewn path and was still hidden within the underbrush, as he intended. Of course, since the perpetrators were looking in the other direction, they might not have seen him, anyway, or any movement he had caused in the foliage.

Damn, but this was frustrating. He wanted to get near enough to at least hear what they were saying, figure out what their plan was, if any.

And then turn his own rough outline of a plan into reality.

Were they all armed? One had shot Pierce. He couldn't assume the others weren't carrying, too. Therefore, what he really would like to do—just dash out there, gun drawn—wasn't a great idea.

Besides, he didn't really want to shoot them, even if they all charged him. He wanted to bring them in, if possible—healthy and whole and able to stand trial. And if they ran away, he definitely didn't want to shoot them in their backs, but how would he stop them? Plus they might all go in different directions, so he would only be able to follow one.

The worst scenario, and perhaps the most likely, was that they'd all go hide among the cattle, in which case there was no way Casey could fire his gun at all.

At least he'd found them, and they remained in one spot for now. This was probably the time to pull Melody's phone from his pocket and call in his backup, though talking here, even softly over the phone, might give him away. He could, instead, reach up and send the signal he and Melody had planned to her. But would she, at the top of the hill, be able to see him?

Would the rustlers see him instead?

What had he been expecting? Something like this, of course. And what was he going to do about it?

Confront them soon. He had to.

First, though, he'd—

He heard some rustling of the undergrowth behind him and pivoted abruptly. Was there a fourth one who—?

Damn. He saw Melody appear at the top of the portion of the path visible to him in the thick foliage. She put a finger to her lips to shush him, as if he'd call out to scold her the way he wanted to, but would then give away their presence.

Without exchanging anything but a challenging look from her and an angry look from him, she sat down on the ground in the middle of the surrounding bushes, pulled out his phone and pressed the button as he'd shown her.

Damn. She surely was aware of the danger they both were in. Scolding was only part of what he wanted to do, like force her back up the hill. Fast.

Was she going to give them away?

Maybe, but he hadn't come up with anything better.

He barely heard her as she whispered into the phone. If all went as planned, she was speaking with Sheriff Krester, telling him where they were and why, and asking for some support to be sent.

That part was good…he hoped. But he turned back quickly toward the view he'd had before.

The suspects remained in the same location, still talking to one another. No indication, fortunately, that they'd heard anything or were worried.

Ah, but Casey intended to change that as soon as possible. But what was the best way to handle things now?

To go back a few feet, where Melody stood, and just wait there with her…after confirming she'd been told help was on the way?

To move forward, gun in hand, and attempt to make sure the bad guys didn't try anything, like getting away?

Although it wasn't his favorite of the available choices, Casey decided to head toward Melody. If he just ran out there and made noises and attempted to scare the rustlers into submission, he doubted they'd accept that, anyway.

And if that was his choice, he had no doubt that Melody would follow him and put herself into further danger. She'd promised not to, sure. She had also promised not to follow him here or do anything except what he told her.

Well, that was an exaggeration. Which gave him all the more reason to inch his way back to where she was.

She wasn't too far from where he had stopped. His phone was in her hand, and, waving it in front of her, she remained grinning, as if she'd done exactly as he'd told her to.

No...as if she'd done exactly as she'd chosen to, which of course was the case.

He wanted to throttle her.

No, he wanted to kiss those lips that were drawn into such a challenging, sexy smile.

Definitely not here, though. Not now. But maybe a kiss in celebration once they were successful...

He'd have to consider that later, when they actually *were* successful.

For now, he quickly squatted down beside her. Though chastising her wouldn't help a thing right now, he wanted to attempt once more to make her understand that she had to listen to him, to do as he said, to keep herself safe.

"You're supposed to still be at the top of the hill," he whispered so softly that what he said couldn't be any louder than a breeze through the foliage around here. Or at least that was his attempt.

"Then I wouldn't have been able to make that call for you, since I couldn't see you before." She, too, didn't sound any louder than the softest of winds. She'd been slightly louder on the phone, but not much—and that had undoubtedly been of necessity, to make sure the sheriff could hear her.

"Help on the way?" he asked her, even though she'd nodded at him after the call, which seemed to indicate all was well.

She nodded again.

"Okay, then. Let's wait here."

He hated the idea of remaining idle, not doing anything but hanging out until they knew backup from his department had arrived.

Still, it'd be safer for both of them. He could stay here with Melody to make sure she didn't do anything stupid, like run out there and try to protect the cattle. They might not even need protection. Not now, at least. No one was getting them to move anywhere at the moment.

And so he sat down right beside Melody. Close enough so their shoulders touched.

She looked at him, and he had an urge for more than their shoulders to touch—but that was old news.

New news would come when all was taken care of here.

He wanted to know when that would be. He had an urge to return to where he'd been observing the rustlers a few feet ahead of where they were now and just watch. But if he did that, Melody would likely join him, and that was a bad idea.

He kept looking there, though…and the smart ranch hand beside him apparently read his thoughts. "If you want to go keep an eye on things now, go ahead," she whispered. "I'll stay here."

He glanced back at her, and she nodded as if to reassure him she wasn't kidding. Of course, that might be her intention for this moment. For the next…?

Well, he'd take his chances…to some extent. He'd go take a look while keeping an eye on Melody, too.

He nodded his thanks, then took her hand in his and squeezed it—for her reassurance, he told himself. But it also helped his own.

This woman made him want to do everything right now and the right way, for her as well as for himself. She was so different from other women he'd known. She put herself out there, into danger, to help not only him, but the animals she cared about.

After one final squeeze, he reluctantly let go, then edged his way back to where he'd been.

Which turned out to be a damn good thing. He heard one of the people standing there speaking a bit more loudly over the continued lowing of the cattle. "Okay, let's mount up and move them out."

Hell, no. Not now.

Instinctively, Casey drew the gun from where it was hooked on his belt, behind his back.

"What—?" It was Melody, still in a low voice but higher than a whisper.

He turned slightly, and only for a moment. "They're

going to herd them again," he said, also slightly louder. "I've got to stop them."

But when he reached the end of the cover provided by the bushes, he stopped.

One of the rustlers had turned sideways enough that he could see her face.

Her face. It was oval and pretty, with sharp features and surrounded by mid-length dark hair. And it suddenly came to him that she actually had received the charm her family had been talking about prior to their nonmarriage. The charm Melody and he had found. The *G*.

G as in Georgia.

His ex-fiancée, the woman who'd snubbed him at the altar—she was involved in this.

Very involved.

Chapter Eighteen

What was going on? Why had Casey stopped?

Had he decided it was too dangerous to continue?

Damn, but Melody wished now that she had a gun. Their backup might be on the way, but for the moment she was the only support Casey had.

And for the moment, though she was watching his back from a short distance behind him and wanted more than anything to do what he needed from her, she had no idea what to do to help.

She felt a vibration in her pocket. Casey's phone. Thank heavens he'd turned off the ringer…although she wasn't surprised. That deputy knew what he was doing in so many ways…

She pulled out the phone and looked at the name on the screen. The sheriff. Were he and his men here, or at least close?

Again speaking so quietly that she hopefully couldn't be overheard, she said, "Hello, Sheriff. Are you—?"

"You need to apologize to Casey and tell him to stand down for now," he interrupted. "We had an emergency here in town—an armed robbery at a clothing store. A lot of personnel are working on it, but we'll get someone to you soon as we can."

"This is becoming an emergency, too," she sputtered at him, though she still kept her voice low.

"Sorry," he repeated. "You and Casey had better be careful. There's something I may try here to get to you sooner, but not sure how long it'll take." And then he was gone.

Melody hadn't lied. Far from it. This was close to becoming an emergency now. Casey had just stepped out from his cover and into the clearing.

What was he doing? She'd figured there was a problem a moment ago when he'd stopped moving, but this surely was a lot worse. She had to tell him that their backup wasn't yet on the way, and the timing was uncertain.

And for now, she definitely had to become his backup. But how?

Once more she wished she'd brought some kind of weapon, preferably a gun. She'd practiced on shooting ranges. She was a ranch hand, after all.

But she'd never acquired a gun herself.

She heard more talking now. Raised voices. Damn! She definitely recognized Casey's among them, and she could no longer see his back. He must be confronting the rustlers, and he couldn't know how bad an idea that was at the moment.

But even if the sheriff was sending some kind of backup now, Melody couldn't imagine any way Casey could end this himself without anyone getting hurt. Without cattle getting hurt.

Worst of all, without *him* getting hurt.

She had to at least observe, and hopefully come up with a way to keep him safe. Maybe some kind of distraction with the cattle.

Yes, that had to be it…she hoped. To figure out what to do and how to do it, she inched forward to the break in the foliage where Casey had just stepped out to look out at what was happening, who was there and where they all stood, and what Casey was doing.

She stopped when she saw something that startled her and made her stand still.

And listen to the yelling, which continued.

The three rustlers consisted of two women and one man, and they were confronting Casey.

Melody was close enough now to hear what they were saying, despite the somewhat distressed mooing of the cattle that were now just behind the people who faced down Casey. Were the cows upset because of the raised human voices?

The rustlers' horses stood off to the side of the small herd of cattle.

And it became clear to Melody nearly immediately how furious Casey was. He was shouting at the people as if he knew them. "You're such fools," he was yelling. "Murderers—Sean, and Georgia and even Delilah. So stupid, all of you. Damn you for starting this, and for killing that ranch hand."

He'd drawn his gun, but it wasn't aimed at any of them, at least not at that moment.

But his shouting or insulting or whatever it was had now apparently escalated the argument even more.

Because the man drew a gun and pointed it straight at Casey's chest.

"WHY THE HELL are you the one who's after us?" demanded the assailant holding the gun on Casey.

And why the hell was Sean Dodd, the man who'd helped to steal the cattle, aiming at him? Sean was his brother's one-time best friend and his ex's brother. Casey might not have been overly fond of Sean, even when Georgia and he were engaged, but he hadn't foreseen he'd become a cattle rustler—and a murderer.

Georgia, who stood slightly behind Sean now, was clearly using her brother as a shield to confront Casey.

Georgia, the too-pretty woman with long, dark hair and full lips that had tantalized him once upon a time. The bitch who had left him at the altar...and had apparently dropped that charm near the broken fence, the charm Casey now assumed was hers.

As with her brother, Casey was surprised. Whatever Georgia used to be, he'd also never considered that she would steal cattle, let alone murder someone.

Georgia, who kept peeking around Sean and grinning at Casey so evilly and challengingly that he was tempted to ignore Sean's gun and go confront her, face-to-face.

But, of course, he knew better than to move, at least for the moment. Sure, he still held his gun, too, but he'd stopped himself from pointing and shooting once he was certain who the suspects—more than suspects—happened to be.

People he knew, even if he hadn't trusted or liked them for a long time. Not even the third member of their party, Sean's wife, Delilah. She was attractive, sure, and wore her black hair pulled back to show off her usual dangling earrings and wide-eyed, pretty face that nevertheless seemed intelligent, as an accountant should be. But was Delilah?

What was she doing out here? Was she involved in stealing the cattle, too? It certainly appeared so, but she'd always struck Casey as a nice, normal person.

Why she'd ever married a jerk like Sean was a mystery to Casey. Not that the answer mattered in the scheme of things, particularly here.

And why the heck were any of them rustling cattle, let alone killing people? Why break the law at all? Were they somehow out of money? Doing it just for fun? It must all be new, since he'd had no indication of their being criminals when Georgia and he were together.

Casey kept his tone as mild as possible when he responded to Sean's question, which hung in the air.

"As you're aware, Sean, I'm a deputy sheriff here in Sur County. It shouldn't be surprising to you that I'm attempting to bring down people who are breaking the law. I'd no idea it was you and don't believe anyone else in my department did, either." He paused. "Not that I'm particularly surprised about you or dear Georgia, and since you're involved I guess I shouldn't be surprised about Delilah, either." He stared at Sean's wife, who stood behind the other two looking off to her side…as if she wanted to be anyplace but there.

Maybe. That could, of course, just be his interpretation, or her ruse.

"Well, I'm not surprised, but I'm also not thrilled," Sean said. The guy looked relaxed despite holding a gun on Casey. His hair was brushed high to reveal his long forehead, and he'd grown a scruffy beard since Casey had seen him last. And when Sean smiled, like now, he revealed even, white teeth. "I'd figured we'd just take these cows and sell them and that would be that. Changed their brand so no one would know where they came from, to SG—Sean-Georgia. Didn't really want an escort."

"Oh, you don't have an escort, believe me," Casey said, taking a step closer but still not raising his gun, figuring that would only cause Sean to shoot him. At least Sean hadn't ordered him to drop it yet. And when he did, would Casey obey? He doubted it. "Now, why don't we wind this down?" Casey continued. "You can go back to town, and I'll get the cattle taken care of."

Sean laughed. Sarcasm coated his words as he quipped, "And then I'll take over the town from Selectman Edison and make a little money that way. Hah, hah. As if." His expression changed from a smile to an angry glare. "Forget that. And I—" He looked over Casey's shoulder, and that expression changed again, to…what? Puzzlement? Or was it a smug look? "Hey, I guess I've found a way to end this stalemate, to make sure you do exactly as I say."

What the hell? Casey had a bad feeling, considering the direction of Sean's gaze, that maybe Melody had stepped out from her hiding place. He didn't turn to look. Maybe, even if Melody had been made, Casey could take control while Sean was distracted by having seen her.

"Hey, come out of there, miss," Sean called. "Melody, isn't it? I did a little bit of research before we adopted those cows, and I learned who worked at the ranch, who Edison's ranch hands were. So, Melody Hayworth, why don't you join us?"

Casey didn't hear anything from behind him. Was Melody still hiding? He hoped so. Better yet, maybe she'd started sneaking her way back up the hill. After all, thanks to her, help was on the way. She didn't need to do anything else.

Apparently Sean didn't see or hear more, either.

"Where is she?" demanded Georgia. "Want me to go get her?"

"No need," Sean told his sister. "I can get her to join us, I'm sure." He raised the gun he held a little more, now aiming it at Casey's head. Casey had an urge to duck and roll up to Sean's feet and pull him to the ground. Anything to help Melody. But when Sean yelled out, "I'm about to shoot Deputy Colton here in the head unless you come out here right away, Melody."

"Stay there!" Casey yelled, still not taking his eyes off Sean. Worst case—he hoped—was that he could save himself the same way, by throwing himself to the ground and shooting Sean.

"Ah, at last," Sean said, though he didn't lower the gun. "So come over here, Ms. Ranch Hand."

Damn. Melody must have walked away from the cover of the bushes. And Casey knew it for certain when he heard some footsteps on the turf behind him, and Melody showed up at his side.

He turned slightly to glare at her, but what was the use? Showing anger at her now wouldn't help either of them.

And the half-defiant, half-petrified expression on her face made him want to grab her and hold her and somehow protect her with his body.

Which wouldn't work, if Sean decided to shoot him. Unfortunately, he wasn't made of armor.

"Hello, Casey." Her tone sounded calm and not scared in the least. "And hi to you, robbers." She didn't mention they were killers, too, as she turned to face them, probably a good thing at this moment. "Guess we're at a standoff here. That's a shame."

Casey wished there was a way to ask her if she knew how far away their backup was.

Better yet, he wished the deputies Sheriff Krester had sent would finally arrive.

How long would it be before help got here?

DAMN. MELODY WASN'T surprised that the guy with the gun—Sean, wasn't it? That was what Casey had called him—had noticed her, even though she'd tried to stay hidden. But she had also wanted to watch what was going on with Casey, so she obviously hadn't remained hidden enough.

She wished she could tell Casey the truth about their possibly nonexistent, or at a minimum delayed, backup.

But there was no way she could mention it now. And how would his knowing help them, anyway?

The best thing would most likely be to get these people talking, hopefully more relaxed, and just pray that the sheriff got whatever help he'd hinted at on its way. Fast.

She drew slightly closer to Casey, who remained standing with his gun still in his hand but aiming downward. She figured that if he moved it, Sean would shoot them.

She looked then at the two women. Who were they? Georgia and Delilah, Casey had called them. Was Georgia the ex-fiancée he had been talking about? Would there be any way of appealing to them to get their apparent buddy to back off?

First, though, she had a genuine question. "You were right that I'm a ranch hand," she said, directing her gaze back to Sean. "Could you tell me why you stole the cattle?"

"Money, of course," Sean said, sounding almost gleeful. "Your boss knows how to breed some nice, valuable cows. We—" he gestured to the women near him "—need quick cash, so we figured some of Edison's cattle would do the trick."

"And that was your idea?" she asked, even though whose idea it was didn't really matter.

"No, it was mine," said one of the two women as she moved from behind Sean to beside him on his left side—as his right hand still held the gun. "I'm Georgia." Melody was more convinced now that this was the same Georgia who'd dumped Casey when they were about to get married, especially when she sent a really nasty smile in Casey's direction.

Melody studied her. What had Casey seen in her?

Well, she was somewhat pretty. Besides, hadn't he mentioned that the woman who dumped him had been his childhood sweetheart? So he probably hadn't known then that she was a potential thief—and killer.

Georgia continued talking. "We've heard those Angus cows bring in bunches of money from other ranchers since they have lots of calves before they become expensive and delicious meat. That's why we gave them a new brand. But now that word's out about their theft, we decided to sell them to a slaughterhouse that wouldn't pay attention to even their new brand and would give us a lot of money for them. We'd hoped to do all of it before anyone even knew they were missing. And we certainly didn't take a lot of them. A dozen, from Mr. Edison's huge herd? Why was he even paying attention?"

Melody stifled an urge to go swat the nasty, less-than-intelligent thief right in her grinning face. "Because they are *his*," she said with her teeth clenched. "And they're valuable, as you said. And no one has any right to steal them."

"Oh, we have any right we want," Sean said in a way so offhanded that Melody wished she had a way to swat him, too, without any of them harming her... or Casey, of course.

But what were they going to do now?

"Look," Casey said, "we've got a kind of standoff here. Like I said before, why don't we just end it? You can go your way and we'll go ours—with the cattle, of course."

"Oh, there are a few other options," Sean said. "Like we could shoot you right here and then continue with the cattle."

"Continue where?" Melody asked. "The ranchers around here will all know these cattle have been stolen. Local slaughterhouses, too. No one will buy them now, no matter what your prior plan was." She moved closer once more to Casey, who'd started to ease slightly forward. Why? To grab the gun from that nasty Sean? That wouldn't work.

The guy had already killed one person during this fiasco of a theft, presuming it was Sean who'd murdered Pierce. He definitely had a gun, although she couldn't be certain neither of the women had one. Maybe one of them had done the killing.

And the two who hadn't done the shooting were still accomplices in Pierce's murder, right?

"Oh, we're just waiting now," Georgia responded. "There's a road just ahead, or are you aware of that? No matter. We've got a couple of big trucks on the way to pick the cattle up, move them...well, I won't tell you where."

"Fine," Casey said. "Go ahead. You can just leave us here, and—"

"And you'll find a way to notify your damn sheriff's department and they'll stop the trucks," Sean hissed. "I don't think so—not with you alive, at least." He hadn't moved the gun away from Casey, and now he took another step toward him.

"Now wait," Melody said, attempting not to sound as desperate as she felt. "If you promise not to hurt us, maybe I can help you. As you know, I'm a ranch hand, and—"

"A useless ranch bitch, that's what you are," Georgia said, sneering at her. "Yeah, I'll just bet that you could help. That you would help."

Useless ranch bitch? Melody found herself breathing harder. That insult reminded her of her ex-husband's insults.

Melody's first impulse was to insult this cattle-rustling bitch in return. These thieves facing them down—including Georgia—clearly weren't particularly bright, if they'd thought they would get away with it. Plus they were horrible—cruel to the cattle they were rushing off like this. And atrociously heartless. They hadn't just killed a cow.

They had also killed a man.

Which indicated they wouldn't have any qualms about killing Casey and her, too.

So, though Melody felt she had to say something, it couldn't be anything that would increase the tension in this situation any further.

After pondering for a second or two, she said to Casey's ex, "I do know how to handle cattle." She wondered how he must be feeling to have this particular woman face him down in this situation as a definite enemy. Melody had hated her final confrontation with Travis, but at least it had been calm despite being nasty. "Let me help you, and I'll—"

"You can help us by shutting up," Sean said, now pointing his gun toward her.

Which she did, even as she grabbed Casey's arm to make sure he didn't attempt to protect her in some way and get hurt.

She nodded, then puckered her mouth to show she wasn't speaking any more, even as she held onto Casey even harder to keep him from talking, too. And she felt him straining at her grasp.

What was he intending to do?

Chapter Nineteen

Damn it all. If Casey had a choice right now, he'd throw his arms around Melody and escort her back into the underbrush to hide, then turn around and confront the deadly idiot standing on the grassy rise just ahead with his gun pointed toward them.

But if he tried it, Casey felt certain Sean would simply shoot him in the back.

Sean. Casey had known the SOB for a long time. He might not have been the smartest tool in the shed then, but he hadn't seemed the type to turn into a criminal.

But who knew? Casey clearly hadn't been particularly discriminating back then, or even afterward. He'd become engaged to Georgia, hadn't he?

Georgia. There was no love lost between them now, that was for certain. Still, would she want to see Casey killed, especially by her own brother?

Or would she be thrilled about it?

Maybe he should sound her out.

At least the cattle had settled down a bit now behind Sean and the others, maybe because none of the humans were yelling at each other, at least not at the moment.

"So what's this really about, Georgia?" he asked. He looked at his ex as if they were sitting across from each other at a restaurant having a serious discussion, rather than out here, opponents in a standoff, on opposite sides of the law. Both wore casual, outdoor clothing to keep them comfortable in the cooling November climate as evening approached, but Casey felt anything but comfortable talking to her. "Would you have stolen the cattle if you'd known I'd be the deputy to come after you?"

She shrugged her shoulders beneath her hoodie and sent a wry look his way. The prettiness that had impressed him once now just looked plastered-on, a facade. Behind her, the cattle moved restlessly on the grassy, rolling turf under the cloud-strewn sky but fortunately weren't going far, so no one needed to go wrangle them at the moment. Georgia had said they would soon be loaded into trucks that were on their way.

"I didn't know you would be after me," Georgia said. "And I didn't know you wouldn't. It simply didn't matter. We need money. I did what I had to do to get it the fastest way possible. And besides, this has worked before."

"Really? This isn't the first time you've stolen cattle?" Casey was surprised. Sure, the sheriff's department had been involved in similar past investigations of other cattle that had disappeared, but not as many as this time, and not as valuable…and not owned by the town selectman.

Georgia just shrugged, which provided the answer Casey sought. He wanted to keep her conversing with him, though. The more time they ate up in nondangerous dealings, the better chance they had to keep things sort of calm until backup arrived.

How far away were they? Enough time had passed that they should be arriving soon, right?

"Well, did you get money before? How do you think you'll get any from this situation? You'll have a lot of legal charges pending against you, and they won't only consist of grand theft of the cattle. I don't know which of you did it, but one of you shot and killed Pierce Tostig—and that's first-degree murder for all of you."

Delilah suddenly moved in front of Georgia. "I had nothing to do with that," she asserted. "I'm just in this partly because I'm married to Sean, and I do love him, but I'm mostly here because I'm an accountant."

"Then you cooked the family books," Casey said, shaking his head at her.

"Well… I do derive income from my own accounting business, and of course we file taxes, and—"

"I get it." Casey figured he'd enjoy letting the IRS know about that, too—not that it would matter much, when this family wound up in prison, hopefully for life. They'd need to spend any money they had on lawyers. Their tax bill would just be another cost they'd have to deal with.

Interesting that Delilah made no attempt to distance herself from the cattle-rustling situation, but claimed, at least, that she hadn't been involved in the murder. Which she was, just by being with those who'd committed it.

"Yeah, I'm sure you do get it, Casey, dear," Georgia said, this time shuffling in the grass to move in front of her sister-in-law. "But look. I'm sure that, as a mere deputy sheriff, you've got to understand what it's like to need money. We're just—"

"You're just committing crimes, for whatever reason," Casey responded, not attempting to hide his disgust. "You know, I was pretty upset at first when you dumped me just when we were about to get married. And back then, you said it was because your wonderful brother here—" he gestured toward Sean with his empty left hand "—didn't think a mere deputy sheriff was good enough. I wasn't even as good as an FBI agent like Everett, who had no interest in you. I admit I felt hurt. Really hurt. But now? All I can do is thank you. I'm really happy I never married you—not a thieving, murderous person like you."

"Why, you—" Georgia seemed to dive for her brother's gun, but Sean pulled it back, laughing.

"Easy now, little sister," he said. "Let's not do anything hasty. Although I have given this some thought. I haven't come up with any good answers about how best to end this, with this deputy sheriff—" he said the words in a mocking tone "—and ranch hand in a way that won't involve my shooting both of you." He raised his gun hand again slightly. "At least if I do, I can say it was all in self-defense, since you have a gun, too."

In response, Casey lifted his empty left hand as if attempting to wave off the threat, keeping his right hand, which held his gun, still pointed at the ground.

"Look," he said. "Let's be reasonable. I know I shouldn't tell you this since I'd rather you be apprehended right here and now, but I'd suggest you just let us go and get out of here. We've already called for backup, and they're on their way. They should arrive at any time."

He saw Melody ease beside him and felt her touch his left arm. What was she trying to tell him?

Was help not on the way after all?

He didn't dare look at her. He needed to keep his attention riveted on Sean and the women who were his backup.

"Really?" Sean raised the gun higher and aimed at Casey's head. "I bet you're lying. And if you're not... well, yeah, maybe I'll let you stay alive now, as our hostages."

"Well, that's certainly better than the alternative," Casey said, attempting to joke. "And sure, if I thought it would convince you not to hurt us, I'd lie. But I'm not lying. And do you really want to take that chance?"

Casey did manage a quick glance toward Melody, at his side. Her lovely face looked pale and drawn, but she nodded as if in agreement with him.

No, he wasn't lying. Last he'd heard, they did have reinforcements coming thanks to Melody's conversation with his boss, the sheriff.

But she'd had time by herself to talk to Sheriff Krester again. She surely wouldn't have told him to call off their backup. But had the sheriff told her they weren't coming?

Casey had come to know Melody a bit in their few

days together, believed he could read her thoughts at least somewhat from her face.

And what he read there right now made him worry. A lot.

OKAY, MELODY THOUGHT. What should she do now?

Telling the truth, the way she understood it, certainly wasn't an option.

Right now, though, she was getting even more terrified of Sean's keeping his gun aimed toward them— especially Casey. They apparently had a history that might even make Sean happy to kill the man who'd nearly become his brother-in-law.

She had to do something. Something to protect both of them. As a member of the sheriff's department, and a guy the people confronting them knew and considered a likely enemy, Casey particularly needed that protection. But what?

She decided to follow through with something she'd suggested before, if nothing else to buy a little time while they talked about it.

Which could wind up being very little time.

"Look, Sean. Georgia. And Delilah, too. You indicated some trucks would be coming down that road soon." She pointed in the direction at the far end of where the cows stood. "I hate the idea of your stealing the cattle that way, but under these circumstances I'd rather you not hurt them while you're loading them up. Let me help you."

"We did okay getting them here," Georgia countered, frowning.

"Except for the one that broke her leg that you then shot." Maybe Melody shouldn't remind them of that, especially in the enraged but muted tone of voice she used. But at least she didn't mention their also killing Pierce.

"Yeah, I think it's a good idea for you to have Melody's help," Casey said. "She knows what she's doing with cattle. And…well, I'd really like to know why you shot poor Pierce." Casey apparently had no qualms about mentioning it, though, she realized.

Melody waited tensely for their response.

"Because he'd caught up with us," Georgia growled, walking slightly down the small ridge where the three of them stood to confront Casey. "Before you did. He threatened us. He was armed, too—and he threatened to shoot us as soon as he confronted us. He seemed so angry about that dead cow, said we'd better give up right away, aimed at us…so Sean shot him."

So now they knew which one was the actual killer, Melody thought. She assumed they now had Pierce's weapon, too, although she didn't want to ask, didn't want to call attention to the likelihood they had at least a second gun among them somewhere.

"I see" was all she said. "Now when are those trucks supposed to get here to pick up the cattle?"

Maybe they could somehow recruit the drivers to help them, depending on how and where they arrived.

She didn't want to get into a situation where other innocent parties, like those drivers, were hurt or killed. Assuming, of course, they were innocent. They might have knowledge of the origin of these cattle, considering the fact they were picking them up in the middle of nowhere.

Behind Sean and Georgia, Delilah was the one to look down at her watch. "In about twenty minutes," she called. Apparently Sean's wife was the most organized, possibly most intelligent one of them. Maybe, if Melody could start walking among them, she could get accountant Delilah to see reality and help her bring down Sean and Georgia—to potentially save their lives, she'd tell Delilah. Otherwise, the people coming as their backup might shoot first before attempting to arrest the armed thieves.

"Okay, then." She glanced around until her eyes lit on the three horses off to the side of the cattle. "Now, as you know, I don't have a horse right here, and herding cattle is easier when you're mounted. Can I borrow one of your horses?" They hadn't agreed she could help them, but they hadn't said she couldn't, either. She might as well act as if it was now a deal.

"What, and gallop away whenever a distraction takes our eyes off you? I don't think so." Sean sneered.

"Besides," Georgia said, "aren't you a big-deal cattle drover? If so, you should be able to get them to go in any direction you want, just by waving your arms and calling to them."

Melody had in fact considered the possibility of racing off as soon as she could, but she'd have been too worried about Casey to try it. She wouldn't tell them that, though. Or Casey. He'd been trying hard to protect her but might resent it if he thought she was further jeopardizing herself to protect him.

"All right, if that's how you want it," she said. "I'd be more help to you if I could be on a horse but I can handle it this way, too. I might wind up giving you more instructions, though, since I won't be able to handle as much myself."

"Oh, yeah, as if we'd follow your instructions," Georgia scoffed.

Melody just shrugged. She'd do what she could to help the cattle—and Casey, too, of course. She would also see what happened when the trucks actually arrived and she had an opportunity to see the drivers and maybe talk with them, and at least show them in some manner what was going on so they'd call for help without Sean and his gang seeing them.

This was it, she realized. Whatever happened in the next hour or less would most likely be the end of this story, and she really hoped she would be able to do something to bring down these miserable rustlers and save Casey and herself…and, of course, the cattle.

There appeared to be no doubt about what the clues they'd found meant. The charm with a G must have been Georgia's. The change in brand on Addie, and apparently the other cattle, signified the initials of the siblings' first names. If Melody recognized it, the smart deputy who was Casey undoubtedly did, too.

She would love to see these people arrested and prosecuted for what they'd done. And hopefully Casey and she would be there to testify against them in court.

But right now she was scared that they wouldn't remain alive that long.

She managed a glance at Casey. He was scowling,

but when their eyes caught she saw something in them that she appreciated. No, despite their nights together, particularly the last one, they had no romantic relationship—although at the moment Melody kind of regretted that. She could die before this was all over, and it might be somehow easier if she died with the belief that someone as kind and determined as Deputy Colton had tried to save her, not just because it was his job, but because he *cared*.

She realized she felt the same about him, no matter what. And if they survived, was there a chance at a romantic relationship?

No matter how much she doubted it—still doubted she was ready for one—she hoped she had an opportunity to find out.

Chapter Twenty

Casey watched as Georgia and Delilah mounted their horses and walked them over the tamped-down grass toward where the nearest cows stood. The cattle stomped and mooed, as if they knew that something was about to happen.

Their lowing wasn't the only sound, though. Occasional planes flew overhead, but, more important, Casey heard vehicles in the distance moving along the road where they'd soon head.

Was that the way their backup would arrive? Assuming there was any, of course. It was a major assumption.

He looked over at Sean, who stayed on the ground with his gun aimed at Melody. Glancing down at his watch, Sean said, "I think it's near enough to the time the trucks are expected for us to get these cattle closer to the road to wait."

"Okay," Melody said. She glanced at Casey, and he read in her expression that she wanted to talk to him. Alone. Which wasn't going to happen.

But what *was* going to happen?

Was backup going to arrive? He'd definitely gotten

the impression that was what Melody wanted to talk to him about, so he couldn't count on it.

He had an unpleasant feeling that Sean was about to shoot him. That way, they wouldn't have to worry about him while they moved the cattle and loaded them into whatever trucks were coming. Of course, he would remain alert and keep his gun in his hand, and use it if he needed to protect himself, though he wasn't sure how effective it would be under these circumstances. Would he be fast enough to raise his gun and shoot Sean before Sean shot him?

He was surprised, then, when Sean said, "You come along, too, Mr. Deputy. You can stay with Ms. Ranch Hand and me. I can see from the way you two look at each other that you've got something going, so I'll use both of you to keep the other under control. Just know that I won't kill either of you unless I need to so I can get the other one to do what I say. First shot probably won't be fatal then…probably. Got it?"

Yeah, he got it. And Casey wondered a bit about Sean's observation. Something going between Melody and him?

They apparently gave the impression they were closer than they were. And that might not help them resolve this situation.

Well, if he ever was to get interested in another real relationship, she'd be at the top of his list of women to check out. Assuming, of course, that she had any interest, after her nasty divorce.

"Got it," he acknowledged aloud, and surprised himself by aiming a wink at Melody where she stood near the cattle as if priming herself to help out with herding them where their captors wanted. She sent back a weak, troubled smile, and he wished he could do something to reassure her. Of course, any reassurance right now could be a lie.

"First, though—hand over your gun now, Casey. I've let you hang on to it as a game, kind of. But I won't be able to watch you as closely now, so give it to me and I won't shoot your lady right now." Sean swung his arm up and took a few steps forward until the muzzle of his gun touched Melody's forehead. "Oh, and your phone, too. And yours, Melody."

Damn. But what choice did he have? Drawing closer to Sean, Casey considered whether he could shoot Sean now and end this, but Sean's finger was wiggling on the trigger as if to taunt him.

Plus, Delilah and Georgia had ridden closer, around the cows, and were watching.

Casey gave him his gun, grip first, and also pulled Melody's phone from his pocket and handed it to Sean, as Melody, too, gave him his phone. What choice did they have?

"Ha, ha!" Sean chortled. "Guess you're finally realizing who's in charge here." He kept his gun aimed again at Melody as he stuffed Casey's gun and both phones into his saddlebag. "And though I'm not sure what I'll do with you yet when the trucks arrive, at least this way you won't be able to call for help if I leave you here." He gestured with his weapon to wave Casey forward. "Let's go," he said. "And in case you need any other motivation to listen to me, Deputy, I'll be nice to both of you for now, until and unless there's a problem. You've already decided I'm a murderer—"

"Aren't you?" Casey asked wryly, unable to help himself from interrupting.

"Maybe, maybe not. But I could easily become one for the first, or not-so-first, time if I get any trouble from either of you. So keep that in mind, will you?" His gaze landed again on Melody, who remained still, and it morphed from somewhat amused to threatening. Casey had an urge to use the opportunity of having Sean's attention at least somewhat diverted to grab him and pull him down, but since he again trained his gun on Melody, that wasn't an option.

"Oh, I'll definitely keep it in mind," Melody said. She rolled her eyes as if she found the man who was menacing her merely stupid, not dangerous, too.

At least Sean didn't react to that. "Excellent. And Casey, how about you?"

"Oh, you can believe it's on my mind." And the look Casey leveled at Sean should tell him that he'd never forget it, never let it go.

Sean walked over to his horse, which he mounted, then aimed his gun again at Melody. "Okay," he said. "We're going to get the cattle to the road. We've done well herding them while we're on horseback, but I know it can be done on foot, too, so that's what you'll do. Let's just all head toward the road and coax the cattle that way, too." He picked up a prod from his saddle with his left hand and waved it. "Haven't needed these much. You've trained those cattle well, Melody, from what

I've seen. They start forward when we do, with one of us behind to wrangle the stragglers."

"That should work," Melody acknowledged.

"And do you have better ways? Bet you do," Sean called to her as he moved a bit away.

"Let's see how this goes" was all Melody said.

Then, with Georgia and Delilah once more on opposite sides of the herd and Sean behind with Melody near him, the cattle moved forward. Sean lagged a bit until Casey got closer to Melody.

"Hey, you can follow your lady," Sean said. "Help her out here, okay, Deputy?"

Casey wasn't sure what he should do, but for now all he did was stay a bit behind Melody but in front of Sean and his horse. The cattle kept moving, which was a good thing.

They went over a small rise, and that was when Casey saw the road ahead of them. There was a fence with a gate along it, so he figured this was part of Over-Herd Ranch, and Clarence Edison had built it out here to protect his cattle from getting onto the two-lane highway.

There was also a wide shoulder along each side of the road, outside the fence—wide enough that trucks could probably park on one side or the other while the cattle were being loaded. Casey figured the cattle would stop on this side of the fence, the gate would be opened, and people would get the cows onboard the trucks one at a time.

Melody could help with that, but he figured she'd hate it. Still, that might be a good time for her to talk to the drivers, if they didn't seem to realize what was happening. Or even if they did but hadn't realized human lives would be at stake.

And him? He'd just have to watch what was going on, wait…and hopefully find an opportunity to get Melody and himself out of this.

The cattle stopped near the fence, as Sean and his group likely wanted them to.

"Okay," Melody said, looking from Sean to Georgia and back. Delilah remained on horseback at the far side of the cattle herd. "You'll soon get these cows heading to wherever it is you're intending to sell them." She stopped for a moment and aimed a quizzical gaze toward Georgia, as if she assumed Sean's sister was the most likely to reveal that information, but Georgia just shrugged.

"You got it," Sean said. "And then we'll be out of here, too."

"You're getting into the trucks with them?" Casey asked.

"Could be," Sean replied.

"Are you also taking the horses?" Melody asked.

Casey figured she hoped they wouldn't so the two of them would have transportation back to the ranch house, assuming they were both allowed to stay there. And what good would it do to take Melody and him along, anyway? They'd just give the Dodds a hard time…as long as they weren't shot first. But Sean probably wouldn't leave horses with them. They'd get back to civilization and send the authorities after the trucks quicker.

If left here without their phones to call for help, they couldn't summon anyone else to go after the trucks. Still, they also would still be alive—or at least Casey hoped that was how Sean was currently thinking.

"We'll see." Sean gestured to Georgia, and the two of them moved a small distance away on their horses and began talking. Casey wasn't surprised that Sean still pointed his gun at Melody and him.

Casey used that as an opportunity, though, to get closer to Melody. "You okay?" he asked. She was pale, but her chin was raised resolutely as if she'd been through this kind of danger before and had come out just fine.

Which he doubted. But he still appreciated her bravery.

"I'll be better when they're gone," she said.

"Yeah, we both will. And even if they leave us here without horses—" He shut up for a few seconds as an SUV drove by, causing some of the leaves on the road shoulder to blow around. "We'll still be here, by the road, and we should be able to flag someone down for help."

"I hope so." She sounded so glum that he figured she believed Sean would shoot them before he left.

And Casey was worried about that, too.

For now, he looked her straight in the eyes, then moved close enough that he could have drawn her near and hugged her for emotional support—and more—if they weren't so visible to their enemies, who might find a way to use it against them.

Sean had, after all, seen some closeness between

them that Casey had been trying not to acknowledge to himself...much.

But now—well, once this was over and they returned to whatever reality they could, maybe he really would see where the familiarity they'd begun could lead them.

For the moment, Casey attempted to put all thoughts of Melody and how they'd get along in the future to the back of his mind.

He needed to watch, wait and figure out what to do to save them now.

THERE THEY WERE—or at least Melody assumed the two semis rolling slowly toward them along the road were the vehicles Sean and his co-conspirators were waiting for. When the trucks began to slow down, she felt even more sure.

"Woo-hoo!" called out Sean from behind her, the ultimate confirmation about whether those were the ones he had hired.

The five of them—the Dodds, Casey and Melody— now stood along the fence with the cattle just behind them. They watched as the trucks came to a stop and parked on the shoulder.

So how would things work out now? Melody knew Sean wanted to have her help get the cattle inside the trailers. Would he also insist that she go along with them in the trucks to wherever he planned to sell the cows?

Sell them. The stolen cows that were her responsibility were about to be finally taken away for good, and she would be part of that, like it or not. They wouldn't even necessarily be identifiable as OverHerd Ranch cattle unless people studied them closely. Presumably the brands on all of them had been changed as Addie, the dead cow's, had been—from OHR to SG.

Where would Casey be when she left with the Dodds? Melody wondered. Would he ride along with them? Stay here, alive and well?

She didn't even want to consider the alternative.

She forced herself to concentrate when two men got out of the cab of the first truck. She assumed the occupants of the other truck's cab would join them, though she couldn't see them yet.

"Gentlemen!" Sean called. "Thanks for coming. Now, show us how we should load the cattle, and we'll begin, okay?"

The two men had reached the gate, where Sean met them. Melody noted that Georgia now held a gun and was trying to be surreptitious about it as she kept it trained on Casey. Was it the same gun that Sean had held? Melody didn't think so—and that made her swallow in sadness.

It might have been Pierce's that they'd taken from him when they killed him.

In any case, it was a symbol that Casey and she had better not tell these other people what was really going on here.

And so she wouldn't—for now, at least.

"That sounds good," said the taller of the two men, who was clean-shaven and wore a gray cap with a logo Melody couldn't see and a dark blue sweatshirt with matching trousers. He'd come from the driver's side of the truck. The other man, shorter and with a receding hairline, was dressed similarly but wore no cap.

Presumably, they knew they'd be transporting cattle in their truck. Was that why there were two of them?

"We'll bring the first cow through the gate as an example, to see how this works out," Delilah said loudly enough for all of them to hear, which Melody found almost amusing since she doubted the accountant would do anything but watch the cows get into the truck.

And what about how they would smell in the trucks? Out in the pasture, their aromas weren't particularly bad in the open air, but inside?

Well, these truckers had apparently been told what they were getting into. Maybe they'd even transported cattle before.

Melody glanced at Casey, who was at her side. He had a bland expression on his face. For now, at least. Would he attempt to tell the truck guys what was going on? Probably, if he had the opportunity, and she would do the same.

He probably wouldn't want to start any trouble now, though, like revealing what the situation was. These drivers were potentially in as much trouble as Casey and she were. If they gave any of the Dodds a hard time, one or more of them might get shot. Casey would undoubtedly try to protect them, too.

Before any of the cows were wrangled through the gate, two more people joined them from the other truck, a woman and a man. They wore similar outfits. Maybe that was standard for this transportation company. The vehicles themselves all had the same logo on them, a loopy, floral thing that Melody wasn't familiar with.

"Hi," the woman called. "Are we ready to get the cattle loaded on board?"

Everyone but Casey and Melody seemed to say yes. Over the next few minutes, one cow was culled from the front of the herd and led through the fence by Georgia, with Melody assisting, per Sean's instructions. There was a ramp at the back of the trailer that the cow was able to walk up, with the people leading her.

The inside of the trailer looked clean enough, Melody thought. She had no idea how many of the cows would fit in here, but since there were only eleven, and two trucks, having six in this one should be okay.

Another cow was led inside by Sean and his wife. Delilah appeared to be fine with helping out here, even if she wasn't as much of a ranch-type person as the others.

Casey accompanied them, and Melody assumed that was because of Sean's insistence…and additional threats, since he seemed inclined to have Casey accompany Delilah and him to the front of the trailer.

As a result, the five of them who'd headed here via the pasture were now inside the truck, along with all four of the drivers, temporarily for now, Melody figured, to get things started.

Only two cows were in there so far, so which people would return outside and lead the next one in? Melody just stood there, waiting to see if she, the ranch hand, was designated to help with that.

And where were Sean and Georgia's guns now? She

didn't see them being pointed at anyone, not even sur-
reptitiously. Did that mean there would be an opportunity to run once they returned outside?

She figured, though, from Sean's prior threats, that
Casey and she would be given their instructions and remain separated, rather than being given the chance to
flee together right now. The threat would remain that
if one was able to get away, the other would get shot
in retribution.

What were they going to do?

CASEY WISHED HE could plan something to save them—
and not just Melody and him. It had become his responsibility to try to rescue the other innocent civilians who
were now involved—the truck drivers.

Although there was something about them that made
him wonder how innocent they were. All four of them
acted like the drivers they were as they stood with Melody and him. But he'd noted that those drivers seemed
to be studying the five of them, as they discussed their
instructions, when the other cattle would be brought inside, and the route they would take to get to the ranch in
northern Arizona where the Dodds apparently intended
to sell the cows. Had they heard of the theft? Did they
know what was going on?

Were they okay with driving a bunch of stolen cattle this way? He wondered how much Sean had offered
to pay them.

Maybe they were watching him for some indication
of whether they could demand more—from the person
who'd stolen these valuable cows.

But there was something about them that suggested there was more to this part of the situation than Casey had figured out.

He'd just have to wait and see.

Suddenly, someone ran up the ramp and into the back of the trailer.

Someone pointing a gun toward Sean.

At the same time, all four drivers also pulled weapons from their pockets and aimed at Georgia and Delilah.

And Casey erupted into laughter, nodding happily as Melody aimed a confused gaze toward him.

The man who'd run up the ramp didn't meet Casey's gaze, though, and he knew full well why he didn't. Instead, the guy used his free hand to pull something out of his pocket—his identification.

"FBI," he said. "Sean Dodd, Georgia Dodd and Delilah Kennedy Dodd, you are under arrest for the murder of Pierce Tostig, an act of violent crime."

"What!" Sean shouted, and he started digging into his own pocket, presumably for his gun. But the female driver grabbed his hands and wrestled them behind his back, where she cuffed him and pulled out his gun, sticking it into her own waistband.

The other FBI agents frisked Georgia and Delilah and apparently found only the one additional gun. Soon they, too, were cuffed.

And as the Dodds were all led down the ramp, one by one, sirens sounded in the distance. Clearly, official help was on the way, so no one would have to drive these criminals to town in the semitrucks.

That gave Casey time to do as he'd wanted to for the last few minutes. He hurried to Melody's side.

"FBI?" She sounded confused. "Why are they here? I wouldn't have thought this was their jurisdiction."

"Probably not, normally," Casey agreed. But he looked toward the agent who'd run up the ramp and begun the arrest process. "Hey," he said, giving the agent a high five. And then he turned back toward Melody. "Melody Hayworth, I'd like you to meet my twin brother, Everett. My older brother, Agent Everett Colton." He turned back to Everett, whose grin was enormous. "So what brought you here, bro?" Casey asked.

Chapter Twenty-One

Melody remained standing next to Casey on the roadside near the trucks. She felt relieved. Was this over at last? It appeared that way. And how interesting that Casey's brother Everett, from the FBI, had been the agent in charge of bringing this to an end. The official Sur County Sheriff's Department black SUVs had already picked up the real truck drivers a mile down the road and they were being interrogated about what they knew about the cattle rustling, if anything.

Melody gathered from the shouted discussion that the FBI agents had commandeered the semis so they could dash out here undercover to apprehend the rogue cattle rustlers—the Dodds. And even if they were cleared quickly of any wrongdoing those real drivers wouldn't be able to take off with their trucks, not with the cows still inside.

Fortunately, the agents had found Melody's phone, along with Casey's, in the saddlebag still on Sean's horse, located with the other Dodd mounts behind the fence near the road. Though the phones would be evidence in the multiple crimes the Dodds had committed, Everett handed them to Casey and her, anyway—a good thing. She really needed hers.

She called Clarence. The ranch owner was thrilled to hear that the cows were now safely in Melody's control, and the rustlers had been apprehended. "By Everett Colton, I presume."

"Yes, and some other FBI agents," Melody responded, keeping her curiosity about what Clarence knew to herself. Getting the cattle back to the main ranch land was paramount.

And, of course, that was Clarence's opinion, too. He promised to send a few other ranch hands there via the road—and Melody promised she'd make sure the five horses, including Casey's and hers, were available for them to help herd the cows back where they belonged. Surely, with the Dodds no longer in charge, that would be the case.

"And you?" Clarence asked. "I assume you'd rather just come back here, right? That's what I want. I need to hear your story about what happened and how it got resolved."

"Fine." Melody felt a bit relieved that she wouldn't be one of the drovers on the way back. She needed some time off.

And…well, she didn't need to remain with Casey right now, but she wanted to. If nothing else, she wanted to learn how he had secretly worked with Everett so that this situation came to a positive conclusion.

But she also hoped to stay in Casey's company just a little longer. No, they didn't really have a relationship, despite their wonderful one-night stand. But she hoped they would see each other occasionally, as friends who had successfully worked together and helped to resolve a difficult situation.

But despite all they had been through together, she still wasn't ready for anything beyond that. Wasn't sure she'd ever be.

Although if she ever was, Casey would definitely be her pick…

And he seemed to value the idea of her being a ranch hand.

In any case, when she ended her conversation with Clarence, she invited both Casey and Everett to join her at the ranch house to provide a summary to the town selectman about what had happened.

"I'm going to check with my fellow deputies about the status of things around here," said Casey from beside her. "Hopefully, we'll all head back to town soon."

"Let's go get our horses before anything else," Melody told him, and they did. Fortunately, both Witchy and Cal were where they'd tethered them and seemed happy enough to be walked to the nearby roadside. The activity around the official sheriff's department vehicles had quieted down, and Melody was happy to join Casey there after they tied up their horses inside the pasture fence near where the Dodds' steeds had been secured.

Casey was soon met by Jeremy Krester. "Glad you're okay," the sheriff said. "Both of you." But the tall, thin man with graying hair leveled his gaze mostly at Casey, his deputy.

"I see you have a bunch of our guys here, too—including Captain Walter Forman and Deputy Bob Andrews." Casey glanced toward Melody. She recalled meeting both of them when the helicopter had arrived to pick up poor Pierce.

She asked, "Is the other emergency over?"

Casey stared at her. "Other emergency?"

The sheriff appeared a bit embarrassed. "Yeah, though we haven't yet caught the perpetrators. Like I said, it was an armed robbery, but by the time we got there, it was over and the perps had disappeared. No indication yet where they are. I probably should just have sent more of our deputies out here to help you."

"Well, we're okay now," Casey said. "Interesting, though, that the FBI helped out this way."

Melody had the sense he was rubbing his boss's nose into his possible mistake, but she didn't say anything.

Still, having a federal agency like the FBI here, represented by a deputy's brother, resolving things did sound a bit off to her—something she might see on TV or a movie.

Everett stood on the road shoulder near the three official vehicles that still had their red lights flashing on top. Melody wished she could bombard him with questions, but this wasn't the time…or, most likely, the place.

But right now, she couldn't have been happier to meet Casey's older brother—who was also in law enforcement and apparently had been instrumental in getting out here to bring down the Dodds and save the cattle.

"Good job," Everett called to Deputy Andrews, who was about to get into the driver's seat of the second SUV. There was a third one, too, behind it.

Melody couldn't help it. She peered inside that second SUV. Sean and Delilah were ensconced in the middle seat, with deputies both in front of them and behind them.

They remained in cuffs, from what Melody could see. And though they'd shot dirty looks at both Casey and her from the moment they were taken into custody, she doubted they'd have an opportunity to exact any revenge.

Speaking of teasing, she had an urge to yell something inside to them, taunt them about their failure, the fact the cattle would go back to their normal lives, but these thieves—and murderers—certainly wouldn't.

But why bother? It wouldn't really make her feel any better. Besides, judging by their posture and expressions, they already knew their despicable escapade was over, and so was their freedom to try to harm anyone else this way, or any other way, including cattle.

Melody considered peeking inside the first of the police vehicles where Georgia was detained, but decided not to. She figured she'd see all of them again eventually.

In fact, she'd look forward to testifying at trial against them.

Everett began talking then, and when she turned back toward him, she noticed he was on the phone. In a minute, his call was over, and he faced Casey, who now stood close to Melody.

"Hey, bro," he said. "We've been officially summoned to the ranch house—you, me and Melody—to provide our esteemed selectman and ranch owner a rundown of all that happened."

Which Melody was already aware of, but Clarence's invitation definitely made it official.

It would be interesting to hear their takes as they described all they knew, all that had happened, to Clarence, along with her.

CASEY WAS FINE with the idea of talking with Selectman Edison again, especially since Melody would be along. Not to mention his hero brother, Everett.

He wasn't surprised, though, that they had to wait until the first two of the three department vehicles, the ones containing the prisoners, took off for the station. Clarence Edison was sending some of his remaining ranch hands to take charge of wrangling the cattle back to their more usual environment in the closer pastures.

Fortunately, though, Clarence was more interested in having Melody join them for their discussion than having her do any herding right now. She'd remain in Casey's presence a while longer, which was fine with him.

He'd talked briefly with Everett and Sheriff Krester. Yes, the FBI team, with Everett in charge, had been the ones to initially place the Dodds under arrest, but that was for convenience, since they'd gotten to this area first, although Casey realized there was more to the delay than that.

However, the local authorities were taking over. The legal proceedings—arraignments, trials and all—would occur in this area, where the evidence and witnesses were.

There were reasons, though, why Everett and his

FBI contingent had happened to be present in Cactus Creek, and the brief mentions in the conversation suggested that Selectman Edison had had something to do with that.

Which made Casey even more eager for this upcoming meeting.

Especially since, fortunately, his initial suspect, Clarence's ex-wife Hilda, apparently hadn't been involved in the rustling, which would have made this conversation difficult.

"Hey, there they are!" Melody, standing near the remaining department vehicle beside him, pointed toward another SUV that was approaching from down the road. The white vehicle sported the OverHerd Ranch name and logo, with the head of a cow on its side.

Four men and two women got out and greeted Melody effusively once she'd approached them, giving her hugs and exclaiming that they hoped she was all right.

Casey felt irritated when the men hugged her, then he castigated himself. Melody and he were just friends. Colleagues who'd gone through a lot.

Two people who'd attempted to ease a difficult situation by having a night of passionate sex...

Which he'd need to forget, or at least not keep thinking about. It was done, it had been a good thing, and now it was over.

Although...well, the fact that Melody seemed even more beautiful now, while she was happy and relieved and surrounded by friends dressed like her in work clothes for a cattle drive, somehow made it harder for him to simply stick the memory of their wonderful night at the back of his mind.

But he would.

In a short while, Melody had helped her fellow ranch hands get the cattle back out of the trucks and secured behind the fence of the ranch land, though one of the men drove the SUV they'd arrived in back to the ranch house.

That gave the semi drivers, who'd been milling around, the go-ahead to take back possession of their vehicles and get on the road, but not before they had been interviewed and gave their contact information to Captain Forman. Evidently they did not appear to have known what the Dodds were up to.

And after that, it was finally time for Casey and the rest to get on the road, too—a good thing, since daylight was beginning to fade, and there certainly weren't any streetlights out here on this remote road.

Casey took charge of the remaining sheriff's department vehicle, promising to drop off Walter at the station before he, Melody and Everett, also riding with him, returned to the ranch to talk to Selectman Clarence.

This had been quite an interesting, revealing day... and Casey recognized it wasn't over yet.

MELODY WAS BACK at the ranch house. Not exactly her home, the apartment in one of the auxiliary bunkhouses near here, but Clarence's house.

This time, she was there with both Casey and his

brother. They'd complied with the summons by her boss, and they had a story to tell.

Melody hoped she learned something, too.

As he had the last time, before Casey and she had gone on their adventure to bring back the stolen cattle, Clarence had them shown through the wooden entryway into his ornate living room to talk. He soon joined them, having a member of the help, whom Melody had seen before but not met, bring them coffee, promising drinks later since he intended that they all stay for dinner.

Clarence took over one of the sections of the room's brown leather sofas. He gestured for Melody and the two Colton brothers to take seats on other portions of the sofa facing him.

Then it was time to talk.

"Hey, you three," Clarence said in his usually jovial tone—the one he used when he wasn't upset about stolen cattle. He started to joke about how lonesome he'd been without some of his cattle and one of his favorite ranch hands—he looked at Melody, which made her smile, despite knowing he was kidding—plus his favorite sheriff's deputy and FBI agent abandoning him for a while.

A good, useful while, he admitted.

Looking at Everett, Casey spoke first. "You know I'm always glad to see you, bro, but why did you happen to be around here to save me?"

"Oh, you can thank our favorite selectman." He turned toward Clarence, whose senior face lit up in a huge smile. "He happened to call my superiors in Phoenix and expressly request that I be sent here with a team of agents because he said some federal laws were being broken and he needed help."

"Help my department wasn't providing just then," Casey said, shaking his head.

"Exactly," Clarence responded. He told the story from his perspective, probably exaggerating a bit.

Melody gathered from what Clarence said that he'd been irritated when Pierce happened to disappear right when she, who was less experienced, headed out with Deputy Sheriff Casey to find the missing cattle. Pierce's job had been to help oversee care of the remaining cattle.

"I wanted him back," Clarence said. "I also considered calling the sheriff about this but figured he already had someone in the field from that office chasing his cattle—Casey. So I called a superior in the Phoenix FBI office and asked him to send our buddy Everett Colton, who knows the Cactus Creek area well, to try to find a missing ranch hand. And, of course, it didn't hurt that Casey is Everett's brother."

Clarence had claimed there was the possibility of a violent crime being committed—one of the areas where the FBI had jurisdiction—although he hadn't yet known of Pierce's death. As a result, with Casey still out in the field, Everett and his team members had been sent.

And Clarence had demanded silence—that Everett not attempt to contact his brother, at least not yet.

By the time they arrived, Pierce's body and the dead cow had been found, making the situation clearly a violent crime. Pierce's horse had shown up soon afterward near the stable. Everett and his colleagues stayed in town to work with the sheriff—and the selectman—in sorting out any evidence. That was why they were there to investigate after Melody called the sheriff's department on Casey's phone for help.

"And it worked," Clarence affirmed as the conversation drew to a close. "Don't get me wrong, I'm generally happy with the job our local sheriff's department does." He leveled a grin at Casey, who nodded back.

Melody noted the word *generally*, but didn't comment. She figured Casey had focused on it, too, since he quickly shared a glance with Everett.

"But, hey, you. Agent Everett Colton." This time Clarence focused directly on Everett. "You're F-B-I like you guys!"

Melody shook her head slightly in amusement. Her boss was clearly back to being himself, now that this nasty interlude was drawing to a close.

He was once again a punster.

He soon shepherded them all into his dining room, where they shared a delicious dinner—most likely the only one of theirs Clarence would pay for, despite the discussion Melody and Casey had had previously. Casey and she had shared their tale of life in the pasture chasing the missing cattle. Not all details about it, though, such as how their nights were spent—especially the last one.

Clarence let them know that he'd sent a couple of ranch hands out to retrieve Addie's remains and bury them behind the barn. That sounded appropriate to Melody.

When dinner was over, Clarence again thanked them

all and then ushered them from his ranch house and out of his company.

"Would you like a ride to town?" Everett asked Casey as Melody stood with them on the front porch, which was fortunately well-lit at this late hour.

"No, thanks. My car's already here. I left it the other day when we headed off to find the cattle."

"Great job with that." Everett smiled at Casey, then gave him a brotherly hug. "I'll probably see you in town, at least over the next few days. I'm hanging around till we're sure the case against your Dodd buddies is getting well-established."

"Great about your staying for a while," Casey said. "And those felons are far from buddies of mine, but I assume Sean and you aren't friends any longer."

"You assume right, of course. Anyway, nice meeting you, Melody." He gave her a hearty handshake, then looked from her face to Casey's, as if searching for something.

Melody sighed inside but didn't say anything. He obviously wasn't about to find anything between them. Which in a way was a shame…although it was for the best.

Still…

Melody at least derived some happiness from the fact that Casey walked her back to the bunkhouse containing her apartment, though he didn't go inside.

Just in case… "Would you like to come in for a drink?" she asked. "A quick one, of course." She said the latter in case he considered that an invitation for more.

"Not tonight, thanks." Casey dashed her hopes of

most likely seeing much of him, if at all, even though he'd limited his refusal to that night. But if there was to be anything more to their friendship, wouldn't he just come in for a minute?

"That's fine," she said cheerfully, anyway.

"Let's grab a drink or a dinner in town someplace soon," Casey said. "No hassle that way, and I'd like to stay in touch. Okay?"

"Fine," Melody said, realizing that this was Casey's nice effort to make sure they went their separate ways.

It certainly was better that way. She hadn't changed her mind about not wanting a real relationship...had she?

Well, if so, it obviously wouldn't be with Casey, no matter how sexy she found him.

And so, under the light by the front door to her building, she stood on tiptoe, reached up and pulled Casey's mouth down to hers for a kiss. A brief one.

It shouldn't feel so hot, she thought.

Well, so what? She moved away and managed to send him a smile. "Good night," she said. "And thanks for all you did to save those cattle."

Then she hurriedly opened the door and dashed inside.

Chapter Twenty-Two

Casey, sitting in his crowded, shared office at the sheriff's department, should have continued to feel delighted several days after his return with Melody.

The Dodds were in custody. Plus he'd had some additional success yesterday, after his return. Along with a couple of other deputies, including Bob Andrews, he had located and arrested the suspects in the clothing-store robbery. A very satisfying conclusion to that situation, too—assuming the criminals were found guilty of armed robbery at trial.

Fortunately, they hadn't hurt anyone during the robbery. And considering the evidence from the robbery that he and Bob had found at the apartment shared by the suspects, a pair of students who were attending college at a Tucson university, that should be a slam dunk.

Casey was, in fact, delighted about that achievement. What he hadn't been delighted about, at first, was his urge to call Melody and tell her about it.

He hadn't seen her since their dinner at the ranch owner's home. That was probably a good thing. And why would he? He had no reason to go to her ranch, and if she'd had any reason to come to town she hadn't told him about it.

Which was fine.

He could have let her know that he had finished providing all the information and evidence that he could against the Dodds right away. From his perspective, the case was closed—and there shouldn't be even a shred of possibility that those killers and rustlers wouldn't be found guilty and put away for the rest of their pathetic lives.

But right now, he was furious.

"Why?" he demanded angrily of Sheriff Krester, who'd just told him the Dodds were out on bail. "You know what they're like. They'll just run."

"And then you'll just have to catch them again," the sheriff said, eyeing Casey with a half-amused, half-irritated lifting of his gray eyebrows. "I'm sure you'll do it just fine."

"Yeah, right. Like last time. But—"

"No, you're right. You shouldn't be put in that position. *We* shouldn't be put in that position. But the Dodds apparently hired some pretty good lawyers—some new criminal attorneys who just opened an office here, I gather. I didn't know them, though I was there in court. The Dodds had their arraignment earlier today and, yeah, they were allowed out on bail, even though the charges include first-degree murder, and bail in that situation might not be legal. How'd they do it? Bribe the judge? Who knows?"

Jeremy came farther inside and sat down on a chair facing Casey's desk. Casey leaned forward on his elbows and clenched his fists. Not that he'd strike his boss, or anyone. It was his fury causing him to react.

Bob was there, too, along with their other officemate, Deputy David Young. Both of them also looked at their boss with expressions that were almost accusatory. But Casey knew full well that the sheriff's department did not have a final say whether or not the judge allowed bail. All they could do was testify at the eventual trial, provide evidence…and hope justice would prevail.

"The thing is," the sheriff said, "it came out at the arraignment that Sean and Delilah have a six-month-old daughter. They'd had a neighbor who also did babysitting for them watching little Kennedy, and they'd apparently planned all along to drop Delilah off in town with her while Sean and Georgia dealt with the cattle."

"Another indication those Dodds are all lowlifes. Poor kid." And it was another reason Casey was glad he hadn't wound up marrying Georgia. But he hadn't imagined any of them would get involved with murder and rustling, let alone insufficient care of a child.

"Yeah," the sheriff agreed.

Something else occurred to Casey. "Well, even if they were granted bail, how could they afford it?" he demanded. "Or even the payment to a bail bondsman? They stole those cattle because they needed money, or at least that's what they told me."

"Obviously we don't have all the answers," Jeremy said. He shrugged and left the office.

Well, the only good thing about that was that it gave Casey a reason to call Melody. She needed to know about the Dodds' release. And the baby? Maybe.

But would they go after Melody, or him, in retribution? If they were smart, the Dodds would simply behave like good citizens and not call attention to themselves, at least not until after their trial. Hopefully then, they'd be in prison for a good long time and not out in the world and able to murder people—or steal cattle. And hopefully they had a relative or two Casey didn't know about who could take care of the baby.

But there was no reason to believe they were particularly smart.

Casey glanced at his computer. It was nearly three o'clock in the afternoon. Not the best time to call a ranch hand, he was sure. But the sooner, the better. Worst case, he could leave a message.

He walked out of his office, leaving Bob behind. He doubted that anything he'd say would be private, but just in case...

First, though, before calling Melody, he found a corner at the end of the hallway. Then he phoned his brother. Everett would be interested in this, too. He and his fellow FBI team members had been the ones who'd first captured the Dodds, after all. He had even hung around for the next couple of days, also helping to put together evidence, though he'd gone back to Phoenix yesterday. While in Cactus Creek, he had also visited Casey, who lived in a small house at the rear of their parents' sizable property.

Casey was quite happy living there. He could spend time with their folks, yet have privacy, too. But he and Everett had visited for an evening's dinner. And he'd soon enjoy Thanksgiving with them, too. Plus there was their upcoming Christmas dinner, an annual event they all enjoyed, and Everett would most likely be around for it, as well, though he wasn't coming back for Thanksgiving, which was usually a much smaller affair and seldom included guests, let alone all family members.

He still believed that Melody would join them for Christmas, after his earlier invitation to her. He hoped so, at least.

"Hey, Everett," he said when his brother answered the phone. "How are things in Phoenix?"

"Fine, but why are you really calling now?" Everett asked.

Casey already knew his brother was smart. He gave a rundown of what the sheriff had told him.

"Damn," Everett growled. "And there's a baby involved, too? What a mess."

Casey promised to stay in touch and keep Everett informed about anything new he heard.

When they hung up, it was time to call Melody. He was eager to hear her voice, even though that was so unwise. But he missed her companionship more than he'd ever thought possible.

He thought about inviting her to town to join him for coffee and he would reveal what had been going on, but he was on duty and it was better to tell her fast.

"Good to hear from you, Casey," she said after answering the phone. "I can't talk long, though. I'm out in the pasture with part of our herd—and that includes the wonderful cows we rescued. They're doing fine."

"Glad to hear that. And the reason I'm calling is to make sure you stay alert." He revealed the information about the Dodds now being out on bail. And because he knew this woman who cared so much about cattle would undoubtedly also care about one of the reasons they probably got out so fast, pending their preliminary hearing, he also revealed the fact that they had a child. But he additionally told her about how they'd abandoned that baby.

"What horrible people!" Melody exclaimed.

Casey could do nothing but agree.

And when they hung up only a minute later, he had another urge to see Melody again.

Bad idea, he reminded himself, and headed back to his office.

MELODY WAS SHOCKED, even as she stared around the part of the pasture where she now rode on Cal's back and wrangled the cattle with some of her fellow ranch hands.

She'd known the Dodds were terrible, but how could they have left their daughter that way? Bad enough they were cattle rustlers, not to mention murderers.

She appreciated Casey's call for the warning it contained. She'd certainly try to stay even more alert, but she recognized that, after all that had happened, she had become watchful and concerned and extremely vigilant, even while doubting anyone would dare to try to rustle any more cattle around here.

And…well, she hated to admit it to herself, but she did miss Casey, his strong and sexy presence while they'd been in the fields together, and, even more, his kindness. And even his sense of humor when he'd kidded her at times about what a ranch hand did.

In fact, after they hung up, she impulsively called him back. "You know, Thanksgiving's next week," she said. "I'm helping to cook a great dinner for the other ranch hands who live in my bunkhouse and would love to have you join us."

"Sorry," he responded immediately, and the word made her heart sink. "But I'll be joining my parents, as usual."

He didn't mention his prior invitation for her to join his family at Christmas and she didn't ask.

It probably wasn't going to happen.

She'd probably see Casey again sometime, in town or wherever.

But she was just going to have to get over him.

THANKSGIVING. DAMN, HOW Casey had appreciated Melody's invitation, he thought, returning to his office.

But it would have been a bad idea in many ways for him to accept. For one thing, his parents expected him.

For another…well, something that could seem even more than an ordinary date, which he didn't intend to follow up on with Melody, anyway, was out of the question. Or was it?

Sitting back down at his desk, he looked at his computer to learn what his next assignment was. He needed to go check on some alleged vandalism outside a local bank.

Good. That would keep him busy for a while.

As did other assignments over the next few days. That made it easier—somewhat—not to think about the Dodds a lot. Except to stay watchful.

And Melody? Well, thoughts of her seemed to creep into his mind, so he cast them aside and found other things to concentrate on. Or at least he tried.

And then, a few days later, Casey received a call demanding his presence at the Sur County courthouse, which wasn't far from the sheriff's department in Cactus Creek. Jeremy Krester was told to come, too.

"What's this about?" Casey asked as they strode down the street on the way to the courthouse.

"Don't know, but I gather it has something to do with the Dodds," Sheriff Krester responded, shaking his head in the cool November breeze so his gray hair wisped around his face.

Casey felt his own hair moving on his forehead, too. "Did they do something else? Did they disappear while out on bail so we're needed to find them again?"

"We'll find out," the sheriff said.

But the reason was quite different from that. The district attorney, Warren Marano, stood up before Judge Morley Ackerman, who was seated on the bench in the courtroom. The judge was fortysomething, stern and wore a standard black robe, with only a fringe of brown hair on his head.

And Marano? There was no mistaking the shock on Marano's face, as his jaw dropped.

What was going on?

It was soon time for Casey to feel shocked, too. Especially when Georgia walked into the courtroom and down the aisle carrying a baby.

Sean and Delilah's? If so, why? And where were *they*?

District Attorney Marano asked for their attention. There weren't many onlookers in the seats, and he seemed to talk directly to the sheriff, who sat beside Casey.

"We have a major development in the prosecution of Sean and Delilah Dodd," Marano began.

That didn't surprise Casey, considering the fact this session was being held and the sheriff had been asked to come.

"It seems that two of our suspects, Sean Dodd and his wife, Delilah Dodd, committed suicide."

Oh, no. Casey might have hated what they'd done, but he'd certainly never anticipated this. Shock pulsed through his veins.

"No!" That shriek came from Georgia, who was sitting in the front row. It caused the baby in her arms to start crying. "They'd never commit suicide," Georgia shouted. "Someone must have murdered them."

How had Georgia wound up with the baby? Had Sean and Delilah left the little girl in her care rather than the neighbor's, knowing they were about to kill themselves? Casey wished he knew the answers to that and more. Ackerman had a clerk come over and escort Georgia, with the baby, from the courtroom, at least for now.

Then Marano continued, describing what had apparently happened. "Last night, they were driving on Sheldon Street, where the town's shopping mall is located. They apparently began speeding and rammed right into the parking lot wall. They both were killed—and there was a suicide note in the car, taped to the dashboard."

Well, there went at least part of the prosecution of those murderers and rustlers. Georgia was still around, though, and she was as much to blame in the whole thing as her brother and sister-in-law.

And what a horrible ending for those two. But according to the note the DA went on to describe, they would rather die than face prison.

Georgia was brought back into the courtroom, the baby still in her arms. She pleaded with the judge to absolve her of all charges so she could take care of her niece.

"You're still out on bail," Judge Ackerman reminded her. "Be sure to return for your preliminary hearing, and bring your attorney. We'll see how that argument goes."

Casey felt sorry for the baby but didn't think a sudden desire to take care of an orphaned family member would clear Georgia. And was that how Sean and Delilah would have wanted things? If they'd committed suicide, they'd probably left instructions for what they wanted for their daughter.

What Georgia had screamed stuck with him, though. When the sheriff and he left the courtroom a while later, Casey excused himself and called Everett to let him know what had happened. "Georgia yelled that Sean and Delilah would never commit suicide. She claimed they'd likely been murdered." He paused. "I'm sure I'm not going to be assigned to look into it, but what do you think?"

"I think I'm going to head in your direction again soon—maybe using a Thanksgiving vacation as an excuse—and look into it, just in case."

"That's my great big brother," Casey said before ending the call. "Look forward to seeing you again soon."

He walked back to the department with the sheriff, who, as Casey also assumed, just chalked up Georgia's cry about possible murder to her grief. "There was a suicide note," he reminded Casey.

Casey didn't bother to mention that could have been planted by the murderer. Had the couple been assaulted before being put into the car and aimed toward the wall?

And would they ever find out?

Well, Everett on the case might be quite helpful in determining the truth.

But more deaths. Sure, Casey might have detested Sean and Delilah for what they had done, but he hadn't wished them dead.

For the rest of the day, what was left of it, Casey couldn't concentrate. Sure, he saw a lot of nasty things as a deputy sheriff, but this somehow really got into him.

People died, however it occurred. Life wasn't a sure thing.

And his life? Oh, it was okay the way it was…yet all of this made him think of Melody again.

A lot.

As his workday ended, he called her, hoping she was back at the ranch. She sounded surprised to hear from him, yet somehow happy. At least she didn't hang up on him. And, yes, it was getting late enough that the cattle were all enclosed behind fencing for the night.

"Can I come see you now?" he said. "I'll come to your ranch, if that's okay."

"Sure," she said. "Sounds good. See you soon."

See her soon? *Yeah!*

As he hung up and closed down his computer so he could get out of there, he thought about seeing Melody. Now—and in the future?

That sounded so good.

Had he gotten over whatever his hang-ups were about starting a relationship?

Maybe.

He had a feeling he'd figure it out that night.

CASEY WAS COMING HERE? Melody was in a stall in the barn, brushing Cal and combing his long, soft mane after removing his saddle for the night.

Why? And why was she looking forward so much to seeing Casey?

Well, she knew the answer to that last question. She missed him. The bond they'd formed while following the cattle, chasing down the rustlers and spending nights together felt unbreakable.

Unless, of course, he was coming here to deliver some kind of blow, like he was moving away, or he'd found a girlfriend...whatever. She'd find out soon.

She finished with Cal and returned to her apartment, where she quickly showered and changed into a nice gray shirt and black slacks, better looking and better smelling than the outfit she had worn at work that day. She left her hair loose, not in its ponytail.

Then she exited the building and walked to the main ranch house, which was the first thing Casey would see as he entered the ranch property again.

She had to smile. It wasn't even Thanksgiving yet, but Clarence had already had at least the outside of his long, one-story red house decorated for Christmas. There were wreaths around the door, and lights mounted around the windows; they weren't lit yet despite the current darkness of twilight. A string of holly had also been attached at the sides of the couple of steps up to the porch.

And most amusing was that he had had mistletoe hung a couple of places from the top of the porch roof. Was Clarence planning on kissing visitors to his ranch?

For now, though, she glanced at her phone after pulling it from her pocket. It had been about half an hour since she'd talked with Casey, so he should arrive anytime now…she hoped. For now, she stood at the side of the porch, waiting.

Maybe, if he'd be here a while, they could go sit on the porch to talk. The mistletoe was spread out enough that they could just ignore it and not walk underneath it.

Although…well, the idea was tempting but unwise.

Sure enough, a car passed through the gate at the base of the driveway. Casey's dark SUV, which resembled, but wasn't, an official sheriff's vehicle, pulled up and parked near the porch.

Casey got out. He was still in his deputy uniform… and looked good in it. And now that they were back in town, he was clean-shaven.

Melody smiled. Broadly. She was so glad to see him.

But she didn't know why he'd wanted to get together that evening. Maybe something was wrong. And so she just stood there, swallowing her smile, crossing her arms in front of her chest.

"Hi, Melody," he called, then joined her where she

stood. She considered giving him a welcoming kiss but didn't.

She still didn't know why he'd come.

"Look, there are a few things I want to discuss with you. Can we just go sit up there?" He pointed toward the porch. "Although, if Clarence is home and he can hear us, that won't be a good idea."

"I don't believe he's home yet. Plus he had his house built to be perfect in every way, or so he says. In any case, it's supposed to be soundproof."

"Hope so." Casey reached out and took her hand, leading her onto the porch, where they sat facing one another on a couple of the fancy vinyl deck chairs there.

"So what's up?" Melody attempted to sound cheerful, but her concern rose. The expression on Casey's wonderfully handsome face was bland, and gave nothing away.

"Let me get the bad stuff out of the way first, okay?"

Bad stuff. Melody drew in her breath. "Sure," she said.

And it really was bad. She certainly didn't like Sean and Delilah Dodd, but she hadn't wished them dead. Imprisoned forever, yes.

The fact that they had a baby they'd left behind during the pasture trek only made things worse. What would happen to the child now? Casey said that Georgia had brought the six-month-old, a girl named Kennedy, to court and was apparently caring for her now, but Georgia still could—and hopefully would—go to prison for a good long time.

Casey had no answer for what would happen to the child, but he clearly felt awful about it, too—as he did about the suicides of Sean and Delilah. Although he appeared not to have fully accepted the deaths were self-inflicted and mentioned that Everett would be around again for a while to conduct an investigation.

"But that's not the main reason I wanted to see you," Casey said, staring at her earnestly.

Oh, no. What was to come? An admission of a girlfriend, a request that Melody keep their night of passion to herself? Something even worse?

"With all that's gone on, all we've been through together…well, I really like you, Melody. I'm not asking for any kind of commitment, but I'd like for us to go out together. On dates or whatever. Get to know each other better. And…see where it leads, if anywhere." He paused, reaching for her hands. "What do you think?"

"I think…yes!" Melody smiled, stood and held his hands tightly as she pulled him to his feet.

Okay, it was silly, meant nothing, but she pulled him to where the nearest sprig of mistletoe hung—and she kissed him.

No, he kissed her. They kissed each other—deeply and sexily and wonderfully. It was a long kiss, and Melody loved feeling his body hard against hers, his mouth searching hers.

And when they both pulled back, it was only for an instant. They kissed again.

"So we're on for your spending Christmas dinner with my family?" Casey said.

"Of course. But that's still weeks away. Can we see each other between now and then—on dates or whatever?"

"Absolutely," Casey said, then he bent toward her to seal that commitment with an even sexier kiss.

Dates together for the foreseeable future. And Christmas with his family.

No commitment, sure. But Melody felt overjoyed. Despite her misgivings before, the idea of having Casey in her life now, and maybe forever?

Delightful!

* * * * *

COMING SOON!

We really hope you enjoyed reading this book. If you're looking for more romance, be sure to head to the shops when new books are available on

Thursday 14th November

To see which titles are coming soon, please visit

millsandboon.co.uk/nextmonth

MILLS & BOON
Desire

Indulge in secrets and scandal, intense drama and plenty of sizzling hot action with powerful and passionate heroes who have it all: wealth, status, good looks... everything but the right woman.

MILLS & BOON

THE HEART OF ROMANCE

A ROMANCE FOR EVERY KIND OF READER

MODERN

Prepare to be swept off your feet by sophisticated, sexy and seductive heroes, in some of the world's most glamourous and romantic locations, where power and passion collide.
8 stories per month.

HISTORICAL

Escape with historical heroes from time gone by. Whether your passion is for wicked Regency Rakes, muscled Vikings or rugge Highlanders, awaken the romance of the past.
6 stories per month.

MEDICAL

Set your pulse racing with dedicated, delectable doctors in the high-pressure world of medicine, where emotions run high an passion, comfort and love are the best medicine.
6 stories per month.

True Love

Celebrate true love with tender stories of heartfelt romance, fr the rush of falling in love to the joy a new baby can bring, and focus on the emotional heart of a relationship.
8 stories per month.

Desire

Indulge in secrets and scandal, intense drama and plenty of siz hot action with powerful and passionate heroes who have it all: wealth, status, good looks…everything but the right woman.
6 stories per month.

HEROES

Experience all the excitement of a gripping thriller, with an int romance at its heart. Resourceful, true-to-life women and stron fearless men face danger and desire - a killer combination!
8 stories per month.

DARE

Sensual love stories featuring smart, sassy heroines you'd want best friend, and compelling intense heroes who are worthy of
4 stories per month.

To see which titles are coming soon, please visit

millsandboon.co.uk/nextmonth

JOIN US ON SOCIAL MEDIA!

Stay up to date with our latest releases, author
news and gossip, special offers and discounts, and
all the behind-the-scenes action
from Mills & Boon...

 millsandboon

 millsandboonuk

 millsandboon

t might just be true love...

MILLS & BOON

True Love

Romance from the Heart

Celebrate true love with tender stories of heartfelt romance, from the rush of falling in love to the joy a new baby can bring, and a focus on the emotional heart of a relationship.